LET ME LET YOU GO

a novel

Jenny Studenroth Gerson

Apple Peach Company

Cover design by: Jenny Studenroth Gerson

*This first one is for Josh,
but I'll never let you go.*

NOW

At seven o'clock, Dolly Weston's alarm tears her from a deep slumber. Beside her is a warm place in the bed where, just minutes ago, her fiancé Michael lay. She can hear the shower water beating down on him in the adjacent bathroom as he badly raps Drake lyrics into its steamy abyss. Dolly stretches her arms overhead, making her body long before recoiling and reaching over to silence the alarm.

It is only Tuesday in a week that already feels like it's been long. Through the window, she can see the mist rising over Manhattan. Dolly would kill to spend another twenty minutes in bed. Even better, to take a day off. Work is rewarding yet downright overwhelming these days—not to mention there is the simple weight of a New York existence in late winter.

Dolly will soon have to make her way up and out into the waiting streets, entering the subway system by way of its sludge-covered stairs, being jostled and crammed-in all the way Downtown to her office. The emails will be stacked up, the lists of deliverables miles long, and it'll be hours until she's back in this bed. It's exhausting just to think about, honestly.

She has, by all accounts, an incredibly stressful job—but she loves it. *Yes*, she *loves it*, she reminds herself, actually nodding her head one time in confirmation before rising out of the bed and padding toward the bathroom. Dolly loves the feeling of accomplishment that comes from signing on a new client, making those connections with business owners and tastemakers. She loves the thrill of turning the pages of a glossy magazine and seeing the businesses she's helped to grow being featured right there for all to admire and support.

Dolly loves the rush that hits her at the top of the red carpet when the lights are on and her microphone has been checked, when the floodgates open and a stream of celebrities sashay toward her and answer her questions with familiarity and charm. She loves the clothes, too, of course. The freebies that are cast aside by her boss (Founder, Principal, and Head Bitch in Charge), Sandra Laisman, who owns at least three Birkin bags and drives a Porsche in a town where most people do not drive at all.

But what Dolly loves most of all about her career, above these tangible benefits, is a feeling: the feeling that she has made it. Dolly Mae Weston from the tiny town of Sugar's Bend, Texas (soon to be Dahlia Weston Peabody of New York City's Upper East Side) has made it in Manhattan. And, yes, her impending marriage to the son of a very prominent New York family and the headline-catching name change that will come with it are part of her newly found social status (*may as well make elegant her first name while doing so with her last*). But most of this was self-built. Most of it came from a hell of a lot of hard work, grit, and the type of determination that only a Southern woman with a dream can muster.

"Well, good morning, Drizzy," she teases in the direction of her still-rapping fiancé in the shower, while grabbing her toothbrush and paste.

"Oh, yeah, because you totally live up to that country-singing name of yours, right, babe?" Michael shoots back, pulling the curtain aside long enough to sneak a peek at his wife-to-be and add a wink to the corny comeback.

Michael is nothing if not a total goofball in jock's clothing. It's part of what endeared her to him in the first place and certainly what keeps her going when she finds herself in a dark mood. For all of the bubbly, girl-about-town, up-and-at-'em charm that Dolly exudes at work and elsewhere, there is a weariness that creeps in at times. There are parts of her past that she'd like to leave behind, parts of her future that feel uncertain and confusing. It's nice to be with someone who understands that lightheartedness and fun are important. Someone who, admittedly, grew up with everything and has always had a cushy lifestyle. Someone who can afford to be an absolute clown when he wants to, to go into work late when his personal life demands it, to take the edge off life's darknesses because his is pretty damn close to perfect.

The steam from the shower engulfs them, the bathroom door having closed behind her. These pre-war buildings, while charming, often feature quirks. Squeaky entryway floorboards, chipped kitchen tiles. Slightly uneven door hinges with a tendency to pull doors closed, unprompted by the human hand. Dolly adores her charming sublet for all its idiosyncrasies and sometimes she wonders how many people have lived in this very apartment before her, have written and rewritten their own New York stories within its walls. Have stood barefoot on this tile floor swathed in shower steam and not quite ready to face another day.

Manhattan is always pulsing with the energy and liveliness of its inhabitants; it's part of why she escaped here in the first place and the main reason she decided to stay. To think about all the people who came before and wonder who they might have been is both overwhelming and endlessly enticing. She may be a Texas girl born and raised, but Dolly is a New Yorker, too, and she wouldn't trade either part of her identity for the world.

Michael exits the shower and reaches for the nearly threadbare monogrammed towel that hangs from the hook beside, despite the fluffier bath sheets stacked in the small corner cabinet just inches away. Etched with her mother's initials and showing its age in bleach spots and loose threads, it is his favorite. Like many of the other curious things about this man she will spend the rest of her life with, Dolly has come to feel that the wondering is sometimes more intriguing than the real answer might be. She's never asked why he prefers to use this one, but maybe using this relic from her childhood makes him feel closer to her in ways he can't express with words. Or maybe he just doesn't like fluffy towels.

Dolly leans in wordlessly to kiss her future husband before entering the shower. She turns the dial slightly to raise the temperature and dips her head underneath its heavy staccato. By the time she gets out and towels off, Michael will have put on a pot of coffee and laid out plates and cups on the kitchen counter. He'll be frying up eggs or placing thick slices of whole grain bread into the toaster, removing her tub of light butter from the fridge to take the edge off its chill before spreading each piece with a thin layer.

Michael is a caretaker by nature, and as a couple they have fallen into a rhythm wherein he often takes on the benign doings at the start of the day so she can float through, eat, and head out for work with little thought or concern. Dolly wonders if these naturally fluid mornings will continue once they're officially living together this fall, or even after they get married next year. It's romantic and sweet, and she feels absolutely guilt-ridden complaining about it to her friends (so she doesn't). But something about the accommodating and swift way that Michael moves through the mornings feels inauthentic... almost as if he's trying to prove something.

It's silly, she knows. Why question a loving guy who's never given you a reason to? Why lament the fact that you're well taken care of in a city, in a world, where so many are not? This is what they call First World Problems, she thinks with a dry smile, snapping back to reality. She cranks the shower to OFF and slips out of the steamy warmth of the small bathroom toward the bedroom, where her wardrobe awaits consideration.

After deciding on a simple, plum-colored sweater dress from her closet and pulling it on, Dolly pours several drops of strengthening oil into one palm and runs it through her thick blond hair. She pulls on a pair of opaque tights and low-heeled black boots, adding mascara and red lips to her face before heading out to the kitchen.

Michael is bent at the waist tying up his white trainers, already wearing his thin Moncler puffer coat to keep warm against a relentless New York winter. As she predicted, his finished breakfast plate is in the sink and on the small kitchen island rests one for her—complete with a scramble of eggs and veggies, one piece of buttered toast, and a glass of grapefruit juice. An empty cup for coffee sits beside the pot, waiting for her to fill it. Michael knows that his future wife doesn't like to let any of the heat escape before taking her first sip.

"Thanks for breakfast, honey," she says, like she always does, this morning facing the top of his head of curly hair. At this point their routine has become so innate that her verbal thanks are practically unnecessary, but again Dolly does realize how lucky she is to have found someone who shows his love in such tangible ways as this.

Michael, spry and energetic, tall and dark, smiles widely in her direction. "No problem, babe. By the way, I think you're going to like this coffee."

"Is it a new kind?" Dolly is a creature of habit when it comes to her coffee.

"Yeah. It's from a super cool little company we're investing in. They take good care of their farmers... and the shit's delicious. Let me know what you think! I gotta go, though. I have an early meeting." He kisses her quickly and heads out into the day before she can return a listener's response on the coffee, eager now to try it and weigh her thoughts for later. These are the seemingly mundane pieces of their days she wonders if she'll remember when they're old and gray. Or even in a few years when they have a couple of kids and life has taken on a whole different tempo.

Dolly eats her breakfast in large, fast bites, pours her leftover happy-farmer coffee into a plastic lidded mug, and pops into the bathroom to briefly run the dryer through her long hair. After a quick appraisal of her reflection in the full-length mirror by the door, she grabs her winter coat and shoulder bag off their hooks and steps out into the long echoey corridor, turning to walk toward the elevator and begin another hectic day.

The streets of New York are throbbing with weekday morning foot traffic, the likes of which an eighteen-year-old Dolly used to find both mesmerizing and intimidating when she first moved up here from Texas. Now that she's been living in this city for over ten years, and feels every bit the true New Yorker, the crowds can be irritating and claustrophobic at times, but are no longer quite so overwhelming. Steeling herself against them now, one hand wrapped around her coffee cup, she makes her way through the peopled flow toward the 63rd Street entrance to the subway at Lexington, and takes the steps as briskly as she can down into the world below Manhattan. One face among millions, one story developing at its own jagged pace.

* * * * *

Dolly's morning commute is no better or worse than she

anticipated, and she enters the lobby of her Downtown office building about twenty minutes before everyone else will start trickling in. This is part of what makes her a good publicist, and a good employee. Dolly has a high standard of decorum and believes in the importance of punctuality among other good manners and best practices. Or, as her boss famously said at last year's Christmas party, "Dolly is annoyingly perfect—I would hate her if I didn't love her so much."

Just inside and to the left of the doors of the grand, modern office building, Dolly pauses to grab a pair of heels from her oversized bag and changes into them, tucking her boots under one arm. She waves hello to the early-morning front desk staffers, swipes her ID card at the turnstile, and click-clacks in her patent-leather heels across the large marble tiles of the lobby toward the bank of elevators at the center of the building.

Dolly spends the first ten minutes of the morning tidying up her desk after leaving the office in a hurry last night. She sits down and switches on her computer, firing up the dual monitors that stare back at her all day with a steadily mounting to-do list that seems to swell even as its items are ticked off. True to form, as soon as she opens the email application Dolly is bombarded. She's recently been named Director, and with the title has come not only a pay raise but significantly more work. *Another day, another dollar*, she thinks to herself with a silent, sarcastic smile. For all the parts of this job that feel glamorous, the grind of her days is almost laughably the opposite. Her phone starts ringing almost immediately and by the time Sandra floats into the office on four-inch red platforms two hours later, Dolly has already secured a big story for a new client and hacked through much of that odious barrage of emails.

"Morning, Dahlia!" Sandra's voice echoes over the newly

scarce office suite. They've recently moved floors; with more clients has come the opportunity for more space. They also, supposedly, will be hiring more help... eventually. But for now it seems Dolly and her closest colleague (or, "work wife") Glinda, have more to do than ever. While their square footage has about quadrupled with the move up from a corner of the third floor to the entirety of the fifteenth, the same five people as before are the only ones to occupy the vast new space. They're just spread out a bit more now and working harder than ever to pay the rent. An intern should be joining them soon, but even that doesn't seem too hopeful.

Sandra's main goal when she floated the concept of this move to the team was to make sure that everyone would have an assistant. Second to that was the plan for a chic space to invite editors and clients over to, rather than always needing to leave the office for quick meetings. Finally, she hoped to design and build a proper fashion closet where they could display and store the clothing and shoes of the brands they worked with, and also facilitate easy loans to any celebrities they had the opportunity to dress on a last-minute basis.

The fashion closet was part of what Sandra had originally referred to as her "two-year plan" with the other bits at the top of the list. Now they are rounding out the fourth month in their new space and no closer to hiring additional help, but the closet initiative seems to be moving along faster than any other. Dolly finds it pretty startling to watch Sandra spend so much of her time chatting with an architect about her "vision" for the dream space when clearly what they need first are the assistants they were all promised.

It's become a point of contention among the team, but Dolly gets it, in a way. Sometimes it's easier to make a dream come true when you've created the perfect space for it to unfold in. Didn't she do this herself when she moved up to New York

City with no friends, family, or connections, and hardly any money?

Watching her boss frivolously concoct a fashion closet before beefing up their staff reminds Dolly of the way she once spent $200 on an antique mirror for the entryway of a studio apartment when she was newly out of college and waiting tables to make ends meet. That week, she hardly had money left over for food or subway fare, but the mirror made her feel like her sweet new home was truly that... *home*. The feeling of stepping into her first "big girl apartment" and seeing that epic mirror just made her happy. It was worth living on boxed pasta and walking all the way home from work for a while to be able to stare at it every day.

"Have you spoken to Joanna at *Fancy* about Carlo yet?" Sandra's sharp, business-like tone rips Dolly back into the moment. And just like that, the mushy feelings of understanding she had just moments ago are replaced with irritation. Dolly has literally done everything else on her day's to-do list and it's not even lunchtime. This very hour, she has spoken with top editors at two other leading women's publications and scored coverage for their newest client, all of which Sandra should know thanks to cc'ing. But of course, the minute Dolly looks up from her desk to think, there's her boss with another deliverable.

Joanna Blair is the managing editor at *Fancy*, a cool new fashion quarterly that's picking up speed with the 30-plus, upwardly mobile fashionista reader. She is also, Dolly knows, currently OOO in Bali with her devastatingly gorgeous new husband. She and Joanna exchanged emails before the trip with plans to catch up over coffee next Monday and talk about coverage opportunities for LAZR's new hair client, Carlo Figuri. Not only does it get frustrating repeating yourself over and over about these things, it also just flat-out sucks to feel like your boss doesn't think you're on top of your stuff.

Dolly snaps her head up to make eye contact with Sandra and offers up her best flight attendant smile. "She's still in Bali, but we have plans to chat hair on Monday." For good measure, she adds, "Thanks for checking in!" The words sound false hanging in the air between these two women who work so closely and yet so differently. Dolly feels her stomach lurch as she wonders if Sandra detects the sarcasm. Luckily her boss seems satisfied with Dolly's response and moves on to badgering Glinda, who's just walked in from a work breakfast and has yet to remove her coat.

"Where are we with that MoMA event, Glin? I'm feeling vaguely concerned..." Dolly slips her earbuds in to steel herself from the relentless badgering, if only briefly. Sandra is not a fan of headphones in the office because she likes to pop in on people and feels her team should be ready to listen and respond at a moment's notice. But sometimes Dolly can get away with a brief jam session of country music on Internet Radio while she drafts up some documents or does other computer work that makes her look too busy to interrupt. That's her goal for the rest of the morning, anyway.

As she listens, Dolly's mind floats away to the back roads of the American South while her body fiercely types and jots, drafts and prints, clips and skims. Jason and Miranda, Kenny and George call her home with their crooning over champagne towns and white liars, American kids and a love without end, *Amen*. Even the Dolly she *wasn't* named after is warm and sweet in her ears this morning, begging Jolene not to do the worst thing any woman can do to another.

No matter how much New York means to her, it will always be her second home. No matter how big her love of cosmopolitan couture, of glitzy cafes pulsing with whirring coffee machines and fresh fancy breads. Of Uptown streets so teeming with elegant people the sidewalk itself appears to vibrate. Of buildings so tall their glitter just about touches the sky... New York will never be Texas. And Texas will always be where it all began.

Dolly is happy here, with a new chapter of life unfolding beautifully before her and no plans to leave—ever. But country music is always there when she needs it, and even when she's not sure if she does. Just like on this bleak and chilly morning, every time she hears the familiar words or hums the bars just slightly out of tune, it's like a journey through the backroads of her hometown. It's like holding hands with the past.

THEN

Dolly grew up down the end of a cul-de-sac in a quiet neighborhood of tiny Sugar's Bend, Texas—a town that was squarely middle-class. Every house on her street had a yellowed-grass square lawn out front and a similar one in the back. Some neighborhoods were slung with white picket fences and some were without. Pretty much everyone had a two-car garage and not much else in the way of bragging rights. There were some kids with less and some with more; none of those details seemed to matter too much to anyone as long as you were kind and showed good face in the community.

Dolly's own parents lived modestly for their means, preferring to save for trips and other occasional extravagances over spending up on a larger house in the outskirts of town like some wealthier recent transplants to the area had done. Most everybody in Sugar's Bend knew each other, or at least knew *of* each other. There was gossip and conflict, solidarity and hope. There were barbecues and by-ways, days that seemed to drag on for far too long, and years that just flew right on by.

Sugar's Bend was the type of town that, from the highway, might appear exactly like what the name implied: just a bend in the road. It was made up of neighborhoods carved out of nothing, where woods or flat green had once been. The 1960's and 70's had laid out and configured rows of houses and narrow roads in those spaces, and up popped a modest town center just a couple of intersections wide. The town was a decent enough drive to Dallas to feel like you weren't in the absolute middle of nowhere, but far enough away from everything to know that you could get pulled into staying put forever pretty easily. You had to *want* to leave... and Dolly had pretty much always known that she did.

She grew up mostly hanging around with the kids who lived in or nearby her close-knit neighborhood—it had always been easiest that way. Dolly was a shy and sensitive child with a pervasive fear of being misunderstood and left behind, so sticking with what she knew felt right, felt comfortable. Her best friend Stephanie Longman was more outgoing and confident, and was pretty much always there to help Dolly navigate the social waters.

Even as little kids down at the community pool in the next town over or playing putt-putt at birthday parties, Steph's eyes and ears were alert to make sure her friend was alright. It was many years later while living in Manhattan that Dolly would learn, sitting across the room from a middle-aged Jewish therapist whose glasses slipped down her nose every time she glanced at her notes, that this was social anxiety. That the thing inside her that told her, almost constantly, that other people maybe didn't like her as much as they just tolerated her, was not because she was inherently flawed or unlikeable. Instead, it was the manifestation of misaligned thoughts she could work through and redirect actively. It was an imaginary if imposing state of understanding that made her feel not-as-good-as, for which she certainly spent years overcompensating. As a kid, she thought she was just awkward.

Growing up shy wasn't the worst thing in the world though. It rendered Dolly humble and honest to a fault. It made her a really good listener and eventually, a good lover, too. But all of that had yet to unfold as Dolly and Stephanie rode their bikes confidently into the summer days that stretched out before them, just after sophomore year of high school and before life started to get complicated.

* * * * *

On the second day of June, Dolly was already headed toward the front door before she heard the rapping on it. Stephanie stood on the porch, striking if understated with the longest legs on any teenager in the county. Her wild auburn hair was pulled back into a messy ponytail and she wore the obligatory cut-off denim shorts just like Dolly's own. Eager to get into town and squander their meager babysitting earnings on manicures at the new place that had just opened up, Dolly hollered goodbye to her parents over her shoulder into the house and slipped out just as quickly as Steph had appeared.

Ten in the morning and outside it was already *so* hot. The humid Texas air filled their lungs without quenching them completely, and was pushed out forcefully with every huff and puff of their cycling toward town center. Dolly could feel sweat collecting between her small breasts, her white t-shirt clinging gently as she pumped her bike faster than she would have liked while trying to keep up with her long-legged, athletic friend.

They didn't talk much on the ride, because best friends don't always need to. Wordlessly they exchanged commentary on what they saw as they rode—neighbors bickering with their spouses on the front lawn, a weird vintage car rolling into town with its top down—sarcastic smiles and head-nods were their second language. Soon they arrived at the nail salon, parked their bikes against a tree and stepped into the cool oasis of the small shop.

Petite, Asian women sat at desk-like manicure stations or on little wheeled stools painting finger and toe nails. They shot back and forth occasional commentary in a language none of the patrons could understand and laughed quietly at their own private jokes. It wasn't the first time Dolly had gone to get her nails done, but something about this tiny place felt instantly special. The ladies in the pedicure chairs were asking their nail techs questions about their lives and actually seemed to care about the responses. She could tell right away that it felt like *community* in here, even though the place was practically brand new.

She didn't even mind the fact that it took a full five minutes for anyone to notice the girls had entered, because the woman behind the front desk was bent over a book with a child and they were pointing at foreign-looking characters, sounding out the words together. *Connecting him to his roots*, Dolly thought. It reminded her of her grandfather on her mother's side. He was a prominent Jewish figure in Dallas society, and even though he'd married a shiksa and agreed to live a largely non-denominational life in a state where religion reigned supreme, he had an affinity for passing down traditions and teachings to his eager granddaughter and her cousins.

As a child, Dolly had loved visiting her grandparents' large home in Highland Park, just north of the hustle and bustle of Uptown Dallas. She'd loved sitting in Zayde's lap after meals and listening as he told her tales about the Old Country and also some from The Book. It was hard, looking back, to decipher which was which sometimes, if she's being honest. So much hardship, so many complicated and weaving tales of sorrow and joy, solidarity and promise. But that precious part of her, the part where people read a language she couldn't decipher and sang cheerful and somber songs to accompany the lighting of candles and breaking of bread, was important. It was history. It was life. It was, well, family.

Dolly snapped back into the current moment as the embarrassed shop owner realized there were two teenagers standing in front of her and asked how she could help them. Dolly answered, "Just manicures, please," and headed to the rows of polish bottles to select her color. Of all the pinks, the purples, the rich creams, and outrageous blues and greens, nothing stuck out.

Stephanie stood nearby, holding up a metallic copper with tiny flecks of iridescent glitter floating inside. "This is pretty, huh?" she asked, having already decided on her own but letting Dolly feel a part of the process by asking for confirmation. Dolly nodded and chose a shimmering opal in the end, deciding as usual that her best friend had the right idea. Shimmer was in.

The girls spent the next hour gabbing and giggling as their manicurists cut, shaped, buffed, and polished them to perfection, and then as their nails dried slowly with the pervasive humidity creeping in somehow from the outside world. Stepping back into the hot Texas air where the steamy small-town sidewalk awaited, the pair couldn't think what to do next, so settled for walking their bikes to the end of the street for a quick milkshake at Beam's.

It was at this local spot where all the kids tended to be that Dolly and Steph's morning moved from a girls' catchup session to a group hangout. And that was fine, but Dolly could feel herself turning inward pretty much as soon as they entered the diner. From across the large dining room where they waited by the hostess stand to be handed menus they didn't need (they probably hadn't even been reprinted, let alone changed, since the girls were born), she spotted a bunch of kids from school that Steph knew better than she did. But as she trailed her friend toward the crowded booth, she noticed her cute neighbor Declan Crue sitting among the others.

"Steph! I haven't seen you in *forever*," came the chirpy little voice of Kimmy Fields, sitting among the pack.

"Hey, girl," Steph returned with a wide smile. "Forever or like, a week and a half!"

"Yeah, close enough. Come sit with us!" Dolly's stomach flipped and she smiled shyly as Kimmy's warm eyes turned to her as well, signaling them both over with a free hand as she reached toward the plate of nachos at the center of the table with her other one.

The girls slid onto the cushy seats of the booth and quickly caught up with the others while waiting for their milkshakes to arrive. Dolly started to feel a small stir of confidence brewing beneath her quiet exterior as they all chatted without her saying much.

Declan had acknowledged both of their arrival with a nod, but a smile lingered on his lips a while after greeting Dolly by name. He was as handsome as they come, in a yellow polo shirt with the collar popped, his sandy hair tousled and hanging just over one eye. She tried not to be obvious, but her eyes darted his way every several minutes. And each time they did, she found his were fixed right on her. Warmly inviting. Sexy as hell. *This is good*, she thought slowly, allowing herself to loosen up and get in on the conversation. Summer was underway, and so far it was looking delicious.

NOW

Dolly is half an hour late for drinks with John-John and she's flushed and breathy as she makes her way up the subway stairs two at a time. For all his eccentricity and flair, her best male friend is always punctual. He might be wearing silk slippers as shoes (and making that work somehow), or showing up with purple-dyed cornrows in his hair, but he seems always to be there and waiting whenever Dolly turns up at their dates, even when she's running on time herself.

Balthazar is just about the best place in Manhattan to meet up with a close friend on a rainy day. It's Sunday afternoon, and after the bender she had last night, staying out way too late with Michael and his associates from the firm, a cozy corner booth and one of their signature hangover cocktails with John-John is exactly what she needs.

Dolly spots her friend right away, wearing leather from head to toe and reading from an independent newspaper with a bemused look on his handsome face. John-John has one ankle crossed over the other and his back is ramrod straight, his long elegant limbs stretched out in the shape of comfort and dignity. She can tell from several feet away that he has already ordered her Champagne Pick-Me-Up and his own Ramos Fizz, but is waiting for her to arrive to start on it. This is one of the many things the two have in common: New York might have taught them about the chic things and how to make it in a fast-paced life, but Southern hospitality and manners will always be essential to who they are.

She unwraps her long cashmere scarf as she approaches the table and folds it up, stuffing it into her oversized Louis Vuitton. "Hi, baby!" she breathes, "So sorry I'm late." John-John waves off her apology and stands to hug her, holding her at arm's length briefly to admire her all-black ensemble.

"I have literally no idea what I'm going to eat," he says. "But by the looks of things, you're off food?"

"Oh, shut up," she retorts, loving the veiled compliment about looking thin. "It's just the stress, I swear. I've been drinking enough wine to fill the ocean, so I'm not sure where all *those* calories are going."

They settle into the booth and peruse the menu quietly for a few minutes before a young waitress with kinky blond curls appears and asks brightly if they need another minute or have any questions. Placing their standard if lightly considered orders, (eggs florentine for him; avocado toast for her), they ease into a typical conversation about work, friends, and lovers.

"I need to tell you about this guy I've been seeing," John-John leans in, eyes dancing.

"I hope he's tall!"

John-John swats away her teasing about his own height (neither one of them understands why women in New York seem so consumed with dating only tall men, but if he were straight, John-John would have a line of female suitors down and around the block), continuing: "Luckily *this* giant doesn't care about that." He sucks in a breath. "Seriously though. Handsome. Successful. *Italian*."

"Oh, get out!" Dolly almost squeals, picturing her fair-skinned Southern bestie with a brown-eyed beau. "I bet y'all look adorable together."

"I don't know, honey, but I'll tell you—I *feel* adorable with him." John-John takes a thoughtful pause, sipping his cocktail and looking away briefly. "It's only been a couple of weeks, so I'm not trying to rush anything, but I haven't been this happy in a long time." And cutting her off at the pass, he finishes with, "And no, you cannot meet him yet! I don't want you and Glinda scarin' the poor man off before he's even had a chance to get comfortable!" Dolly throws her head back, giggling. They both know she and Glinda can be a tough crowd to bring new suitors around.

"Fair enough," she concedes, lifting her glass to clink his. "But when you're ready, I'm there. And I promise I won't ask too many questions. Well, except this one: What's his *name?*"

"Roman."

"It's not!"

"It is. I'm telling you... legit, old-school Italian." John-John lifts a hand to fan himself. "Ooh, girl. He is just... well, whatever the Italian word for hot is?"

"That's amazing," she emphasizes. "I love this!"

"Yeah, so what's up with y'all? How's Michael?"

"Oh, you know," she sighs. "Doing his businessman thing, working out too much. The usual. I guess he's invested in some fair trade coffee company? Tastes pretty darn Starbucksy to me, but apparently there's something special about them. Who knows?"

"Who knows?" He repeats, puffing out a sigh designed to blow imaginary bangs up and fan them out. "I guess that's the thing about relationships, right? You gotta act like you care about whatever it is they're obsessed with for the minute, so they'll do the same for you later."

Dolly snorts, practically sending her cocktail up and out her nose. "I would die to have Michael act like he cares about what I'm obsessed with." She laughs, but means it. "Can you imagine? I come from work and he's all, 'Love that vintage DVF, babe!'" Now they're both dissolved.

"Somehow I don't see that happening ever," John-John concedes, his eyes dancing. He raises a glass, gestures for her to do the same. "To putting up with men who don't get it—"

"And loving them all the same!" Dolly finishes.

"Chin-chin, darling," he says with a hard clink. "As long as he's paying the bills once y'all move in, I could care less what he thinks of your wrap dresses."

"Fair," she says with a smile. "I'll drink to that, for sure."

Brunch is lovely and warm. Gossip sneaks in as it's wont to do when you find a few precious hours alone with one of your closest friends. A little celebrity chat and some lamenting over the fact that even with the big stuff like Fashion Week and Awards Season over, they're both so perpetually slammed at work. Sundays seem to be the only day they can consistently get together this time of year, and even then, they both often have only a few precious hours before they have to get home to prepare for the coming week.

John-John is a highly esteemed makeup artist who seems to have gotten almost too popular; he's so busy these days she can hardly nail him down for coffee, let alone brunch. His rise was the stuff New York fairy tales are made of, but they only unfold this way for truly special people. Assisting some of the greats backstage at the New York shows got him picked up to do a few low-level shoots and once his work was out there, he became a *Name*, fast. The past few years since the two met, Dolly has swelled with pride watching her friend move up the ranks from that of an overworked assistant living in a scary sublet in Queens to earning the coveted title of *Vogue*'s One to Watch and then finally breaking out into full-blown success.

Makeup artists with any degree of talent are important but they're a dime a dozen. What sets John-John apart from anyone she's ever met in the profession is the way in which he treats each face like the unique canvas that it is. Even when doing a uniform makeup look for a show or a shoot on the designer's orders, John-John always figures out a way to work the colors and angles into each model's skin to bring out her uniquely beautiful features. This compassion, this understanding that every single person you meet is their own special individual who should be celebrated, is not only what makes him an outstanding makeup artist, it's also what makes him such a good friend.

Today, the busy pair have enough time for a brief shop-around after brunch, so once they've finished up their meal and split the bill, they bundle up and walk arm-in-arm from the restaurant out into the soggy, late winter afternoon. SoHo is alive with tourists and locals—New York doesn't care about the weather or rely on it to pulse on. People of every age and style move briskly along the overflowing sidewalks and pour out into the cobblestone streets in every direction.

Dolly can detect a different language at every corner, from Japanese to French and Spanish to some she doesn't recognize at all. Working in fashion means coming in contact with tastemakers and talents from all over the world. She has picked up key phrases in many languages and likes to make a game of trying to decipher what strangers are saying in a crowd. This morning though, winter's chill holds steady and there isn't much time to focus on anything other than getting to their destination with faces they can still feel.

"What the *fuck* is up with this endless winter?" John-John says then, speaking her own thoughts aloud.

Dolly laughs, shuddering against her friend. "I'm so over it," she admits. "Kinda makes you miss the South."

"I don't know about all *that*," John-John retorts.

As much as Dolly (mostly) loved growing up in Texas, she knows that her friend's upbringing in Arkansas was anything but bliss. And while John-John doesn't like to dwell on the past, he's dropped plenty of hints in the time they've known each other and gotten close about how hard it was for him back then. Being born gay in a revered military household and conservative town left him feeling alone and intimidated a lot of the time. He mentions his mother and siblings from time to time in conversation, but Dolly honestly has no idea if he still keeps in touch with any of them, let alone with his strict father. For all the confidence in the man who stands beside her today, John-John's past is riddled with sadness and insecurity. And clearly, part of his present is too... just a little.

So while he might miss the weather on days like this (*who wouldn't?*), it's not enough to ever want to return. Dolly bites her lip. Maybe she shouldn't have said that, but John-John has moved on already, suggesting Rag & Bone as their first stop and steering her in its direction briskly. "I could use some jeans," he explains.

"Oh totally, me too. I mean, we *need* so much more in our closets!" They both laugh, knowing their wardrobes are already out of control.

"Sometimes I worry about my closet," John-John says, in

mock-confession. "Do you think it gets overwhelmed?"

"Same," she agrees, blotting away a laughter-tear from the corner of one eye. "I seriously feel bad for mine. I'm also a little scared that when I move in with Michael and he sees the bags and boxes coming in, he might call off the wedding."

"Girl! You should be worried. That man is *not* prepared."

"Okay, let's take it easy today then," she says.

"Yeah, just the essentials."

"Like a thirtieth pair of jeans?"

"Something like that," he says with a wink, opening the heavy glass door of their first stop to let her inside.

The next few hours are light and easy, with comfortable lulls in conversation and plenty of exclamations of "Chic!," "Sure," and "Hard no" as they both hold up and try on clothes and sunnies, hats and bags. The afternoon soon turns to evening and they part ways, cheek-kissing and promising to catch up midweek. Dolly feels cocooned with the love of friendship as she heads into the subway and back Uptown.

Beneath the real world, where Manhattan pulses with visitors and natives, shoppers and workers, traffic and trends... the subway is a yellowed space frozen in time. A reminder that this all existed long before you did and will be here long after you are gone. When she first moved up to New York, subway travel seemed daunting. With its color-coded map and all those tiny dots, connecting here and veering off far into the distance there, she felt certain she'd never figure it out. But, if you want to be a New Yorker, you need to woman up, walk down, and learn to appreciate the wind of an approaching train as it hurls toward your station to pick you up and get you wherever it is that you need to go.

Tonight, she has a mountain of paperwork to go through, and once she's above ground her phone will refresh with emails she needs to handle. But for the next forty-five minutes of underground travel and transfers, she is alone with her headphones and the soundtrack of a chilly Sunday evening. A moody playlist fills her ears and body with songs of love and loss, longing and remembering. And despite the slop-coated tiles beneath her feet and the harsh yellow lights of the Uptown 6 Train, she is comforted by the sweetness of a day spent noshing and laughing, shopping and slowing down a bit with her dear friend.

Birdy's "Skinny Love" catapults her unexpectedly to a time when life was sexy, simple, and uncontained. She walks the several blocks from her subway stop to her apartment building beneath a dimming sky, glancing down from time to time at her patent-leather boots but otherwise lost completely in reverie as the city keeps up its pace around her.

Memories of a time keenly innocent and sweet take hold; flashes of the softest and most startling kiss she's ever received come across her consciousness. *My, my, my...* the sound of this song both confusing and dear to her, goes on in her ears as she remembers the feeling of his hand at the small of her back, the way he pulled her in and kissed her untouched lips that summer day. The way childhood melted away in an instant and was replaced by something much more exhilarating, much more important and... what?

Real.

The way the choices made by two teenagers in love could be so erratic and yet purposeful at once. And the way a pair of inexperienced, lovesick hometown sweethearts could become intricately connected for the rest of their lives, even if they were never to see each other again.

THEN

The first time she noticed him wasn't the first time she saw him. Growing up on the same street, riding bikes with the neighborhood kids, and eventually hanging out on the playground in groups of angsty teens had been the norm. Shared jokes and memories ran deep among the lot of them. But after that first lingering smile at Beam's in early June, a hand started to rest just a beat too long on her shoulder when they all hung out together. And soon there were two straws in one milkshake at that same diner, an electric rush that ran up and down her leg when his fingertips grazed her thigh on his way out of the booth. These were the slow and natural beginnings of the type of love reserved for the young.

Early that summer there was a shift. To him, her cut-off shorts no longer looked the same as all the other girls' did, and to her, his crooked smile suddenly meant a lot more. That summer being sixteen... the start of what they would become. *That* was when she truly saw him.

"Hey, stranger," Declan said one morning in mid-June, standing unannounced at her doorstep, all mud and sweat and summer sun. "Whatcha up to?"

Dolly paused, searching for an answer that would live up to the cool-girl status she wanted so badly to achieve. After a moment she settled on returning the question, for lack of something more interesting to share.

"I should be asking you the same. You're all dirty, Declan!" she teased, instantly wondering if that was too far.

But he was light and easy, true to form. "Me and the boys took Flynn's dirtbikes out by the creek earlier. Gotta get it in before the sun comes on too strong." She smiled as he changed the subject back to her, "But I asked you first."

"Oh," she said, forgetting for a minute to try and be cool, to try and act like Stephanie would. "I was just reading," she shrugged. "Predictable."

"That's not predictable at all, except it'd be a lot more fun if you'd hop down off that porch and come join me for lunch at Beam's."

Was there any turning that down?

"I'll grab my wallet," she said.

"Don't bother," he said, And then she knew... this was a date.

* * * * *

Flat-chested, quiet, and into books and facts, Dolly had often felt she didn't quite live up to her name. It was the name of bawdy, outgoing girls that jumped into cars with boys they didn't know, snuck out, didn't run home and tell their mamas everything. Girls who owned their womanhood at the dawn of adolescence, who didn't just try to look pretty for attention's sake but who planned to actually do something about it. Girls who were kind and empathic, sure, but who also didn't shake like a leaf when they had to do something on their own.

But none of that was what Sally Weston had been thinking when she picked out the moniker for her only daughter. Dolly had asked her mama about it, just a couple months back. And curled up on the couch with a bucket of microwave popcorn between them, she had explained.

"Have you ever seen a dahlia, the flower?"

Dolly nodded slowly, not making the connection. "I think so."

"Well, I wasn't going to go right out and name you after a flower... but it's in there." That was when Sally explained the language of flowers, a Victorian system of communication where each one had a purpose, a message. "And the dahlia is not only gorgeous and bursting with color, baby. It is the flower of dignity and elegance. It symbolizes the bond that lasts forever, just like ours." Giving her hand a squeeze, Dolly nodded.

"Thank you, Mama. I love that. And I love you."

Now, when Declan said her name she felt the power in it, the grace and beauty of its floral connotations. She understood herself to be a new Dolly this summer, but also just an extension of, a more developed version of, the person who had been blooming inside all along.

* * * * *

The walk over to Beam's was slow and a little quiet, at least on Dolly's part. While she'd been thinking about Declan nearly constantly ever since they'd started to exchange those secret smiles and a little flirting here and there, now that they were officially on a (*was it really a—?*) first date, she was starting to feel shy.

"I've been workin' up the nerve to ask you out for a while," Declan deadpanned, right as they turned the final corner toward town.

"You were?" Dolly still was having trouble understanding that this was all happening.

"Why do you find that so hard to believe?" He stopped walking then, turning toward her. Dolly followed suit, locking eyes with him.

"I don't know," she answered honestly, searching for a way to describe her doubts without scaring him off. "I guess I'm just used to all the guys being into Stephanie."

"Yeah, well..." One side of Declan's mouth turned upward as his eyes took in her whole face, pausing momentarily at her lips. He was so close she could smell his minty breath, see the tiny flickers of his nostrils as he breathed in. "Stephanie doesn't have what *you* have."

Feeling suddenly bold, Dolly pushed. "Oh yeah? And what's that?"

Declan shook his head then, for the first time ever looking almost shy to her. He was smiling though, wide and goofy. "You just haven't figured it out yet is all," he said finally. "But you will one day... Brains and beauty. It's a toxic combination."

For a moment she thought he might kiss her right there, but instead Declan pulled back and turned to face the direction of Main Street, taking her hand in his again. "Let's get that lunch, yeah?"

"Yeah," she replied, her cheeks warm. "I'm starving."

Dolly was surprised how easily they caught up over burgers, laughing like the closest of old friends even though they had never hung out one-on-one before. She hadn't expected him to share so many of her memories and observations, nor her opinions on school and mutual friends. Around the group in the neighborhood and at gatherings of the football and cheer teams, he'd always seemed like your average, loud and confident jock. Now a tenderness emerged between French fries and sips of his Coke. The genuine way he threw his head back in laughter at her witty jokes delighted her. Feeling their knees touch under the table sent that now familiar electric current up her legs and more than once, made her forcefully catch her breath.

This was happening.

They walked hand-in-hand back toward home as the late afternoon warmth swelled around them, sticky-hot but not its typical bother. He slowed to a stop unexpectedly, and she followed suit, turning to face him. "You look really pretty today, Dolly," he said with his eyes downcast, shifting from foot to foot.

"Thanks." It was just a mumble. "But if I'd known you were coming over I would've—"

It happened there. Mid-sentence the kiss came at her, both a natural progression and an utter shock. A moment of awkward mechanics, moving lips and tongues around each other to find the right fit. And then the softening of everything, as he placed his hand around the back of her neck, pulled her in. *So this is what it's like*, she thought. *This is how it begins.*

It was a dizzying mix of kissing, walking, whispering in the shade of the tree-lined street. They found themselves at the end of their shared road, a spot so familiar, feeling now completely different. As different as it could ever be. Even as it was happening, Dolly could hardly wait to tell Steph about kissing Declan. Of course, Steph had already had her first (and many subsequent) kisses, but Dolly felt a bit lucky that hers was happening on top of slowly developing feelings. Not in a hidden corner of a house party with a near stranger, alcohol-induced and messy, like many teenager's first times would be, she imagined.

Kissing Declan was like watching shooting stars and rainbows exploding at the backs of her eyelids. He tasted like salt and cherry ice cream; his tongue warm and firm against hers. *I'm falling for the neighborhood boy*, she thought. *What a goofy cliche.* With his arm slung low around her back, his hand fit perfectly in the pocket of her jean shorts. Maybe it had been a fast-paced day for a couple of friends, but in retrospect she could track the lead-up.

All those times sophomore year when he'd come around wanting to make sure she and Stephanie would be joining the gang for dinner, at the county fair, to watch the rodeo. Maybe it wasn't just because she lived right down the street, and apparently it hadn't been about Stephanie at all. Maybe it had been more the whole time... like the mornings at the bus stop when he'd asked her seemingly random questions about a class, a homework assignment, a friend they had in common. Casual conversation, she'd thought. Just a kindness to the shy girl. But it wasn't that. Now, she could see clearly from the other side of it. It was *definitely* more.

"See you in the morning then, Dolly Mae?"

"What's happening in the morning?" She wasn't sure how to play it cool, but also felt so emboldened by what had just happened that picking out the right words didn't seem to matter as it had just hours ago.

"Thought we'd take a walk, maybe grab a little breakfast."

"Alright, then. I'll see you in the morning."

She did see him in the morning, and pretty much every day after that. The next few weeks unraveled like the front end of a country song; he picked her flowers from the side of Mrs. Hunter's bushes that hung over the fence into his backyard, tied them with a piece of pink ribbon stolen from his mama's sewing box. They kissed for hours, and started to think about doing a little more. At night it was cookouts in someone's yard and movies on the couches of each other's living rooms. Usually they were flanked by friends, but they often felt like it was just the two of them together, despite the crowd around them.

Always the token shy girl in the group, Dolly found herself newly pushed toward front and center by his side. Maybe they had all started to see something new in her, felt the energy of her new-found confidence, or maybe it was just the two of them. But things were different now, that was for sure. She was Declan's girl.

* * * * *

He came to pick her up at exactly six his first night as a licensed driver. It was still almost 90 degrees outside and the gauzy cotton of Dolly's dress clung to the backs of her legs. She'd pretty much given up on makeup at this point in the relentless heat, but wore some pink lip gloss, grateful her complexion was clear and browned from the summer sun.

She hopped up into his hand-me-down white Chevy truck cautiously, settling herself before glancing up to catch his gaze. Those crystal blue eyes were like puddles in the sun, multidimensional and reflecting the light right back at her. They would be the pair that set the tone for all future eye-gazing, which was probably a large part of why many of her subsequent relationships failed; they just couldn't compare in any way to Declan, starting with the eyes.

It wasn't just that. There was also the dusting of friendly freckles that gave a boyish look to the manly face he was starting to grow into. A strong jaw with a little bit of baby-faced cheek remaining just above. A mop of sandy hair in desperate need of a cut, mussed from a day under a hat, but spruced up lightly with some gel before heading out the door. And those broad, proud shoulders that only slouched, only turned inward and down, when he leaned in toward her for a kiss. Everything about Declan made her feel special and rare. That's the thing about first love. It turns you into the person you always hoped you'd be, while you drink in the best features of the one you're falling with.

"What?" he asked, a slow smile creeping up on one cheek.

"Nothing," she returned with flushing cheeks.

Declan shook his head slowly, reached over to grab her hand in his. "Well. You look prettier than a picture tonight, Miss Weston. And *that's* not nothin'." She leaned in closer, rested her head on his shoulder. The cab of the truck smelled a bit musty, but she didn't mind.

Is this how it goes?, she thought. *Do these dizzy, aching feelings stick around, or will it eventually turn into something else?*

She didn't want to dwell on it. Didn't like the possibility that there could ever come a day when she could hop into the shotgun seat of his truck and not feel warm and buzzy at the sight of those gorgeous baby blues; in fact she feared it. A day when anything, or everything, could be different. Because she'd been waiting a long time to feel what this was like, and now that she had it, she couldn't imagine ever letting it go.

BEFORE

Dolly's mother grew up Sally Day in a sprawling stucco mansion in Highland Park, Texas with every comfort a child could want. She was outfitted in a carefully constructed wardrobe of summer-weight wool and linen, soft silks and stiff brocades. Cara Walsh Day, her mother, purchased most of her three daughters' clothing at high-end boutiques and had the rest commissioned for them exclusively.

Cara and her husband Sol were a unique couple on the Dallas social scene; she was Irish-Catholic and he was a Polish Jew who had emigrated during World War II and shortened his name from Danglowitz. They weren't WASPs like most of their fancy neighbors, but both their families had worked hard to build small fortunes and the Days were accepted and invited among the Dallas elite for their cash and their class. Or as Sol would often joke, "We blend."

Actual talk of the atrocities of what Sol and his family had experienced during the war was very rare, but the lingering pain and the lessons learned during that time were never entirely out of the family consciousness. It was in the way Sol would insist on using every tube of toothpaste down to the point of having to cut the back open for a final squeeze, despite their fantastic wealth. And the way he insisted on lighting Shabbat candles every Friday night even though they rarely went to services as a family. Cara had her own complicated relationship with feeling "othered" in Dallas society, so she didn't harp on Sol's idiosyncrasies. Not too much, anyway.

Despite their healthy financials, the Days made no attempt to hide their roots. And so they fit in, but didn't, at the same time. They enjoyed a cushy lifestyle in the posh northern section of Dallas where everyone had country club memberships and butlers. They, too, played tennis and vacationed in Boca Raton. They, too, served caviar at cocktail parties and could decipher a fine bottle of wine from a decent one with a single sniff.

In her pink pillbox hats and Chanel suits, Cara was a Jackie Kennedy emulator and lover of all the fine things. Her own family had found their success in New York City before packing up and heading west and south for a simpler life in Oklahoma where they could enjoy their wealth with a side of privacy. Meeting Sol and creating a life in Dallas where he managed the Southern branch of his family's business in a lucrative but hands-off manner, worked for everyone.

Sally's parents didn't participate in the rumor mill and one-upping of the 1950's and 60's Dallas elite like her classmates' families did; they were accepted and enjoyed among neighbors and in the philanthropy world. They threw great parties and kept up, but despite their large social circle, only a precious few made it past the gates of their hearts. Cara was known for her lavish parties and at those, everyone who was anyone was present. But she could count on one hand how many women were ever invited to turn up in casual clothing for coffee and a cigarette. Her secret hope was that her three daughters would make husbands out of the sons within *that* circle.

When her youngest and most precocious daughter met a young bank clerk from East Texas at a gala Uptown and came home with stars in her eyes for him, Cara bit her tongue but hoped it was a phase. In keeping with the style of a refined Southern woman, she kept her mouth closed, silently willing

Sally to move on and turn back in the direction she was supposed to be going... up north in the country, or at least on the social ladder.

NOW

February, while technically the shortest month of the year, is droning on relentlessly. The piercing chill in the air is a perfect match for the stale place Dolly has fallen into at home and at the office. Michael has been so busy with work this week that they've barely shared a conversation, let alone a meal or any semblance of quality time. She feels adrift and it's hard to fight the loneliness of it even when she has her own work to keep her occupied.

And as for that—Sandra still hasn't hired any support staff leaving Dolly and Glinda to share an intern. The college junior is about as green as they come and can only be at the office two days a week when she's not in class. Dolly wishes she could find the twenty-year-old's wide-eyed optimism a comfort and a genuine help, but so far the only task she seems to consistently get right is the coffee order, and even that took a lot of training. Any hope of lightening Dolly's actual workload so she can focus on new or more ambitious projects is out the window for now. Glinda, who's usually about as relaxed as PR girls come, is also getting annoyed. On a cold and rainy Thursday, the two women nip out for a quick lunch a few blocks away to escape the stress inside their marble and lucite prison.

Their sturdy boots pound in unison against the Fifth Avenue sidewalk, black-tighted legs in step and their skirts—one pleated, one twirl—swishing breezily in turn.

It is a funny thing how, having known each other only a few

years, Glinda and Dolly have become so close and sisterly, it's as if they were always friends. Dolly often wonders if it's kismet that they both applied for jobs at this particular firm in that exact time period. With so many directions in which a young fashion major with an interest in advertising and editorial could start her career, why did they both land at LAZR when they did?

And on days like today, when she and Glinda have turned up at the office wearing nearly identical outfits, or at times when Dolly reaches for her phone to text her and sees a message coming in from her that very moment, she is reminded of the goodness and promise of fate. That sometimes in life you lose people that mattered a lot, but that you can start fresh. That you can forge new bonds that are even stronger than the old ones were. Or at least just as important.

Over chopped salads and Diet Cokes, the conversation with Glinda moves from work frustrations to the ups and downs of dating in New York. Glinda hilariously details her one-night-stand from last night with a guy whose name she mortifyingly cannot remember, but whose skill in the bedroom has her craving another meet-up.

"I literally saved him in my phone as Bar 6," she admits, as that's where they met. "I texted him this morning to see if he wants to hang this weekend, but nothing yet..."

Glinda's wide gray eyes look out the window of the salad spot where they sit on high stools along a countertop facing out. She has enviable cheekbones and smooth skin, a pixie-like look that matches her whimsical name. Glinda is goodness and light and everything earnest in the world, so Dolly worries about her in moments like this when she seems so hell-bent on sabotaging her chances at happiness in a world too cruel to comprehend.

Why would you pine away for a one-night-stand who won't text you back? Dolly wants to implore, her thoughts resting briefly on Michael. Her strong and caring fiancé has never left her hanging. Not once. From the moment he practically barged into her life, he's been a steadfast pillar of Doing What's Right. He has his quirks (like the off-key shower performances) and downright infuriating tendencies (like leaving wet towels slung over the backs of velvet furniture or sweat-soaked workout clothes in a heap on hardwood floors), but he is a lover and a caretaker with a tender heart. Glinda deserves that kind of security, that kind of protection.

"He's probably busy with work," Dolly returns her friend's open-ended statement carefully.

Shaking out of her moment's daydream, Glinda shrugs. "It's all good. Honestly, he was hot as fuck, but it's not like I'm wanting to get wifed up anytime soon." After a beat she murmurs, "Sorry," in the direction of Dolly's large engagement ring.

The two women's situations are so vastly different that Dolly feels a slight jolt at the fact that a sliver of comparison has been made. "Oh, please. It's fine... Anyway, I kind of miss one-night stands, to be honest!"

But it isn't until she utters the words aloud that she realizes they might be somewhat true. Glinda is too kind to push the issue and instead gives her friend a gentle shove on the forearm and roll of the eyes as if to say, *Yeah, right*, before sighing and concluding their lunch with the truth: "We should probably head back to the office before Sandra sends out a search party."

* * * * *

That night, Michael comes in late from work and she awakens

to his fingertips, cold and gentle on her shoulder blades. Half-asleep, she breathes him in, the scents of wool and sweat, cologne and bourbon filling the space between them.

"You look too pretty. I had to wake you up," he whispers, tracing his hand down her side and reaching around toward the waist of her leggings slowly. Feeling herself getting turned on, Dolly whispers, "Hi," and turns her face backward over her shoulder toward him for a kiss. Soon her torso follows and she presses against his body, tasting his tongue as his hands move her elastic waistband out of the way, one wrapped around her back and the other with two fingers lightly hovering on the outside of her silk thong.

After their bodies melt together, rhythmically pushing the day away, Dolly relaxes into the arms of her shirtless fiancé and breathes *Goodnight* as she closes her eyes and prepares to once again find sleep. In the quiet dark of her bedroom, wrapped up in the arms of the man who will soon become her husband, she is reminded briefly of that surprising confession she made at lunch. But the comfort and relaxation of this moment are enough to override any truth in the statement— because as much as she might miss the single life from time to time, this is better than any one-night stand she's ever had. *Maybe that's why we get married anyway,* she thinks while drifting back to sleep.

Maybe the whole point of getting married is that sex alone isn't enough to keep us satisfied for the rest of our lives. But sex *and* companionship? That does a pretty good job.

THEN

Stephanie confessed about two weeks into the budding romance between Dolly and Declan that she had "totally seen it coming." It was so like Steph to try and claim some ownership over the most important new element of Dolly's life.

"If you *knew* he liked me, why on earth didn't you tell me?" Dolly implored over Cherry Cokes one late June afternoon. The girls were barefoot and perched on the top of Dolly's back porch stairs.

"I thought it'd be more fun to sit back and watch y'all fall in love, I guess," Steph said, as straight-faced as she could muster before dissolving into giggles.

"You're such an ass," Dolly said with an elbow-jab.

"What should we do tonight?" Steph asked. There were parties going on in various corners of town and just as plausible was the offer to go to an R-rated movie with Dolly's mom and eat their weight in popcorn and candy without spending a cent of their babysitting money. Declan was out of town overnight on a camping trip with his dad, and Dolly was actually glad to have a little time to solely focus on her oldest and dearest friend. Every other summer had been theirs and theirs alone, and a part of her missed the endless days in Stephanie's carefree company.

* * * * *

The summer before, the two had made a pact on this very

porch. A promise that by this time the following year, they'd each have had their first kiss. Not surprisingly, Steph had ponied up to the task almost immediately, making out with some senior boy at a party just weeks after. Dolly had never confessed to her friend, but when Stephanie came back inside from the bushes at the side of the house where the kiss had gone down, pink-cheeked and wild-eyed, ready to confess, she already knew what had happened.

It had been about twenty minutes since Dolly had excused herself for the bathroom and emerged to find Stephanie no longer in the kitchen. She didn't exactly panic, but that fuzzy, angry thought bubble that tended to pop up in times like this was flying high: *You are alone at this party with a bunch of older kids who don't know you. Steph is cooler than you and has taken off to have fun while you awkwardly look around for her like a lost puppy. Also, your outfit kind of sucks.*

She had gulped inadvertently and calmed her breathing so that she was able to focus on the moment and try to get through this murky, uncomfortable bump in the evening unscathed. Obviously, she knew her best friend would not always be able to accompany her to absolutely everything in life. At a certain point, Dolly was going to need to learn how to make her way through a house party with a genuine smile on her face and probably even say hi to someone she didn't know.

But tonight was not that night.

Fumbling with her bag, Dolly decided her best course of action was to go outside and get some fresh air. She didn't have a cell phone like some of the kids at school had started getting, but she had a compact and a lipstick. These could serve as a decent excuse to be standing off from the crowd for a minute, not that anyone would notice that she'd left.

Once outside, the nagging question of where the heck Stephanie had gone to was answered almost instantly. A rustle in the bushes just off to the side of the wide, wrap-around porch caught her attention, and several feet from where she stood, she could make out a mess of auburn curls and a tight white t-shirt being lifted slightly at the waist.

Stephanie was locking lips with a tall boy in a collared polo shirt. Dolly could tell by the biceps bulging out of the cuffs of his short sleeves and the manly cut of his jaw that he was definitely not their age. Here they were, a mere two weeks into their kissing pact, and her best friend was making out with some hot, older guy while Dolly stood awkwardly on a stranger's porch alone.

It wasn't a great feeling, but Dolly was mature enough to understand that this wasn't about her at all. So as not to risk being caught inadvertently watching them in the bushes, she quietly shuffled back into the house and made her way toward the kitchen. She pulled a can of beer out of a cooler that sat on the floor beside the kitchen island, cracked it open and took a sip. It felt bubbly on her tongue. She'd had a small glass of wine with her parents at dinner from time to time this past year or so, and *this* tasted nothing like that. Dolly placed the beer can on the countertop and, to busy her hands, loaded up a napkin with Doritos. She tried to smile at random people as they passed her by in clusters or alone.

It was right then that Dolly became convinced for real that it was time to come out of her shell. She didn't yet know that it would take almost a year from this very moment before she finally got that coveted first kiss. But in the months that unfolded after that awkward night Dolly would slowly start to transform herself bit by bit into the person she wanted to be.

She would soon shed the more juvenile outfits she'd worn throughout much of ninth grade and ditch the ribbon from her hair. She would finally pack away the dolls that still lined her bedroom shelves. She would flirt a little bit, lift out of her comfort zone. Maybe it would take a lot of practice, but now she was determined that it was time.

Stephanie did eventually burst back into the kitchen at that house party to rescue her shy friend. She confessed about the kiss—bushes, nameless stranger, and all. She challenged Dolly to a one-upping that they didn't know they'd both be waiting eleven months for. She linked arms with her best friend, grabbed her own beer, and guided Dolly through the crowded kitchen and out onto the back deck.

"This is my best friend, Dolly Weston," she said, introducing her to some older girls she knew from her church's youth group.

"Hey, Dolly, I'm Allison," said a petite brunette with perfect chiclet teeth and a high ponytail.

"Hi, is this your house? It's really nice."

"Aw, thanks. No, it's actually my uncle's but I'm sort of house-sitting for the weekend. Which reminds me—I've got to grab the mail and put it inside before I forget and have no excuse to be here!" The girl giggled and disappeared down the deck steps, toward the gate in the fence.

"Well, look at you being conversational with a stranger," Stephanie lightly teased her friend.

"Oh, fuck off," Dolly said. But both girls laughed because it was funny and true.

* * * * *

Even once you've decided you're really going to change, you still need a friend by your side to give you a little push. Stephanie had always been that friend to Dolly and she planned to keep it that way. If you had told either one of them that warm summer night of Steph's first kiss or even a year later as they sat on the porch swinging their legs and sipping their sodas, that their bond wouldn't last forever, they wouldn't have believed you.

Tonight, though, there was a movie to see and treats to enjoy. Much to Sally's surprise and delight, the girls decided in the end to skip the party invites and join her for a night at the movies.

"Oh, isn't this so much *fun!*" Dolly's mother practically squealed as the three of them pulled up to the large cinema at the center of town. Inside the icy movie theater, the sweat-pant-clad teenagers and pretty mom in white jeans waited in line for their movie tickets and then snacks. One of the many reasons Stephanie's own mother had never quite warmed to Sally was definitely her appearance. Though the women were close in age, Sally wore it better. Her hair was shoulder-length and a deep golden color (what her dad had always called, "Jewish blond").

Sally was sunny and kind, with a wide smile that revealed large, straight teeth, and oversized green-blue eyes that held your attention. While her husband Dale was attractive in his own right, it was a running joke around town that Sally could've had any man in Texas. Despite being unprovable, it was probably true.

The girls were uncomfortably aware of Stephanie's mom's jealousy of the other woman, thanks to little jabs and jokes made behind her back through the years. But Sally would never let on that she knew, even if she did. For her, taking Stephanie Longman under her wing as a second daughter was just as natural as making sandwiches for the pack of preteen boys that hung out in the cul-de-sac on their bikes on the weekends with nothing else to do. She was just... *like* that.

And, looking up now at her mother's arms overflowing with popcorn and sodas, having stuffed boxes of candy into her oversized purse, Dolly felt for a second like she might cry just thinking about it. "I love you, Mama. You're the best," she whispered when Stephanie was off to the side, using Sally's cell phone to let her own mother know their plan and when to expect her back home.

"I love you too, sweetie," Sally returned with a smile. "Thanks for coming with me tonight. It seems silly, but this is so much fun for me." She elbowed her daughter softly, not having a free hand to place on her, and then moved back, cheerfully asking Stephanie how her mom was as the other teenager rejoined them and the trio made their way into the theater.

In the months that unfolded after that sweet June evening, Dolly would let go of this sliver of memory in favor of much more exciting things than a connection with her mom. Things like Declan, of course. Things like cheerleading and fashion magazines, malt beverages and MTV. But many years down the road when she was grown up and elegant herself, this memory of their quiet movie theater exchange would rest calmly on her heart. With all the bends and ebbs of the teenage and college years, as natural as they were, she would develop a certain grief inside of her when moments just like this one, were no more.

No matter what—or who—else came into or walked out of her life from that point on, it was always in the back of Dolly's mind somewhere that her first love had been her mother. That beautiful truth would stand the test of time, even when very little else did.

NOW

It's a late winter's day in New York City: bleak and cold with brief shots of sunshine reflecting off skyscrapers. The sidewalk beneath Dolly's feet is covered in a slippery layer of half-melted slush, thick with dirt and the occasional glint of glitter. March is holding on firm with no hints of spring to be found, and the overall scene is bleak.

Tonight, she has drinks booked at the Monarch with a new client and their team. First thing tomorrow morning, she'll be on a plane to a rented car to a freeway to a dirt road home. Where Michael will make his way into the next 24 hours is beyond her, but she pulls out her phone anyway to send a quick text:

Client drinks tonight. "Dessert" after? x

An eternity (or about 30 minutes) later, she's at her desk, wrapped in a chunky scarf against the unrelenting cool air that seems to push through the office vents all year round. Any sun that earlier snuck between this morning's clouds is now completely gone. Outside, the sky looks so dark and foreboding, it seems for a moment inconceivable that she's expected to be anywhere but her own apartment, tucked into bed.

A whole day's work lies ahead, though: a scattered yet packed to-do list staring back at her from the demanding computer screens. Needy clients and hard-to-get editors; resumes to read and emails to respond to. It's all important and it must be done, but Dolly is lost in thoughts of tomorrow. She pauses a moment to stare out the window beside her desk, at that gray sky. Against it are a cutout portrait of buildings in dark shapes, fuzzy at the background and sharper way up front. She can hear the shouts and sirens from below despite the closed windows, can feel the pulsing of city life all around even in the near solitude of her fifteenth-floor office suite.

New York, she thinks sarcastically. *Good old New York.* Where she always hoped she'd end up. The city of fabulous things, where careers are made and magazine-quality dreams become real life if you're willing to work hard enough to make them come true.

New York... where sweet small-town girls meet modern Prince Charmings, their crowns replaced by gold Rolexes and multiple framed diplomas hanging, slightly off-center, in bachelor pads. A tableau of overpriced leather and lacquer, a mix of hand-me-downs from wealthy parents and first-big-job purchases. Boys like Michael. *Men* like Michael.

And with the thought of him, the words, *I'll miss you*, flicker across her consciousness.

The phone's vibration startles Dolly to the point of actually jumping in her seat. A quick glance confirms it's him responding to her text from earlier: *Sounds good. Will come over after gym.*

This man and the gym, she thinks with a passing smile. Not an athlete anymore, but always working toward an impeccable form he doesn't need for any practical use. Personal training sessions in the mornings and cardio or weights after work, almost daily. Sure, there's the wedding to think about. But only just engaged, they have over a year to get there. Taking a bite of her everything bagel with scallion cream cheese (one *definite* perk of living in New York), Dolly is grateful for that year.

K. See you then x

Working through lunch and into the early afternoon to secure a new salon client front-page coverage, she finally escapes for a coffee break to give her father a quick call. "Helloooo, Dolly!" The old refrain brings both an instant smile and a soft hint of sadness. She feels suddenly homesick like she hasn't in months, not only for a place but for a person... for herself.

"Hi, Daddy," she presses the phone to her ear, leaning up against the mirrored lobby wall.

"What's shakin' sugar? What time you gettin' in?"

The sound of his voice washes over her, and suddenly she's eleven years old again in a pleated skirt and polo shirt, navy blue. It feels like she could reach across her shoulder to find the strap of that old Jansport right now, smell the library books and pencil shavings within. See the high sheen of the gym floor as the day wound down and the few kids whose parents were running late huddled together by the hallway payphone to determine a new plan.

Oh, Daddy. Where did all the years go? She wonders silently. In just a few weeks, her childhood home will be packed up and torn down. Daddy and the surrounding neighbors have sold their houses to a developer for decent chunks of change. *Can't stop progress*, she thinks, wincing.

"I land just after noon and will be home well before dinner!"

"Okay, honey," he says with a confidence edged in loss. "Thanks for doing this, Doll."

"Of course. It's nothing, Daddy. See you soon."

* * * * *

At drinks last night, the new clients delighted in hearing about

Dolly's Texas routes. *Do your parents hunt? How'd you end up here? Where's the accent?* It's not often that she comes across Northerners with superiority complexes who barely veil their judgement of a small-town Texas girl at the table, but when it happens it annoys her terribly. People like this tend to think that anyone born in the Northeast has a birthright to starting their careers in New York City, but that a Southerner, and one who hasn't quite dropped the use of the word "y'all," doesn't belong. If only they knew how much this city meant to her, and how hard she worked to get to exactly where she is in it.

Now she has her right hand raised at the street corner, a wheely bag in the left. Off to JFK in a yellow cab, allowing herself a mental break from work for the morning as she'll be busting out her laptop on the plane. She knows Sandra well enough by now to understand that special privileges like last-minute requests for long weekends off are not something you want to mess with. If you got it, and you want to get it again, you had better keep your shit together while you're gone.

Michael *did* come over last night, but it was clear the gym had done him in. After wolfing down a power bowl of grilled veggies and chicken over quinoa, he passed out on her couch in his workout clothes, snoring deeply with the TV remote in his hand. So much for "dessert." Michael isn't always the most reliable when it comes to evening plans. Sure, the gym is a part of his life and an escape that he deserves, but shouldn't you want to see your girlfriend, *nee, fiancée!*, the night before she heads home to Texas for a long weekend?

It wasn't enough to wake him and start a fight over this morning, but now she finds herself missing him and feeling restless. In the cab she looks out the window. Behind her oversized sunglasses in the lifting fog post-dawn, the city is still sleepy and has lost its edge of night. She loves this time of day in

New York, when the only people competing with her view are quiet, small-business owners sweeping the sidewalks outside their storefronts, delivery men with packages strapped to their bikes.

It's weird, she thinks, to be headed home and living in it at the same time. Dolly can't wait to step off that plane into the Dallas sunshine (Texas wouldn't dare freeze you out in March like New York does!), but she is also a little sad to be flitting away from New York without having had a proper kiss from Michael on her way off. She lovingly watches her new home go by in a blur, now barrelling up the Belt Parkway toward the airport, thoughts of deadlines and emails she needs to answer intermingling with the promise of the weekend to come, a few days to spend at the slower pace of Texas.

Dolly will always be a small-town Texas girl at heart, with long messy hair and knobby knees and a love of country music that nothing could ever extinguish. But she is now also a New York woman with a big life, caught in between the memories of what she had… and the reality of what she's created. Now she has a massive diamond ring on her left hand and the Plaza booked for a Saturday next June. A handsome fiancé with dark brown curls who forgot to wake her up last night but damn sure will make up for it when she gets home in a few days. She aches for him a bit now, the way Michael's smoldering eyes watch her with a sense of familiarity and adoration whether she's practicing a pitch or burning toast.

And speaking of pitches, she's got her recent promotion and a wardrobe her old friends would lose their minds over. The dream. The whole damn thing. *This* is home.

And yet, and yet… Texas-bound to collect, organize, and purge the belongings of the woman who made it all possible. Packing up the house that raised her up. Saying goodbye to the first version of herself. Closing a chapter, hand-in-hand with the only family she has left.

* * * * *

Dolly doesn't notice eyes falling or fixating on her as she removes her shoes at security or settles into a blue leatherette chair, but that doesn't mean they don't. In her own estimation, Dolly is average looking: five-foot-five and willowy, "all leg" as Mama used to say. Her hair hangs straight, sheet-like and pale blond. When she first arrived in New York it remained its natural honeysuckle in waves, but after her first batch of comped highlights at Sally Hershberger a year or so into her job at LAZR, she was hooked. The hair—the whole person—started to change. She is now classic, New York chic. Capable of blending in a crowd. Easy to trust with a warm smile, but tough as any man underneath. It's not that she doesn't think she's pretty; it's just that she knows everyone else is, too.

In the eleven years since moving here and creating a life for herself, Dolly has changed along with her hair. Once the dirty-blond girl next door, freckle-faced and pillow-lipped wearing nary more than a sweep of mascara, she is now glamorous in almost perpetual black from head-to-toe. She often wears crimson lipstick on weekday mornings (even put-together Mama would think that's a bit much) and her hair is just about as blond as she can get away with. The freckles are really the only piece of her old self that have stayed exactly the same, but on this elegant, late-20's version of her, even *they* look chic and refined. Of course, she's learned the tricks of the trade in lessening their contrast against the rest of her skin. And John-John, whose opinion on all things makeup and face-related she would take over anyone else's, insists that the freckles keep her looking unique in a sea of fashion girls all grasping for the top. "It's that whole young-and-flirty thing, honey. Keep 'em."

But Dolly is striking, even if she doesn't know it. Dressed casually for traveling today without her typical "face" on, she is beauty itself, Americana-plus. From the upturned nose to the glossy pout, she has become a gorgeous combination of her past and her future. The hometown country girl may glow in expensive elixirs, wrapped up in the best fabrics, but her radiance comes from down deep inside.

Smiling now at the barista and then the ticket attendants, leaning down to pick up the fallen toy of a crying toddler whose mother has her arms full with a younger baby, Dolly has a generosity of spirit and an emanating kindness that shows in her grace and the way she speaks to people. It's part of why she's been successful in her career: unlike some of her more cutthroat contemporaries, Dolly has risen quickly because she's humble and takes care to write thank-you notes, to follow-up without pressure. She can delight just about anybody with a smile and a brief conversation or kind gesture. Some may call it Southern charm: she just thinks of it as what's right. Kindness. Grace. The things her mother taught her from the first days of life until the very last ones they had together.

* * * * *

The plane touches down in Dallas and Dolly is on her way home within an hour. In the rental car, it takes a few minutes to get used to actually driving. It's a skill that seems to become rustier the longer she lives in New York. Soon, though, the familiar sound of her back-home radio station comes through the speaker, washing her worries away. She is at peace, if only for a little while. She needs to be on call for work… but not when she's driving.

It is a thrill to hear some older country music come on the radio. "Strawberry Wine" starts playing and suddenly she's back: sixteen again and in love with the boy down the street. A song Michael would never in a hundred years understand. He'd probably laugh, actually, if he could see her now. Belting out about the hot July moon, recalling being tangled up in an old handmade quilt on a neighbor's musty couch, or in the bed of a truck. A teenager hearing the song for the first time and knowing that she'd one day look back and reminisce on just that. So many feelings. The sweetness mingling with the losses, and before she knows it, a tear rolls down her cheek.

That's another thing New Yorkers don't get to do: listen to music alone in their cars and have a good cry.

But the sunshine feels good surrounding her rental car from every angle, and warming her skin in the process. That hot Texas sun is nowhere near its seasonal peak, but in March down here it already feels like the beginning of a New York summer. The glow of it is like a literal hug and the symbolism of this switch from yesterday's slush and gloom is not lost on Dolly.

By the time she nears Sugar's Bend, muscle memory has taken over and Dolly realizes she hasn't read a sign or contemplated a turn in almost an hour. Off the highway and onto smaller, local roads, the reminders of her roots start popping up left and right.

Soon she approaches the center of her hometown and can feel the familiarity of it flood the car. There, the billboard that the high schoolers would dare each other to climb up and repaint under the cover of darkness. Up this bumpy road and two left turns to the creek where they spent summer days skinny-dipping after telling their mamas they would just be at the mall with the girls.

And of course, finally, just down the street from her house is the most poignant landmark of them all. There's no way to avoid this spot on her route; no tricky, backroad, "long way" when it's right at the entrance to her own street. Dolly's heart just about stops as she passes by the site of so many weighted memories, trying not to look but seeing it all the same.

Powder blue with white shutters, his dad's old Dodge parked out front. The Crues always liked to keep the driveway clear of cars for visitors, but she best remembers his own truck parked right there. Unthinkingly lifting her hand to adjust her sunglasses, and reaching for her lip gloss, Dolly smiles at this silly gesture.

He won't be there, and even if he were, a glitzy pair of sunnies and some trend-right lips wouldn't change a thing. She's engaged to be married and he's a ghost from the past. It's a shame though, isn't it? How sometimes in life, the ghosts seem to walk among us.

Dolly pulls into her old driveway at the end of the road, just one house down from where it dead-ends. Before rushing inside, she pulls out her phone to check in with Michael. Knowing she'll get swept up when she gets in the house, she decides now is a good time for a quick "hi."

The phone rings four times before going to voicemail. Dolly hangs up to send a text instead, and sees he already has.

Hi babe. So sorry about last night. Make it up to you next week, promise...

She smiles at her phone and punches in a response. *Landed safe. Just got to my dad's. Next time I leave town, don't forget to kiss me goodbye! xx*

Dolly tucks her phone back into her bag and takes a deep breath, looking toward the house. Everything feels so familiar and yet so far from her new reality. With fresh eyes that haven't seen it in almost a year-and-a-half, she can see that the place clearly needs a facelift, but that isn't why she's here.

She came down to pack it up, clean it out, and get Daddy

ready for his next chapter. The house doesn't need fixing up just to be torn down. The ranch-style home of her childhood, an ample front lawn dry-yellow even in March long before the summer scorch; the house with its chipped paint and brick-faced in all its late 70's glory, will be no more.

Compared to whatever glamorous home she and Michael will one day choose among the sky-rises of Manhattan or the lush suburbs of Long Island, this 40-ish-year-old Texas classic isn't much on the eyes, despite how well her parents always kept it up. *Oh, but it's mine,* she thinks for a second, the emotional pull catching her breath. Or it is for a few more days anyway... and then it will be gone forever.

Daddy's waiting inside and she could use a sweet tea. On with it, then.

THEN

The best thing about being young and in love is the natural abandon that the feeling creates. Suddenly all of the other things that used to trouble you greatly, seem to matter less. Distress over an argument with a parent or the loss of an object seem less profound because something bigger than a momentary setback is happening to you. The limits of your life grow wider while your focus fine-tunes on the minute details that ultimately build up into the thing that feels like the biggest piece of it all: *love*.

As Dolly and Declan spent that summer stretched out underneath the Texas sun, this is how things went. Though they hadn't actually said the words, they both knew what was brewing beneath the surface. They hadn't done more than kissing and running their hands up and down each others' bodies, but even that intimacy felt deep and changing. How many nights had they spent tangled up in a mess of limbs and long hair, sweat beads forming on the ends of their noses, lips interlocked and breathlessly holding back words?

Words. So often in life they serve to make things worse. And even the best ones can come crashing in at the wrong moments and make someone run scared. So, while she had started to fall for him soon after that first kiss, over a month enveloped them before Dolly let herself put a name on it, out loud anyway. But the day it happened was one she'd never forget.

Declan was more impulsive than she was, bringing out a spontaneous side she'd never known existed. One late July morning he showed up at the usual time and asked if she had the whole day free. *For you?* She thought, *Forever and a day.* Instead, she nodded with a simple, "Sure."

They hopped into the truck and drove for miles before he finally revealed their destination. "When was the last time you went out to Dallas?" he asked, those blue eyes dancing.

"Oh, um, it's been awhile," she said, realizing suddenly that she'd never been to the big city in the capacity that she was about to. All of her childhood (which was what life before this feeling had been), Dallas trips had always included her parents. Usually, she went to Neiman Marcus with Mama to pick out a dress for some special occasion and then stopped by Zayde and Granna's for a brief visit and a bite to eat. Often around Christmastime to see the city all lit up. Occasionally with Daddy to watch the Cowboys play a home game. And plenty of times to spend a long weekend or holiday at her grandparents' home. The thought had never occurred to Dolly to hop in a vehicle and head out to Dallas with another teenager, especially a boy. But of course now that he suggested it, she couldn't think of any better way to spend a day.

Declan kept his eyes on the road for most of that hour-long drive to Dallas, sneaking glances her way when he dared. Dolly tried her best to act natural and not nervous, but something in his demeanor said today was going to be important.

"How's your summer been, then, Doll?" he teased, breaking the silence with a chill smile. The question was obviously a joke, since he'd been there for all of it. But she decided to play along.

"I don't know, it's been alright..." she offered slyly. "How about yours?"

"A hell of a lot better than I expected," he shot back, sneaking another quick glance in her direction. After a beat he continued, surprising her. "You went from my crush to my girl this summer, so I'd say it's been one for the books."

"Declan!" It was still hard to believe that she'd ever been anyone's crush, despite Steph's prior confession that she'd "totally" seen all of this coming. Dolly's mind went back again to last summer, standing awkwardly on that porch outside a party with the floorboards vibrating to the music from within. Catching sight of her best friend making out under the moonlight, while she herself felt like the least desirable or interesting person there. How long had the hottest guy in her neighborhood been checking her out across the table at their favorite local diner? How long had she secretly been... seen?

And she saw him, too. Of course she did. But until that June day he'd made the first move, she never would have even dared to imagine that she'd be sitting shotgun in his truck by the close of the summer, joy-riding all the way to Dallas with sexual chemistry practically surging between them, covering them in a heavy cloak of teenage feelings.

"I had no idea you had a crush on me..." she said, placing her hand on his thigh.

"Well, I'm just glad I finally worked up the nerve to ask you out," he replied, turning the radio dial back up a smidge at the sound of a favorite song, but not loud enough to drown out the conversation. Just about everything Declan did was adorable, even the way he cussed under his breath when someone cut him off on the highway. Over the medium-volume poppy twang that emanated from the truck's speakers, they talked about everything and nothing. Swapped stories of childhoods similar in scope, taking place right on that same street.

Both of them only children, there were familial bonds that ran deep. A responsibility to their mothers, who had each stayed at home to raise their children. Who were both now middle-aged women with a seeming bud of lacking purpose developing as their children grew older and more independent. Of course, as teenagers it was difficult to find a way to describe or understand that completely.

"I honestly think my mom enjoys doing my laundry," Declan said with a chuckle.

"Same!" Dolly retorted, laughing. It felt a little wrong to discuss her mother like this, to expose and analyze her as a person, as if they were on the same level. As if she had a right.

Shame swelled somewhere deep within her, but she suppressed it. This is what teenage girls do, right? Ride around in trucks falling for cute boys, make little jabs about their parents. This is life. *Lighten up*, she told herself fiercely while saying a private apology to sweet Mama who didn't deserve the mockery. Because after all, it was her mother who was the center of it all. Her dad worked hard, yes, managing the biggest branch of a successful chain of local banks. He'd played the stock market well and put away money for college for Dolly, while treating his wife and daughter to occasional splurges like a Disney vacation or whatever bag or piece of jewelry they coveted on any given Christmas. But Mama did everything else. Literally, all of it.

The Westons lived a pretty simple life in their sleepy Texas town. Barbecues, bake sales, and BINGO were the best excuses for her parents to get out of the house. Mama, a Dallas society girl at her core, had given up the glitz of city life and moved to this remote suburb after meeting Daddy at that fated dance and spending three years in love prior to a brief engagement and a simple backyard wedding.

While the glamour of her own youth was never too distant a memory, Sally Weston embraced the country life. She'd approached it in the early years with a sort of amused detachment; learning how to bake a pie and mend a sweater was like memorizing lines to a play you had read and enjoyed but never seen performed. As their marriage grew roots, and a daughter was born, it became harder and harder to think of herself as anything other than a small-town wife. And she was happy here. Sincerely, she was. Dallas would always be her past, but Sugar's Bend her future.

But fashion doesn't fade too far into the back of a society girl's memories. It was from Sally that Dolly developed an early love of all things beautiful. Imported silk scarves from France; leather handbags and shoes from Italy. The scent of expensive lipstick; the difference between proper perfume and eau de toilette. What it felt like to really take your time getting ready, and step out at a restaurant or any social gathering looking and feeling your absolute best.

Her mother had no idea how glamorous she was. Few women in the 80's and 90's were still wearing stockings with sundresses on warm Texas days, but Sally Weston was. In her bathroom, Mama kept a tube of lipstick beside her toothbrush and paste, so that every morning as soon as her hygiene routine was completed, her beauty one began.

It would be hard to put into words what her mother had done for her over the years, what she'd taught her about life and love, about respecting yourself and other people. But what she did know was, thanks to her mama's dignity and kindness, thanks to a certain responsibility she'd always felt to make her proud, she had toughed out the waiting period and found her way to the perfect first boyfriend. Dolly had no idea what the future held for her and Declan, but she did know that this particular here and now simply might not exist if she hadn't been raised by the exact mother that she'd been blessed with.

They arrived in Dallas before lunch time and Declan parked the truck on the main avenue. The day dripped with sweetness and felt grownup to Dolly in a way that nothing else ever had before. Though the city wasn't built up then quite like it is these days, they strolled what had been minted the "Uptown" area about ten years back, stopping on foot for tacos and bottled lemonades at a cute Mexican spot unlike anything they had in Sugar's Bend.

Declan was a gentleman and a boy at once—opening doors and giving her light elbow jabs as she teased him. Paying for everything but leaving the decisions about where to go and what to do, to her. He was funny and kind, all the things she'd known about him as a friend as far back as their elementary school days. But now there was another layer, now his jokey tendencies and glowing smiles felt intentional and hers alone.

They talked for hours, popped into a book shop and she introduced him to her nerdy side, asking him what his favorite book was and approving of his answer—*The Catcher in the Rye*. When he returned the question, she was embarrassed to admit it was technically a children's book:

"*The Secret Garden*," she replied, "by Frances Hodgson Burnett. Did you ever read it?"

"Can't say I have," he said with a teasing glint in his eye.

"It's silly, I guess, but I've always loved fairy tales. And that's the most realistic one I've ever read. It kind of makes you feel like magic is real. I know that sounds ridiculous..." she drifted off, looking away for a moment. Declan reached up with two fingers and slowly turned her chin back so that they were locking eyes once more.

"It doesn't sound ridiculous at all," he said, and kissed her right there in the book shop. Dolly could practically feel the eyes of the old ladies shuffling around the Christian Literature section burning holes into her skin, but she didn't care.

"Let's get out of here," he whispered, pulling back gently and grabbing her hands in his own. Dolly nodded conspiratorially, holding back a giggle.

They made their way back to the parked truck and hopped in. Dolly figured they'd head straight toward home, but Dec said there was something he wanted to show her first. He drove up McKinney and merged onto the highway, the music turned up loud enough that it wouldn't allow much conversation. Honestly, she was fine with that and enjoyed looking out her open window, watching the lights of the city whir by as they emerged to meet the ending day.

They drove over a bridge and off of an exit ramp, down around a gritty bend in the road where the visibly down-and-out mingled in groups of threes and fours, where stray dogs wandered in hopes of finding their next meal.

Dolly took in the scene with widening eyes, having never seen this part of Dallas before. Despite all those trips out here with her parents, she'd never been too far outside the main streets of the city. Not in this direction, anyway. With her wealthy grandparents living in Highland Park and every other plan she'd ever had out this way pretty clearly constructed, Dolly guessed she probably had never seen much of the sprawling city at all.

"This is kind of... depressing," she said finally, turning toward Declan who was stopped at a red light.

"I mean, it is..." he paused thoughtfully before explaining, "because a lot of people here are hardly making ends meet. But there's so much potential, too. Sometimes the most beautiful things come out of the hardest parts of life." After a beat he found the next words that fit while she took in what he said, understanding. "Someday I'd like to do something out here. Open a shop, or a little venue with live music. I don't know... help some of these people tap into their talents somehow."

"I love that," she replied, watching concrete and chain-link fade to green pasture as they drove on through. Eventually, Declan pulled the car over into what looked like an abandoned parking lot a ways outside the city limits. She looked at him with eyes that asked, *What now?*, and with the engine idling and his baseball hat pulled low over one eye, he returned her gaze with a smile. He had just bared himself to her, let her in on his passion and secret goal. They had spent the day wandering around Dallas like a pair of young adults in love. He trusted her. He cared about her. She was interesting... she was someone Declan Crue wanted to be around. These facts all came at her a million miles a second, as Dolly suddenly had a glimpse of what it might be like to *really* be together. As adults. Could it be happening, this fast and this real?

Since the time she was about nine years old, she'd watched the movie of her adult life on a screen inside her head. Road trips with her parents were spent looking outside at the green-brown scenery, concrete and billboards. She'd imagined what it would be like to be 15, 18, 21, 30. To be self-possessed and gorgeous in body-skimming jeans and a red lip, to be alluring and melodramatic in the sweetest way. To have a boy, later, a man, with his arms wrapped around her waist, and hers dangling at the back of his neck. To be fiercely and freely alive, in the throes of a great romance. To be admired and adored, for both her quirks and her effervescence.

As early as fourth or fifth grade, she and Steph would talk

about it—about growing up, about falling in love. They had kept "dream boxes" filled with magazine clippings of elegant women in sexy dresses, of handsome bachelors standing against eccentric-looking walls, waiting to fall in love. They swapped tips they'd heard from older girls about how to breathe when you were making out, or about what kind of underwear boys liked. It was all part of a big, snowballing fantasy of what the next stage of life would be. Last summer Steph might have had her first taste of it, but she still hadn't experienced anything like this yet. Despite having dated a few boys this year, she'd never reported back on a day this special and this... what was it?

Grown-up.

The afternoon progressed into what would be one of the pinnacle moments of Dolly's life—the shift from child to adult, in a way—and in the back of her head she was looking forward to revisiting it all with Steph the next day. Going over every minute detail, decoding and reliving it as teenage girls do.

She'd known that there was a passionate person inside her for years. But what others saw in real life, she assumed, was something entirely different. Lanky in ill-fitting jeans, awkward in the way her words came out. A reader, a deep thinker who didn't mean to, but did flash knowledge trivia-style, or correct her friends' grammar simply by using her own properly. She *was* a bit of a nerd, really. Despite the goddess that lived within her waiting for a grand-scale escape, she had seemed for so long to be no one to be noticed.

Only Steph had ever known who else was in there. Her best friend assimilated more easily into the popular crowd and wasn't as bookish as Dolly, who focused on good grades and pleasing her parents. Steph was more applied to succeeding in her cheerleading career (a passion they shared, but one which was better suited to Steph's intense personality and enthusiasm) and, of course, to boys. They were still young teenagers, sure. But they were also girls feeling the pull of womanhood starting to take shape within.

Now, Dolly's world was changing in the front seat of a pickup truck. So many feelings, ones she'd imagined possible but hadn't fully understood, swelled in her mind. Sheer, beautiful, enveloping romance... the momentary but terrifying jolts of reality (high school would be over and they'd be on to their adult lives in less than two years. *Then what?*). The fear of being picked over by another girl... It was a lot.

And while, in the end, it *would* be another girl that ended things between them, she couldn't know that now. And she wasn't afraid enough to *not* dive in.

Dolly pulled down the car's passenger side sun visor and glanced at her reflection in its mirror. The light freckling of late summer seemed more pronounced at this time of day; a slight pink at the tip of her nose was showing, too, after their few hours spent wandering the streets of Dallas. Dolly pulled her lip gloss out of her purse and spread it across her lips slowly. It wasn't an act she really needed a mirror for, but she was already looking, so why not?

Declan leaned in for what she'd later think of as the last innocent kiss, smeared her lip gloss in the process. She wouldn't remember later whether they said much after that, but their bodies did. A slow, quiet nod of her head and then the world tilted on its axis.

Parked in that lot just off the corner of any world she'd ever known, a few miles outside the reaches of the beams of street light and with a clear view of a dumpster no one had probably utilized in months, Dolly's life was about to change. It was maybe not the most romantic spot for one of the most transformative moments of her young life. But it was theirs, and that was that, and here began the switch over from puppy-love to a real, grownup, relationship.

NOW

Inside the house, Daddy looks everything and nothing like she expected him to. Dale Weston always slept well and had boundless energy when she was growing up; now he looks tired. Dolly and Sally used to laugh at how his snoring was enough to keep them both tossing and turning for hours, but he always slumbered right through it. Ever since Mama's death, though, he's expressed having trouble sleeping. Many nights, she knows, he probably nods off upright in that plaid La-Z-Boy in the corner of the living room, letting an inane sports or war documentary ease his brain into the OFF position.

She now notices too, an extra ten or so pounds resting on his formerly trim waist. Hair thinning and graying far beyond what it was this time last year. Yes, Daddy has changed outwardly, but his exuberance and joy at seeing his only daughter is exactly what she'd hoped for. Especially after so many months passing since they last saw each other.

"Honeybee!" he booms, taking the room in a few steps and wrapping his daughter in a bear hug. After what feels like a sufficient embrace, he extends his arms to hold her back for a good view.

"Well, look at you," he says, smiling with just the softest hint of a sigh. "You're all grown up, sweetie."

"Oh, Daddy, come on," she bats his hand away with a smile. "It's only been six months; I look exactly the same."

Shaking his head, a happy(?) tear running down one cheek. "No, sweetie. You don't." He fumbles, reaching for her left hand. "Let me see that sparkler anyway!"—a fake gasp—"Well, I'll be!" Pause. "Boy did a good job."

Dolly extends her left arm to take a peek at the four-carat emerald cut solitaire. "He sure did, Daddy. I—I love my ring. And him. Very much."

"Would'a been nice if he'd shown up to ask me, but I'd say the rock makes up for a 'rocky' beginning." His eyes are shining at his tiny pun, but the low-level hurt is apparent.

"Oh, Daddy," she sighs, knowing that there is truth to the words. "Stop it. That whole 'asking for the hand' thing is so archaic. And anyway, he *did* ask... just... over the phone."

"Yup. I remember. I was there. Just as I'd always pictured it... this Manhattan preppy I've met all of twice calling me up at 10 o'clock at night to ask if he can have my Dolly's hand..."

"Daddy, I—"

Shaking his head to toss all that to the side, he stops himself. "Never mind." He lifts a hand as if to sweep away the awkwardness of this first exchange. "I'm happy for you, Dolly Mae, I really am. I know you wouldn't marry a guy that didn't deserve you." He pauses to think for a half-second. "Of course, as your dad, it's hard to imagine anyone does... but that's another story." Daddy winks and pulls her in for another brief embrace. "Let me grab your bags."

As he bounds out the front door, grabbing the key to the rental car off the foyer table, the shape of the old, happy-go-lucky father she knows so well re-emerges. The way he's always moved around a room, taking up more space than his body with that big personality. The way his joy and gratitude for life just makes everyone around him feel that same way. Dolly smiles, and then takes in the scene around her for the first time since walking through that door.

It's not that the house looks bad... it just doesn't look good. Technically it's clean, but something is off. Plenty is off, actually. It takes a moment for Dolly to place it, but soon what clicks is that nothing has changed, not even the things that really should have by now. Through new, aghast eyes, Dolly looks around the foyer and living room, realizing that Daddy hasn't moved a *thing* in the almost-eighteen months since Mama's sudden death. And we're not talking about furniture.

In what appears to be part homage to the woman who made this house a home and part ineptitude at how to put a space together, Daddy has apparently left every last decoration as she had it, even the seasonal ones. It was October when she died, and the living room reflects that it has been even longer since anything in here was moved or spruced up. A brown flannel throw blanket here, a pumpkin-motif pillow there. *Gosh, fall kitsch strewn about in March... Mama would just die,* she thinks. She is mildly amused for a split second before feeling sick at the thought of the word "die."

From the front she hears Daddy re-enter. He calls out that he's headed to the john and will be back in a few. She walks into the kitchen and it's more of the same: the fridge, always orderly but filled with personality, reveals invitations to weddings and baby showers that have long since taken place. These unborn babies are now a year old, Dolly thinks, sick to her stomach. A class schedule for Sally's gym hangs here, too. October, the year before last. Has he been... What? *Dusting* them? It's not even like everything looks tired and old and stuck in its same position, untouched all this time. It's more like he's been preserving it all.

What the fuck!, she wants to scream. These papers, full of false promises, feel like a slap across the face. Parties to which Mama would have worn a pretty dress, toted a lovingly thought-out hostess gift. Exercise classes where she would have joked breathlessly with her friends in the next row about how good those mimosas were going to taste after this burn. A standard couple of months spread out before Sally Day Weston, an ordinary stretch of time in a life she'd crafted carefully. A life that would be stolen from her, from all of them, by a careless teenager who shouldn't have even been on the road. So... outrageously unfair. A deep rage stirs within her, and Dolly is only half aware of what she does next.

A sudden rush of pulling, ripping, and shoving into the trash is punctuated by a guttural scream from somewhere deep within. And in a matter of seconds, the refrigerator is bare. The haunting fliers, invitations, and schedules that no longer matter, never got to matter, are where they belong. In the trash.

So begins the emotionally wrecking process she came here to complete. But first, she is going to need a glass of wine.

* * * * *

The shock of her tantrum has settled for both of them, and for the newly sparse kitchen as well. Daddy is in there now, standing over the stove top quietly sautéing chicken sausages and bringing a pot of rice water to boil. He might be a bit of a scary bachelor now, but Dolly smiles softly at the comfort of having always known her father can find his way around the kitchen. It's not that Mama didn't cook; most nights, she did. And she did great. But Daddy was raised by a single mother who couldn't afford help; he grew up helping in the kitchen and so doing the same for his family was just a given. He also derived a certain joy from cooking that neither his wife nor his daughter ever did. In that way, this one moment feels very similar to her old life. She holds onto the feeling a beat, then exhales. "I miss seeing you two together in here," Dolly says finally, breaking a silence that feels both natural and slightly awkward.

"I miss it, too, Doll," he says, not looking up from the stove. The flood of memories she's been able to shove deep down living in New York is just starting to rise to the surface. Even over the weekend of the funeral she hardly stepped foot in the house. Every time she's seen him since the loss of her mother it's been somewhere else. In another, emotionless city. In a hotel or at a relative's happy home. Sitting now on a familiar, comfortable kitchen island stool of her adolescence, Dolly is hit again with the understanding that she no longer has a mother. This is how it unfolds, in shockwaves unfamiliar and unexpected. After losing a parent, the reminders never seem to stop. It's like the roof gets ripped right off your life, and the rain can start pouring in at any time.

She also realizes how incredibly hard this all must be for Daddy. Sure, she can shove it down underneath her career and wedding planning; under the layers of silk and leather, the third or fourth espresso martini. While her father, in the same house alone, has had to go through the motions of daily life over and over since that fated day, without his missing piece beside him.

Mama's floral-print apron still hangs on a hook in the corner of the kitchen having escaped the grip of Dolly's wrath earlier. Over there beneath the window sits a glass she used to fill with fresh flowers every week, empty now but not put away. It's like she is still here, but not, at the same time. Just like the fall decorations in the living room and, as Dolly will discover in the morning, just as in the sad and unfulfilled details lurking in nearly every corner of the home.

She's already completely lost her shit and hasn't been in the house more than a few hours, so it's probably not the best time to go room-to-room with a critique for her poor, aching dad. Not to mention the fact that she flew down here to help him pack it all up. There's no need to mention the out-of-season throw pillows, the empty vase. He's been through enough. Instead she will focus on cold, crisp white wine and the chance of a lighthearted conversation with her father whom she misses and loves. After a long day, with eyes gritty from the airplane, and in the wake of the emotionally raw outburst that brought papers to the bin, she just can't say—or feel—anything else deep right now. Can't allow the ache take over.

* * * * *

Down the hall, past the bathroom and to the last door on the right, Dolly lingers at the doorstep of her childhood bedroom. The door creaks like it always did, a welcome rush of feelings waiting to take over. The walls are still covered with magazine clippings she obsessively used to decorate the space back then, their edges now curling but their meanings frozen in a time capsule of memory.

Untouched belongings of a teenage girl with big dreams, tenderly upheld and maintained by two parents who wouldn't dare hold her back. Of *course* Daddy would have loved nothing more than for Dolly to stay in Sugar's Bend, to have taken a job at the bank where he could secure a decent salary and proper benefits. They could genuinely have used her quick wit and modern sensibilities as they expanded into Oklahoma and beyond. She could have gone to a local college, married an upstanding Southern gentleman and had a pack of kids that came over for dinner on Sundays.

But those were his dreams, not hers. And so he kept them inside, mostly.

They weren't Mama's either, if the truth could be told. And this little room, Dolly's own space, is honestly where she feels her mother most of all. Because all those conversations, the hard ones and the hopeful ones, the fashion-focused and the tear-stained, the ones about boys and the others about endings, took place right here. On this ditsy floral bedspread beneath a wall covered in magazine clippings, in a collage of dreams worth pushing toward.

To a teenaged Dolly, the world was two things at once. First, there was the strong, aching pull toward Declan and those dreamy eyes. Plaid shirts handed down from his dad, cut-off at the sleeves and buttoned several spots from the top. Driving down to the creek with the bed of the truck loaded up with friends; buzzing a few beers deep and ready for a dip in the cool water. Clothes cast aside. Stars in her eyes and the warmth of his hand in hers. Losing abandon, losing fear... losing her virginity. It all built up into one whirling hope that maybe they could become something more, could solidify something longer. Something that would last past high school and on into the next exciting chapters of life.

And then there was the fact that she could not stop thinking about doing something with her passion for clothing. For as long as she could remember, ever since those early trips to Dallas with Mama to buy dresses for special occasions, clothes did something to Dolly. Something different and more than they did to other kids her age, even Steph who loved a label just as much as the next girl. Dolly could close her eyes now and distinctly remember the feel of heavy, textured jacquard, or the slight grain of a quality silk against her nine-year-old fingertips.

She would watch Mama in dressing rooms or at home, pulling on an elegant day dress and zipping it up the back. She loved the way clothing could make a person feel, the way it seemed to change everything. It was in the calf muscle that became instantly defined when the foot slipped into a high-heeled shoe.

It was in the new contouring that happened when a good pair of black tights were pulled onto a pair of legs. The way a waist could emerge with the simple fastening of a belt.

Dolly loved fashion because to her it wasn't just about clothes. To her, it felt alive. It wasn't the way the other girls would beg a ride to the mall an hour out of town to gab over coffee drinks and pull as many trendy t-shirts and mini-skirts off the racks as they could afford on their babysitting or fast food checkout wages. It was in a way that felt a lot bigger than that. Fashion moved her and made her feel hopeful and strong.

As much as she wanted Declan (and Heaven knows she wanted him by her side forever...) there was no future in fashion for Dolly here in Sugar's Bend.

It was thus a back-and-forth that second half of high school. Between the fantasies of two different lives that she wanted, and the tiny spark of hope that she might figure out how to merge them in time. How to be both, how to *have* both. To be a wife and a part of the industry in which she desperately coveted a role. To marry the hometown boy and build a career the other girls in Sugar's Bend—even Steph—couldn't possibly imagine. To see the world, and to do it with that first man she loved right by her side.

Now, here she sits, wrapped in a cashmere cardigan, down from the big city for a brief visit home. A diamond ring weighing her left hand down elegantly, if that weight is only imagined. Dolly's got the career. She's built it, to be more accurate. She goes by Dahlia in professional circles and will soon legally change her name to that, solidifying her sophisticated, grownup identity. She is right at the center of the dream she once cut out and taped up all over this small bedroom, of this modest home, in this nowhere town.

Working for a solid and growing boutique public relations

firm. Meeting with some of the top names in fashion and wearing them all, too. She has major photographers, household-name catwalkers, and world-renowned hairdressers in her cell phone contacts, saved under their first names or even just their initials beside a heart-shaped emoji. At twenty-nine-years-old, Dolly is a few quick steps from the top of the ladder, working closely with the owner of the firm and making great strides all the while. And soon she'll be married, working toward the family part, too. Promising a future to a handsome man who loves her. In a way, she's (sort of) lived out both aspects of the dream.

And yet...

Her eyes trace the edges of those teenage thoughts in every direction. Here, a model on a runway in a frothy peach dress. Plastered beneath a separate clipping with the words "*Make your mark*." Hundreds of faces, fierce and free, bedecked in what was the height of fashion at that time. Words and glitter, cemented in time and space with Mod-Podge.

Adjacent, a collage of another kind. Not of dreams, but of a teenage reality experienced by only the lucky. The photographs of young love, printed at the drugstore and made up of moments marked by disposable cameras held at arm's length. Hopeful, goofy teens. In love with each other and in love with their sweet and simple life.

There was no social media back then, so the photos themselves felt different. They were tangible and not always a click away. In fact, it's been ages since Dolly has actually seen these images and she pauses a while to really take them in. There she is with Steph, arm-in-arm standing by the creek. In cutoff denim shorts and bare-footed in the late afternoon sunshine. She remembers that white crop top Steph is wearing so well. She borrowed it soon after this photo was taken and spilled barbecue sauce on it at a party. The thing about Steph was, she was always so easygoing about stuff like that. *I miss you*, Dolly breathes, looking intently at the glossy, auburn curls and huge, unabashed smile splashed across half the photos on this wall.

It would take no more than three minutes to pull her up on social media. Even easier, to shoot her a text, send a message and just let her know she's in town. Ask: *What's new? How are the kids? Would you like to grab a coffee?* Her number hasn't changed, even though much else has. But something stops her. A fear of how it might be returned? The last time the two were in the same place together there was a lot going on, Dolly wasn't the kindest to her, and now so much remains unsaid.

Dolly places those thoughts on hold and soaks in the rest of the photos. There, sweet Declan in his Baylor sweatshirt. Arms around her waist, not looking at the camera but instead planting a kiss on her cheek. She can still smell his hair gel, tropical and coconutty, blending with a hint of Tommy Boy cologne that lingered after a day of grilling hot dogs and sweating in the late summer sun.

We thought we were so cool, she thinks, catching the start of a laugh at the back of her throat. And just like she used to reach out and touch those dresses at Neiman Marcus, her fingertips now do the same to the photos that encapsulate her first romance. Gently, gently, running across the edges of a chapter she so firmly put behind her. Now, raw and real the feelings rush back. Two teenagers acting out an adult love. Trying like hell to create something worth hanging onto. Laughing and dreaming and looking to a future they both kind of knew would not actualize.

But what is young love, if not hopeful? What is life if not enjoyed moment by moment, running together and future-bound? Right here on this very bed, how many nights did Dolly wonder aloud to her mother about a possible future with Declan? Now pulling onto her bare feet the trusty old sherpa-lined slippers that have been resting on her closet floor for over ten years, Dolly sets up some pillows at the head of the bed and grabs a box from beneath it. She's home to go through things, after all. So what harm can starting here do?

In a moment, she's back. Back wondering what life would be like if Declan would have given up his stubborn streak. Traded in the truck for a one-way ticket to New York City. But then again, there's more to the story. So much more. An unexpected wedge Dolly never saw coming between them. A girl that muddied their edges. A love that twisted them both too far beyond their capabilities. A teenage romance ruined by reality. So young, too much damage. Now it's all just a memory she wished she could let go. But wishing doesn't seem to be cutting it. Not tonight, anyway.

THEN

That night in the parking lot beyond the Dallas city limits was a mess of sweat and tender abandon. Dolly gasped for air, her heart and body thrilled while her mind raced with possibility and yet fell soft and blank in his arms. Declan, a gentleman and a school boy at once: "Is this okay? Can I touch you here?" with urgency. Just as he ripped off his own Levi's and pulled her onto his lap.

When it became absolutely obvious to her what was about to happen, Dolly relaxed into the moment and let the waves of the as yet unknown wash over her. First a hand on the small of her back, then two on her hips, tugging gently and feverishly at the same time. Panties pushed to her ankles. He lifted her up with ease, having cranked the driver's seat as far back as it would go.

Slowly, slowly, blue eyes fixed on her with razor-sharp focus, he pulled her down toward him. She let out a quick gasp, shocked and simultaneously thrilled by the sensation of him inside of her. He grunted, deep and long, reached his arms up and around with his hands on her shoulders, pulling her down again.

"You are so fucking beautiful," he whispered. And for the first time in her life she believed it. Wholly. Relaxed into the feeling. Looked softly over his shoulder at the stitching of the upholstery on the headrest. The hoodies and Coke cans that littered the cab behind him. All these ordinary objects developing new meaning with the warm, glowing pleasure of intensity rising from their laps. Sweat beads dripped down her neck and he leaned in, pressed his lips to them. Whispered something she couldn't quite hear, but understood.

As most teenagers' first times, it didn't last long, but to her it felt like a minute and an eternity at once. The slow and steady thrusting grew quicker, anxious, and hungry before he pulled back and finished clumsily on the seat. Her breathing had quickened and she stayed, half bent over him letting it calm before she spoke. He reached into the back seat and grabbed a t-shirt to clean the mess, then collected her in both of his arms and fell into her like a child. Vulnerable and open, she knew they both felt it. And so she said it first.

"I love you." It was almost a whisper. "I hope that's—that's... okay to say."

She couldn't see his face with his head still resting on her shoulder, but she could feel him nodding. She traced the expanse of his back with her fingertip, noticing vertebrae and tiny freckles. Watching it expand and contract with his slowing breaths.

"I love you, too," he said finally.

And that was both the beginning and the end.

NOW

Dolly wakes with a start, realizing in that uncomfortable dead-armed way that she has fallen asleep sitting up. There is a sharp pain in her neck from the awkward positioning against her pillow, and a quick glance at her phone reveals that it's 4 AM... and also that she's missed two calls and a text from Michael.

WTF Dolly? I'm worried...

Dolly rubs her eyes with a distracted fierceness, trying to figure out a way to explain innocently the act of falling asleep while looking through a box of old photographs and love notes from an ex-boyfriend. She settles for not doing that.

Sorry babe. Exhausted. Left my phone in my room & fell asleep watching a movie. Talk in am love xxx

But she knows despite her best efforts, this is it. There will be no "in the morning," because she's up. This is the morning. That's the thing about insomnia... and unresolved emotional drama from the past. They don't work too well together at four in the morning. So she reaches down and frees the edges of her floral quilt from the mattress, wraps it around her shoulders like a massive parka, and heads out to the living room to put on some mind-numbing TV.

Amid the glow of the television screen and the petty banter of vapid reality stars, Dolly's eyes finally do close. And they stay that way until the overwhelmingly nostalgic aroma of bacon awakens her senses three hours later. *Welcome to the South*, she thinks, the edges of her mouth turned up into a quiet smile as she sits up and begins to stretch out her limbs.

At home in New York it's usually that simple, healthy, Michael-made breakfast in the mornings. If he's stayed at his own place the night before she'll stop on her way to the office and grab a $13 egg-white omelette with veggies. This is washed down with a green juice and a bottle of ice water, and considered a v, *v* hearty breakfast. Dolly smiles, wondering what Glinda would think if she could see the Texas breakfast she is about to devour with abandon.

"Bacon is worse for you than cigarettes!" She remembers Glinda declaring to their fashionably drunk crew in an over-stuffed diner booth one night after too many cocktails. "I can't believe they even have it on menus still," she continued, not satisfied with the few grunts of acknowledgment and other-wise complete avoidance of her statement, ignoring the fact that she was, by all accounts, turning into a bit of a smoker.

The group erupted into laughter, but none of them ordered the bacon (nor have they since). This will be the first taste of it in months for Dolly and she is ashamed to admit she's pumped about it.

"Now that you mention it though, Glin, I *could* go for a cig," John-John had said with a laugh once they'd stepped outside into the brisk night air. And so he and the rest of their group including Dolly, Glinda, Adam, and Langley (two new design-ers at the start of their success peaks who sort of worked to-gether but not always), and sweet, wide-eyed Veronica (who'd only just moved to New York and was starting out as a print model), went off to procure a pack.

These were the scenes Dolly hadn't quite been able to imagine, but had always hoped for when she dreamt of a life in New York. Banding together with tastemakers and rising stars in the fashion world, finding their way and having their laughs in a whir of music, drinks, and beautiful fabrics. That night was just one of so many that were incredible for their simplicity.

It was a hope that a teenaged Dolly could never explain to Steph or her other friends, let alone to Declan. It was something that sat deep within her, the feeling of belonging with a crowd of high-heeled, Dior-decked friends. Risky behavior, sure. But so, so much love underneath it all.

New York loves you simply for being you. Or if it doesn't love you, it at least lets you exist as your authentically flawed self.

Texas loves you for fixing your hair the right way and saying "please" and "thank you." It loves you for staying humble and kind, appreciates your efforts to what's right even if that sometimes comes at the expense of your happiness. And Dolly still loves Texas, her forever home... will never not appreciate the bends in these very back roads surrounding where she grew up. Will never not feel grand and special while staying at her Zayde and Granna's Highland Park manse; will never not love the sleek and funky beauty that is Uptown Dallas.

But the landscape that New York lays out before you not only accepts your differences, but encourages them. To Dolly, this has mattered a lot as a woman who fought hard to create a career for herself from scratch. She learned fast in her early days outside of college that this was not the Good Old Boy's Club she was walking into and trying to bend the ear of.

There is no head-patting, no little woman bullshit in New York. She is respected at the table because she made it to the table. That's it. And it feels so good. Stepping outside of herself, she loves that New York loves her friends, accepts them for who they are and nurtures their souls in a way a lot of their hometowns do not.

Like in the case of John-John. Growing up scared of his own heart, he now lives in a place where it's not a shock to witness two young men holding hands in the street, or deep in the scotch, making out in their stools at the middle of a bar. A world away from Arkansas and the acidic rumor mill that would reduce men like him and their families to pathetic, embarrassed dust should he show affection to another man in public. In New York, he and his new man Roman (whom she cannot wait to meet) can dance in the center of the room, sweaty and relaxed, honest and quietly falling in love. And the only reason anyone would care is to be jealous that they've found something beautiful and rare.

Back home in Texas, and elsewhere throughout much of the South, being gay is something that is forward-facing acceptable in most circles. As in, most people seem to know that it's considered wrong to criticize it publicly, but will whisper behind closed doors. And worse yet, there are plenty who believe it's a sin and will let you know it. Loudly and everywhere, from their church pews to the supermarket. Even to the people who understand that it's not their business or problem who loves whom and why, there is usually a grandma or an uncle or even a friend that they just don't talk about this with. Because it's hush-hush.

Well, not in New York. Dolly didn't grow up in a particularly religious household, especially with her mother being half-Jewish and not committed to any one faith at all. They went to church sometimes but it was all pretty basic and not in-your-face. And certainly Mama didn't raise her to judge.

However, as much as she loves this bacon-frying man who now stands before her, she has to wonder what he'd think if he was ever up visiting her in New York and John-John turned up at dinner holding hands with a guy. She wants to believe he'd be polite at least, nonjudgmental and natural at best. But as for his colleagues, their neighbors? Probably not so much.

Maybe this is why she can't make her thumbs do a quick search in her phone for Steph's old cell phone number and reach out for coffee or ice cream. Maybe it's not so much the dark rift that has formed between the girls over the years, one that could probably be mended if they both felt compelled to get together and talk it through. Maybe it's the fear that life has moved them too far in opposite directions. OK, and it's also probably because Dolly would sooner pass out and disappear into the abyss than sit through the awkwardness that might unfold if Steph were to join her and her new friends at a dinner table. They're just too darn different from each other now.

Guessing at and judging where Steph sits on social issues isn't fair, she knows, nor is casting her aside mentally as a small-town Plain Jane and too different from her now to ever be friends again. But it's probably the truth. Because sometimes there are parts of yourself that you left behind for a reason. And sometimes those parts are made up by the people you left behind, too.

Anyway, back to that bacon.

"Morninggggg, Dolly Mae!" Daddy booms from across the kitchen island. It's funny how you can see the sadness on people's faces right at that exact moment when they're trying to show you the happiest parts of themselves. None of it is supposed to be this way, of course. They should be seeing each other often enough that neither one of them has to put on airs or try so hard for a connection... but here they are.

When Dolly picked up and moved to New York City, the idea was always that her parents would fly north frequently for weekend visits and that she'd come here every chance she got, too. In college Dale and Sally visited a bunch and she came home during most breaks, relaxing and luxuriating in those

Southern summers. But there was definitely a shift after that. The more her career picked up, the less time she had for her parents. And now with Mama being gone, the entire landscape of a visiting schedule has all but evaporated.

Once Dolly graduated and started working, things got harder on everyone. Dolly would come home twice a year or so, usually at Christmas and once in the late spring. She'd step off the plane at DFW pulling an oversized wheely bag stuffed with designer scarves and bottles and tubes of the most coveted, not-in-stores-yet products for Mama. See her sweet parents waiting to receive her with welcome arms and usually a few tears.

Over dinner she always regaled them with stories about the designers and makeup artists behind the scenes, and after bed she'd toss Mama's old jars of very decent night cream in the bin in favor of La Mer. Make things over for them while they slept, infuse a little bit of the big life she was working on, right into this worthy home.

Her parents were never going to leave Sugar's Bend, but she hoped that when and if they did move out of the house, it would be to a condo that would be closer to the center of town and easier to maintain. In her mind, they'd have a terrace and enjoy their retirement sitting on it, drinking coffee and wine. Golfing. Deciding on a whim to spend a long weekend in Manhattan with their daughter and (one day) the family that she would create.

Eventually, they'd plan Dolly's big celebrations right here in her hometown. Engagement parties and baby showers, weddings and Christmases with the eventual flock of towheaded grandkids climbing all over the place. And at the center of it all, of course, would be her mother. Mama, the Dallas society beauty who always made any setting feel grander than it was.

This was a simple East Texas ranch built in '75. Bricks, long lines, and modest finishings. It was a middle class home with no aspirations to be anything else, though they did reside in what was considered a better corner of town with decent-sized yards and located a good bit of distance from the main drag. The inside of their home, though, despite the exterior similarities, didn't look anything like that of the other houses on the block. Sally decorated it like it belonged to a social-ite... she kind of was one, after all.

A grand chandelier with an air of modern glam hangs from the low ceiling of the foyer. It doesn't quite match the scale of the space, but Southern women can hardly be bothered with silly details like that, at least not when it comes to lighting fixtures. The couches, lavish too, have been replaced since Dolly's childhood. They reflect a more upscale and clean aesthetic popular in recent years, than the Trisha Yearwood-inspired kitschy 90's look that was prime when Dolly was growing up.

The sofa is modular and cream-colored, a choice Sally made valiantly at the thrill of knowing that the messy elementary and teen years were over. The moving out of their young daughter with all its associated sadness also brought with it the sigh of relief that chocolate milk—and later, caramel frap-puccinos—would no longer be a daily threat to the furniture.

It wouldn't be a Southern, suburban living room without a plaid recliner chair in one corner, but even that Sally spruced up with a lush, white faux fur throw. The blanket still lies there now, washed occasionally she's sure, and always care-fully put back by Dale just how his wife would have kept it.

Looking around at the soft, geometric patterned rug and pops of taupe leather throughout the room, Dolly can't help but smile at how much pride Mama put into setting up this space. The backdrop for baby showers and book club meetings, Tupperware parties and all those Christmases when half the neighborhood showed up for cookies and coffee after gifts and before dinner.

And now here she is, eating a home-cooked meal at the breakfast table of her childhood home for what will be one of the last times. Dale is already under contract and every house edging out on the cul-de-sac and the rest of the street too, will soon be bulldozed down; a five-bedroom yuppy McMansion will soon stand in place of Number 206 and the two homes on either side of it. While there is a certain sadness over the state of these bricks and planks, mostly Dolly just wishes against everything that Mama could be right here with them, wanting to know all the latest gossip about the celebrities and begging for a discount off Dolly's friend at Ferragamo. Making light of a heavy situation with banter and lipstick. She was always so good at that, exactly when you needed her to be.

If she were here now, she'd be going on and on about how cool their new adventure was going to be in the modern condominium near the shops. She'd be pointing out audibly, and repeatedly, how much easier life would be when she could just pop downstairs and stroll up the block to grab her morning cappuccino, could walk home in five minutes after just about any get-together with her book club gals or the planning committee from the latest charity she was pouring her heart into. Because that's just how Mama was: positive, bright, and ready for a challenge.

Sally was no fool. With her parents' money and social clout, the obvious choice would have been to stay in Dallas or head to another big city to marry an elite bachelor who could provide her with the same lifestyle that she grew up with. The country clubs, the exclusive concerts, the posh trips to Europe. The things that felt important in her youth, and that she surely enjoyed. But it turned out they were not enough to turn away from the life that could await her in a tiny suburban town. Married to a local banker with a mortgage and a last name that didn't mean much to anyone.

They could have taken her parents up on their offer, too, for a down payment on a big house closer to Dallas and even a high-up job for Dale at the family business that would rake in more cash. But she—they—weren't interested. Instead, they were comfortable being comfortable and didn't need more to be happy. Sally was proud to be married to the man whose green eyes lit up when he saw her in the morning and whose jovial spirit kept her feeling upbeat when other things tried to drag her down.

This morning, the conversation between Dolly and her father is low and spotty over breakfast, both of them putting off the inevitable. Last night with its trip down Memory Lane and bouts of crappy sleep are put to the back of Dolly's mind for now. Today there is work to do and neither she nor Daddy can ignore that fact.

But linger they do over hot coffee, sipping slow and resolute, reminiscing to break up the loudness of the silence in between. Trying to fill it with familiar stories that always make them smile. Like the one about that time when Dolly stayed out way past curfew with Declan and came home fearing Sally's wrath.

"Your mother was smart not to tell me about it until months later," Daddy chuckles, the beginnings of tears glinting at the edges of his eyes. Dolly can't tell if they're from the laughter or something else. "She had a way of dealing with a teenage girl that I just couldn't have mustered..."

Dolly shakes her head, thinking back on how embarrassed she'd felt that night. Fairly drunk and wearing something completely different (and skimpier) than what she'd left the house in, coming home to find her mother waiting on the couch was a literal teenage nightmare. "I expected a screaming match, but it wasn't that bad. I'll never forget the only thing she could think to say was, 'What would your grandmother think?'"

Daddy is red-faced with laughter, probably remembering the version of the story his wife eventually told him.

"I thought for sure I'd be grounded 'til college, but she just wanted to know where the heck I'd stashed my other clothes, what with how tiny our dumb purses were back then." Dolly shakes her head laughing.

"They might have been tiny, but their price tags sure weren't. I remember that much!" He lets out a sigh, smiling. "Anyway, I guess I should start with my stuff," and she nods in agreement. "Let me know when you need my input." Neither one of them has mentioned Dolly's outburst over the papers in the kitchen last night. They're both a little ashamed—she of her behavior, and he of the fact that all that trash was still hanging up there in the first place.

Dale looks around now and sees the home for what it is: a depressing freeze-frame of what used to be a happy life. A moment stuck into eternity that should have been long since forgotten, a late October evening that robbed him of absolutely everything.

He often wonders what might have been. What if he had gone out instead of letting her do the errand, taken the "long way" as he always did to avoid local traffic and listened to an extra country song or two? He could have avoided the whole thing. Sally's car never would have crossed paths with the other one.

It was a simple task: pick up a few bottles of wine for the dinner party she'd decided to throw last-minute. And in a matter of minutes, it was all over. If he's honest, it's something he should have *wanted* to do. Help her out after she'd planned and shopped for the entire menu, prepped everything, made handwritten place cards for the table. Damn. She'd even built the whole friend group from the ground up. *And I couldn't just pick up the fucking wine?!*

Wreck. An interesting word, really. An idiot teenager answering a text message when his eyes should have been on the road, Dale thinks, anger rising again like it does every time he lets himself think about it. He knows how Sally would have wanted him to handle the situation: with understanding and forgiveness. He tried throughout his early healing process and continues to try now, to channel her class and grace. But he'd be lying if he said he wasn't gritting his teeth the whole time while not pressing charges on that boy.

You always hear about wrecks on the radio and roll your eyes at the consequential traffic delays and complications that come as a result. You don't think about the aftermath that can stick with everyone involved—forever. You don't think about the brokenhearted and the broken-homed. About a refrigerator covered in invitations to parties that will never be attended.

Or about how in the hell a middle-aged man, still in love with his bride, will pick up the pieces and try to rebuild his life out of a pile of emotional rubble. How he'll help their daughter plan a wedding that could have only been done perfectly under the careful guidance of her mother. Or that rolled up into the word "wreck" is really what a wreck one can make of an entire family, of even the lives that it has spared and left behind.

No, he thinks, this is why "accident" has never felt like enough to him, not since losing Sally. When running into old friends and former business associates who mention how sorry they were to hear about the "accident," he still always flinches. *Do you people not realize that this was the moment that completely destroyed my life?!*, he wants to scream, instead just shaking his head at the tragedy and thanking them for their condolences.

For Dolly, the loss is just as profound, but different. Rolling up her sleeves and looking around the living room brings a fresh wave of pain over her. All morning she's been able to pretend this is a visit like any other, but now that the time has come to actually start the work, she's overwhelmed.

What would Mama be thinking right now?, Dolly wonders as she starts to collect the fall decor and stack it against the wall. She can't look at the leaf decal pillows and brown mono-grammed trinkets anymore. It's bad enough that the house is being packed up and half its belongings trashed. Flattened to the dirt beneath its floorboards in just a few weeks' time. But the terribly off-season decor has become a garish and hideous reminder that the woman at the center of this home isn't here to see any of this process through to its completion.

Sadder still is the fact that she'll never get to see the condo Daddy has picked out, never get to touch it with her impeccable sense of style. Squabble with him over the importance of finally getting her dream closet and, of course, get her way in the end. Saddest of all will be actually going through her belongings and making the difficult choices of what goes and what stays.

After corralling the fall decorations and boxing up the couch cushions, Dolly attaches a sticky note reading SELL to each large piece of furniture in the room except for her father's recliner and heads down the hall to the master bedroom. Daddy's still out in the garage puttering about, so it's a good moment to tackle Mama's wardrobe. While this is the most dreaded portion of the program, Dolly figures it'll be easier to get through it without him alongside her in the same room sorting through his own keepable plaids and holey socks.

Opening the closet door delivers the instant surge of pain Dolly expected, and she lets the initial sting of it settle before actually beginning the chore. She was ready for a stomach lurch at the sight of her mother's clothing and bags, but for some reason the thought had never occurred to her that the closet would still smell like Sally: Narciso Rodriguez "Her" hangs ever so gently in the air. Despite the bottles of adventurous fragrances from Bond No. 9 and By Kilian that Dolly would bring or ship home the past several years for her mother, Sally was a creature of habit like most Southern women and her favorite scent is thus embedded in her wardrobe where it belongs.

This hurts.

If losing her mother so early was a robbery, this moment feels like the bitter aftermath. Like a discovery that even more is gone than originally assessed. It won't just be the birthdays that go by without that glittery voice on the other end of the line and the random, occasional surprise of a dozen pale pink roses showing up at the office to say, "Happy Tuesday."

It isn't only the understanding that never again will the two of them put way too much on a credit card at Neiman's and giggle about it conspiratorially over salads and bellinis at the Zodiac afterward.

It's more than the pain of not having had that conversation with her about which floor-length black sheath to wear to her biggest client's upcoming charity event and the fact that they never got a chance to discuss the latest book they were reading together, long distance, in a little book club just for two.

It's so much more...

Those things all revealed themselves like one blow after the next in the days and weeks following Sally's sudden death. But now that Dolly is finally starting to adjust, however painfully, however awkwardly, *this* suddenly feels like too much. This act of making decisions about bras and scarves, photographs and journals. This tangible proof that Mama is never coming back to decide for herself. This knowledge that when the house is packed up and its contents removed, it'll be forever. And many of these things, she will never see again. Not reorganized and upright, color-coded or alphabetically displayed. Not on a bookshelf or in a shadow box. Just... not. Nowhere and no longer needed.

Oh, but Mama, you are...

THEN

Everyone knew that Dolly had the coolest mom on the block, even if she hadn't always been that cool herself. Sally Weston possessed the kind of universal appeal that just made everyone want to be around her. Babies and toddlers adored her, little kids felt understood in her gracious presence, and awkward middle-schoolers and new moms alike flocked to her for a sense of comfort and a word of advice they could count on.

But there was a particular way she had with teenagers that made the Weston home a great way to spend an afternoon or evening. And that didn't let up when Declan and Dolly started dating. While Dolly didn't come all the way out of her shell among the neighborhood kids until that fated summer, they had been hanging around her home for ages. Her house's position at the end of the block had always made it a great spot for snacks and bathroom breaks as the kids from up and down the street played hopscotch or jumped rope; later practiced bike tricks and hacky sack, or just loitered to get a break from their own parents. Sally had been a sort of unofficial Neighborhood Mom in that most good-weather weekend days and plenty of afternoons during the week, she was prepared with homemade cookies or other treats to bring outside for the kids. And she got to know them each and all, despite her own daughter being the quiet one in the group.

All these years, the kids had flowed in and out, hung out in the living room dipping tortilla chips into fresh salsa while sharing their minidramas with bubbly and wise Mrs. Weston. And now that they were teenagers with more complicated problems, they seemed to need her more than ever. This was a positive development for Sally as her own daughter (and even Stephanie who'd always been a fixture on their couch and was now dating another neighborhood boy), were less and less emotionally available to her.

Dale Weston wasn't the biggest fan of the constant waves of teenage angst draping itself across his couch, but since having kids over at the house all the time meant knowing where his daughter was, he put up with it. And as Dolly and Declan grew inseparable, the rest of her social circle strengthened. While she'd always been a part of the group, and technically their excuse for hanging around the "cool house," that summer before junior year she really started to feel like she had an actual place among them. Maybe some of that eccentric sweetness that dripped off her quick-witted mother was finding a voice and a home in Dolly, too.

Or maybe it was the confidence that young love sparks in any girl. The feeling that all of a sudden the person you knew was hiding inside you has finally burst to the surface. The caricature of yourself that you used to picture acting out the poignant scenes in your favorite love songs is now a real part of who you are.

And so it wasn't just him that she gained that summer. It was her.

* * * * *

After the first "I love you's" had been said and the relationship taken to the next level, Dolly's fears of *what might happen next* actually lessened. Having lost their virginity to each other gave her a sense of confidence in the relationship. She felt he was more hers than he could be someone else's. It might not last forever; not much does. But at sixteen years old she had started to figure out how to feel more sure of herself. Even though it was brought on by romance and not some intrinsic change in herself, her parents were pleased with this change and new confidence in their daughter.

On the last day of summer break, Sally asked Dolly if she'd like to drive out to Dallas for some back-to-school shopping and lunch. She would much rather have spent the day with Declan, truth be told, but she knew he and his dad had plans to go fishing and toss a football around, so that option didn't exist anyway. This would be the first time in months that she and her mother would be spending the whole day alone together, and the first half-hour of the drive was kind of quiet between the usually chatty pair.

"So, you and Declan have been seeing an awful lot of each other this summer, huh?"

The dreaded icebreaker Dolly had anticipated was another reason she had hesitated before agreeing to this shopping trip.

"We're just having fun, Mama," she said finally, rolling the window down a crack to feel that warm August breeze in her hair.

"You don't have to tell me anything you don't want to, honey. But I know young love when I see it." Dolly didn't catch the glint in her mother's eye behind the oversized sunglasses, but she could see the hint of a smile forming at the edge of her lips.

"I... it's just a lot right now. I know we're young, Mama. I really get it. But I do love him..."

"And that's wonderful, Doll." Sally's eyes remained on the road but she reached her right hand over and gave Dolly's arm a quick squeeze. "You don't have to make any big decisions right now. You're sixteen years old. You can enjoy your life without losing sight of your dreams," she said.

"I know that, Mama." After a pause, "Like I said, we're just having fun."

Sally nodded with conviction, a gesture that said, *The conversation is finished then.* She turned the radio volume up and within a few minutes they were both singing along to "I Hope You Dance" as if they held microphones in their hands. Off-key and without inhibitions, just like they'd always been, the mother-daughter pair barrelled west toward Dallas, giving themselves, and each other, a much-deserved day off from reality and all its associated concerns.

Dallas welcomed them like it always did. Sally valeted the car at Neiman's and together they headed right to the contemporary section to dig through the sale racks and jeans displays. She had always taught her daughter about the importance of quality and design, but they did have a budget. Even though her own affluent parents sent unasked-for checks a few times a year to "help" their daughter and Dale furnish a nice lifestyle, she aimed to teach Dolly the value of a dollar, and to avoid spoiling her. Also, she preferred to live within the actual means of her own family on what her husband's salary at the bank provided. They might not be rich, but they were comfortable. Her parents didn't get it, but that was okay. This was *her* life.

They picked out a couple of must-have pieces for back-to-school at full retail and a bunch of cute transitional stuff left over from summer on double-discount that Dolly could layer up and wear through fall. The best thing about the forgiving Texas weather was how long you could drag out a summer wardrobe. Years later, Dolly would remember this with a pang of envy at her former self. Fall shopping in New York often meant that you'd have to pay full price or freeze; and on an assistant's salary, she learned quickly that high-end department stores were no longer an option. It would be years before she could afford to shop like this again, like she used to with her mother. And when that day came, she would wish more than anything that she could trade in all her credit cards to have her mother's physical presence back in her life instead.

After losing Mama, Dolly would also look back on this particular shopping trip to Dallas with a mix of nostalgia and regret. In fact, when she received the call telling her that her mother had been killed in a car accident, for some reason the memories of this exact day at Neiman's would come almost instantly to mind. It wasn't because it was the best or even the last time they'd come here. There would still be more Dallas trips in their future together after this school-shopping jaunt as a rising junior. But it was probably because, and she couldn't have known it yet, this would be the last time that she and her mother spent the day alone together before her life completely changed.

The loss of innocence is a really challenging and conflicting way of looking at things, and it varies from person to person. While many people might look back at a story like Dolly's and see the watershed moment as the one that took place in Declan's truck a month earlier, she'd later find that losing her virginity made her no less innocent to the hardships of the world than any other part of her life had up until then. Perhaps it should be looked at more cumulatively than that, or perhaps the fact is that losing your virginity to a good guy who loves you doesn't rob you of anything (until you lose him). Maybe instead it re-infuses you with all the hope and naive thoughts you had since childhood of what it would be like to be an adult. Maybe it *keeps* you innocent, in at least that sense.

It wouldn't be until several months after this day at Neiman's when reality ripped Declan right out of Dolly's arms, that she would experience a feeling adjacent to the loss of innocence. It wouldn't happen as the result (well, not the direct result anyway) of the joyful, tender act of their lovemaking but instead come as a consequence of young love that she hadn't deeply considered. A way that brought other people in the way of their happiness, splintered their bond. So many tears were still to be shed over that relationship, and the majority of them would be soaked right into the t-shirt sleeve of the woman who sat across from her at lunch, today.

But they didn't know any of this yet. And blissfully taking in the sun-soaked department store café in August, with several shopping bags at their feet, the two women slowly chewed their endive salads and giggled about their "accidental" splurging. They swapped predictions on how this year's hometown football team would hold up, avoiding all direct chat of Declan. It was the kind of light, easy mother-daughter talk they had always loved, but the missed-opportunity feeling would creep in later.

Dolly would look back on this day and wish she'd asked her mother some questions. Something other than what she thought that red scarf would do to her favorite black Marni turtleneck she'd scammed at a warehouse sale. Something about what she'd wanted to study in college, and if she'd ever regretted not going. Something about why she'd fallen in love with Daddy when stacking him up against the fancy young men her parents had tried to fix her up with. Something about the summer she'd spent in Paris figuring her life out before returning and picking out a silk floor-length gown to say "I do" in. Something... more.

After lunch the two took the quick drive to Uptown Dallas to meet Granna for a brief hello. Sally parallel-parked in her typically awful way that had them both in a fit of hysterical laughter and, luckily, no tail lights harmed. They met up with the glamorous and difficult yet loving Cara and strolled three-abreast along the main drag, got glitzy manicures, and stopped for a frozen yogurt before hopping in the car and making the drive home.

When "his girls" pulled in the driveway, Daddy was waiting in the kitchen with George Strait on the radio and a bottle of red uncorked. "Wash your hands, ladies, because we're feasting tonight!" he called out over the familiar tune.

Dolly retreated to her bedroom to change into a t-shirt and cut-offs. She took a few extra minutes to lay her new pieces of clothing tenderly across the bed. She could picture the new jeans with a hint of sparkle on their cuffs, carrying her through junior year with aplomb. She knew the cozy cardigan would be a staple on chilly winter mornings, and that she would have to find a special occasion worthy of the little champagne-colored dress they'd had no excuse to buy other than impulse and 60% off.

Dolly smiled while turning away from the clothes, thinking about the mystery that was her mother. So low-key and almost bohemian in affect, and yet so polished in appearance. She was probably the only woman in the entire South who had encouraged her teenage daughter to pick up a spaghetti-strapped cocktail dress as part of their "back-to-school" shopping trip.

But that was Mama—a lover of fashion and an understander of teen girls. One day, she hoped to be half the woman her mother was. For today though, she just felt lucky to have her. Dolly stopped in the bathroom en route to the kitchen and splashed some cool water on her sun-warmed cheeks. Catching a glimpse of herself in the mirror was a bit of a surprise.

Dolly hadn't touched up her makeup all day with Mama and most of it had worn off. Since she and Declan had started dating earlier this summer, hardly a day had gone by that she hadn't thought about her appearance, hoped without obsessing that it was enough to keep her romance going. Tried probably a little too hard with the outfits, wore eyeliner for the first time ever. But right now in the early evening with remnants of sun on her cheeks and her hair pulled back, she looked for the first time in months like the girl she'd always been. No push-up bra, no lip gloss. It wasn't exactly how she'd leave the house to see her boyfriend, but she was surprised that it didn't bother her either. Dolly turned out the light and headed back toward the other end of the house, stopping in her tracks at the sight of white tennis shoes on the floor by the front door.

"What in the—?"

"Hey, Dolly!" she heard the goofy exclamation emerge from behind the refrigerator door. There was Declan gathering condiments and a pitcher of iced tea. "Your dad invited me over for dinner." At her stunned silence, the continuation: "Last night of summer... how'd that happen?"

How manly and grown up he suddenly seemed, helping her parents arrange dinner. This act startled her with the same intensity that catching her own baby face in the mirror had just moments earlier. She'd always believed that teenage boys were immature and somewhat ridiculous. In competition with each other over immaterial things, they were not necessarily people that could be counted on. Of course Dec had proven a lot of that wrong this summer by being not only a gentleman and hilarious best friend but a caring, kind lover. Still, in this context he looked like an almost-man... and it was shocking.

The sweet surprise of Declan having chatted with her dad behind her back to earn a dinner invite tonight, to come through for her anyway and spend time with her on the last day of summer when she'd been disappointed thinking they wouldn't have the chance, was all too sweet. The pressed linen shirt and jeans he wore in lieu of his typical graphic tee and basketball shorts, the confidence with which he moved around her family's home, filled her with a kind of hope she hadn't dared allow herself before this moment. *Maybe this really is it,* she thought, leaning in for a hug once his hands were free.

At dinner the hot topic was back-to-school. Declan would also be a junior, but the two had pretty much opposite schedules. In such a small high school, this was a bit of a surprise, and Dolly had been bummed about it since getting her schedule in the mail a few days earlier. "We don't even have lunch together!" she lamented between bites of chicken-fried steak and garlicky turnip greens. Under the table, he squeezed her leg to tell her it would be fine.

Dolly looked around for a moment, took in the scene. Here on the back patio, in the waning hours of daylight, was a glimpse of what her future might look like. Daddy, so handsome and freshly tanned from a summer spent outdoors every chance he could get there. Mama, throwing her head back laughing at her husband's gentle teasing over how Dolly was just as sentimental and needy as she had been back in the day.

Her mother's shoulder-length, deep blond hair turned up at the ends, so perfectly coiffed this morning, was now letting a few strands free. The way she was sitting with the setting sun to her back it was almost like a halo, her hair. She reached up with one hand to play with her single strand of pearls. So effortlessly glamorous, completely unbothered by the fact that her white linen shirt was rumpled from the day. She reached for her glass of wine and clinked it to her husband's as an almost afterthought, moving onto a new (old) story about their courting days.

God, Dolly hoped she could be that chic one day.

Declan was transfixed, as everyone always seemed to be when Mama talked. He chewed his dinner quietly with a slow, mild smile creeping up the sides of his face throughout her stories.

Those blue eyes that had captured and roped Dolly in the first time he'd really turned them on her. The wavy piece of sandy-blond hair that fell across his eyes now and then, flicked back quickly with an instinctual gesture. She couldn't stop staring. Perhaps it was thanks to the small glass of wine Mama had poured for each of them, now getting to her head.

She could almost see him in a tuxedo, could almost feel the strength of him by her side in an unnamed future. She could even picture a baby nestled in those bear-hugging arms. Was this the wine? Or maybe it was the fact that life felt so delicious in this moment she couldn't see any other possibility. Something about it was so real. All summer she'd been along for the ride and eagerly soaking it up. She'd worn the right things and said what she felt and let him into the deep workings of her mind in a way that she'd never done with anyone else. It was weird, though, how you could be so close to someone but at the same time look at them sometimes with new eyes. Where she'd been seeing the high school romance, shielding herself from the inevitable pain of a future that held their demise in its hands, now a different thing was happening when she looked at him.

By the time the table was cleared and her parents had shooed them out of the kitchen, excused from dish duty on this last night of summer to go relax, Dolly felt both thrilled at the revelation she'd had about Declan and terrified that she might say too much and scare him off.

"I'll walk you home?" she offered, feeling suddenly shy and unsure of herself. It was funny how that could happen when you were standing beside someone who knew all the secret parts of you. Someone who had quite literally *been* inside of you.

"A whole block and a half, he could definitely use the protection!" Daddy chimed in from across the kitchen island, flushing her cheeks even if he hadn't meant to.

"Exactly!" Declan played along, but grabbed her hand briefly and thanked them for dinner. "Maybe she can just walk me to the end of the driveway," he said. Mama came over to give him a quick hug and wish him a good day tomorrow. Daddy shook the teen's hand and thanked him for coming which was returned with, "No, thank *you*, Mr. Weston."

"That's Dale," he called out a beat later as the pair made their way toward the front of the house, and Declan nodded gratefully.

Once they were out front and Dolly had pressed the door closed until the latch clicked, she wasn't quite sure what to say. She looked up at him and saw suddenly that he was feeling the same.

"Thank you for coming tonight," she mustered. "It was a nice surprise." She knew it was silly but she felt quite sad about the fact that they wouldn't be seeing each other so much in the coming days.

As if he could hear her thoughts, Declan said, "We'll have the weekends, Doll," and reached his arms around her waist to pull her in. She rested her head on his chest, let out a sigh. "And," he whispered, "every time I see you pass in the hallway I'll picture you wearing a lot less than you really are." She warmed at the hint of their sexual chemistry, the reminder that he indeed felt the same way about her that she did about him.

"I'll miss you, though," she said. "I can't explain it."

He pulled back a moment, moved one hand so his finger was under her chin, lifted it up so they'd be eye-to-eye. "You don't have to, because I get it. You just have to trust that I feel it, too."

Later that night Dolly would toss, turn, pour over photos of them, and basically not sleep. But for now, she pressed herself into his strong chest, letting his words soothe her fears. How had she gone from looking at him in the setting sunlight and seeing her possible one-day-husband, to now facing the irrational fear that not sharing a lunch hour would rip them apart? It was almost laughable, but of course it was high school—that's just how it is. You have to embrace your ridiculousness while also acknowledging that sometimes the worst outcomes you can imagine will come true. And even some you can't imagine, will too.

For now, she had his arms. And although there was no music, their hug started to sway a little to one side and then the other. The crickets were at it and the sun was legitimately down. The summer was over and the next chapter would soon begin.

NOW

Sifting through the items that belong to your dead mother brings up all sorts of feelings, an assortment that don't usually hang out together at the same time. There's the deep, under-lying feeling of loss and sadness that gets frequently inter-rupted by pops of laughter at the memory of an item in use. There's the swell of hope that is felt when seeing something that might work perfectly in your own home as a memento, followed by the tinge of guilt about coveting it when it should still belong to its original owner. There are myriad memories attached to things that bring your mind here, there, and to the farthest reaches of your love for her. This hurts and helps at once.

And then difficult, too, are the items that are unfamiliar. The scarf you've never seen before reminds you of the winter you said you'd fly down and didn't. The beautiful cocktail dress with its tags still in place, as she was excitedly saving it for New Year's Eve in New York City. A trip that never happened, bringing with it the cold reality that Mama would never see another Time Square ball drop, not in person or on the TV. All of her eventual New Year's Eves were deleted, cancelled by fate, and with them had gone all the other holidays, too.

These are the jumbled thoughts that assault Dolly's mind as she takes care to go through every single item in her mother's closet. It's hard to part ways with any of it, but she manages to collect a small DONATE pile in one corner of the room. Any-thing worth selling, she wants to keep for herself, and most of what's not? Well, she wants all that, too.

The cards and photographs, as well as Mama's leather-bound journals and spiral date books, Dolly can't face right now. She fills up one big box of sentimentals and marks it MAMA: PAPERS. Daddy will understand why she wasn't able to sort through it now, and likely he won't be ready for a while, either. This type of thing cannot be done properly when you are surrounded by piles and working on a deadline, but it boxes up okay.

Once the papers are packed away for the move, Dolly gets back to accessories. She laughs here and rolls her eyes there in the silence of the closet at some of Mama's favorite—and least understandable—fashion choices. Crushed velvet from the 80's and even those weird slide-on shoes everyone loved in the mid-90's. *Why did she keep these?* But Dolly knows why. Her mother was always so sentimental. And, while Dolly is always one to point out the best of every era, there are plenty of things in any small-town suburban woman's closet that probably shouldn't be there anymore. *DONATE.*

At a certain point, autopilot kicks in and the work gets going faster than it did at the onset. By noon, Dolly has created a small pile for Daddy to look at, as well as a huge heap of pretty dresses, fun poplin tops, classic designer shells and perfect cigarette pants to ship home to New York. Dolly then boxes up the best pairs of shoes for herself, even though it'll be tough to shove her solid eight-and-a-half's into Mama's narrow 8's. The rest she places in the DONATE pile. Not sure how to handle what she can't let go of, and with another large corner of the closet to rifle through, Dolly decides it's time to take a break.

The house has such an eerily quiet feeling, she notices as she makes her way toward the living room. Realizing simultaneously that it's past noon and that she's starving, Dolly opens the refrigerator to assess her options. Suddenly she's back in high school again, barefoot and seeking out a snack in the kitchen. How many times did she stand here like this, staring into the abyss of an expected assortment of items before turning her nose up at all of it and settling for pretzels or a piece of fruit?

True to form, she shuts the doors and grabs a banana, not in the mood to prepare a proper lunch or go find Daddy and ask what his plans are for the meal. The sun is streaming through the windows of the front of the house generously, and that Vitamin D is exactly what she needs right now. Dolly heads out onto the front porch, letting the screen door swing shut behind her.

Though it's been a couple hours since she saw Daddy, she's not concerned. Men and their boxes upon boxes of formerly important electronic paraphernalia is something to which Dolly is accustomed. She's sure that within the hour he'll reenter the house to grill up some cheese sandwiches and regale her with tales of the random memorabilia he's unearthed in the garage. This is why she's here after all, she thinks with a smile. If packing up this whole home was left up to Daddy alone, he'd still be standing in the middle of the kitchen selecting which one of the three cheese graters to keep, when the bulldozer came to demolish the house for good.

Dolly turns the edges down to the last of her banana and pops it in her mouth, folding up the peel and placing it on the top step of the porch. It's been all day since she's looked at her phone, and she's not quite ready to catch up on email or the rest of her real life. She should call Michael, though, she realizes. The idea of taking a little walk comes to mind, seeming like the best way to work through all the feelings she's had about Mama this morning. She picks the banana peel up again, goes inside to toss it in the kitchen bin, grabs her phone, and scrawls Daddy a quick note to say that she will be back soon.

Visiting your hometown when you haven't been back in over

a year feels sweetly nostalgic and a little sad. Dolly's not even really sure where she's going, and the thought passes that if she had a dog to walk, this excursion would make a lot more sense. In Manhattan, people walk everywhere and the sidewalks are always bustling. Even on weekend mornings it's rare to have a block to yourself, and heading out for a stroll to clear her mind has become second nature to Dolly.

At least she has her phone. Dolly calls Michael from the end of the driveway and he picks up on the second ring.

"Feeling better, sleepyhead?" he teases, and they fall instantly into their usual rhythm.

"I don't know if it was the plane ride or all the sunshine I'm not used to, but yesterday just knocked me clean *out*," she responds.

"You sound so Southern when you're down there. It's cute."

She could protest the statement, but she knows it's true. Dolly *feels* more Southern when she's down here. "I miss you, though," she says, toeing a patch of grass at the edge of the drive.

"I miss you, too, babe," he says. "I think I'm gonna play a few rounds with Dad later. What are you up to?"

"Also Dad things, but not as relaxing as golf," she laments. "There is so much crap in this house, Michael. I just left to take a little walk and escape for a bit."

"Well, you're good at organizing. You'll burn through it, and before you know it you'll be home." *Home.* The word sounds good coming from him.

"I know." She takes off walking then, letting the conversation dwindle as they both have things to get back to. After saying goodbye to Michael and hanging up, she zens out far enough to focus on the simplicity of one foot in front of the other, fresh air, sunshine, and a much-needed break. So it comes as a complete shock to the senses when Dolly's walk is interrupted by the unexpected sound of her name:

"Dolly! Dolly Weston... is that you?"

She turns toward the voice and can't help but smile at Nancy Crue, Declan's mother. The years haven't been as kind to her as they were to Dolly's own mother, but she's still no more than a size six and her hair hasn't changed shades in at least two decades.

"Mrs. Crue, what a nice surprise," Dolly says, walking up from the sidewalk toward the flower bed where Nancy Crue has risen from her knees and placed both gardening gloves into one hand.

Never big on physical contact or emotion of any kind, it's a surprise to Dolly when Mrs. Crue places her arms around her shoulders briefly, into what is nearly a hug. "I don't think I've seen you since your mama passed..." she says, holding Dolly's shoulders at arms-length now. Her big brown eyes move back and forth between Dolly's, as if she's searching for something more to add.

Mrs. Crue's shoulder-length, bottle-blond hair is so curly and dense, it takes on a life of its own. The sun visor she wears looks practically threatened by all that hair, hanging on for dear life as its wearer remains completely unfazed by the curls and the sun itself. Dolly has never known anyone else as unwilling to pull their hair back under any circumstances.

The thought pops up briefly of the time Declan was telling the group about the look of horror on his mother's face when he showed up with some football buddies after practice and his mom had her hair in a messy ponytail, looking "unkempt." That night, after they left, she'd let him have it for invading her privacy. *So silly*, Dolly thinks, standing closer to this woman than she has in years, or maybe ever. The parts of ourselves we try to hide.

"No, I haven't been back in a while," is all she can think to say. There are so many reasons she hasn't been back, and none of them she feels like discussing. Not with anyone, but least of all with her high school boyfriend's mother. "It's really good to see you, though."

"Absolutely, you too. You look great, Dolly. So grown up!" Dolly smiles. "So, where's your dad headed then, out of town or...?"

"Oh, he found a condo downtown actually. It's small, but really nice. He can walk to the bank. See his friends and stuff... he's..." *looking forward to it? That's not right.* "I'm here to help him pack up," she finishes.

"Good girl. Declan wasn't so pleased with our decision to sell, but in the end it just made the most sense. Of course, I'm still out here tending to my flowers as if they aren't about to be turned into some fancy person's open floor plan living room, so who am I to argue with him?" She laughs a little, but it's the kind of laugh that people put on when they're trying to cover up something else. "We're headed to Oklahoma actually. Got family out that way..." Nancy trails off.

"How *is* Declan, anyway?" the words come out before Dolly has decided if they should. On one hand, it would be very weird to run into the mother of anyone you knew in high school and not ask about them. But at the same time, the question feels loaded when asked to this particular person, even if it's not.

Isn't it, though?

"Oh, yeah, yeah, he's good. Got a job in California actually." (Dolly knows this already. Thank you, Facebook). "Doing really well out there, 'sfar as we can get out of him!"

"That's great!" she manages, not sure what to say or where to go now.

"Well, I better get inside and fix some sandwiches. Bill's partially retired now, so he comes home by lunchtime every day."

"It was good seeing you, Mrs. Crue." She shocks herself by meaning it.

"Yes, Dolly," she says, placing one hand on Dolly's upper arm in another unexpected touch. "You be well and tell your dad we said 'Hello.' If he needs anything, anything at all... Well, he knows where to find us!"

Dolly nods. "For sure. I'll tell him." They lock eyes for another slightly awkward moment and then Nancy seems to suddenly understand that her hand has lingered too long on Dolly's arm; this casual hello has gone on long enough. "See you around, then, Dolly," she says, a hint of something like sadness flashing quickly across her face, and turns to disappear into her house.

By the time Dolly has absorbed both the shock of the encounter and the surprising ease of the unexpected meeting, she's back on the sidewalk again with still nowhere to go. Enough time has passed that Daddy is probably confused if not slightly worried, so instead of more ambling in the general direction of town with no wallet on her, Dolly turns around and heads back toward home.

When the screen door slams behind her, Daddy beckons in from the kitchen almost immediately. "I made lunch, Dolly girl. Let's take a break!"

Over BLTs (Daddy never was one to make less than a whole package of bacon at once, so there's plenty left over from breakfast) and lemonade, the two watch a spring wind sweep across the grass out back. It's weird to Dolly how they always had so much to say to each other when Mama was around, but now that she's gone, they both seem to struggle with even the lightest conversation.

It's not lost on her that the normal thing would be to discuss Michael and her life in New York. To gush about the beginnings of wedding planning or at the very least regale Daddy with the latest funny or interesting stories about her job and friends. But in the midst of all they are dealing with, a conversation like that would just feel flat and awkward. Actually, the silence feels appropriate, if in nothing but homage.

Boisterous, happy-go-lucky Daddy has never been one to let a meal go by without at least some idle chit-chat, but it's clear that similar thoughts plaguing her are with him as well. So, quietly they sit, chewing and sipping and looking around the yard, each grateful for the bright sun and the existence of natural distractions like birds and butterflies to follow with your eyes when your voice feels unnatural.

"That was delicious, Daddy," she breaks the silence slowly and he looks her way with a fast smile as if all of a sudden remembering he isn't alone on the back porch.

"Oh, good, sweetie. Well, it's nice to have someone around here to feed. I'll tell you, it's easy enough to make excuses for frozen dinners every night when it's just you!"

"Don't I know it!" she laughs. "For me it's microwave most nights, too. That or delivery. Life is just too busy nowadays." She carefully omits the piece of information that includes

Michael being there for almost all of her dinners these days, not least of all because her father is now, technically, single. She knows the sting of loneliness all too well and hates that he has to feel that, has to live that, every day.

"I can imagine," he says slowly. The broad smile has crept away but its memory rests in the corners of Daddy's mouth. After a beat: "Hey, whaddya say we mix it up tonight and head into town for dinner? Maybe to L.B.'s? They've got a new menu down there and live music on Saturday nights."

Swallowing her last sip of lemonade, Dolly nods. "That'd be great, Daddy." To be honest, the thought of going out tonight is a bit nerve-wracking. In a small town full of people you used to know, there's almost no doubt that you'll run into someone you don't necessarily want to see, especially on a Saturday night at one of the most popular spots in town.

But then again, the thought of sitting through one more quiet meal at home with Daddy, surrounded by boxes neither one of them feel they had the authority to pack, makes her want to crawl out of her skin and hitch a ride to the nearest airport. So, dinner in town it is. At least in a public space, they'll have music in the background, coupled with the voices of other people's joyful dinners, first dates, and family gatherings to distract from the growing near-silence between them. And of course, from the loud presence of Mama that lingers in the air here at the place that won't be home much longer.

"Okay, Doll. Let's keep on for a few more hours then, and head to dinner around 5."

"Sounds good, Daddy," she says, standing up slowly. She kisses Daddy briefly on his forehead and reaches to clear both of their plates, heading into the kitchen through the back porch door.

How many times did she sneak through this door?, she wonders with a private smile. By the time high school came around, Daddy had installed automatic lights up the front walk toward the porch and all around the sides and back of the house. But there was one little spot between sensors that could be swiftly crawled through and get you to the door without detection. It took some trial and error, but she and Declan had figured it out that sexy fall, right before things took a turn.

THEN

The first day of junior year was exactly and nothing like she expected it to be. Dolly woke up earlier than necessary so she could take her time getting her hair perfect. Mama had offered to curl it the night before so that it would fall into soft waves this morning, but it turned out she was just too nervous to sit still last night so she declined and was now blowing it dry, up-side-down, trying to create some volume that just didn't want to exist. Something bigger than hair nagged her though, and the morning left a chewing feeling on her insides.

It was more than the summer being over and the worry that not spending those long days and nights together would tear her and Declan apart. It was more than the fact that their class schedules couldn't be less of a match. She hated to admit it, even to herself, but weighing heavily on Dolly's mind was the fact, too, that at the start of every school year, there was a fresh batch of pretty girls to compete with.

Freshmen. When Dolly herself had been a freshman, she remembered feeling both terrified and absolutely thrilled. *High school*. Finally a step closer to adulthood—to dating and secrets that had merit and importance. To being encouraged to make more of her own choices, from quitting the violin in favor of cheerleading, to branching out socially and not just hanging out in the hallways or at the lunch table with the same pack of kids who lived in her neighborhood. Even if it took her a while to actually do that, the possibility of new friends buzzed around her.

As a freshman, Dolly had been way too scared to kiss a boy, or even to really flirt. But she had no problem rolling the waist of her skirt over twice before walking out the double-doors at the back of the school past where the track team practiced. She knew her slender but shapely legs were eye-catching and she would throw her head back and laugh at a joke a friend was telling, even if it wasn't all that funny. Just for the sudden, secret thrill of being looked at by the older boys who were standing out there, warming up for practice. Even though she didn't really intend to do anything about it, she wanted to be noticed. Who doesn't?

While bookish and geeky, untouched by any boy until Declan this past summer, the beginnings of a flirtatious existence had started to form freshman and sophomore year so she could only imagine it would be rampant with any incoming ninth-grade girls who possessed more confidence than she had. Would they be flooding the halls in tank tops showing off gorgeous summer tans and age-inappropriate makeup, their own skirt waists rolled twice and trying to be noticed? Would it be Declan's eye any of them tried to catch?

Of course, he was hot. It would be hard for anyone not to agree. With that sandy hair and chiseled face, shoulders broad from football and fishing. The laid-back way that he wore his clothes, usually something quite casual, but for the first day of school it would probably be a button-down and some nice shorts. Opened just one spot lower than it was when he walked out the front door and said goodbye to his mother.

But to her, he was so much more than his exterior. Declan was laughter and understanding and a soft place to fall. She had a great life already and she knew that, but he had unlocked something deeper within her. When she and Steph had dreamt about what it would be like to fall in love one day, they never could have imagined a reality like this.

It was in the way he trusted her, the way he let his emotional walls crumble in her presence. Curled up beside him for a stolen hour on a couch or in one of their beds, even hovering in his lap making out and talking on-and-off, she had learned a lot from him this summer. When his hand held hers and their fingers danced back and forth running over each other's knuckles, whispering into the darkened sky on one of their back porches, this was when she felt most alive. And he had taught her by responding, by showing her his joy, that it was okay to have interests outside what the other girls talked about. That the deeper parts of her were the parts he liked best. Like the fact that she was a reader even though he definitely was not. Like the fact that she mostly did Cheer because it was the only sport that came with a good outfit.

And Declan was more than a hot football player, so much more than his type cast. She guessed, or was starting to learn, that most people were probably more than theirs, too. It was a hopeful discovery. A quiet introvert who had been drawing conclusions about others for years, she was excited to learn that sometimes all you had to do was dig a little deeper and you could find a goldmine. But Dolly didn't need anyone else to know this much about Declan. Didn't want some cute freshman girl sidling up and scratching the surface of her thoughtful and humble boyfriend. She didn't need anyone else to see the deep pools of hope his eyes could look like in moonlight.

Which is why, when she saw Declan right after second period, she felt both pure happiness and a knot in her stomach. Dolly's guess had been right: he was wearing a pale blue Oxford shirt with the sleeves rolled up and the top couple buttons undone. His signature flip-flops were on, and despite the school policy against the wearing of hats, his well-loved Texas Rangers cap was hooked around the top loop of his backpack, ready to put on his head the minute he stepped outside those double doors to freedom.

From where she stood, Dolly could see him laughing with a pack of buddies exiting the math wing as she approached. She smoothed her skirt and stood up a bit taller, feeling suddenly naked because she was not standing and chatting with a friend. She had two options: make it weird and scurry past, waiting for him to notice her; or approach the group confidently and say hello.

Luckily, he looked up in enough time to make the decision for her.

"Doll!" he exclaimed, that familiar broad smile stretching across his mouth. He parted from his buddies long enough to grab her into a bear hug, whispering in her ear, "You look so hot, babe."

The warning bell rang, signaling thirty seconds to get to class, so they parted just as fast as they'd met up, but that moment was enough to get her through the rest of the day. The summer might be over, but she knew they weren't. Freshman girls be damned; they could look all they want. He was hers and she was his, and that was that.

The day was long and busy. Dolly had a swell of anxiety each time she had to find a place to sit in class, but it hit the worst when she entered the lunchroom. Seniors had the privilege of leaving school during their lunch periods, but juniors had to hang back with the younger kids. How she ached for that freedom to cut and run—even if it was just to avoid being seen on the outskirts, trying to find a way in.

It had been nice sharing lunch with Steph the past two years, but now that Dolly was on an AP track taking a bunch of college-level courses, the girls were separated for much of the day, including this critical 35-minute span.

Dolly walked into the orange tile-floored lunchroom with a lump in her throat, reaching across her chest to adjust the shoulder strap of her backpack. She hesitated a minute at the edges of the room, scanning for an approachable face. It was a small town, and they all knew each other. It wasn't that she didn't see people she could sit with. It was that thing—that inner voice of doubt making her feel like she'd be a burden at anyone's table without Steph there.

And so it served as a complete shock when Flynn Beaufort, one of Declan's friends on the football team, tapped her on the shoulder from behind and asked if she was coming or going.

"Oh, uh, this is my lunch period. I was just..." she trailed off.

"Cool, me too. Let's go find everyone."

Everyone? Was she part of a group of "everyone" now? It felt too good to be true being steered through the lunchroom by one of the most popular kids in their class. Dolly played it cool, smiling and nodding as he chatted away while leading her toward a corner table where a bunch of the football guys and their friends sat together.

Being officially "invited" to sit in the group, Dolly chatted naturally with the other girls at the table, some she knew from Cheer, and things felt comfortable and light soon enough. "Dolly, your hair looks so cute today. What did you use on it?" asked Taylor Grieves, a sophomore on the cheer team who'd likely make Varsity this year due to her insane tumbling skills.

"I literally just blew it dry upside-down and hair sprayed the crap out of the underside," she admitted, and both girls laughed. Inside, Dolly felt the most incredible little nugget of hope and warmth forming. She couldn't wait to get home and tell Mama about this lunch period. She knew looking around the table that not a single one of these friends-of-friends of hers would have any idea how much their kindness meant to her. She felt included. Admittedly, she felt pretty darn proud of herself for not resisting this, for not turning away and mumbling to Flynn some lame excuse that she had to go beg off and spend lunch working on the school paper or chatting with a teacher. Creating emotional buffers to stay within her shell was a speciality of Dolly's, but it didn't serve her. This had been exactly what she needed, and the memory of their simple inclusiveness would be precious in the months and even years to come.

It would not be an easy year to navigate, she could feel that now even if she didn't know all the reasons why. There were just so many changes stemming from within, including the fact that this was her first year of high school with a boyfriend. As for their relationship, it would be the first time they experienced any kind of roadblock, or a schedule mandated by anything other than the rise and setting of the sun—and parental curfews. But by the time she ran into Declan again at the very end of the day, long after the final bell had rung, she was already feeling ten times more confident and happy than she had been this morning.

* * * * *

He was in a good mood, too. Declan could make out the shape of his girl walking across the parking lot toward his hand-me-down truck the second she opened those double doors. Her skirt was shorter than any he'd seen on her at school before, but he wasn't complaining. Her hair was loose and long, reminding him of her mother's. She was a lot like her mother, actually, even if she didn't realize it yet. Powerful. Strong. Funny. He was proud to call her his. She looked like a sunrise even right here at the end of the day.

* * * * *

"Baby! How was your day?" She asked after their hug came to its natural close and they pulled back for a minute to look each other in the eye.

"I made Varsity," he said without much emotion. "Well that, and I missed the shit out of you."

"Yeah. Same. Same on both counts," she replied with a tender smile.

"Congrats, baby," he said, tracing her left cheek with his thumb. "I know how bad you wanted that." She shrugged and displayed a toothy grin. Making the varsity cheerleading squad for junior year was a vindication and an accomplishment. But she knew that for Dec, this was not the big exciting development that it should have, or could have, been.

She squeezed the hand she held with wordless communication passing through them like lightning before letting go and climbing into his truck. They sped out of the parking lot and peeled toward their shared street in silence, hand-in-hand to the sound of Kenny singing about the good stuff. This was the good stuff for sure.

Here's the thing about football and Declan Crue. He was good, better than he really wanted to be. Dolly wasn't the only one who knew that his heart wasn't totally in the game, but she was the only one who understood why. Declan was dealt a lot of pressure from his father to stick it out, especially after this summer when he'd confessed to his parents that he was considering leaving the team. His parents wouldn't hear of it. A football scholarship, even one to a D3 school, was his best shot at a college education, they said. And that was the only thing the Crues cared about, probably more than their son's actual happiness or passions.

127

The Crues weren't like the Westons. Declan's mother had never worked a day in her life, believing that women's work took place squarely in the home. While Dolly's mother was also comfortable in the role of housewife, she had taken odd jobs here and there throughout Dolly's childhood to afford her favorite splurges when Dale wasn't making as much as he was now.

Declan's parents were likely at the top of their budget living in the nicer area of town down the street from the Westons, and his dad didn't make nearly as much as Dolly's. Even with in-state tuition they wouldn't be able to afford Baylor, and if he didn't get in there Declan was pretty sure he wanted a break from Texas before coming back home to start his own quiet life. So, begrudgingly he stuck out the football thing. Committed to playing the sport while burying his bigger dreams deep within. This fact saddened Dolly but also empowered her. It was nice to know you were the only person in the world that someone trusted with their secrets.

It wasn't just that he'd let her in on his dream of one day owning a little shop or bar in the outskirts of Dallas; it wasn't just his hope of making a better life for the people over there who had very little. Urbanizing and coolifying a rough part of the city. Dolly was about ninety-nine percent sure that if his parents caught wind of such a lofty (and surely by Mrs. Crue's account, frivolous) goal, there'd be hell to pay.

But Declan's parents also didn't even know that he owned a guitar. That beneath the rugged, athletic exterior of their son that the rest of the town saw, which they revered as his penultimate trait, there was a creative person dying to get out. Doing it in secret. They didn't know that he'd saved up his Christmas money from his grandparents for three years running and eaten a bag of chips a day to hoard his lunch money all of sophomore year to buy it.

Dec had a part-time job helping Hank Bowie down at the auto shop a mile outside of town, but his parents knew exactly how much he made there and insisted that any dollar he didn't need for gas for the truck was going into a savings account for college. (Admirable, sure, but also a *little* rigid, Dolly felt).

Since his mother was always around, it was hard to get time to practice the instrument, but he figured it out. He kept the guitar hidden in the back corner of his closet behind childhood paraphernalia where his mama wasn't likely to look. And then one night just before the close of this summer, he had pulled all of the pieces of Dolly together when he drove her out to a clearing in the woods, parked, and said, "Gimme a second."

* * * * *

They were expected at a party at Jimmy Lavery's house in half an hour, but it was clear he wanted to do something special for her first, so she wasn't going to question it. Dolly smiled as she sat still in the front seat of the truck, her fingers fiddling idly with the clasp of her seatbelt. She was wearing her favorite dress, a pale pink floral with halter straps and a completely open back. When she had hopped into Declan's truck just twenty minutes earlier, she could see Mrs. Crue peering out through the curtains, her mouth set in its signature straight line of judgement.

Dolly could tell that her dress wasn't a mama-pleaser, but what did she care? Her own mother had purchased it for her, so it couldn't be that bad. Sure enough, Declan looked her up and down and twirled her around by the hand to see the dress from every angle. He didn't say much, but his eyes did enough talking. She knew he liked it just as much as she did.

Now he was clunking around in the back of the truck and she willed herself to keep her eyes forward. Finally he came around and opened her door, holding up his hand to help her down. There were about two weeks of summer break left and though the sun was slowly beginning to set, it was still plenty warm out. "I didn't want to share you with anyone tonight, so I thought this would be better than goin' to Jimmy's."

They walked around the side of the truck and there on its bed was a scene that made her gasp. Declan had laid out a large plaid blanket and set up candles along the sides. There was a small cooler sitting open with a couple of beer bottles inside, and to her surprise, a guitar rested against the back windshield.

"What—?"

Wordlessly, he motioned for her to sit down as he cracked open the top of a beer, handed it to her, and got one for himself. He took one slow sip and then placed it down beside him, picking up the guitar and giving it a quick tune before he began to play.

Dolly felt at once like she was in a movie and like this was the realest moment of her life to date. Yes, she'd lost her virginity to him in this same truck not long ago. And said *I love you* and had all the other firsts. But this felt like another kind of first, one that many people probably never even get. The first time that someone feels close enough to share the deepest and most beautiful part of themselves with you. And discovering that that part is as pure and as beautiful as the feelings you already have.

Slowly, a tear rolled down her cheek and she quickly wiped it away with her pointer finger as she lifted the beer can to her lips.

The tuning of the guitar turned into chords and the chords morphed into a song and before she knew what was happening, the boy she had come to love was singing to her in the back of his truck. She was so engrossed in what was happening that she didn't start to absorb the words until he reached the hook the second time:

"...And I will wait for you,
And I will see this through.
And you will not see me break free.

And we will stick this out,
And we can withstand doubt,
And we can reach forever, Dolly..."

The sudden realization that hearing her name meant this was an original song, and one about her, was almost too much. Now the tears were flowing more freely and she didn't bother to stop them. By the time Declan finished playing the song and looked up from the guitar, Dolly was a mess. She was sure all her makeup had slipped clean off with the tears. He set the guitar down and grabbed an edge of the blanket, coming closer to her to wipe them away before lifting her up onto his lap.

"You... you play guitar?" was all she could manage, and he shrugged, sheepish.

"I wanted to wait until the right moment to tell you," he said. "It needed to be the perfect song."

"Did you write that for me?"

"No," he laughed. "It's about my other girlfriend named Dolly." She gave him a light jab in the ribs before leaning in for a kiss.

"Am I your girlfriend then, Declan Crue?" Weirdly, with everything else that had transpired that summer, they hadn't quite made it to the actual labels. Suddenly, she needed this to be a "yes" with all of her being.

He nodded, kissing her slowly. "If you'll have me."

Years later, she would listen to the CD recording he later made her of that song, over and over again. Crying different tears and wondering what might have been, deep in the throes of regret.

But for this night, and for the next while, those words stuck with her when she needed them most: *And I will wait for you // And I will see this through...*

Young love. So full of hope and so unaware of how easily life can take a turn that changes everything before you even know it's happening.

NOW

She can sense Michael giving her some emotional space while she's down here, outside of their brief and intermittent catchups. It has never served them well to get too deep while far away from each other. Michael knows enough about Dolly's past to be aware that in a small town, unexpected encounters can always happen. He's never been down to Texas with her, but when she came last time, she drunk-dialed him from a bar downtown in the middle of the night, laughing maniacally and asking him why he was such a square. It didn't go well from there.

Dolly had just lost her mother and was in town for a few days after the funeral. It was a little weird, but despite having promised her dad she'd stick around through the weekend, she couldn't quite bring herself to linger at the house. Staying at a hotel the next town over seemed like the best option, but then the chilling loneliness of nightfall set in hours after the post-funeral dinner at which she couldn't stand to eat a bite.

She and Michael had just started dating, and while he offered to join her for the week, the suggestion felt rushed and uncomfortable. But now that she was alone in a crappy hotel room with half a bottle left of cheap wine procured from the lobby and drunk on an empty stomach, she desperately regretted declining his offer.

Hoping to drown out the sound of her own lonely, aching thoughts, Dolly called a taxi service and headed back into Sugar's Bend, to the only spot she knew of that would be open at this hour, with any promise of being fun.

Luckily, most of the people she knew from high school that were at the dive bar, weren't close enough friends to pry. After quick condolences and hugs all around (it was a small town, after all, and the details of the fatal accident were still very much being discussed), a round of drinks appeared and the pool sticks were raised. Dolly saw Stephanie across the room, lingering in the dark. Her lurking presence felt unemotional, rude. Dolly would deal with that later.

Three hours after arriving at the small-town bar, Dolly was properly wasted and standing outside sharing a cigarette with Starla-Sue Herring, who'd been a freshman her senior year. It's funny how once you're all adults, the slight age differences that mattered so much in high school mean absolutely nothing. That one year of high school they'd shared, Dolly had considered Starla-Sue like a kid sister. After not making JV she hung around Varsity Cheer practice trying to learn from the older girls. Dolly, in need of friendship and support after all the chaos that had overwhelmed her junior year, found something sweet and calming in Starla-Sue. Their friendship had been brief and not terribly close, but Dolly had occasionally checked up via social media to see how things were unfolding for her young friend in the first several years after moving out of Sugar's Bend.

So, it was jolting to see her in person now with a wedding ring on her hand, whipping out her phone to show off photos of the two babies and hunky husband she had waiting at home. Dolly didn't know him, but she might as well have. He looked like how she used to picture Declan would as an adult—tall, hot, and Southern. Pudgy baby fingers and tiny spouted pigtails flashed across her vision as Dolly experienced a whir of conflicting emotions. She felt joy and warmth at seeing the photos, but they also brought forth a pang of jealousy she couldn't quite place.

It didn't help that she could make out the form of her old best friend from growing up lurking in corners and shadows at the bar, refusing to come over and talk to her. All she wanted was a hug, and instead she found herself smoking and swapping life details with a random acquaintance from the past.

Being in Sugar's Bend, drunk, and not talking to Stephanie was hard enough. Now sharing a cigarette with someone who was happy and who had not just lost their mother, set Dolly over the edge. She said goodbye to Starla-Sue, leaning in for Juicy Couture-scented hug and waving, sloppily, to the small group of old friends and acquaintances standing nearby.

Before she knew what was happening, Dolly was in the backseat of a taxi calling Michael to brag about the home-town crowd and how *cuuuute* Starla-Sue's husband was. She wouldn't remember much of the conversation, and Michael was enough of a gentleman not to fill her in on the other bits —*ever*. But she could tell by his face when she showed up at his place that following Tuesday night, a line had been crossed.

"Look, Dolly," he'd started. Always a negotiator, always clear-headed even at the worst of times, he was letting her off the hook. "You just lost your mom, and you're in pain. So I'm going to let this one slide. But please... the next time you're drunk in your hometown, do us both a favor and don't call me."

Those words haunt her now, almost a year-and-a-half later. Things with Michael progressed pretty peacefully and joy-fully after that, but she got the message loud and clear. Dolly has been careful not to mention the crowd back home, not only because of what had happened after the funeral, but also because they're irrelevant. She has a life in New York and they are working toward a future together. All that's left for her in Sugar's Bend is her father, and there isn't much to say about him. Not today, anyway.

Widowed and semi-retired, Daddy started playing more golf and throwing himself into a social scene. She's been proud to see him getting out instead of muttering about the house or wallowing in his plaid recliner. But there is a sense of guilt at the base of their relationship these days, because she knows every time she calls him that talking to her is the absolute best part of his day... something she should do more.

That's why this trip mattered so much to him, and why she is here.

Empowered by these thoughts, she pulls up Michael's name in her contacts, hits the call button, and listens to two short beeps before he picks up. "Hey, babe."

"Hey! How was golf?" she asks. Her voice feels far off, like someone else is saying the words.

"Fine, the usual. Absolutely no improvement in my handicap and a bit of a sunburn." He isn't usually self deprecating. Is this insecurity over her being in Texas? "What's up with you guys? I mean... y'all?" And cute Michael is back.

Dolly smiles into the phone. "Heading out to dinner in town tonight. Hoping I don't run into any ghosts."

"Ah, it can't be that bad. Just think... when you grow up in Manhattan, you see them everywhere."

Dolly's never thought about it like that before. Everyone she knows in New York, aside from college friends that have been in her life on and off for ten years, is new.

"Ten-mile island," he continues. "Millions of ghosts."

She manages an actual laugh now, realizing that running into an old friend of Declan's or a history teacher who'd hoped she would stay local and teach English at SBHS, won't be the worst thing in the world. It's never occurred to her that Michael with his confident gait and easy smile would dread running into anybody. Sometimes, she realizes, she carries on like she's the only person she knows who has a past.

"I miss you," she says weakly, the distractions of the day draining from her consciousness suddenly as she pictures her new life in New York. "I wish I was hopping in the shower to come meet you for dinner..."

"I know, babe. I miss you, too. But I'll take you out this week, okay? Go enjoy your dad tonight. Try not to think so much about all the... heavy stuff." Michael sighs audibly through the phone, the realization clicking for Dolly how much he gets it.

Buried deep inside Michael is the loss of his own mother, which happened twenty years ago when he was just a young boy. Dolly often wonders what's worse: losing a parent before you have time to create beautiful memories and a loving relationship with them, being robbed of the time? Or losing a parent who has become your closest friend in the entire world, and not knowing how you will go on without them? She still hasn't decided. She probably never will.

"Well, I'll call you tomorrow if you're going out tonight...?" she offers brightly, redirecting the ship.

"Yes, that's good. Might meet up with some of the guys after the gym. I'll text when I'm in, though. I love you."

"I love you, too."

She hits the red circle to end the call, now wrapped in the tight hug of Michael's pull. She's been in some kind of daze almost since landing at DFW, and this first proper conversation with him has reminded her of who she really is now. Thinking back on the past and what could have been and what was, looking through photos and boxes and reminiscing on times best left forgotten. All the while not thinking enough about the person who will be her future.

It's strange what a place can do to a person, but stranger still what a person can. Thanks to his encouragement, Dolly is back to herself again—the version of herself that she *wants* to be —and ready to put things where they belong. Ready to pack away the vestiges of her high school romance and friendships and focus on helping Daddy pack up the rest of the knick-knacks that need to go. Ready to get on a plane back to New York. Back to the man who has picked her up every time life has knocked her down ever since they met. Who will meet her at the altar next June and with whom, one day, she hopes to start a family.

Dolly holds the phone close to her chest for a moment before putting it down on her nightstand and standing up slowly to stretch. What she wouldn't give to go to a yoga class right now, she thinks, reaching her arms up overhead and letting them fall slowly to her sides. Her body craves the stress release and her mind needs it even more. But in order to get to a class she'd have to drive half an hour out of town, so she decides against it.

Monday night. Monday night she'll be back in New York and by the middle of this week she'll be doing a sunrise flow with Glinda before work. Just a while longer in Sugar's Bend and she can put all of this behind her. Let go of the past and move boldly toward her bright future.

If only it could ever be that easy.

* * * * *

Last night when Dolly was looking at all the photos on her walls and in boxes, it sort of casually passed through her mind that she would need to do something with them. But now that she has spoken to Michael she's feeling reenergized. Armed with a couple of empty shoeboxes from the back of the closet and a large plastic trash bag, Dolly slowly starts peeling her big fashion collage down from the walls.

It's hard but cathartic at the same time; she doesn't need these pictures like she used to, because now she has what she always hoped for, what they symbolized. The dream of making it in New York is unfolding and the outdated fashion tear-outs are tossed in the garbage bag. Next to come down are the snapshots of those happy days by the creek, in parking lots, and other meaningful places past the edges of town with the old crew; the cheerleading snaps, the once-precious photographs of her and Declan—young, tan, and falling in love. Savage as she was in discarding the magazine clippings, she can't bring herself to do the same with these. Instead, she places them gently in shoeboxes and stacks them up in a KEEP pile on the floor beside her desk.

Daddy's new condo will have a second bedroom for her to stay in when she visits, and he's already said that the movers will take whatever it is she wants to keep and set it up in that room for her. A swift transfer. Almost as if nothing is changing, when really, everything is. Dolly is keenly aware that she doesn't need most of her old sweatshirts and pajama pants, but she can't bring herself to get rid of any of it after the emotional work of doing so with Mama's stuff this morning. So, instead she consolidates everything into a few drawers and slaps another KEEP Post-It onto the front of the dresser.

A lot of her favorite items have come north with her over the past several years, and Mama cleared out most of what was truly unnecessary a year or so after Dolly left. Daddy should be fine with holding onto these few pieces of furniture and boxes. The paperweights, banners, and books she wants to keep will all be packed up by the professional movers as well. All they've asked is for the house to be cleared of what's not going across town to the condo, and the walls to be stripped down. She doesn't need the few posters that remain, so she peels them off one by one and takes a last look at each before crumpling and tossing them in the big bag of trash.

When she's satisfied with the state of her room, she heads out to check on Daddy, who's finally finishing up in the garage. They agree to take turns showering and get going into town within the hour, leaving the kitchen and dining room for tomorrow. "I can handle the bathroom, assuming there's nothing left in there you want," he says. She nods her head to give him the go-ahead.

At five o'clock, they climb into Daddy's sporty two-door Mercedes and head into town for an early dinner. After Mama died, he traded in his sensible sedan for something faster and more fun. Now that the totaling of the SUV has taken her life and all but ruined his, it's like he doesn't want anything in the driveway that was there before. Funny how the house still sat up until last night exactly how it had been the day she died, but the driveway received a full overhaul. *Men's priorities*, she thinks with an inner chuckle.

But then again, we all do things like this. Make choices, move things around. Almost like parts of us feel compelled to move on and heal fast, while others stay exactly where they were for as long as humanly possible.

The meal is not nearly as quiet or awkward as the others have been up until now. As Dolly hoped, being surrounded by strangers and vaguely familiar faces enjoying supper at a crowded restaurant (with a live band, no less!) takes the edge off. She and Daddy each order a glass of chardonnay and enjoy it a sip at a time while taking in the scene. Daddy seems happier to-night, lighter from having the bulk of the housework behind him. He's telling her about some of the cool (and completely useless) things that he found in the garage today, boasting that there are more TOSS or DONATE boxes than KEEP.

"Mama would be so proud!" she says, and he nods in agree-ment, smiling. The mention of her seems not heavy, though. It's like she's in on it all.

"How'd it go with her things?" he asks then. "The closet and such? I don't want to erase her, Dolly. But I can't take it all…"

"I know, Daddy. I know. She wouldn't want you keeping it all. I'm holding onto my favorite clothes, and I left a bunch of stuff you might like. I couldn't touch the papers or photos yet, ei-ther. But there's a lot we can give away that women without anything would love."

"That's what she would want," he agrees. "Absolutely. We can worry about the papers another time… when I'm settled." He flashes that old confident smile she remembers, the one she hasn't seen in a while. This is nice… *really* nice.

"So did you uncover any old gems of mine in the garage, or just your weird Dad-stuff?" she teases between bites of her salad.

"Ha! Not today, but did I ever tell you a few months after y'all left and headed off to college, your mama and I found your old stash of empties out there?"

Dolly nearly snorts wine straight up her nose, the memory of hiding a bunch of bottles that final summer coming in clearly. Her parents knew she had a drink here and there with friends, but one weekend they'd had a few too many bottles to safely bury in with the recycling and they'd panicked. Looking back now it seems ridiculous that they thought they'd get away with it, but when Steph had suggested stashing them behind bins of old baby clothes and slowly offloading them in the coming months, it had made sense.

Like the idiot teenagers they were, they'd totally forgotten to do any of that. And apparently her parents had found them out quick.

"No, you never told me that! God, Daddy, that is so embarrassing."

"Your mother was mostly horrified at that terrible shit you were drinking. I'll never forget her"—he is red in the face now, a laughter tear forming at the edge of his eye—"looking at the bottles and back at me, saying 'Didn't we teach her better than *this*? Flavored wine?'"

Dolly lifts up her glass now, through laughter, and motions him to do the same. "To Mama—who would definitely approve of this oaky chard!"

"To Sally!" He clinks glasses with her and smiles. "That she would, honey. That she would."

They swap some of their favorite old stories about Mama for a bit. Then, Dolly's phone buzzes. She hasn't had it handy all weekend and while everything is fine with Michael, she worries about not being on call for Sandra. It's outside Daddy's realm of understanding why anyone would have their mobile device out on the dinner table on a Saturday night, but he isn't a Director at a fast-growing PR firm trying to secure a six-page spread for a major designer client at one of the most read women's magazines in the country.

It *is* Sandra calling, so Dolly begs off to take the call outside. She feels a bit guilty that she hasn't checked her email all day, so it's a relief when, on the other end of the line, her boss simply fills her in on some benign details about an event from last night and issues her some follow-up reminders. It is easy to get lost in the work-stress, because it's so much easier to handle than the other kind.

Dolly makes a mental note of it all, "yessing" and "sureing" and wishing Sandra a nice rest of the weekend, too. They hang up briskly and she starts to walk back into the restaurant, but a familiar voice stops her before she reaches the door.

"Dolly?" The voice is soft and sounds almost as nervous as Dolly feels hearing it.

Years and pain, secrets and misunderstandings may have un-folded, but the sound of your first best friend's voice isn't something you'll ever forget. Dolly turns around slowly, and there is Stephanie. Tall and striking, her deep red hair hanging in loose ringlets just past her shoulders. It's only been a year-and-a-half since they were in the same room, but Stephanie looks different. Dolly aches to run to her, to grab her in a hug and pack ten years of missed opportunities into the 90 seconds until her entree is likely to hit the two-top that awaits her inside. But she can't do that. Her body won't let her.

"Stephanie, hi." It comes out so coolly; she is rooted to the spot.

"What are you doing in town?" Steph manages, ignoring Dolly's icy reception. Her eyes are hopeful, soft.

"I came down to help my dad pack up. They're dozing the whole neighborhood and putting new houses up there, so everyone sold." Steph nods as if now recalling news she's heard already. Dolly can't help but wonder, for a split second, if it was Declan she heard it from.

"How long are you down for, then?" She looks sad. Until this moment Dolly has only considered her own feelings. Despite the hard things they've faced together and separately, they once were inseparable. That can't be easy on Steph, either. Especially after the tension that ensued the last time they were in the same room together, and the combative text exchange that happened afterward. Dolly cringes at the split-second thought of it.

"Just until tomorrow..." she starts, and then feels her phone vibrating in her hand. She looks down to a text from Daddy. "Listen, Steph, I've gotta go. That was my dad and our food is out."

Steph nods, and then suddenly her look of longing is replaced with a stiff lip and a nod to seal the conversation. Dolly is almost sure she catches Steph noticing her large engagement ring then. She has to wonder if it instills a pang of jealousy, or if her former best friend is beyond caring about anything that's happening in Dolly's life anymore. She's married, anyway, but to an incredibly unspecial boy they knew in high school. Her life is nowhere near as glamorous and exciting as Dolly's. Dolly is disgusted at herself for that thought. "Enjoy your dinner, Dolly. See you around..." And she's gone just as fast as she appeared.

*   *   *   *   *

Right after the funeral, Dolly and her dad had driven wordlessly from Dallas home to Sugar's Bend. It was a journey she had taken countless times, but never had it felt so long. She was numb from the inside-out, hands resting awkwardly in her lap with the palms half-turned up toward heaven. Her mouth felt thick and dry, cotton forming around any word she tried to pull out from within. There was nothing to say.

This was the first time in her life that Daddy seemed unable to lift the mood with banter. Always chatty, always funny, his boisterousness had gotten them out of so many hard times. Like in high school when things had all fallen apart, Daddy was about the only part of her day that brought genuine belly laughs. Now, he was eerily silent, his joy washed away and erased, buried with his wife. Dolly could picture Daddy in swirls of happiness leaving his own body like smoke, curling and settling around Sally in the grave, disappearing beneath the dirt.

She shook her head, shoving the image away. Finally, a safe topic pinged up in her weary mind.

"I'm glad Steph was able to make it. It was good to see her."

Daddy said nothing. The warm air circulating luxuriously around them started to sprout sweat beads at the back of her neck. Used to the austere backseats of taxi cabs, riddled with germs and never the right temperature despite the steep price, Dolly realized then two things at the same time: first, that it was a downright luxury to be able to reach out a hand and turn your air temp down in a vehicle. Second, that Daddy looked pissed.

"What?" She didn't mean it to, but the question came out like a demand. Another long pause filled the space between them with static. With silent, angry noise.

"It's nothing, honey. Just talk to Stephanie when you can," he finally said. Quietly, he reached over to pat her thigh in warmth and empathy. "It was sure good to see her. Hopin' you two can talk some time... work through some of your stuff."

Dolly shrugged, satisfied if a bit confused. But late that night when she ran into Steph at the bar, her old friend was nothing but a shadow. At the funeral she'd mouthed "Hi" and, later, "I'm sorry" when catching Dolly's eye. But later when they both found themselves at the late-night dive in town,

Dolly tried to approach her and couldn't get close. Dolly was drunk that night, yes, but later she would form a clear picture of Stephanie hanging out in a group of unfamiliar faces or standing in dark corners turned into her phone. Avoiding her. Avoiding confrontation or just being ice-cold? The obvious thing was to come over and talk to Dolly, throw her arms around her and tell her, out loud, that she was sorry for her loss. That she missed Sally, too. Something... anything. It shouldn't have been on Dolly.

After pouring herself into a small-town taxi and berating her new boyfriend over the phone, she endured a nausea-induced drive back to her hotel. By the time she arrived, Dolly could think of no other outlet for her rage than to punch out a text to her former friend. Confused and angry, she wrote:

WTF Stephanie? Come to my mom's funeral for brownie points but can't say hi to me at a bar?

In the morning, after a fitful night of drunken slumber, she awoke to a half-answer from Stephanie.

Sorry. We should talk at some point... last night just wasn't the time. You were wasted, and I have a lot to tell you. How long are you in town?

Dolly stared at the screen, unsure what to feel. Daddy's visible anger in the car last night and her own feelings of rejection from being avoided by Steph in the bar resurfaced. Tumbling back to her mind came all the old feelings of insecurity and doubt surrounding their complicated and storied friendship. And she was tired. So, so tired. She had just lost her mother and now she was being criticized by a lifelong friend? Of course she'd been wasted last night. What the hell else happens after leaving your mother's funeral, after processing her sudden death?

Fuck you, she typed and deleted. Twice. The words looked harsher than she could stand to send, even though they felt authentic. Across town she pictured Stephanie watching the dot dot dot form and disappear, form and disappear on their text chain.

I'm leaving today. I guess you missed your chance. Dolly hit send and then deleted the whole exchange, which included months- and even years-old tiny hellos and brief memory swaps she'd coveted.

The stormy silence between them had remained intact ever since, and though it would be several months after that awful weekend that Dolly would learn the whole truth about Daddy's problem with Stephanie Longman, it wouldn't be her that she heard it from. It would be him.

* * * * *

Seeing her tonight, all that remained was the dry aftermath of a too-long grudge that stayed put even when you didn't want it to. So she walked away, hoping to avoid the topic altogether.

When Dolly arrives back at the table, she doesn't mention seeing Stephanie. "Sorry, my boss was just following up on a few things for this week." He brushes her explanation away with a quick wave of his hand to say, *"Not to worry,"* and they tuck into their nearly identical orders: chicken and waffles, his drenched half-and-half in maple syrup and gravy, hers bone-dry. Daddy shakes his head with a small chuckle, remarking as he always loves to at the lack of condiments on her plate. *"So* not Southern," he teases.

She laughs too and shrugs, "I'm a simple girl, what can I say?" And now something has officially changed; they can both feel it. The heavy cloud that's hung a few inches above their heads this whole visit is starting to dissipate as father and daughter find a way to enjoy this new version of what their family is. While phone calls have always been natural enough, sitting down at meals with Sally absent has felt claustrophobic to both of them this trip.

They probably expected it on a base level, and that's why the past few times they've seen each other in the year-and-a-half since Mama died were somewhere other than home. There's always been an excuse: Dolly had an event in Miami and flew him down to get a few days on the beach with her. She was working most of the weekend, but they had a chance to get out a bit and sightsee together. And doing the past two Christmases in Oklahoma with Daddy's cousins was a welcome change from the hustle and bustle of New York. It was also an opportunity for him not to have to feel the marked agony of waking up alone on Christmas morning in the house he'd shared with Sally for nearly thirty years, of going to church without her and coming home to a kitchen that didn't smell of fresh-baked pie.

Escape. That's what they've both been doing for the past year and a half, but now it is time to face the past and move on. If they can.

* * * * *

The morning light breaks fast and strong on her last day in town, rolling in through the windows of her childhood bedroom like it did throughout her youth. Dolly groans, a day of travel lying before her when she wishes she could just snap her fingers and be back on the Upper East Side.

Groggily, she makes her way out to the kitchen where Daddy's put on a pot of coffee and is fully dressed in an ice blue polo shirt and khakis. "Morning, sleepyhead," he greets her, looking up from his paper long enough to catch her eye over the rim of his reading glasses. "Any interest in seeing my new place today on your way out of town?"

Dolly wasn't expecting this. The sorting, discarding, and packing all made real enough the fact that this will no longer be their family home in a matter of weeks, but the thought of actually seeing the new one in person seems a step past her comfort zone.

"Oh, I don't know... do we have time?"

"Sure! You just follow me over there in the rental, and hit the highway from town."

"Oh, okay. Yeah, Daddy, that should be fine." She has no justification out of his plan, and realizes then that maybe he needs this. Maybe the errand is not just to let her see the condo, but to make him feel better about everything. He deserves that.

After breakfast and once the rental car is packed with her weekender and purse, Dolly pauses a moment in the foyer, the engine of Daddy's Mercedes purring just feet from the porch in the drive. She looks one last time out across the collection of rooms that held her through her early triumphs and losses, lets herself picture her mother standing there in white linen. *I will miss you,* she breathes inaudibly into the space before turning to close the door behind her forever.

Her father's cheerful face peering at her through the windshield of his fancy new car says everything she needs to know: *This is going to be okay.*

It's only a short drive to the section of town just past the shops and restaurants of Dolly's youth, where a smattering of smart condominiums have been constructed. The entrance to Daddy's new neighborhood is flanked by rows of evenly trimmed shrubs and announced by a sign saying "*Willow's*

Crest: Homes available from the low 300's!" in red. She follows his car to the second row of housing inside on the left, noticing with a snort that there is not a single willow tree in sight. Daddy parks right outside a white two-story home that is cookie-cutter identical to everything else on the row outside their cheerfully and variably painted shutters and front doors. His are black and salmon, respectively.

They park and get out of their cars, standing feet from his new front door. The home might not have endless Southern charm or even much of a personality, but it has its own entrance with a garage behind and it's brand-new, free of problems. Free of memories.

"It's really nice, Daddy," she says, giving him a wide smile.

"Thanks, honey. Wish I had the keys so I could show you around, but I don't pick them up 'til next week." He turns then to look at her. "Think you'll be back again before too long?" There is a pleading in his tone and his eyes, despite the upturn of his smiling mouth.

"Yes," she promises, meaning it. He wraps his arms around her like he hasn't since the funeral, and for the first time since then, Dolly feels the roof over her beginning to repair. She still has a family. She still has a *parent*.

She almost doesn't want to let go.

THE OCTOBER
BEFORE LAST

Sally stands in the kitchen, barefoot in a green velvet wrap dress. Her hair is pulled into a low, loose bun at the nape of her neck. She is writing out place cards for the evening. Throwing impromptu dinner parties has always been one of her favorite things, and with a Friday night opening up unexpectedly, she decided to call a few of their favorite couples to come over for fish, salad, and wine. Simple, peaceful, fun.

Dale comes into the kitchen looking sharp, if tired, in a blazer and pressed shirt. At the end of the work week, it's a wonder that he's agreed to clean up and entertain, since usually about now is when they would be changing into sweatpants and popping corn for a movie on the couch.

But with Dolly so firmly an adult, off in New York living her wildly different life, and with the season of grandparenthood still quite far out of reach, Sally has grown somewhat bored with her routine in recent months. During their daughter's college years she was on edge a lot, ready to fly up to New York at a moment's notice. But that was a while ago and like the rest of the mothers in her circle of friends, Sally has blossomed from a newly empty-nester to a seasoned one with a life far outside the demands of motherhood—even college-aged motherhood.

She has always been a social person who strives off an active calendar. Dale has said from the time they got married that if it wasn't for her, they'd have no friends at all. After a summer of endless cocktail parties and cookouts, her homebody husband needed a break and she obliged. But recently she's been craving a small get-together. She *needs* this tonight.

He has acquiesced by taking a second shower and changing into clothes that are not pajamas. She stands here now, trying to figure out how to ask him to go pick up wine so she can make the dressing for the salad and finish setting the table before touching up her makeup in time for their guests to arrive. But as he's already visibly annoyed by looming social plans he could have done without, she can tell it'll be a tough sell. She tries a soft angle, giving him the chance to make himself useful:

"Honey, I have a few more things to do here, but I can pop out to get the wine for tonight…"

It's clear that Dale isn't only *not* going to go to the liquor store; he isn't even listening at all. His back is to the kitchen, and to her. He reaches for the remote control, clicks on the baseball playoffs, and wordlessly takes a seat at the edge of the couch.

Okay, then. She'll have to cram a trip to the liquor store in between now and the arrival of their friends in one hour, while simultaneously finishing up the food prep. Sally grabs her keys, slips her bare feet into a pair of leather driving moccasins that are waiting by the door, and wraps a cashmere pashmina around her shoulders. "Be back in a bit then," she says over the lull of baseball announcements and stats she cannot understand and doesn't care to hear. Dale mutters a "Bye, drive safe" that sounds like one word all smashed together.

Neither one knows this will be the last time they speak. That this is the last opportunity they'll have to look one another in the eye and say "I love you." These are the thoughts that will hit her in her final moments before she loses consciousness forever.

Her beloved, her sweet Dale with his fun-loving personality...

Why hadn't she taken that evening she didn't know would be her last to lie with him on the couch and watch a terrible movie together? Why hadn't she agreed to spend New Year's Eve in Paris with him last year instead of planning another trip to New York to see Dolly? Why was it always about their daughter, or herself, and not enough about him? Why had she allowed so many opportunities to let him make the decisions pass them by?

He, too, would have regrets. None so bitter as the one about holding his line and not going out for the wine that night. About practically ignoring her not-so-subtle hints that she needed help. The scene would continue to play over in his head often as the months unfolded in the wake of the wreck. Not the scene where he arrived and saw flashing lights and blood everywhere. Not the vision of her reliable, sporty SUV with its left side crunched beyond recognition. Not even the part where he said goodbye to her sleeping face, kissed her ruined forehead, wept and prayed audibly at the bedside of a woman who was already gone.

No. For Dale Weston it would always be that vision of Sally in green velvet. The knowledge that he'd taken note of, but not mentioned, how damn pretty she looked that night. When he walked into the kitchen and saw her, spaghetti straps in October, narrow waist accentuated by the same style dress she used to wear when they first met, his heart had fluttered.

And his grumpy, no-good, old-man attitude had pulled him right over to the couch to sulk. Why hadn't he walked across the floor to her, removed his sports jacket, rolled up his shirt-sleeves, and offered to help? Squeezed the lemons for the salad dressing, grabbed his own stupid car keys from the hook? Gone to the store, lightened her load a bit? Done this one thing to make all of her effort feel worth it...

Worst of all, why hadn't he kissed her fucking goodbye? Told her how beautiful she was, one last time?

Yes, the accident had robbed him of his wife, of not only their lovely if pretty average life, but of their future together. The accident had taken the most important part of him away and replaced it with a hollow, vacant longing. But he had had a hand in it, too. Because that night he wasn't the husband he should have been. And though it wasn't technically his fault, he couldn't shake the knowledge that if he had done things differently, she would still be here.

These are the types of tragedies you don't just walk away from unscathed. You might grow and heal, change and persevere, but they stick with you always, just beneath the surface. And part of Dale's tragedy will always be wrapped up in that green velvet dress. The last chance he didn't take to tell her she was everything.

How do you ever let something like that go?

NOW

It is a quick, easy flight home and an expensive cab ride from JFK to East 68th Street. Despite all of the photos, the intense quiet that opened the door to reminiscence... the rush of memories, and even the encounters with people from her past that made her think of Declan, Dolly is breathlessly excited to see her fiancé. And maybe it's more than Michael, but also an urgency to return to her life. Her apartment, her clothes, her art hanging on her walls. A place that is light and airy, untethered and free from the complications of the past.

To return, after a brief hiatus, to her schedule with its rush of panic and too-frequent client drinks. Her myriad excuses not to focus on these huge, deep losses: first, her mother and now, the house she grew up in. (The other stuff too; the stuff she can't even touch right now). A good and full distraction from the dissipation of her roots. Her new home, a new life, and the future that it all promises her, just within reach.

Yes, Michael. But everything that goes along with him, too.

She has probably checked her lipstick five times in the dim overhead light of the taxi, wanting to look perfect for him tonight. And when she turns her key in the lock and spots him, smiling, across the quirky vintage decor of her small corner of New York, she knows the reunion will be exactly what she hoped it would be.

There he stands in the kitchen, five-foot-eleven and handsome from the inside out. In fitted blue jeans and an untucked shirt, clearly having showered and changed after the gym. He gives her the look she loves, the one that takes his face from a grinning Manhattan socialite straight out of *Page Six* to the sweetheart in her living room. He is holding a bottle of rosé, looking fresh and sexy, exhausted and relieved.

Michael has two distinct sides and this is part of what she loves about him. The night they met comes back in flashes at times like this— it's hard to look at that half-grin (so similar in some ways to the first smile that ever took her breath away...) and not feel instantly at ease.

She was working a client event on the night that started everything between them. Having dated a string of the wrong guys (including a fifty-two-year-old client: that was a huge oops), Dolly was weary (and wary) of the New York dating scene. All of her friends were constantly being wined, dined, and dumped by hot actors or bartenders, interesting colleagues or bankers, alluring ER doctors, young politicians, or friends of friends. It was the same thing on repeat, and none of it was good. What of the New York love story? What of the dream she carried in her back pocket?

It had started to seem at the time like no matter where you looked, the pool was getting smaller and the need greater. Dolly was twenty-eight and ready to meet the one; nowhere near old by New York City standards, but as a Southern girl, she could hear the clock ticking. The little voice in the back of her head (and sometimes, gently, Mama's tinkling voice on the other end of the phone) reminding her that if she were in Sugar's Bend, she'd be married with a decent pack of kids by now.

Meeting and falling in love with the perfect guy wasn't at the absolute top of her to-do list, but it was a pretty close second to her career aspirations. Ever since losing Declan in the splintered and slow-burning way that she did, Dolly yearned to fill the void he'd left behind. In college that meant a lot of casual sex with terrible matches that would lead to nothing but heartache, boredom, and tears. She dated a few contenders among the duds in the years between college and Michael, but none of them were a fit. Dolly had a laser-sharp focus on her career and wasn't going to give any guy who didn't respect that the time of day. So, she was pretty heavily single for most of that period.

By the time she had secured her position at Sandra's firm and moved up a rung or two, the old shame-voice in the back of her mind that used to tell her she wasn't good enough had quieted. She was making her way in a city with hard edges where glamour, romance, and thrill seemed to pulsate in the air. She had important, cool friends who made her feel valued and respected. She earned a totally decent salary and had access to any clothing or cosmetic item she desired. Falling in love was the right next step and the thing she wanted just after another big promotion at work.

That was the Dolly that Michael met just over a year and a half ago. And the one he was confident enough himself, to fall in love with. They laugh about it now, but their very first encounter was anything but romantic.

* * * * *

Michael is known for under-dressing (a habit his buttoned-up tycoon of a father finds absolutely mortifying and one he is now working to improve). When Dolly saw him, honest-faced and adorable in a classic New York way, she assumed he was one of the product models for the event and chastised him for not being in the right spot.

"I need all the paid minglers in the ante room for roll call and assignments," she offered in his general direction without looking him in the eye; motioning flippantly toward what was honestly an oversized coat closet off to the corner of the lobby. Michael looked down at his simple slacks and white button-down, and then back up at her, his big brown eyes dancing. "Oh, yeah?"

Now she was getting frustrated. This was the first time Sandra was letting her run logistics at an event and it *had* to go well. The client, owner of a burgeoning makeup start-up who'd found massive recent success with a line of vegan lip glosses that lasted from sunup to cocktails, needed to come out and see fluid, joyful partygoers and expertly functional space fillers—everywhere. Otherwise, LAZR risked losing the account, and it would be Dolly's fault. She didn't have time for cocky seat fillers.

"Yeah," she said, matter-of-fact, pulling out her clipboard. "Are you with the agency or temping? Pretty sure we sent out a detailed assignment email earlier today," she said quickly, not even looking up from her Blackberry which was vibrating incessantly.

"You think I'm a model, huh?"

The words stunned her enough to make her glance up briefly from her phone and take in his appearance again. "Are you not?" she deadpanned, "Because if not, I'll need to see your press pass."

Michael leaned in close then, a gesture that totally freaked her out at the time but now fills her with nostalgic butterflies. "I'm Michael Peabody," he said in her ear. "I don't have a press pass, but I'm probably on the list."

Shit.

There was no hiding her deep embarrassment at having accidentally bossed around the son of the event's key sponsor.

Now that she looked at him, of course Dolly recognized the son of M. Gideon Peabody, a revered socialite with generations-old New York railroad money. The Peabodys owned a successful liquor conglomerate among other lucrative local businesses for what Dolly's boss referred to as "fun money," and Michael was a frequent fixture in the society pages of the local news. Also, their wealth and fame made Dolly's somewhat-important Dallas grandparents look like unimpressive paupers. Not that that mattered... but, it wasn't *not* true.

"Oh gosh, I'm so sorry," she stammered, stashing her Blackberry in her purse. "I—I have to go! Enjoy the party!"

"I will, now that I know someone like you took me for a model," he called after her as she hurried to the top of the red carpet, cheeks flushed.

Dolly dove back into handling the flow of the press and celebrity guests, making sure she secured every sound bite her client needed, and ended up nailing the event. By its close, she was exhausted yet happy in the way that only the young professional can be after a big, busy, heart-racing night where you did everything you were supposed to do and then some. Where you impressed your boss, received a breathy compliment from a Kardashian, *and* had a mild flirtation with a cute socialite. Not bad!

It was still all so new and foreign to her the way she seemed to have a totally different personality when it came to work. This was probably the best part of her job, to be honest. Whereas she'd always been the shy girl with one foot out the door, being a publicist forced her into the spotlight. The demands of her job made her feel more confident, gave her a voice if for no other reason than she needed one. And damn, it felt good. Shy teenaged Dolly Weston from Sugar's Bend, Texas teetering on the outskirts of the lunchroom would be beaming with pride.

Exhausted, Dolly walked outside and decided to treat herself to a rare cigarette before hailing a cab home. She tucked into a 24-hour convenience store to buy a pack. As she was standing on the corner of Essex and Stanton Streets with her back pressed gently against the wall outside the bodega's storefront, Dolly struck a match, lit her cigarette, and inhaled deeply.

What a night behind her and what a morning to come. In a mere five hours she'd be back at her desk sending out the press release her boss's assistant was no doubt currently writing up. Her ears buzzed with the leftover commotion they still felt from inside the party. Her heart lurched at the realization that she'd mingled with some of the most important celebrity journalists in the city. Her cheeks burned and she felt an inner giggle brewing at the fact that she'd accidentally taken society darling Michael Peabody for a paid stand-in.

Dolly rested her smoking hand against her side for a moment, felt the sequins of her dress pressing into her wrist. Dahlia Mae Weston, once Dolly down the cul-de-sac, had reinvented herself, spruced up her given name into something that would match better. But now that she was here, she felt as authentic as she could. *New York.*

New York was home now, in its glory and with all its demons. A mix of French restaurants and subway rats, the highest of fashion and the lowest of blows. The place that turned you from an innocent hometown girl into a woman who thought she knew the world. *New York, you are beautiful and complicated and scary and such a thrill,* she thought, breathing in deeply on the cigarette she knew Mama would snatch out of her fingers and stomp into the sidewalk so quick Dolly's head would spin, if she could see her right now.

And at the thought of Mama and what she might think of

Dolly's impressive career moves tonight, and of the chic little Versace slip dress she wore that she'd scored for a mere $50 at Century 21 last week, Dolly tossed her stubbed-out cigarette and headed to the corner to catch a cab back Uptown. Her arm extended and her eyes practically ready to close from exhaustion, Dolly hardly noticed his approach. But before she even found a taxi, Michael found her. She'd soon learn that he and some buddies had popped across the street for a bite to eat and he'd not-so-accidentally kept an eye on the door to the venue, hoping to get another chance to talk to this mystery girl with long blond hair and kind of a bad attitude.

She'd later tell people the story with a sense of that rushed, impassioned New York energy that made even the most mundane and sometimes even creepy how-we-met's seem like the ultimate in romance. Theirs almost ended before it even began, actually, because neither one of them had a scrap of paper and both of their phones were dead.

"Is this our fate, then?" He was wide-eyed and his hair was wild. "I waited for an hour outside the hotel and find you smoking outside a bodega... Can we at least make sure next time it takes a little less effort?"

Dolly reached into her purse and pulled out an eyeliner pen, rolled up his boring sleeve and scrawled her number on his arm. "Don't shower before your phone is charged back up," she warned, hopping into the cab that had just pulled up. "That's not waterproof!"

* * * * *

When she thinks of that night, the old butterflies often return, because unlike the other guys she's dated in this town, Michael is every bit as sweet and adventurous as she'd thought and hoped he might be from that first meeting. The eyeliner is a distant memory and that cigarette was one of the last few she ever smoked. The past year and a half has both flown and meandered. Their bond is strong and solid, and Michael has been permanently etched on her heart.

When Dolly lost her mom a mere six weeks into their relationship, things were hard and she often wondered what the point was of any of it. But there he'd remained and here he is now, her Michael. The dream that life was deciding to let her hold onto. The love that wasn't going to disappear when things got tough.

"Hi, baby," he smiles now.

"Hi," she breathes back, wrapping her arms around his waist and draping them at the small of his back.

"Oh, God, I missed you." Michael stands back a moment, holding her at arm's length and looking into her eyes. "Let's order Chinese?" he suggests.

"Yes, yeah. Let's do that," she answers quietly, feeling suddenly shy, which is odd.

Dolly shakes off the feeling, which is probably fueled by the weight of her recent visit home. It might have been only a long weekend, but the magnitude and purpose of the trip pull heavily on her heart. Not to mention the unexpected run-ins with figures from the past.

Saying goodbye to the house forever this morning and seeing Daddy's new digs with her own eyes brought on its own complicated swell of emotions that hit on the plane. Despite Daddy seeming fine with the adjustments, she knows deep down he's hurting, too. It can't be any easier for him to say goodbye than it was for her.

Goodbye to linoleum and a back porch door that squeaks in the summer heat, to glass vases containing marigolds in August, daffodils in March. Goodbye to 70's brick-face and the site of Mama's vegetable garden that he just couldn't keep up after she was gone. Goodbye to the spot where every argument took place, and every Christmas morning, too. (Well, not the last two, but every one with Mama). Goodbye to the plantation shutters Sally had insisted they splurge on that one fall and had loved so dearly; to wall collages and ceiling fans, stolen high school kisses and the place that held your first dreams, heaved under the weight of them.

Goodbye, too, to something nameless and less concrete, something she can feel but not quite explain: the feeling of Mama in the air. The trace of her perfume in the closet, sure. But also to that thought, however silly, that remains even long after someone is gone... That you can be sitting in their home and allow yourself to wonder for just a silent moment: if you closed your eyes and breathed them back into being, would they maybe surprise you and come walking around the corner? Goodbye forever to that childlike hope.

For the corners will now be gone, and no one will be coming around them again. Least of all someone who's no longer there, no longer anywhere.

Dolly and Michael order chicken and broccoli with the brown sauce on the side, steamed vegetable dumplings, and a large hot-and-sour soup. They eat half-reclined on the couch, their feet up on Dolly's hand-me-down glass coffee table (a gift from her aunt Judy in Dallas who briefly owned a lovely pied-à-terre in New York when her marriage hit the rocks, and offloaded most of her best stuff to Dolly when she moved back home).

They use chopsticks and plastic forks on-and-off, depending on which bite of food they're going in for. They drink a bottle of not-quite-chilled chardonnay after polishing off the rosé. (Michael remembered to buy the wine, but not to place it in the fridge before she arrived). The edges of their feet are touching, the heart of their routine is falling back into place.

Here, in her home with its bohemian fixtures and soothing colors, snuggled close to the man who will marry her next year, Dolly can finally breathe. The complications, the messiness, the sadnesses of the past few days are starting to lift. Even the awkward coming back together that hit her when she first walked through the door has dissipated. She feels playful once more and can almost pretend it's just a regular evening.

After the food is finished and the containers rinsed and added to the recycle bin; after the wine is gone and before they can both tuck into their phones to get a headstart on tomorrow's emails, Michael leans in with the kiss that moves things from the couch to the bed. And Dolly, with both love and lust in her heart for this man who makes the world feel simple and clear, falls into his arms and lets her body do the rest of the talking.

* * * * *

Dolly wakes up easily to the familiar sound of her alarm and is instantly catapulted back to reality. Last night was romantic and draining. She and Michael had sex three times between dinner and finally closed their eyes around 2 AM. Today her schedule is so packed, Dolly's starting to feel a bit panicked. But as usual, she takes care to block off a couple of hours, one in the morning and one just after her lunch meeting, to pretend she has an appointment and use the time to hack through her unanswered emails.

She steps out onto the sidewalk and is given her first reminder that she's no longer in Texas. March in New York is anything but willingly sunny, and today is a particularly harsh reminder of that. The wind is biting and there are tiny, stinging drops of rain coming down so fast she almost can't even see them. Shivering inside her mother's Burberry raincoat that she was smart to have worn home on the plane yesterday, Dolly decides to try for a cab instead of roughing it on the subway.

Usually, having lived here for ten-plus years and knowing the subway system inside and out, Dolly stands up a bit straighter, elbows out, and faces the crowd even when it's bound to be a grumpy ride. But today she feels delicate, an emotional hangover from the charged weekend not completely out of her system. She doesn't have the heart to try for a seat or to risk getting mud on the cuffs of her brand new Helmut Lang pants. As luck would have it, an older gentleman is getting out of a taxi at the top of the block and no one else is around to nab it. Careful not to fall, Dolly sprints toward it with her arm extended and manages to hail the cab as he's about to depart. "Thank you," she says, breathless, to the man who has just exited the taxi.

"I never had cab fare when I was your age," is his response, to which Dolly just shrugs awkwardly. *People are funny*, she thinks, sliding across the seat toward the middle and pulling the door closed against the spitting rain.

"Mercer and East Eighth, please," she tells the cabby before folding herself into the right-hand corner of the backseat and pulling out her cell phone. With traffic she figures she's got about forty-five minutes of commuting time ahead, so she decides to check Facebook before hopping into Outlook to respond to the most pressing work emails. After scrolling for about a minute she sees a notification at the bottom of the screen. Not one to typically send and receive Facebook messages, Dolly doesn't think much of it, but realizing it might be a client's assistant (some of these younger girls do literally everything via social media), she clicks on the icon.

Suddenly, the parts of her pieced-back-together world, all of which seemed whole and sexy last night after coming down from a hard weekend, are blown back to bits. Because the message has nothing to do with social media-happy assistants or client events, nor is it one of her eccentric friends inviting her to drinks at a new spot:

Dolly, hope you're well. I heard you were in town this weekend. My mom says she ran into you? Hope the packing wasn't too stressful. I don't even know why I'm writing... Love, D

The message is, in fact, from the last person she would expect to hear from now, or ever. And just like that, she's back where she shouldn't be... in the past.

* * * * *

If Declan doesn't know why he's writing, she sure as hell doesn't know what (or how?) to write back. What do you say to your high school boyfriend who didn't show up to your mother's funeral? How do you keep yourself together while actively picking at an open wound? Does there ever come a time when you can read and respond to a note from an ex and it doesn't have to mean anything... doesn't have to feel like a huge, heavy deal?

And what's with the *"Love"*? It feels almost like an afterthought, but that is the type of word no sane person would just toss in at the end of a message like this to someone from the past, especially not someone that was your first love... first everything.

Right?

Dolly is confused and breath-taken, annoyed and not a little jarred. She is also *engaged*. And completely unsure how to handle this message from the ghost at the center of her complicated past. Dolly is twenty-nine years old and going to be married. Shouldn't that right there be enough to deter her from responding to her high school boyfriend, or at the very least to make her realize that her response doesn't much matter?

But Declan isn't just an ex, and she isn't just someone else's fiancé. The whole mess that took them from where they started and where they fell apart, to where they are now, is layers deep. Michael doesn't know; almost nobody does. About that winter and spring of junior year and how everything got blown to bits. About the girl who would come between them and change their relationship beyond repair. About the very real, very adult dramas that can happen to teenagers. And about how those things can change us forever.

* * * * *

At her lunch meeting, Dolly is completely preoccupied. Under the table, she click-click-clicks her stiletto heel onto the white tile floor at The Smith, wishing she could find her way to a serene beach somewhere. Somewhere warm and without cell service, where she could contemplate this stupid message in peace and try to come up with something to say in return. Or if she should even respond at all.

This lunch meeting is with one of her favorite clients, too. Anderson Jones has a small fleet of boutique hotels launching downtown over the next six-to-twenty-four months. He's cool, kind, and disarmingly not cocky. Despite coming from family money and dressing like he wants you to know it, Anderson is laid-back and funny. He's probably in his early 40's but loves to gossip as much as the next intern. He smiles with his whole face, talks with his hands, and doesn't care who's looking. Dolly adores Anderson, and usually a lunch with him is a joyous escape from whatever other work obligations and personal dramas are weighing her down, even though it's technically business.

Today, though, she can't stop mulling over that confusing Facebook message. Between bites of her kale salad and sips of sparkling water, Dolly can't help but think: *You don't even know why you're writing?... Then don't fucking write!*

Anderson is in the middle of telling an apparently hilarious story, and Dolly's grateful that both his assistant and her intern are here, too, because their laughter makes it less obvious that she isn't paying attention. Snapping back into the moment, Dolly orders a cheesecake with four forks and tries to get in on their conversation, but fails. She's missed too much and it's too late to ask for more details now, so she smiles brightly and throws an "Oh my God!" in where it feels natural, then enjoys the diversion of the shared dessert when it finally arrives.

After lunch, Anderson pulls her aside a minute while the PA's gather coats and umbrellas. "What's up, Dahlia?" It's jarring to hear her reimagined "New York name" as Michael calls it, after being home for the weekend.

"What do you mean?"

"Something's off, girlfriend." After a beat, "That hot fiancé of yours better not have pissed you off, because I can get him blacklisted from every club in this city if I want to!"

Dolly bursts out laughing and reaches in to hug her client-turned-friend. "Oh my God," she says, "No. It's... worse." She hasn't planned on telling anyone about hearing from Declan, but now feels the universe placed this particular friend in the middle of this particular day to help her figure it out. Anderson is far enough removed from her "real life" that she risks nothing in telling him about the weighted message, but he cares enough about her that she knows he'll give her some solid advice.

"My ex... from high school..."

"Mm-hmmmm?" Anderson's green eyes seem to have grown a full size as he folds his arms in front of his chest and dramatically lets out breath, upnods quickly to shift a piece of hair that's fallen across his forehead.

"I don't know. I was home in Texas this weekend and I ran into his mom. He messaged me this morning and I just don't know how to respond. *If* I should respond."

"What's he look like?" Anderson deadpans, reaching for the phone she's holding in her left hand.

Dolly playfully swats his hand away. "That's totally not the point!"

"Well, maybe not, but it could change my opinion on how to proceed," he replies wryly. Dolly opens Facebook, clicks on her messages, and opens Declan's, holding the phone close to her chest for a moment as she makes him promise not to respond for her.

"I won't, I won't. Fork it over." Anderson takes the phone and peeks at the message, clearly clicking on the profile of its sender before forming and voicing an opinion. "Damn, girl!" he declares, going back and forth between the message and the profile a couple of times before returning the phone to her open palm.

"I think you need to respond."

The assistants are now approaching, rain gear in hands and panicked eyes wide-open in looks of "you-need-to-get-to-your-next-meeting."

"He doesn't even know why he's writing!" she hiss-whispers to

Anderson as the two air-kiss each other's cheeks.

"Yeah... but you do."

THEN

The first few weeks back at school were a decent enough adjustment. Once Dolly got used to not seeing Declan as much, the cadence of their new schedule took hold and things began to feel easier. While the lazy days that ended under the stars and picked right up again early in the mornings were pretty much through, they still had fun on the weekends and found opportunities to sneak a kiss before football and cheer practice. Most days, their practice end times were close enough that she was able to catch a ride home with him rather than having to rely on her dad. Those were the best times, when the sun was lowering in the sky and the radio was up loud. The windows down and the refreshing late-September breeze whipping through her long hair. His hand on her thigh, firm and loving.

When Declan's mom was feeling generous, she would let him have supper with the Westons on a weeknight. Dolly's parents were more laid-back in general than his were, but it wasn't like they'd let them hang out in her room with the door closed either. Dinner was nice, but Dolly missed their physical connection, the freedom that summer had allowed them to spend alone together during the day.

She felt even more sexually charged than ever around Declan now that there were fewer opportunities to get close to him. Which is why on a Thursday night in late September, when her parents surprised them by going out bowling with friends after inviting Declan over for dinner, she was more than ready to have him to herself.

"Listen," Daddy said, reaching into his wallet to pull out a twenty-dollar bill. "Y'all order in some pizza and enjoy. But no alcohol, and no leaving the kitchen and living room area." Dolly almost laughed, realizing her parents still thought their daughter's virginity was intact. The strict, no-bedroom rule had kept up all summer in both houses, but had been ignored as often as humanly possible. Also—did neither set of parents realize that there was a truck involved? And river banks and pantries, mall dressing rooms and couches in their friends' basements...?

It didn't matter, though, because fifteen minutes later they were alone in her living room with a pizza on the way and their mouths and hands all over each other. "I missed this," he said, grunting as he picked her up and turned her to lay on her back. "So." *Kiss*. "Much."

Acting out their very adult feelings of passion had become a part of their routine, yet to two lovesick teenagers it was anything but routine. By the time the pizza delivery boy rang the bell, Dolly had no idea where her shorts had gone to, so she wrapped herself up in an afghan that was draped over the back of the living room couch and motioned for Declan to answer the door.

They ate their pizza in front of the TV, ordinary, happy, and relaxed. Chomping on dinner and taking sips of Sprite in each other's arms with the TV drama that buzzed in front of them serving mostly as background noise to their intermittent kissing. She would miss this later.

By the time her parents came home, they were dressed and the mess had been cleaned up. Dolly tried to look and act like she hadn't been rolling around on their couch naked with her boyfriend for half of the evening, and it worked because Daddy even made a comment about how good it felt to know he could trust them alone for a few hours. Cringy.

Sometimes it was hard to think her parents had ever been teenagers themselves. Did they really think nothing was going on between Dolly and Declan, on top of pizza-eating and a little making out, perhaps? Was it because their daughter had always been so quiet and shy, or was it more that they just didn't *want* to know? Whatever the reason, she had her parents' trust even if she didn't deserve it.

* * * * *

In school the next day, Dolly caught up with Steph by her locker. "I feel like I haven't talked to you all week," she said, not realizing it was true until the words came out.

"I mean yeah, Dolly, you're completely preoccupied with Declan," Steph shot back. The words stung and filled her with shame. Even though they'd been best friends for years, a part of Dolly would always feel a sliver less significant than Steph. Steph was taller, first of all, and infinitely more striking. She had thick, auburn hair that did all the right things without needing to be cajoled, coiffed, or sprayed into place.

Steph also had boobs, which in high school were a hot commodity. Later, as a publicist working largely in the fashion industry, Dolly would learn that there was a beauty and an allure to her flat chest. The same with her generous sprinkling of freckles. But as a teenager at Sugar's Bend High School, the two traits in combination made her feel anything but sexy.

And when your best friend is in line to be captain of the cheer team next year, and has all the boys' eyes on her when she walks down the hall, you develop a bit of an inferiority complex. So that if she tells you that you're wrong, you have to believe her even if you don't think she's right. Such is the pecking order of high school female dramatics, and so it continues for much of life, Dolly will find out in time. You have to physically break down these dynamics to see an even playing field; sixteen-year-old Dolly wasn't there yet.

"I had no idea you felt that way," she said honestly. "I'm sorry. We—we've all been hanging out all summer," she continued. "I don't see why that has to change?"

"I don't know, Dolly, maybe if you'd taken the time to call me back last night, you'd know that Jimmy and I broke up. So yeah, us all hanging out together is gonna have to change."

Dolly reached out to hug Steph and received the icy edges of a sharp chin nestled in her shoulder for a second (with no return on the embrace). "It's fine. I'm fine. Let's get to class," was the end of the conversation, but probably the beginning of the rift.

That afternoon at practice, Steph was cold and distant. Dolly felt awful about not returning her call but it was so late when Declan left she didn't want either of them to get in trouble. Why hadn't Steph caught up with her this morning? What was the point in punishing her for not realizing her friend was going through a breakup?

Steph was as breathtaking in heartbreak as ever. Tall and slender with muscle tone, she stood near the front of the squad as she was being groomed to take over a captain spot next year. Her legs held onto their summer tan while Dolly's had already started to fade back to that girl-next-door peachy tone. Steph might have been going through a hard time, but she didn't let it stand in the way of her toe-touches or her ability to catch the eye of practically every boy on the football team from across the field. Even, Dolly noted with an inner stomach-flip, Declan.

It was only about twice a week that their practice times and locations overlapped, but this was one of those days. And while Steph took over the warm-up, calling "ONE!" to receive a round of "TWO" from the squad in unison, and so on through their group stretches, Dolly's cheeks burned with a mix of furious jealousy and shameful regret of that first emotion.

Steph was her best friend and wounded. Going through a breakup and feeling lost. Dolly hadn't been there for her and was now paying for it, but should she have to pay by watching her own boyfriend glance in this general direction when there was no way he could see her? Leggy Steph was at the front of the pack, now bent over demonstrating a new stretch and Dolly sat facing her, in the second row lost in a sea of nearly identical ponytails. She stood up when it was time, but was too late to catch his eye.

Just last night, she told herself, slowly and with a deep breath. *Just last night he was on your couch, telling you he loved you.* That had to mean more than a pair of tanned legs. High school is a real bitch when it wants to be, and so, too, could Steph be. But this was nonsense, she decided. And she wasn't going to let her own silly jealousy get in the way of any good thing—not her best friendship nor her relationship with her boyfriend.

The herkie drills and stunt building wore on for the next two hours and by the time practice drew to its natural and exhausted close, Steph and Dolly were linking arms again and the ickiness of the afternoon was mostly gone.

"I'm sorry about last night," Dolly offered as they headed to the sidelines to grab their bags.

"I know," Steph replied. Dolly gave her a playful shove which ended in a hug and the two were repaired, for now.

That's the thing about high school. It pulls you up and it drops you down, shows you some of life's most beautiful truths and then rips them away without warning. You never know on a given day which way things are going to go and so many hard times wend their way between the good ones. But the best you can do is keep trying, hold your head up high, gather some good people by your side, and hope like hell they don't tear your young heart to pieces.

NOW

Dolly won't lie to herself and pretend that Declan's Facebook message isn't weighing heavily on her mind. But with all the feelings that emerged this weekend she isn't sure she knows how to respond... or if she should at all. Not to mention that he clearly doesn't know what he expects to hear back, or even why he's writing. With all the time and emotionally charged space between them, it's a joke to think for a minute that they could ever become anything resembling friends.

Also, Dolly is engaged. To a good man. Who loves her. Life is complicated in this moment with work stress piling up and Daddy's pending move, but she's handling it. She will be okay and will go on to spend the rest of the year planning her fairy-tale wedding. What space does an ex-boyfriend have a right to take up in all of that? Dolly can't think of one reasonable way to explain to Michael having contact with Declan, nor does she have any desire to keep things from him. The choice to not respond and simply leave the message festering in her inbox is the clear winner.

And yet, that night when the lights are out and Dolly is lying in bed beside her husband-to-be, the pull of the past is strong. New York's Upper East Side serves as a surprisingly serene backdrop to the endless, busy noise inside of her head.

Dolly sits up, restless in a black tank top and gray sweatpants. She turns momentarily to watch him sleep, her forever. Bare-backed and facing the opposite wall. With one fingertip she gently traces his spine. She tries to conjure him as a husband

and father. Weirdly, she can see him in a tuxedo at the top of the aisle but has trouble going further than that in her mind. Michael is strong and sweet. He's never given her a reason to doubt him and he's stuck by her side when things were bad. They've spoken about kids, even joked about baby names, more than once. But watching him in sleep, ribs expanding with the deep breaths of slumber, she can't see past the aisle.

Dolly looks out the window and down at First Avenue. She notices how odd it is, the serenity that can exist in a city that never sleeps. Down below the confusing emotional reverie taking place in her bedroom, life looks simple. Chaos is the routine. This is New York City.

Cabs beep their horns and midweek bar-crawlers swap jokes and smokes. Despite the closed windows, Dolly can hear the owner of the bodega on the corner telling someone to pick up after their dog. It's well past midnight and she thinks about what's probably happening in Sugar's Bend right now (a whole lot of not much at all…). If you ever saw someone out walking their dog at this hour, you'd assume they were either losing their mind or in the throes of an argument with their spouse. But in New York, the cycles of day are staggered for everyone. It's just as natural to get home at 7:30 PM as it is to start your routine at that hour. You're never alone in New York, and that is probably what has kept her here for so long.

Tomorrow will be a big day of meetings and proving herself. While many in this town work on a set if unusual schedule, hers is unpredictable and trying. She's got to be downtown at 8 AM for breakfast at Egg Shop with Celestine True, a journalist that she's planning to toss three beauty pitches at in the space of an hour. After that it's meeting after event-prep after meeting, and finally she'll be home long after dark, since she's got press drinks and a dinner to follow. So many clients, so many deliverables and goals, so little support staff.

The thought of the day ahead—her life in general—is dizzy-ing and Dolly can't quiet her mind to find the sleep she so desperately needs. Reluctantly, she settles down, lays her head against the pillow. In college when insomnia would hit, she used to recite one of her favorite poems in her head. Its mean-ing darker than most understand, but its cadence a comfort to her when she was feeling dark herself. *The woods are lovely, dark, and deep // but I have promises to keep...*

With all of this beauty around her, Dolly isn't sure why she feels a bit empty. How many women are lucky enough to build a career from scratch on brains, grit, and good manners? She didn't come to this town with a single connection, not even a friend. She secured an internship out of college that paid noth-ing and waited tables to make rent. She met Michael by chance and he turned out to be the best thing that could have hap-pened to her, in every sense. She made this life, all of it. And it's just as it should be.

Now, she is mentally preparing to leave this charming Upper East Side sublet for which she underpays. The apartment has served as a gorgeous if modest home base to the comings and goings of her New York life these past seven years, a step up from that crappy studio downtown where she lived the first six months out of school.

This place has been the perfect backdrop for nights spent high as a kite with friends and low as a heartbreak on the couch alone. It has held her in the way that only your first real, big-girl home-away-from-home can do. It has welcomed her back at night and when she didn't make it in until morning. Has for-given spilled champagne and strewn lingerie, too many guests to count, and (regretfully) the occasional late rent payment.

Soon, she and Michael will move in together officially and she'll have an oversized loft in Brooklyn to decorate. She'll miss this sweet piece of heaven she's called her own, but life is catapulting her in the very direction she always hoped it would. It's happening so fast and so flawlessly that she feels thrilled, but also like she can't breathe.

This world that Dolly has constructed for herself, against the landscape of Manhattan and all that it has given her, is so beautiful it hurts to look sometimes... But here she is now at—what? 1 AM? 2? Tracing the letter "D" on the edge of the bedcovers with her finger, in spite of herself and in spite of every bit of good sense left in her.

And miles to go before I sleep // And miles to go before I sleep.

THEN

The late summer weather wended its way from warmer nights to the cooling reality of fall's onset those first couple months being back at school. Dolly and Declan stayed together, but their academic loads and scattered sports practice schedules didn't leave much time for socializing. On weekends they carved out time for each other between games where he played and she cheered. Both of them spent a bit too much of those games without their heads in it, which made them each wonder about themselves, and each other: why all this dedication to things that kept them apart for little plausible reason?

In the beginning of December, Dolly had to miss the last game for a stomach bug and spent the morning on the couch worrying that Declan was going to go off with his buddies afterward and forget to call her. As she sprawled out with ginger ale watching MTV reality trash with Mama vacuuming and disinfecting maniacally in the background, and Daddy hiding from her germs at the indoor driving range with some of his colleagues-turned-friends, Dolly heard a surprising knock on the door and her stomach about flipped over itself.

Declan opened the door gingerly. She could see him from the couch—fresh and dirty from the field, six-foot-one with worried eyes and bare feet in her foyer. "I left my shoes on the porch," he called out in the direction of Mrs. Weston before tiptoeing over to the couch in his socks to lean in and plant a kiss on her forehead. "Missed seeing you out there," he said and she returned his thoughts with a tired smile. "I missed you, too."

"Now, Declan Crue, you know I just adore you, boy. But you better march on home and get you some fresh clothes on before you pile up on my couch," Mama called in from the kitchen. Declan laughed and let her know he was going down to Beam's for burgers with the team but had just stopped by to say a quick hello. "I'll call you later, baby," he said softly before turning and heading out the front door just as quickly as he had shown up.

"That boy..." Mama started, but Dolly was too fatigued and felt too sick to engage. She did notice the hint of a smile forming around the edges of Mama's mouth as she turned back to the kitchen with the Lysol and started to attack the cabinet handles.

"He sure does love you, though, Dolly Mae. Of that I'm sure."

* * * * *

Dolly was sure of it, too, and so the weeks leading up to Christmas brought anticipation and security. She and Declan stole kisses in the hallways and before practice. Football was over and he was in off-season training now; cheerleading never ended and there was always more to work on, more to perfect. On the weekends Dolly and Declan spent every moment they could together, soaking up every last drop of reasonable weather out by the creek as Texas's version of winter didn't seem too eager to crash their parties quite yet.

Steph was often with them, single now and happier than she'd seemed in months. She had cheerleading to focus on and had recently secured a part-time job at Fashion Spot, the only decent clothing store in town. Steph said her motivation for the job was just extra cash, but a part of Dolly couldn't help but wonder if any step her best friend could take closer to the world of "fashion" would make her feel she was quietly one-upping her at her own game.

For Dolly's part, an after-school job wasn't her focus. She was in all honors classes, on the cheer squad, and an editor at the school paper. Her parents gave her spending money when she needed it but were more concerned about her getting into a good college and following her bigger dreams than they were about whatever small sense of responsibility and meager paycheck a part-time job could give a sixteen-year-old girl living in Small Town, USA.

This was a sticking point for Steph and it came up too often, as it did that one Saturday night when the months of quiet tension between the two of them blew up into the kind of fight that no one could be sure they would ever come back from.

Dolly was waiting for Declan at the edge of her brick front walk, wearing her tightest-fitting jeans and a long-sleeve white peasant top with floaty sleeves. The look was ethereal and relaxed, so she had her hair down and was wearing large silver hoop earrings to bring it all together. Paradoxically, it had taken a lot of effort for her to achieve "effortlessly chic," but tonight she felt just that. It was mild outside for December, with temperatures holding steady in the low-70's at 8 PM. She and Steph had made plans to meet out front of her house; Declan was going to pick them up and drive them to a party at the Hamilton's place just outside of town.

Marjorie and Jane Hamilton were curious transplants from up North. Dolly didn't actually know the girls much at all but had learned bits and pieces about them from mutual friends. She was kind of in awe of what she'd heard about the mysterious twins who were, actually, New Yorkers. Dolly had always had a secret obsession with that city she'd never seen; she was curious what these girls who were from there would be like, what their house would be like.

The Hamilton bloodline hailed from New York City where some family heads had made tons of money back in the 1800's. Marjorie and Jane, the twins, were descendants of a cousin of the famous family. Though their father's own wealth had developed under murky circumstances, the family was revered locally for being two things: generous and friendly. They were nothing like the Yankees you'd hear gossiped about for their pomp and arrogance. This comforted Dolly and confirmed her suspicion that living in New York one day wouldn't ruin her character.

Every time the Hamilton girls threw a house party, word was that the alcohol would be in generous supply. Dolly had never actually been to one of said parties, but had heard about them and was eager to see what the fuss was over.

It probably should have dawned on this small group of friends that driving the 15-plus miles home from the Hamilton estate later, under the influence of alcohol, would be a mistake. But they were sixteen and careless, desperate for a good time and that inimitable feeling of fitting in.

So, drive they did.

Always the gentleman, Declan drove down to Dolly's end of the street to pick the girls up that night, even though it would've been easy enough for them to make the short walk to his driveway. The windows of the truck were open and the girls could hear the bass from his stereo all the way down the block. Dolly was pumped. This would be the first time she'd be going to a stranger's party with an actual boyfriend. All summer the group had hung out as a unit and with other kids they'd all known for ages. The thought of entering the expensive home of a slightly intimidating set of twins from New York on Declan's arm was exciting.

"Hop in, ladies," Declan said as he slowed to a stop outside of Dolly's house. He reached across the passenger seat to open the door from the inside and watched as his girlfriend and her best friend climbed in. "Alright, then. Let's go have some fun, y'all."

It could have been awkward arriving at the Hamilton's as a group of three now that Steph and Jimmy were firmly a thing of the past, but Declan's light nature made even potentially weird situations feel more natural. He had learned in their time together that she needed a little more support and care in social settings, and they had an unspoken agreement that they'd walk into unfamiliar places hand-in-hand. But he was too much a gentleman to make any of this feel weird for Steph. They made a good trio.

Dolly was exhausted from an unusually stressful week of school work and deadline catch-up with the paper which she'd contributed to all throughout high school, but was now editing most of. But she was committed to having a good time tonight, not least of all because her outfit was cute. Declan's hand on her thigh was a steady reminder that they were together and everything was going to be okay. This would be fun.

The threesome pulled up to the Hamilton's twenty minutes later and it was clear that the party was well underway. Since the home was situated outside of Sugar's Bend, the SBPD had no jurisdiction and wasn't likely to know about the house party or find an excuse to break it up. But Dolly wondered as soon as she got out of the car if coming here had been a mistake.

For a clean-cut girl like her, who rarely went against her parents' wishes (well, unless you count couch-sex that was only supposed to be pizza and a movie... or truck sex that was supposed to be, uh, not that), even approaching the party made her stomach flip. The music was louder than it could have ever gotten away with in the heart of Sugar's Bend and most of the kids standing outside were visibly drunk or high. Dolly could smell the sweet smoke of someone's weed coming from somewhere she couldn't see, could hear the awkward, too-loud flirtatious shouts of girls who'd be better off at home in their pajamas.

Steph recognized a couple of freshman girls who showed promise on the JV cheer squad and veered off immediately to say hi. Declan reached over and grabbed Dolly's hand in the dark, guiding her up the dimly lit cobblestones toward the front of the oversized house.

While the homes in each neighborhood of Sugar's Bend were all pretty similar in size and scope, this manse was markedly different from anything the teens were used to seeing. Not built in the 70's or 80's with the same predictable floor plans the rest of them had grown up in, the Hamilton's house was a new-build on easily ten acres, with a sprawling front porch and dramatic, angular construction. The house was three stories high and looked unable to decide which style it belonged to: Was it a modern palatial dream home, or a Southern plantation style sitting on no actual plantation? The generous front porch with its multiple seating areas and large wicker swing seemed to be in place to remind visitors in an overstated way that this was Texas. But the rest of the construction, including a two-story tall door, said "trendy transplant."

As Dolly climbed its steps, she noticed some familiar faces from school. The Hamiltons went to a private school closer to Tyler, so their parties notoriously included a very mixed group. A lot of the girls on the cheer squad revered these get-togethers as the perfect opportunity to meet guys from other towns, but to Dolly it was the allure of something new and different that brought her here tonight. Well, that and Declan.

She had met one of the twins in passing and knew plenty about them by word of mouth; their wealthy and devoutly religious parents were active at the Catholic church where Steph's family belonged. But Dolly wouldn't be able to tell them apart, which to her meant she really didn't know them at all. Did she actually belong here tonight, even on Declan's arm?

As soon as they walked through the door, Dolly could tell why everyone liked to hang out here. The home felt stylish but welcoming at the same time. It was large, certainly: the Hamilton's foyer could have fit the majority of the Westons' "living area" right inside. Its floor and walls were marble, and columns sprung up where it was obvious they weren't needed for any structural purpose. A large, lush, fur rug covered the center of the entryway and two mirrored tables sat on either end. There were dozens of cascading white flowers in crystal vases on every surface in sight, and cheerful photographs of the family in white frames dancing up and down the walls on both sides. Dolly couldn't place her finger on what style this was, but contemporary upscale homey chic was the group of words that came to mind.

"Declan Crue!" a twin said, appearing around the corner in a crop top and straight black skirt. "Thanks for coming!"

Dolly and Declan had never discussed their personal contact with the twins, so she'd assumed he didn't know them any better than she did. It was hard to hide her surprise at how familiar they seemed with each other. "Hey, Marj, thanks for having us," he said, hugging her in that loose way guys did when they weren't sure what was appropriate and necessary. "This is my girlfriend, Dolly," he gestured toward her without looking away from Marjorie, which was sort of okay, but also not at the same time.

"Of course! Hi, Dolly. It's nice to see you again," she said with a thin smile.

"Hi," Dolly returned coolly. A brief and heavy silence followed, and then like an automaton Marjorie led them into the sprawling kitchen several feet to the right. Inside, a keg sat in one corner and there were bowls of chips, bottles of wine, and red plastic cups littering the otherwise pristine countertop.

"Help yourselves to a drink... and let me know if there's anything else I can get for you," she said warmly, to Declan. Marjorie disappeared into the large crowd and Declan wasted no time getting beverages for Dolly and himself. *That was weird,* she thought, not wanting to verbalize her annoyance and start an unnecessary argument.

Steph was now long gone into the throbbing scene of the living room at the left, or maybe she was out back? At this point, with this many kids and most of them strangers, it was hard to tell exactly what was going on where. Dolly wondered what kind of confidence you had to have to throw a party like this. Confidence in yourself that you'd timed it right, confidence in your parents to stay out all night, and confidence in the Law to not come knocking at your door and ruin it with shame, arrests, or worse. Knowing secondhand that the twins had religious parents who wouldn't allow a party, Dolly had to assume they were gone for the weekend.

Because the twins' parents clearly weren't here at all. Dolly had been at house parties before where the parents hung out upstairs or in the basement and turned a blind eye, but nothing on this scale. None of this was really her problem, but the little anxiety ticker in her head was always going. She worried about the white rugs and the crystal vases; the possibility that everything in this fancy house felt so... susceptible.

Her only responsibility tonight was to enjoy her time here with Declan, make sure he stuck to two beers tops and got them out of there safely. The awkward encounter with—which twin had it been?—wasn't a memory yet, and Dolly wanted desperately to just relax and enjoy the party. She was in high school. Isn't this what high schoolers do? They go out, they drink. They flirt loudly over the music and squeeze each other's waists. Take hits of a joint as it's passed around.

The thought of smoking weed had never appealed much to Dolly, but the air was thick with the scent she knew was that, and if Declan took a hit, she had decided, she would, too. She really needed to lighten up. What were the chances that a single other teenager at this party was looking around and worrying about the *furnishings*?

As she settled into the scene, music pulsing in her tired ears, his arm quietly slung across her waist, Dolly took a sip of the drink Declan had grabbed for her. It was a wine cooler, and way too sweet, its alcohol feeling aggressively pungent in a way that surprised her. But she swallowed back a few more sips so as not to make him worry that anything was off with her tonight.

With pretty cool parents of her own, Dolly had had a glass of wine or beer here and there at family events or important dinners and had definitely gone too far at a river trip or two this past summer. But the saccharine nature of this drink coupled with her general unease didn't pair well. She also was starting to wonder if she'd actually fully recovered from that stomach bug a few weeks back, as the smell was making her a bit queasy. Excusing herself, Dolly found the nearest bathroom and dumped the contents of the cooler into the toilet. Replacing the nasty liquid with cool water from the tap, she figured she'd found herself a loophole that would get them home safe even if Declan couldn't.

And then, the night took a turn.

Leaving the bathroom, Dolly took two rights to where she'd last seen Declan in the kitchen. The smell of the weed was pervasive now, but it didn't exactly bother her. It was just strong. There were about twenty kids standing around the kitchen in their best *looking-like-I-don't-care outfits,* that totally revealed how much they all did.

For the girls, the uniform was a standard-issue denim cutoff skirt and doubled-up, pop-collared polos or skinny jeans and a sequined top. The guys all looked comically like copy and paste versions of each other. Pastel, gingham, checked, or other preppy button-downs not tucked into their navy or khaki shorts or vaguely distressed denim. Taking in the scene and glancing down at her own more bohemian outfit she'd felt good about a mere hour earlier, Dolly considered this life she was living for a moment and how meaningless it all seemed.

From where she stood, she couldn't see Dec, but she knew he wouldn't have gone too far without her. Probably mingling over the sounds of hip hop pulsating through the sound system that seemed to be connected throughout the entire house (*pretty excessive, no?*), she figured her popular, football-playing boyfriend could do without her for just a few minutes.

No longer kitchen-bound, Dolly went back the way she had come and headed in the opposite direction toward the side of the house that seemed completely unpopulated by kids. Everyone was pretty much focused in the kitchen, foyer, and living room off that side of the house, and she could hear the shouts, laughter, and general teenagerness coming from outside in both the back and front, as well.

But here was Mrs. Hamilton's obvious sanctuary, a sitting room so white, so carefully put together that Dolly felt guilty standing in it. Holding her water-filled wine cooler bottle, Dolly timidly walked toward the center of the room, pausing a moment and leaning down to take in the contents of the oversized wooden table behind the white leather couch.

On it, someone had arranged mementos from a life that looked markedly different from her own. While Dolly had grown up with beautiful things and a mother whose upbringing was pure society, in Sugar's Bend things were quiet and humble. (Some might even say hokey). The photographs on the Hamilton's living room table depicted New York City at Christmastime and a luxurious beach decorated with uniformly striped umbrellas on the Fourth of July. There were tall buildings twinkling with countless lights; smiling, Burberry-clad family members. Celebrities with their arms slung around the shoulders of the red-headed twins, appearing as if they were normal people when everyone who saw the photographs would instantly know that they weren't.

In what must have been a photograph from Mr. and Mrs. Hamilton's wedding, a striking red-headed bride donned an absolutely resplendent gown that cascaded down the front steps of what Dolly knew from her obsessive research on New York was the Plaza Hotel. The handsome groom was looking away from her, toward a happy springtime crowd throwing tiny white specks of something (*flower petals?*) in their direction.

The bride was dripping in what were obviously diamonds and beyond the close-standing onlookers who were clearly family and friends, the photograph revealed blurry dots as far as the eye could see. Random passersby, sneaker-clad and mesmerized no doubt. Snapping photographs themselves to capture the happy couple they likely didn't even know. It was all so impossibly chic, like a scene from a movie. *Most of the good ones take place in New York, don't they?...*

What this family was doing in the outskirts of Sugar's Bend, carting their upscale Manhattanite teenage twins to a Catholic school a few towns over, and setting up camp on what was essentially farmland, was beyond Dolly. The girls were cool enough. Throwing parties and volunteering in the community. But, why? And better yet, how? How would this place ever be enough for them, she wondered, and in so doing sparked the inevitable question in herself:

How would this place ever be enough for her?

Lost in thought and realizing suddenly that she had stood still in a seemingly off-limits room for too long, Dolly meandered back toward the kitchen wearing a look that said she was simply lost on her way back from the bathroom. But by now, Dec was no longer a brush of dusty blond in a sea of chatting teenagers. He was gone.

It seemed unlikely that he'd go back out to where they'd entered without telling her, and the screen doors out to the back deck had been left open. It was obvious a sea of kids had moved the party out back, so that's where Dolly went next. Across the din of the party, throughout which most of the lights were off or low, she could make out forms of people tucked into corners kissing or passing around joints. Or something else?

Dolly had never tried hard drugs and had no interest, but Steph had described her one encounter with cocaine and Dolly figured it was the type of thrill she just didn't need or want. The music was so loud it could give you a headache if you stayed in one spot for too long, but Dolly was determined not to. Instead, she felt eagerly, almost desperately, compelled to find Declan and get the hell out of here.

Something in her gut was telling her she just shouldn't be here tonight and neither should he. Out on the ample back deck, Dolly felt a renewed sense of panic as she looked around. Declan was nowhere to be found, and there were strange faces everywhere. Maybe she'd underestimated just how unfamiliar this crowd would be? Her expectations had been to mingle with a few friends from the football and cheer teams, hang on Declan's arm all night, and have some laughs. But none of their other close friends had shown. And Steph and Dec were now nowhere obvious, which made her feel isolated and insecure as she walked back and forth the length of the large deck twice.

Realizing her panic was probably showing on her face, Dolly decided to stop for a moment and get her wits about her. She stood, leaning against the railing with sweat beads prickling at her temples and hairline. Something just didn't feel right, but then again she was the only person at the party drinking water out of a wine cooler bottle. Everyone looked relaxed because they *were* relaxed, when she was in her head concocting some drama that didn't need to exist.

She smiled at a few girls huddled nearby, wearing the predictable, bright-colored polo shirt and denim mini skirt combo. One returned it with a warm-eyed glance and the others didn't seem to notice her at all. Cigarette smoke wafted up from the ground below, where a group of kids had set up a makeshift table for drinking games and were lined up, sloppily flipping red plastic cups over and cheering when they landed on their heads.

"What the fuck are we going to tell Dolly, then?" She overheard the exasperated words before she could see their source, but you know your best friend's voice when you hear it. Dolly felt her hands go ice-cold as her cheeks burned hot, a weird mix of sensations stemmed in anxiety and nameless rage.

"Stephanie?" she managed. "Steph, where are you?" Dolly demanded in the general direction of the voice she'd heard. Luckily everyone standing nearby seemed too drunk or too focused on their own conversations to notice, but Dolly could feel a spectacle coming on even though she had no idea over what. Finally, she spotted them. Stephanie's eyes looked panicked, and his manic, shifting back and forth between the two girls as Dolly approached, with a desperation she hadn't seen in him before.

Everything happened really fast from there: she saw Declan and Stephanie off to the side of the bottom of the deck stairs, apart from it all. Later, she would chastise herself for not asking and listening, not trying to get to the bottom of the situation. But she was a teenager and they were supposed to be the closest people in the world to her. All she felt was betrayed.

Dolly chucked her not-wine cooler over the railing, taking the wooden steps two at a time, running head-on into her best friend with fists up at the bottom.

"Dolly! What the hell?" Stephanie's face twisted in hurt and confusion at once.

"You tell me!" She managed, reaching angrily for her best friend as Declan pulled her off. *Had they hooked up? How could Steph do something like that to her?* She wanted to ruin that porcelain skin, wanted to hurt her the way she was hurting.

The ordeal was over in under a minute, and it would take half an hour to get the truth out of Declan. But the emotional mess that remained between the teens would last months. In retrospect, it was all ridiculous. But young love is complicated and painful, as was this night.

Apparently, in the twenty minutes or so that Dolly had gone to the bathroom and wandered off on a self-guided tour of the Hamilton's sitting room, Declan had made the ill-advised decision to try cocaine for the first time. Three bumps off a key that a twin pulled out of her jeans pocket. Enough that when

Stephanie found him on the side of the house doing said, alone with who she knew was Jane, she panicked.

Not only did Jane Hamilton have a crush on Declan which Steph had tried to protect her best friend from, but he was supposed to deliver them home safe to their parents in two hours or less. What right did he have doing coke on top of drinking? What kind of person risks other people's lives like that? These were thoughts building up to Stephanie's question, not the remnants of an accidental kiss or other illicit encounter as Dolly worried when she heard those panicked words uttered.

But Dolly had attacked her best friend with a drunk, laughing, and confused audience. Had embarrassed them all and created the type of scene no one ever wants to be a part of. Declan pulled the girls off each other with the help of a nearby football buddy, held Dolly tight to his chest and begging, convinced her to take a walk with him away from the scene. They stood now by a cluster of trees that provided enough privacy for a brief conversation. Dolly's cheeks burned and she felt hatred pulsing through her, a new feeling for a girl who always took the high road.

"What the fuck, Declan?" she implored.

"Dolly, I'm a mess. I'm sorry," he fumbled. Sweat beads scattered across Declan's forehead, his eyes wild. "You don't know how much pressure I'm under... I wish I had parents like yours," he managed.

"Football and homework stress don't justify doing coke at a party, Declan," her voice was raw and icy. Dolly was mortified, furious, and mostly exhausted, but she also was melting for him again, at seeing him vulnerable. "Let's just get out of here," she said, barely above a whisper. She pressed her forehead lightly into the bones at the base of his neck, brushed her lips across the dipped-in space below. "I want to go home."

The pair left hand-in-hand, pretending not to hear Stephanie's words hurled at them on their way out. *"Spoiled little bitch,"* she spit in Dolly's direction while she sat in a corner with Marjorie and Jane, holding a bag of ice against a pulsating bump under her left eye.

Dolly and Declan decided that a learner's permit and a very limited amount of substance was the better choice in a driver than an actual license plus two beers and three bumps, so she drove home. She took the roads slowly with her hands gripping the wheel tight enough for white knuckles, not a single word passing between them throughout the entire twenty-five minute drive.

She loved him, deeply and wholly and enough to let this night go (eventually). Honestly, a little experimenting with drugs wasn't the big issue to her, so much as sneaking around a corner with a rich redhead she barely knew. Conspiring to lie. It was all confusing and her head was pounding and all she wanted to do was get home. Declan's truck puttered eventually into his driveway and Dolly turned the key and handed it to him. Despite their mutual silence the whole ride home, he turned to her now and asked if he could see her in the morning.

"Go to bed, Dec," she breathed. Lifted his hand and kissed it, exited the driver's side and made the short walk to her own front door.

In the round foyer mirror, Dolly's reflection looked more wild and ragged than she'd expected. There was blood on her chin from where Steph had scratched her lower lip, fighting back. She hadn't even noticed much of a pain there really, but now that she saw it the rush of memories seemed to revamp the sting. Her mascara streaked down her cheeks from tears of anger. If a stranger saw her right now they would shudder, but her mother coming around the corner did just the opposite.

There are women who are born to be mothers, and whether they know this from an early age or not, it all clicks into place when they first hold their children. For Sally Day Weston who had always hoped for one precious child to lay all her love on, this had been the case from the start. Dolly was her real-life baby doll, hence the name she'd selected despite the rolling eyes of family and friends. "It's such a country-girl name, Sally," her own mother had protested, wanting her to select something more refined, more classic. Mary. Elizabeth. Rose?

But Dolly she was always meant to be, with just the hint of the dahlia flower imparting the strength, dignity, and elegance she hoped her daughter would grow into. Sally was okay with her daughter standing out, having a name unique among the Michelles and Jennifers. She would not be born to fit in with the other girls, of that this woman was sure. And so watching her become a reader, a thinker, a collagist with a passion for the beautiful things in life and a growing obsession with a city she had never seen, a place on which she cast her gorgeous fantasies, was exciting to this woman whose main life purpose was to love and encourage her daughter. She knew her teenager would soon be a woman, though she couldn't anticipate the twists, losses, and pains that were barrelling her way, even on this seemingly standard weekend evening, suddenly ruined by drama.

She had wrapped a light wool robe around her narrow shoulders, covering her silk pajamas in case Declan was with her daughter and needed to be sent home. It wasn't that late, and she wasn't terribly worried, but something compelled her to greet Dolly when she heard her key in the lock. A nameless need to fix a snack or pour a glass of water or ask her nearly grown child how the night had gone. These feelings intermingled with a certain sadness, too. As she pictured her daughter at three, at five, at eleven. All the other times she'd wanted to hold her close but knew she had to let go long enough for a half-hour dance class, a full-day kindergarten program, the first night of sleepaway camp.

Such is the push-pull of motherhood. The swelling pride in watching them grow and flourish rests hand-in-hand with the exquisite pain of wanting to hold on just a little longer, or maybe forever. Tonight she had no proper motive for meeting her daughter at the door. But once she did, and took in the disheveled hair and bleeding lip, Sally felt all those old feelings of fear and then some.

"Dolly!" She rushed to her not-so-little girl and placed her hands softly on her shoulders, reaching a hand up to lightly inspect the source of the bleeding. "What happened?"

Dolly's mother smelled of almonds and baby powder. Her honey-colored hair was swept back in a loose bun. Her eyes looked older suddenly, and tired. It had probably been months since she'd seen her without makeup on, or even this close up. Life had been moving both women in opposite directions. Sally catapulted toward strengthening friendships and getting more involved in volunteer work. The impending if eventual departure of her daughter for college and then adult life weighed heavy. She wanted to have a life when Dolly left, and was hard at work setting up the various avenues that it would include.

And Dolly, lost in a teenage romance and preoccupied with cheerleading and schoolwork, knew she hadn't been the most attentive daughter lately. She looked up at her mama now, wondering when was the last time she'd asked her anything meaningful about herself. She knew she had to answer the question, had to tell her about the fight. (She would leave out the detail about the cocaine, edit it with a drink too many as the secret she mistook for something worse between Declan and Stephanie).

So began the verbal unraveling of the evening, over tea on kitchen stools.

"I just can't believe you attacked Stephanie," Sally admitted, struggling to suppress a chuckle. She treated the small cut below Dolly's lip.

"I can't either," Dolly admitted, sheepish. "I just didn't know what else to think."

"Declan wouldn't do that to you," her mother said, the words serving as the final say. "That boy loves you, though he's young."

"How am I going to fix this, Mama?" Her voice was pleading.

"Oh, honey. I think a little bit of time will fix this."

Sally had once been young and in love, so she took Dolly seriously despite the seemingly needless high drama. While her mind moved around, taking in the landscape of her young daughter's life from a bird's eye view, she knew that logically there were so many higher highs and lower lows to come. So many bigger dreams to pursue than ending up with Declan Crue. So many larger goals to solidify her status as a woman in the world. Sally could see both the plastic princess crowns of Dolly's youth and a corner office in her future; envision her as a blushing bride in a gorgeous sheath with a veil cascading to the floor. And one day, God-willing, experiencing motherhood for herself. But tonight it was a house party and a fight with her dearest friend.

A part of Sally wanted to tell her daughter to pick her head up, not worry so much about these trivial dramas of high school. But she knew that it was her job to take her daughter's words as facts and to advise without pressure. While the world had bigger things in store for Dolly than girl-fights and broken hearts, she also remembered what it felt like to be talked out of her feelings by her own mother in the face of adolescent pain. And she wanted more for Dolly.

Neither Sally nor Dolly knew as they sat on those kitchen stools, sipping tea and swapping stories, changing the subject and letting the night wrap up in eventual laughter, that this fight with Stephanie and the stirrings of mistrust in Declan were just the beginning of a year that would be marked by immeasurable pain for Dolly and thus for her mother, too.

Tonight they had country hits playing quietly in the background and soft-baked cookies intended for Sally's book club that they mischievously broke into. Tonight they had secrets and memories and a quiet womanhood of two. And despite the rest of what had happened earlier, and the lingering, painful question-mark that was her current situation with Declan, Dolly clung tight to the hope that was in the air. That her mother's soothing words were correct and that in the long run, tonight wouldn't mean much at all.

She wasn't exactly right. But for now, it was all okay.

NOW

Late May in New York is hazy and warm with the promise of summer so close on the horizon, Dolly can feel it in her bones. The days are getting longer and she's taken to hopping off the subway a few stops early to walk some of her commute home. With the wedding just over a year away now, planning has been kicked up a notch. This weekend she'll go shopping for her dress; she's been pushing out of her mind for weeks how hard the milestone event will be.

After deliberating for months over whether to go it alone or bring friends to help with the gown selection, Dolly decided that the only thing sadder than being without your mother at the bridal atelier is being there without *anyone*, so she asked Glinda and Veronica, who will serve as bridesmaids, as well as John-John (her voice of fashion reason), and Sandra's assistant Taylor who is the most organized and clear-headed person she knows, to come along to her appointment at The Mews in Chelsea. Daddy has already called in his credit card information and everything is in place. John-John will definitely sneak in chilled prosecco, and the day will be good. It will. She knows it will because that's how it should be, how it has to be, and she's going to make it be that way despite the gaping, Mama-shaped hole at the center of it all.

It's now a Tuesday afternoon and Dolly takes the blocks north of 60th Street slowly and with a meandering sense of purpose. Since the days have started growing warmer and longer, she and Michael have both experienced more of a marked interest in preparing some of their own dinners in lieu of ordering in, so she ruminates on what they might cook tonight, what things they'll pull from the fridge to nosh as they move around the kitchen.

Recently, they've enjoyed lingering at the pop-up farmer's market on the weekends, picking out herbs that look promising and little purple carrots that might be used for a summery salad. Dolly is nothing much in the kitchen (a surprise after growing up in a home with two culinarily skilled parents... or maybe it's because they did too much for her), but experimenting with Michael has been fun and given their evenings a new sense of purpose.

So, too, has the acceleration of wedding planning. All of a sudden, appointments are on the calendar. Here a meeting with the executive chef at the Plaza, and there a cake tasting with Christina Tosi of MilkBar fame. It's exciting and nerve-wracking at once.

In their normal daily life, Dolly is able to forget that her fiancé is a Peabody and well connected in the New York social and philanthropic scenes. Despite his father's gobs of money and frequent insistence on taking them out to expensive dinners or sending them away for extravagant weekend trips, Michael himself doesn't like to show off. Nor does he really see his old crowd so much, at least not the splashiest among them. He doesn't keep up with the loud money or the people whose priorities are skewed. He might have grown up with boundless means, but he can't stand people who act like they did.

In the absence of both their mothers, Mr. Peabody (*"Call me Mike!"*) is trying his best to be the fill-in parent to get things done and celebrate their impending marriage. His way of doing that is to ensure the couple is connected with every single best-of-the-best person and experience they can get along their wedding planning journey.

Dolly breathed a word of her long-standing dream of getting married at the Plaza and the next thing she knew, there was a June date (unheard of!) secured. She mentioned a love of the famed birthday cake from MilkBar and (boom!) they were being scheduled for a custom wedding cake appointment with the founder and head baker herself. There would be no fretting over the cost of the wedding, as Mr. Peabody waves his hand in a gesture of "I got it" whenever the topic arises. And the honeymoon, three weeks in the North of Italy, is locked, loaded, and prepaid. There is something guilt-inducing about all of this fanfare and expense, but it's only now that the planning is launching full-scale that Dolly is able to put her finger on it.

A tiny part of this girl from Sugar's Bend, Texas who was raised to be humble and grateful is ashamed to admit she loves this feeling. The knowledge that her dream wedding will be exactly that, and that unlike some of the other couples she knows who are still paying theirs off years later, she and Michael can just do it and not look back for a minute.

There's a magical quality to knowing that your wedding is going to be a New York social event. That a photograph of you in your gown at the top of the aisle (or maybe afterward with lilacs strung up around you and the late afternoon sun turning your first married kiss into silhouette), will end up on *Page Six* and on the cover of the *Sunday Times* wedding section. That celebrities and tastemakers will be there; that life is starting to look a lot like the photographs of the famous families you always wanted to be a part of.

It's all vaguely reminiscent of those strange Hamilton sisters whose family photos Dolly stole a contemplative look at that long-ago night of the house party outside Sugar's Bend. She never did find out the details of that family or why they really moved to a tiny corner of East Texas. The best she could uncover after rekindling her friendship with Steph and having a chance to get to know the twins a bit in passing was that their parents just wanted a fresh start, a chance to relax. A teenaged Dolly couldn't understand the appeal there, and if she's honest, she still can't.

There is something unexpectedly cool about the drama and attention that is coming from planning a wedding to a prominent member of New York society. It doesn't seem to matter how many organic purple carrots she pays for with her own hard-earned cash or how much of her furniture is thrifted. Dolly can't deny that along with this little bud of pride that is starting to form in the center of her lifestyle, there is also something that feels like shame. Because all of this wealth, all of this attention, has nothing to do with her, nor even with Michael. It is nothing more than an offshoot of his father's fame and success. Meanwhile her own sweet dad, feeling like a big man for calling in his credit card information to the bridal atelier and offering her a "no-budget" budget, has no idea the scale of contribution from the other father.

Sure, Daddy is aware that the couple has decided to break tradition and not have the bride's family pay for the wedding. He was baffled and a bit hurt about it at first, but Dolly spoke his concerns down by explaining that the Peabodys were in business with the Plaza (not directly true) and that they were offering them a bit of a "family discount" (not at all true), so it just made sense. Daddy acquiesced and offered to swap roles, taking on the rehearsal dinner, a fair trade. But Dolly has to admit, if even just to herself, that she feels a bit icky about the whole thing.

Her parents, having one daughter and being low-key financially successful (by small-town Texas standards, anyway!) had always prepared to pay for Dolly's eventual wedding. They surely envisioned the nuptials taking place at First

Church in the town square, followed by a reception at one of the beautiful outdoor venues found locally. Simple, lovely, and sweet.

Dale's wife isn't here to help in the planning and preparation, and now Dolly has taken all of the above from her father, too. He'll never say a word about it, but just as his face fell for a second upon first viewing her diamond ring, she knows that deep down, Daddy feels a loss in all of this. Something has been taken from him and given to Michael Gideon Peabody, Sr., a man who hasn't bothered to so much as introduce himself to his son's future father-in-law.

These thoughts come out in panicked spurts late in the evenings while she lies awake in bed. And sometimes on her walks home, as now. But she pushes them down to focus on the good things as best she can. She has table linens and blowouts to think about; flowers and photographs to obsess over. That is much more fun.

Though she's been engaged for several months now, Dolly is finally feeling her identity is more than partially comprised of being a *fiancée*. The word has romantic overtones but is also intrinsically connected to responsibility and the work of setting up an event. And since neither one of them has a living mother, related celebrations and details like the bridal shower and rehearsal dinner will fall to Dolly as well to organize. It's enough to give a girl a headache, despite the splendor and extravagance of it all.

Michael has been nothing if not a model fiancé, doting and romantic when they're together, detail-oriented and patient with her many texts related to the wedding. Despite the cuddles and the dinner prep, though, there is a sense of purpose in their togetherness. Weirdly she always thought she'd be way more plugged in to the planning of her wedding, and because there is this void in her lately she's found herself over compensating a bit, forcefully throwing herself in and paying more attention to the details than she really cares to. This is giving her control. Luckily, Michael is adaptable and unconcerned.

This evening, she hasn't exactly gotten off the subway 20-plus blocks south of home in order to soak in the balmy air and the passionate noise of New York's Upper East Side. She has done it to delay her arrival at the apartment. Not ready to face another evening flipping through bridal magazines and dog-earing pages with Michael to bring in to her dress appointment, Dolly wishes she could get out of it. Have a night to herself. While Michael's interest in linen colors and cake fillings is limited at most, the one thing he cares about is the dress.

It's weird that a guy who dresses so notoriously plainly has such an impassioned concept about her bridal gown. Over a year out from the event, Dolly imagines, most guys wouldn't even be thinking about that detail. But Michael has made numerous comments about how he envisions his "princess" in a big, dramatic gown. It's not that Dolly can't imagine herself in said, especially with a venue so classic and glamorous as the Plaza... she is a Southern girl, after all.

In the back of her mind, though, is one of the very few conversations she ever had with her mother about her someday-wedding. She doesn't want to let Michael down, but also can't imagine not following through on something close to what they envisioned. It's moments like this when Dolly starts to feel alone despite being surrounded by loved ones and friends. No matter how many people come into your life, after your mother leaves it, there will always be something missing.

* * * * *

In the late hours, she paces back and forth past the foot of the bed to the irritating melody of Michael's snoring. She feels guilty, but something tells Dolly that this is not the moment to find her dress. So she texts the group and lets them know that the salon had her double-booked and she'll reach out with the new date ASAP. *In the meantime, let's grab brunch tomorrow instead!* Then she crafts an email to the salon director claiming a terrible case of the flu and a request for a new date later in the summer.

It scares her a little how easily the lies come to her, pouring off her fingertips and out into the ether. But she learned at an early age that in your most desperate moments, sometimes you just need to figure things out for yourself.

BEFORE DECLAN

Just about six months before Dolly would fall in love with Declan and everything in her life would change dramatically, there was a conversation between her and her mother that would stay with her forever. It was the fall of sophomore year and late in the season, between Thanksgiving and Christmas. The two decided on a whim to drive to Dallas to pick up some dresses for the holiday season, so they packed into the car and set off with warm coffee in their travel mugs. Driving to Dallas with Mama was always something Dolly would cherish; today's trip would linger in her mind for years to come.

The pair wasn't even pulling off the highway and making the familiar turns to Neiman's when Mama first mentioned it: they were both singing along to the radio as they always did, not particularly well but feeling free. The song had a happy ending: boy meets girl, asks for her hand, and they dance on and on forever. Dolly wouldn't remember what the song was, but she'd remember the conversation they had to follow.

"Have you ever thought about your wedding, Doll?" Sally asked with that classic, softly smiling face of hers. It occurred to her that as a little girl growing up in Dallas society, her wedding was the big event she'd always dreamed toward, and yet she and her own daughter had never really discussed a similar fantasy.

"I mean, I have, but not in great detail," Dolly shrugged and went quiet. This was the part of her future goals that she couldn't seem to decode within her own mind. There were two halves of her very hopeful heart and they couldn't seem to agree on much of anything.

On one hand, she could picture a wedding right here in Sugar's Bend. Have the ceremony at the Episcopal church in town where they didn't belong but went often enough. Wear a big white dress with a pair of cowboy boots underneath it. She couldn't imagine anyone specific among the cute guys at school, but there was plenty of time to meet a boy from another town or catch the eye of someone on the home team. It could work. She could be a wife and mother. After all, she'd learned from the best.

Dolly also felt the conflicting need deep down to try a life in the fashion industry, to dissolve her small-town Texan accent and trade it all in for a whole different life. To say goodbye to Sugar's Bend and learn a new way of dressing, a new way of being a part of things. Knowing she had followed a dream.

It was not that that life couldn't include a husband, couldn't include a wedding. It was more that she had no idea what to begin to expect or hope for in the romance department should her life actually take her where her goals wanted her to go. Would she travel abroad in college, take up with a small business owner in Milan and split the calendar year between Italy and the States? Would she fall in love with, and marry, a devastatingly handsome, if maybe too old for her, New York bachelor and move her parents to the big city to help her raise their kids?

The possibilities were endless and dizzying, the daring within her so deep to entertain a dream like this. The creeping idea of potential was based on nothing more than passion, really. Many of her friends—her best one especially—not only thought, but *knew*, that they'd end up in Sugar's Bend or a small town just like it. There were some who planned to go to school in Waco, Dallas, or Austin and hoped to end up on their outskirts. Those were big dreams, too. Big plans. But the most carefully guarded secret she had was that none of that seemed to fit her just right.

"Mama?" Lost in reverie, Dolly hadn't spoken for a few minutes. But Sally was a patient person who understood important silences.

"Yes, babe?" She could tell a confession of sorts was coming, but she wasn't scared. She saw a lot in this daughter of hers, and admittedly most of it was bigger than the potential she'd ever seen in herself as a teenager.

"I do think about my wedding sometimes, but I think a lot more about other stuff. Like, where I'll want to work... or maybe where I'll live after college."

She looked over at her mother timidly, the truth now about to fall out of her. It was too late to pretend that her big-city dreams took place in Dallas now.

"Well, what are you thinking?"

Everything came out fast and excited, not in the right order, but without a missing detail.

"Have you ever noticed I've been sneaking your magazines from the recycle bin for years?"

Sally's laugh was light and twinkly. "Yes, I suppose I have..." her mother's reply was the type intended to get you to keep talking.

"I keep my favorite outfits and articles cut out, in a box underneath my bed," she admitted sheepishly. "They're kind of like inspiration to me?" Sally didn't respond, so she spoke on. "I don't even know what kind of inspiration; I'm no writer... but I see myself in that world, Mama. With the lights and the energy and the clothes. I guess I just want something more. Something *else*." She corrected herself, not wanting to hurt Mama's feelings. She liked Sugar's Bend just fine, but it wasn't big enough for her dreams. "I need to be somewhere that I can turn all these thoughts and dreams into a career. Somewhere like... New York City."

It was hard to miss the raise of Sally's eyebrows at those words, but her mother kept her mouth firmly shut while Dolly went on. "Maybe I want to make y'all proud in my own way. I just don't know if that involves a big Texas wedding."

Her monologue reaching its rambling and breathless end, Dolly looked at her mother and searched her face for signs of disappointment. Sally was still looking at the road, her large navy hexagonal sunglasses making eye contact impossible. But slowly, the corners of her mouth turned up into the hint of a smile, then they turned back down quickly, a flicker of remorse. She opened her mouth, then closed it again, choosing her words more carefully than she had before.

"I'm sorry," she managed.

"What? You didn't do anything. It's nothing about you or Daddy or Texas... it's just something inside me that I can't put out."

"No," Sally laughed suddenly, lifting the mood in the car. "I'm not sorry to hear about your dream of moving to New York. I'm just sorry I didn't know sooner. And I'm sorry about how it came out. I shouldn't have asked you about your hopes for the future by starting with a wedding."

Dolly reached over and gave her mother's arm a quick squeeze. They were pulling into that familiar parking lot now, the sun high in the sky and a valet attendant waving at them, his bright white teeth almost blinding. Sally shifted into park and lifted one pointer finger up to signal, "Give us a minute," at the eager parking attendant.

Swiftly with the same hand, she removed her sunglasses and turned to look her daughter in the eye. "Dolly Mae Weston," she said, her big open eyes looking like home. "I do not want you to ever dumb down or apologize for the light within you. If you want to go to New York and work in fashion, then that's what you'll do. We'll miss you, but honey, we'll figure it out."

Dolly could feel relief washing over her like a cool shower at the end of a long day. Sally patted her hand idly then and said, "Okay, now let's get in there and do some shopping."

They got out of the car and headed inside for some special occasion dresses, Sally placing a folded-up twenty into the attendant's hand as he helped her out of the car. "I apologize, Sir. My daughter and I were just finishing up an important conversation." Her cheeks were flushed at having been rude, having kept him waiting. He shook his head, smiled at the unexpected gesture.

After about an hour of shopping for dresses, and a delicious lunch upstairs, the pair unexpectedly found themselves standing just feet from the bridal salon. Though Sally had felt guilty for bringing up the topic of weddings earlier, they shared a conspiratorial smile now. "Should we poke around, just for fun?" Dolly asked, to which her Southern mother nodded in agreement, eagerly and right away.

After explaining to the sales ladies that they were just looking for fun and had no wedding to plan (which they smiled tightly at and definitely found irritating), the two wended their way through the salon gasping, nodding, tsk-tsking, and otherwise sizing up all of the designer wedding gowns before them.

At one floor-sweeping, shining silk, fitted 1920's style sheath dress, they both stopped still. The beading at the neckline was subtle and elegant, the cut of the fabric designed to emphasize the wearer's waist and hips perfectly. The bottom of the gown had another hint of sparkle, but so tastefully and subtly done that you wouldn't even notice the embellishments were there until they glinted softly in the light with each step the bride took down the aisle.

In a sea of strapless ball gowns and frothy lace, this spectacular dress stood out. Mama reached her nude-manicured hand out to gently take it by the waist and pull it from the rack, watching the fabric swish against a neighboring dress and then fall in a cascade of silk and tiny specks of crystal to stillness.

"This is the most beautiful dress I have ever seen," Sally declared, in the definitive way that only she could, that way that really made you take her opinion as fact.

"Me, too," Dolly agreed, willing herself not to look at the price tag. She was years, maybe even decades, off from needing a wedding gown and by then, presumably, she would be able to figure out how to get the one that she wanted. Something about this moment felt so important though, and she couldn't quite place why. That *dress* felt important, and she wished she could just take it, own it, and hang it in her closet at home waiting for the special day—years from now—that her mother would help her put it on.

They weren't going to do any of that, of course, but it felt good to pretend for just a second. Dolly rested her head on her mother's shoulder and sighed, looking at the gown that was still being held on one side, gently, between the thumb and pointer finger of the person she loved most in the world. "Let's commit it to memory," Sally said with a sigh, leaning her head onto her daughter's, as they still fit like Tetris pieces for one of the last times. Soon, Dolly would shoot up a good four inches and this particular standing cuddle would be impossible. Neither of them knew that at the moment, but what's worse is that neither of them knew the day would never come that they'd get to shop for wedding dresses for more than "just fun."

"Okay, Mama. We won't ever forget it."

And they never did.

NOW

At home (*her* home, for just a bit more sweet time), Michael is already simmering a pot of vegetable stock on top of the white, twenty-year-old stove in Dolly's kitchen. He's wearing a pair of medium-wash jeans with the faintest distressing at the knees and a plum-colored t-shirt that is spotted with a few drops of errant liquid. This is a pretty cute outfit and she almost teases him about all the fashion magazines he must be reading in preparation of the wedding, but his immediate body language tells her not to.

Noticing her enter but not actually greeting her, Michael gestures with his free hand in the direction of an open wine bottle and says, "I was expecting you an hour ago, so I broke into the shiraz." Dolly tip-toes up to kiss his wine-tinged mouth, reaches around his back for a glass off the drying rack behind him, and pours herself an inch before heading into the living room to remove her shoes and decompress.

"I thought I told you I've been walking home," she offers in the general direction of the kitchen, as much an afterthought to her as it is a pinnacle reminder to her vaguely puppy-doggish fiancé. Bold, handsome, and annoyingly attached to his workout schedule, Michael is known among their friends as some sort of walking billboard for stereotypical masculinity. But recently he's become the type of doting, nearly pathetic boyfriend who truly gets offended if you're running behind schedule and (apparently) leaving him unexpectedly alone with the shiraz and the soup.

While this isn't exactly a fight, Dolly can feel the energy of the apartment requiring egg shells, so she goes ahead and tucks the bridal fashion magazines into her work bag, ignores the urgency of the soup that's likely ready to serve, and returns to the kitchen in nothing but her lace thong and the new Dolce & Gabbana bra John-John snagged for her at his last *ELLE* shoot.

"Don't take the pads out, sister. You're gonna want those," were his completely honest words as he tossed the four-hundred-and-fifty-dollar, cheetah-print lace undergarment in her direction two Saturday nights ago, between puffs of an incredibly strong joint. At the time, Dolly felt ridiculous accepting the extravagant, if unpaid-for gift, but like most luxurious items tend to do, it grew on her fast. While her initial reaction was that the bra was an insane way to spend that kind of money and nothing that would be worn in real life, a mere ten days later it has become a logical and lovely addition to her collection. Not to mention it felt damn good walking around all day today knowing she was wearing hundreds of dollars worth of animalistic lace under her black silk button-up tank, so anyone who tried to mess with her had pretty much been ignored.

And now the only person worth messing with in any real way is forgivingly reaching around to undo its single clasp, kissing the bottom of her neck while gently tugging her hair with his free hand. "Fuck the soup," he whispers to her genuine apologies about lateness and a home-cooked meal. "Or better yet, fuck me."

All is forgiven in a moment and animal instincts have taken over, so Dolly says a quick and silent *grazie* to the D&G... and to John-John.

THE OCTOBER BEFORE LAST

The headlights of the other car come at her so fast and so frighteningly, Sally gasps audibly and reflexively turns the steering wheel. There's nowhere for her SUV to go, though, and she was stopped at a red light anyway, so any acceleration will be negligible. There's no getting away, no avoiding the fatal accident she knows is about to occur.

It's a split-second's thought process, but a loaded one. Knowing your life is about to end is at once absolutely terrifying and inherently nostalgic. In flash succession the highlights and low points of Sally's fifty-two years on earth flash across her visual field: high school prom in floor-length, melon-colored chiffon; her elegant wedding just a few years later that comes in only black-and-white. Five-year-old Dolly holding up a dried-out dandelion and making a wish in the backyard, eyes closed and giggles audible.

Every person who has ever been loved by her is a part of the absolutely beautiful and incredibly too-fast montage that works hard to counteract the terror over what is about to happen, what is definitely happening. Clinging to the fear of the crushing blow that's about to come but drawn to the beauty of the life that she has lived, Sally thinks vaguely, "So this is what the end looks like..."

The next several seconds will see blood and crushed glass, dramatically crumpled metal and the dispatch of an airbag that turns out to be useless if not detrimental. Sally comes in and out of seeing and feeling what's happening as her life pitches toward its early end.

It happens so fast in reality, but for Sally, it is experienced in slow motion. The pain is sheerly life-altering and shocking; her ragged, hopeless screams are barely audible to her own ears, but if anyone else were in the car it would be all they heard over the slam of the impact. She feels as if she's swimming underwater, a sea of pain she wades through briefly before her mind takes over and she begins to lift away from the scene toward a light that calls her home.

In her mind's eye she catches her precious, sturdy Dale. The curves and edges of his handsome, stubbled face that has only just started to show some age. She wants to reach out and place a hand on his cheek, whisper a secret in his direction, hold on to another moment with their little family. A family of three. *Oh, sweet Dolly.*

Sally smiles now, the pain dissipating as her mind starts to slowly climb away from her ruined body. Thinking of her precious girl. And then bitterness takes over for a moment, now knowing she won't be there to do the rest of it with them. A rush of blood warm on her temple and the renewed sharpness of pain in her left side where the other car has T-boned her and her own car parts have struck her, crushed into her.

Awareness of sitting within her physical body has returned long enough for her to take in the scene. People, people everywhere on this downtown street at dusk, screaming and making phone calls, clamoring to try and help. It is the tail end of rush hour on a Friday evening and this is certainly not how anyone driving through this corner of town planned to spend it, what they thought they'd see this evening before returning home to a slow-cooked dinner, or spritzing on fresh perfume and heading out for sushi or cocktails.

Sally manages to turn her head slightly for what will be the last time, looks in the direction of the impact and fixates, fleetingly, on the stunned teenager sitting in the offending driver's seat. Despite the darkening sky, she can make out red hair and a familiar upturned nose. Some of the widest green eyes she's ever seen, staring back at her. Awestruck, immobilized with fear, dread, and regret. He has not gotten out of the car, and she has not seen him in probably ten years. But the adorable, knobby-kneed kid-brother of one of the pack to whom she served a sandwich and lemonade on more than one occasion when he was trailing the big kids, is there looking back at her now. It's unmistakable.

Sally opens her mouth to speak and it closes again right away, nothing more coming out at this point. Right before she lifts out of her physical body once more, not to return in time to have a chance to kiss her husband goodbye or tell her daughter the same, she receives the only real farewell she will get. As her daughter's best friend Stephanie's younger brother, Avery Longman, his eyes filled with tears of knowing he has officially killed her, mouths: "I'm sorry."

THEN

The immediate aftermath of the fight between Dolly and Steph was tough. Dolly knew that it had been almost entirely her own fault, so she would be ready to apologize to Steph first thing Monday morning, in person, and hoped to start smoothing things over.

But that Sunday morning, she had Declan at the front of her mind. She was embarrassed and annoyed, too, over his stupid choices and also the fact that he hadn't called. After what seemed like the slowest and shittiest morning of her existence, Sally knocked gently on Dolly's bedroom door with the offer of coffee and breakfast: "You can't stay in there all day, honey," she reasoned, though they both knew she could—and had before. "How about a drive out by the creek... we could take a little hike?"

Exercise and fresh air was what Dolly needed to take the edge off her depressive state of mind, but she didn't want to try. "I think I'd rather be alone, Mama," she said honestly. And her mother nodded, understanding.

"I'll bring you lunch in a few hours then. But if you need anything in the meantime, just let me know."

It was nice that Mama was able to push aside the obvious misgivings of the night before and the natural consequences that should come with them: underage drinking, driving without a license, and lying about where you were going, to name a few. Dolly appreciated this at the same time that she allowed herself to wish for a slightly more normal family dynamic where everything didn't have to be discussed to death and you were able to keep your secrets.

Like in Declan's home, where there would have been absolutely no talk of what transpired the night before. As she paced and fretted, sniffled and overthought, he was likely sleeping in and pretending to have had a perfectly uneventful Saturday night of teenagehood. His parents were no fools, but they also would never suspect him of trying cocaine at a party.

The Crue parents' biggest fret this morning would be their exhausted football player of a son sleeping in rather than attending church. Meanwhile, down the cul-de-sac his girlfriend and her parents had all been touched with the very beginnings of the true pain, regret, and heartache that teenage romance and friendship can create.

Finally, the kitchen phone rang and it was him and she agreed to meet for a milkshake in town. Dolly pulled on her favorite jeans and a simple white v-neck long-sleeved tee, the type of outfit that served as a blank canvas for difficult conversations. She had no idea if their milkshakes would be two separate or one shared. She couldn't predict if the meetup would end in hands being held or hearts being broken. She couldn't even decipher which of these options she actually wanted, if she was honest.

Things were unclear and it was obviously more than the fact that he had tried a hard drug at a party and not planned to confess. It was the question that swirled above her head, not quite ready to come down to earth and touch her lips. She knew she loved Declan, but would it last? Would it be enough to pull through the tough stuff? Where were they going? What was the point of any of this? Were they in love, or were they just playing at it?

Rather than head over in Declan's truck and face awkward silence or uncomfortable small talk en route to a relationship-
defining conversation, Dolly asked her dad to drop her off at
Beam's to meet him there. She felt hopeful enough to add a
sweep of mascara and a touch of lip gloss to her tired face before hopping in the sedan and heading into town.

She felt nervous and Daddy looked it too, as he heaved an
audible sigh and turned the key in the ignition. The drive to
Beam's was short and quiet, his eyes focused on the road the
whole time. Dolly shot quick glances in his direction, wondering what he was thinking. This was the type of errand usually
reserved for Mama but she was preparing a week's worth of
dinners for new neighbors who were expecting a baby fairly
soon.

Since he was needed to give her a ride into town, Mama was
unable to shield her husband from the news that the teenagers
were struggling. But, she had tried to minimize the drama of
the night before, simplifying Dolly and Declan's issue with a
shrug: "You know how it is, Dale," she had said. "We were
young once, too."

That was all it took to put Daddy in a funk, but Dolly could
feel him holding back from asking for details as they made the
quiet drive into town. Shania belted a ballad over the radio
waves but the volume was so low, you would have to know
the words to hear them. Dolly did, but she wasn't much in a
mood for mouthing along. Instead, she turned her head from
her father to her window and watched the small town go by.

Too soon they pulled up at Beam's Diner and Dale let the car
idle for a moment while reaching into the center console for
his wallet. "Let me give you a little money, sweetheart," he
said, figuring that if he couldn't protect her from an awkward
conversation, he could at least pay for her meal.

She accepted and thanked him for the twenty and unclipped her seat belt, turned away to leave the car. Suddenly a force bigger than her and bigger than the wave of emotion she'd been riding all day took hold and she turned back toward him and wrapped her arms around his neck.

"Daddy, I love you," she said, surprising them both with the blurted-out sentiment. Dale was an affectionate guy, but the emotional embrace took him by surprise and he found himself unsure what to do with his hands, settling on patting the top of her head as she rested it on his shoulder for a minute.

"I love you too, sweetie."

Dolly could feel the fine grain of his cotton pique polo shirt growing warm as her tears soaked it through. He was not one to press for conversation; it was like her eyes knew they could release it all right here and she wouldn't have to say a word. She pulled back finally and reached into the glove box for a tissue, dabbing her eyes and apologizing about the black streaks of mascara on his pale green polo. But it wasn't until she looked back up and made eye contact to say goodbye, that she saw her dad as she never had before.

He wasn't a crier, but for the first time since probably the day she was born, he had let a few tears loose. They stared at each other a moment, neither sure what to say. "Don't take any bullshit from that boy," he said finally. They both smiled as she promised she wouldn't.

"But will you stay nearby in case I need to make a quick exit?"

"Of course. I'll be right in the parking lot with my paper until you're ready for me," he promised.

The two of them would never talk about their tears in the car that day, and it wasn't something Dale would go home and share with his wife either, but he also wouldn't soon forget it. In the years since holding his daughter for the first time, thinking about this part was what had scared him the most. That one day she would fall in love and things would go awry and there wouldn't be a damn thing he could do to fix it.

Paralyzed by the realization that they had suddenly arrived at that seemingly far-off "one day," her tears had immediately sparked his own. As his beautiful, nervous, lovesick sixteen-year-old wept into the collar of his shirt, all he could think of was the painful reminder that he would never again see her in pink fleece pajamas with the footed bottoms. Never again experience her shrill whoops of joy over a surprise ice cream cone; never tiptoe past her room and overhear the made-up mini-dramas she created for her Barbie dolls, lined up in a row. Dolly was growing up—not *one day*, but this very moment. And along with all the hard things she was about to endure, he was now face-to-face with the seemingly impossible task of saying goodbye to his "little" girl.

* * * * *

Beam's Diner was the place where it had all begun, where they'd had their first shared milkshake, but also where the crew had been going for years. It was a small-town stalwart that people who visited from elsewhere always had to try. But stepping out of Daddy's car and onto the sidewalk at the edge of the parking lot, the sweet nostalgic pieces of her hometown were far from Dolly's mind. Today, the diner looked tired and hopeless, just as she felt.

She took a deep breath and abandoned her tears in the car, stiffening her face to keep it together on her way in. A quick glance in the sunshade mirror had confirmed that her lack of mascara would be fine, actually. Best not to look like she'd tried, best not to look like she cared too much.

Inside, she was greeted by the familiar formica countertops and bright leatherette seats that had probably been there since her parents were newlyweds. Dolly preferred the small-town places over the newer restaurants that had shot up in recent years; it was what she'd grown up on. This was also the only place outside their own home that a town native would go for an important conversation, let alone as a high schooler on the edge of potential heartbreak.

There he was in the second booth on the left, shifty and hand-some, commanding and undone. Wearing one of his dad's old plaids with the sleeves rolled up and the top two buttons open, he looked exactly as he always would in her memories in years to come. She sat down slowly, aware that it was ob-vious she'd been crying and also oddly empowered by a new sense of self from deep within—something that made it okay to let him see her emotions right out in front.

"Hi," was all he could muster, and after a brief pause they both smiled a little at that.

"That's all you got, Dec?" she teased, shaking her head as she surprised herself by realizing that she was willing to let it all go and move forward. The waitress came over and took their order (a plate of cheese fries and *one* large vanilla shake, two straws), filled in the quiet space between them. Their eyes shifted back and forth, catching each other's and letting them go. At first, neither could speak.

Dolly wanted so badly to not be the one who broke the silence, but finally she gave in. Whatever this talk was going to accom-plish between them, it was about time it started.

"I don't care that you did coke last night," she said, just above a whisper. "I just wish you hadn't tried to keep it from me?" (*Where was that dang power? She was starting to state her feelings as if they were questions).*

"Yeah. I get that, Dolly. I really do. It's just—" (*Words no girl is ever fond of hearing...*)

"*What?*" She demanded, searching his face with her eyes a minute, thinking back on last night. Was it weird that she'd wandered off alone, scoped out the Hamilton's house alone? Had she been gone too long, made him worry?

"You're so... good, Doll." His face looked like an apology. His mouth wasn't quite closed, the milkshake had arrived and sat between them, untouched.

"I don't—what the fuck does that even mean?" Dolly thought back to replacing her wine cooler with water. What a loser move... but there's no way he could know about that, so, what was it?

Declan reached for a fry, put it back down. "Sometimes I just feel like you're so good, you might not like me as much when you find out I'm not." Unlike her statement that came out a question, his should-be question sounded a hell of a lot like a statement.

"Uh... no I won't. I *love* you," she said, now suddenly desperate to get the real him at the table, back in the conversation. Find their way back to the other side of this. "And 'good' in what way?"

"I don't know!" he said it too loud, got them a few stares. "I don't know," quieter now. "I like to party and stuff. I thought going out last night would be fun but then we got there and right away I couldn't even *find* you and I just..."

"You just *what*, Declan?"

"You're a better person than me. Isn't it obvious?"

His face said the rest, the words he refused to say out loud. Declan reached for another fry, put it to his mouth and chewed slowly. Dolly found it shocking that he was able to eat in the middle of breaking up with his girlfriend and making her be the one to say it. It was all so clear, though... everything was different. That desperately sweet, romantic young man she'd spent her whole summer with and had just last night felt was hopelessly in love with her, had left the room. Or that part of him had, anyway.

The warm, soft edges of his smile that had shone her way all those beautiful times was replaced with a set jaw, eyes looking back and forth between hers with intent. He almost looked like he might cry, too, for a second (*Shit, she was crying again!*) but he swallowed hard and unlocked his gaze from hers long enough to get out the next terrible words.

"I just feel like we're headed in two different directions. This is *high* school and—"

"So you're breaking up with me because I didn't do coke at the party last night. Wow, Declan. What an exit." But it was she who was about to make one. Because not only had she just said those words, loud, in public at a small-town restaurant, but the tears were running down her cheeks in more than a mild flow at this point and she could feel her voice catching.

The sobs were coming and she had to get out of there. Couldn't let him even finish his stupid speech. She shoved the milkshake at him (*Okay, that part felt good*), and ran out of the diner. Breathless, she rushed to the front door and stood outside it a minute, scanning the parking lot for Daddy's car. Just as promised, there he was, idling at its edge with the windows down. She could make out the top of his newspaper through the dash.

Angry and confused thoughts rushed through her as she bolted across the parking lot into her father's waiting car and again throughout the drive home. Sure, this was "just high school," but wasn't it real love? Where less than an hour ago in this same spot she had wondered for a moment if this was the real thing, all she could think now was that *of course it was*.

Hadn't they fallen at the same time and the same place, into the same thing? Felt those things deep in their hearts and stayed up at night longing for the next kiss, the next laugh, the next touch? No, she had no idea where the future was going to take either one of them, but she'd always hoped, deep down inside, that somehow there *was* a future for them. Or at the very least, that this shattering moment could be postponed until graduation at the earliest.

She didn't even tell Daddy what had happened; her face said it all and more. The drive home was even quieter than the one there between them, but at least this time they had the radio up loud enough to hear. She could tell it was the best and the worst song possible from the first chord of Carolyn Dawn Johnson's "Die of a Broken Heart." Daddy, realizing the awful timing, fumbled with the buttons to change the station, but she broke their silence to stop him.

"Turn it up," Dolly said, putting on the sunglasses Daddy kept in the glove box and letting the tears fall as she looked out the window.

Take me fast or take me slow
I don't really care how I go
In the daylight or in the dark
Just don't let me die of a broken heart.

And kill her this wouldn't, but Dolly vowed silently to let this heartbreak take her under as deep as she needed to go before finding her way back up. There was an unexpected feeling pulsating through her as she and her father rode the rest of the way home, in the same car they'd driven in countless times to church, out for ice cream, and even for a joy ride or two with Mama for no reason at all, just to get out of the house.

Life would not go in one straight line and she was going to have to get okay with that, going to have to learn to follow its turns deliberately and with gratitude. Her parents, so devoted to each other and so revered in their community, had not been high school sweethearts. Mama had hinted at other boyfriends from the past, and Dolly knew that with those piercing eyes of Daddy's, and his fun-loving personality, he'd had to have seen other girls before her as well.

But they were good and happy and life had taken them out of those relationships and into what was a solid marriage. They were more, much more, than what they'd been in high school. Dolly didn't want the ranch-style Texas brick-face anyway, was done with small towns and charming diners. The hurt would recede, she could already tell that despite how potent and sharp it felt now. And beneath it a fire was starting to burn inside of Dolly, one that said it was alright for her to keep her dreams big and start to take Declan out of them.

In a year she'd be applying for colleges and soon after that, headed to New York. High school would be a thing of the past and so, too, would that sandy hair, those tired and sexy plaids. She had so much to look forward to. A big future that would be brighter than she could even imagine.

In the same moment that she tried to conjure an image of herself in the big city, dressed in black and donning enormous sunglasses, all of Texas a faded memory she no longer needed... the tears rushed right back in. Because she knew none of it mattered.

Maybe teenage love wouldn't define her. Maybe this wasn't the end of her story. But oh, was it a sweet chapter. And right now, she needed Declan like nothing else. The future was murky and meaningless. The only thing she had for sure, was a broken heart.

NOW

Friday nights of Manhattan summer are particularly special for the young and unattached. Rooftop drinks, fairy lights, and the bellowing laughter of close friends. Rosé with bubbles and, in the case of Dolly and her pack, very chic little outfits borrowed or purchased at exclusive discounts from the most coveted names in fashion.

Maybe you've decorated your little place in tapestries and topiaries. Maybe you've bummed some exquisite serving dishes and crystal off your parents or scored them in a great sale at Barney's. Maybe you've just started out and have none of this yet or maybe, like Dolly, you were lucky with gifts from clients, associates, and friends before you'd saved enough to start doing some of the decorating for yourself, too. But the place where you put together these pieces of a twenty-something New York City life, the place where you spend your time before pulling on going-out clothes, the place where you roast broccoli ever-so-slightly too long or fix the cocktails just this side of too strong? This is a place you will never, ever forget.

And in summer, with the windows thrown open and that warm evening air flowing through your linens and lace, it can start to feel like real-life magic for sure. That's how tonight was starting off, anyway.

Last night Michael told her that his dad needed him for a prospective client meeting on Martha's Vineyard this weekend. He kissed her sleeping eyes this morning and took his black Prada weekender off into the early light of dawn, leaving a note behind to tell her he'd miss her and signing it with *x*'s like they always did.

Admittedly, Dolly is relieved to have a weekend off from wedding planning. She'll miss Michael, but is content in the knowledge that he isn't working *all* that hard. It might not be the weekend he envisioned, but it certainly won't be terrible either.

It always gives Dolly an inner chuckle to imagine a group of men chatting around a golf course, eating steak dinners, spending thousands of dollars on a getaway and calling it a "meeting." Old School Manhattan and its business dealings are still very much alive and well, but she feels good knowing that the Peabodys are major philanthropists and all-around good people. The deals they've been working on hardest lately are to save and repurpose old buildings, bring new life to neighborhoods that need a lift, and build companies that will create jobs for veterans and the disabled. Business is business, and it has its ugly sides. But she knows she is marrying a good man who was born of a very decent one, and that's about all she needs to know for now.

Tonight will be all about her friends though, and Dolly is looking forward to it. Laying out on her velvet couch, windows wide open to let in the fresh air and streaks of early evening sunset, she takes a minute to just *be,* something she realizes she hasn't done in weeks.

In New York City, your tiny space feels like a precious shrine. It is a cocoon in which you protect, nourish, and recharge yourself before emerging into the busy, chaotic, and passionate world that exists in the streets below. Dolly loves both aspects: the messiness and busyness juxtaposed to her own quiet, serene space. Sometimes, like now, she allows her mind to wander timidly and curiously to what it will be like to officially live with Michael come fall. Though he spends a lot of time and frequent overnights here, it is still *her* place. Will she ever feel like this again, this complete sense of peace just lounging around in the home that belongs to her? Will sharing an apartment completely and permanently make her lose this ease and the opportunity for stillness that living on her own has brought?

It's silly, really, to question what living with Michael will be like. He'll pay the bills and her life won't be stressful. She'll continue to work because she loves her career, but the pressure will be off. They'll put their Brooklyn home together bit by bit, one candle and picture frame at a time. She might even hang on to this precious old couch. Despite a little wearing in some spots, it has become one of her favorite things in the universe. Maybe bringing it with her to their new apartment will help that space feel like home.

Dolly is about to convince herself to break the daydream and start getting ready for the night out when she sees a notification pop up on her phone. Hoping it's one of her friends finalizing plans for tonight, she hoists herself up on one elbow and reaches out with the other hand to grab it. A text from a number she doesn't recognize is revealed on the screen. Not thinking anything of it, Dolly punches in her four-digit pass code, reads the text, and instantly her mood shifts.

I never heard back on FB so thought I'd try texting. Got your number from Steph. In NYC this weekend. Can we please talk Dolly? It's Dec btw.

As if he needed to tell her who it was. She didn't recognize the San Francisco area code, but there is only one person in the world who would send a message like that. And also only one person who knows Stephanie, and doesn't also have Dolly's current number.

What the hell? Ever since Daddy revealed that it was Stephanie's brother who'd killed Mama on a teenage joy ride, she'd been actively trying to avoid that girl. A "best" friend who can't reach out and attempt some kind of apology was not a best friend, which is why she found it impossible to be friendly when they ran into each other back in Sugar's Bend this spring.

True, we aren't responsible for our family member's wrong-doings. Dolly has reasoned and re-reasoned this over and over in her head for months. *But still! Own your shit. Give me a hug. Tell me you are mortified, bereft. Accept that your stoned brother ruined my family. Or, you know, sure. Dole out my phone number to an ex-boyfriend without checking with me first. That totally works, too,* she snorts drily.

She was actually kind of starting to feel proud of herself for ignoring the Facebook message. Clearly, this problem is not going to disappear simply by ignoring it. Dolly is annoyed and a little angry that Declan won't just stay in the past where he belongs. She can't help but wonder if his sudden need to talk to her is stemming from jealousy over having noticed that she recently changed her Facebook relationship status to "en-gaged." Despite Michael popping the question this past win-ter, her desire to keep her private life private won out until recently. But then it started to feel a little weird booking cake tastings and dress appointments while appearing to all the world like there wasn't a ring on her finger and a coveted venue booked for next June.

It has to be more than that, though, and this is the part she always tries to ignore, tries to push down. What happened be-tween them back in high school started out like all the stupid small-town romances that go nowhere and it ended similarly, too... at first. But the chaos that unfolded throughout the rest of junior year and into that following summer, the challenges they faced together and separately, are the type of things that you never really can put behind you.

Dolly moved to her dream city, changed her name, and tried to forget it all... but really, it was unforgettable. Sure, she'd always hoped she'd make it in New York, but there was never a doubt in her mind that part of her motivation was because of how things ended with Declan. So many words left unsaid that maybe never should be shared. The things they saw, the things they did, and then the other part, the part that became the real end for them... it's almost too much to bear thinking of, even now.

She heads to the bedroom and flips through her closet trying to find a suitable outfit for wherever tonight will take her. Black sequins and leather, gauzy white cotton and studded denim, long silk floral all stare back at her looking wrong. The pain comes on unexpected and strong, like this particular one always seems to do: she wishes more than anything that she could call her mother right now. Ask her what to wear for a summer evening that could take her from casual drinks to perhaps a nice fusion dinner and dancing downtown. Tell her about the unexpected text and work through together what she should do. Drink a gin fizz over the phone and figure the fuck out of her bizarre, twisty life with the only person who ever really got her.

Friends are wonderful and she knows she can hand her phone over to John-John and Glinda later to weigh in. She'll let them read the messages from Declan and decode the words while helping her make sense of the mess going on inside her own brain. They'll listen. They'll give solid advice.

But they aren't her mama, and of course, they don't know the whole story. They don't know the half of what their "Texas Flower" has lost.

And there in her closet, standing in one shoe, Dolly puts her face in her hands and begins to sob.

* * * * *

The only person Dolly wanted to rehash her first date with Michael with, was her mom. Since Sally was an hour behind her in time zones, Dolly had watched the clock passionately that morning. She wasn't a huge morning person, but that day the buzzing energy that had pulsed through her all night on the town with this exciting new guy, remained.

Finally, at 9 AM in New York, she figured her mother would be awake and padding toward the kitchen to fix herself a cup of coffee.

"Mama!" She practically squealed into her cell after Sally picked up the landline on the second ring, her voice gravelly.

"Oh, hey honey. This is a nice surprise on a Sunday morning."

"I know, sorry. It's so early. I just have to tell you about my date last night!"

"Oh! One second, dear. Let me take the phone onto the porch so I don't wake your father." Dolly could hear her mother moving through the kitchen, the clink of her spoon against the edge of her coffee cup, the porch door slamming behind her. "Okay. Tell me everything."

"Oh my gosh, Mama, he's such a gentleman!" Dolly gushed. She knew these were the details her friends in New York wouldn't care about nearly as much as what kind of wine he ordered at dinner, what he did for a living. But Southern women prefer the sweeter details, the parts that feel like home. Mama was the perfect audience for the way he placed his hand gingerly on her back when guiding her through the restaurant, for the way he texted her an hour after they parted ways to make sure she was safe at home.

"The whole night was so romantic. I mean, this restaurant he picked I probably would have never heard of! He told me his dad took his mother there for their first date, *thirty-five years ago*. Can you imagine? So sweet."

"Does he have a Yankee accent?" Sally couldn't help but ask, the two dissolving in giggles.

"I mean, yeah, he has a *New York* accent," Dolly corrected, teasing back, "but it's not bad. He was raised on the Upper West Side, not in *Queens*."

"Well, I don't know what any of that means, honey, but if you're happy I'm happy. Remind me of his name?"

"Michael. Michael Peabody, *Jr.*," she elaborated. "Don't Google him though. The cameras have been following the poor guy since high school. His family is pretty well known up here."

"Is that a good thing?"

How far removed her mother was from New York society. Dolly could feel a headache coming on, and it wasn't just the barolo from dinner last night.

"I mean, they're society, Mama," she tried feebly to explain. "Think about it like Dallas but with a lot more newspapers to print the gossip."

"I get it, honey. I'm just having a little fun here. I promise not to Google him, okay? As long as you promise not to give it up before the third date."

"*Mama!*" Somehow they'd managed to get through high school, college, and several subsequent years of young adulthood without any allusion to Dolly having a sex life outside the semiannual reminder from her mother to keep up with her birth control.

"Well, I'll admit I did Google him once, and wow—the man is gorgeous! You couldn't be blamed."

"You *did* remember his name."

"I remember everything you tell me, sweetheart. Sometimes I just like to hear you say it again."

"Well, I'm glad you approve. I just had to fill you in, because it's been a while since I felt this way. And... I don't know. I just wanted you to know."

"And I'm glad to know it. I can't wait to hear how it all pans out, darling. Yankee accent and all."

They wrapped it up casually, her father waking up and piping in briefly to say hello before giving the phone back to Mama.

"Talk to you soon, honey. Don't spare me any details! It's been a while since I got to watch a love story unfold right in front of me."

Six weeks later, she would be dead.

THEN

Returning to school on Monday after physically fighting her best friend and being dumped, was not exactly a dream scenario. Dolly tried faking a cold that morning but Sally, usually inclined to let her daughter take "mental health days," sat on the edge of her bed and told her something important:

"I know you want to hide from them, Dolly Mae, but here's the thing—skipping a day of school isn't going to make this any easier to face tomorrow, or the day after that. You need to go in there and hold your head up high. Show him you're getting on with your life. That's what's going to fix it."

"And what about Steph?"

"You and Stephanie have been friends for a very long time and that's just not the type of relationship anyone throws away over a disagreement. Take her aside after school. Let her know how you feel. You girls will work this out, honey. I know you will." Sally said, stroking her daughter's hair. "Now, you need to get up and put yourself together."

Spitefully, but out of options, Dolly grumbled her way out of bed and padded down the hall, biting her lip to hold back tears she just couldn't stop from flowing. She also felt like shit, which didn't help matters.

Her mind was doing two things at once and it was absolutely maddening; just as yesterday in the car, she felt equal parts despondent over the breakup with Declan and hopeful about what a future without ties to a high school boyfriend could mean for her. There were moments of elation in which she reminded herself that she'd always felt called to a bigger life outside this gossipy town. What did she need her inferior high school boyfriend for anyway, when the world had such better things in store for her? Then seconds later she'd get lost in a memory of his hands, his eyes, the way he said her name, and the crushing rejection would wash all over her once more, like it had the very minute he'd broken her heart in the diner she'd never be able to look at the same again.

Dolly took her time applying her makeup (waterproof mascara, naturally) and doing her hair. She pulled on a very tight pair of jeans and a black top that would show off just a tiny bit of stomach when she raised her hand in class. Packed her school bag. Headed out to the kitchen.

Though Declan often drove her to school when he didn't have morning practice, it wasn't unusual for Daddy to drop her off on his way to work. With everything that had transpired yesterday, it was clear he knew that the job was his exclusively now, and would be for a while. She entered the kitchen wordlessly, wishing she could erase the past 48 hours of her life or maybe just the past three years. Go back to being younger, more innocent, and free of the complications that come with growing up.

Dolly observed Daddy standing, bent over the kitchen island with a cup of coffee in front of him, its steam wafting up in soft swirls. He always drank his coffee black, which she and Mama teased was one of the few rugged, Southern things about this cooking, cleaning, gentle giant of a man they loved. Now, once again, back to being the only man of her heart.

"Ready, honey?" he asked, sensing her in the room. He half looked up from the paper while reaching for his car keys. "I've got a meeting this morning and need to make a few calls when I get in."

"Yeah, Daddy," she took a deep breath. "I'm ready."

Yesterday, and what happened between them, wouldn't be mentioned unless she wanted it to be, and Dolly was grateful for that. For his ability to lock up the emotions box when it needed to be done and let the routine move them through the hard things and back to normalcy. Later, when they'd lose Sally suddenly and have only each other to turn to, they would pass this torch back and forth. Now the strong one, now the mess of tears. Now the fortress, now the reed in the wind. But those teen years and all the trials they had brought and would continue to bring, would have been ten times worse for Dolly if her dad hadn't let her just... be.

In the beginning of the school year she'd bemoaned the fact that she had very few opportunities to see either her best friend or her boyfriend at all during the day, but today their mismatched schedules made things so much easier. Familiar with Declan's routine and his typical pathways throughout the school, she knew which hallways to avoid and between what periods to linger where.

In turn, she walked three times the distance in the wrong direction and back around just to not pass his locker and risk eye contact (or worse, no eye contact). If this was what the entire rest of the school year would be like, it was going to get exhausting quick.

Dolly was relieved at lunch to discover that a huge benefit of having had the fight with Stephanie at a party just outside town, was that word didn't seem to have spread too far if at all. None of the girls she sat with brought it up, and if any of Dec's football buddies at the table knew about the breakup yet, they were kind enough not to mention it. Everyone seemed oddly normal against the panicked swells that had engulfed Dolly's mind all morning. She was able to pretend for that thirty-five-minute block of time that this was just a typical Monday. It was nice.

Cheer practice, though, was brutal. It was obvious to anyone who looked at Stephanie that she'd been hurt in the face. A tiny, angry cut was etched into the area right above her cheek below the eye, and it, oddly, made her bright eyes look even prettier, her face even more striking.

Dolly expected the silent treatment, but instead Steph issued her a tight, sarcastic smile every time they made eye contact and made a rude comment under her breath every chance she got.

Under the pressure of Steph's watchful and nasty eye, Dolly fumbled her stunts, not straightening her arms enough and falling off count often. She couldn't keep up, couldn't keep count, and was out of breath after only twenty minutes.

"Do we need to sub you out?" Steph demanded in her direction without actually looking her in the eye.

"No, I'm fine. I just need some water," she replied and walked off the rolled-out mats, to the sidelines of the basketball court to grab her bottle.

Well, at least she'd avoided Declan.

* * * * *

The next few days passed similarly. They were not horrible, but not exactly great either. Dolly buried herself in her schoolwork, a tendency that came naturally, and tried to focus on the positives. Like the fact that, so far, it didn't look like Steph had told anyone about the fight. And despite how public, awful, and embarrassing it had felt the night of, most of the people who witnessed it had probably been drunk.

Things weren't exactly looking up, but at least they hadn't gotten any worse. Yet.

NOW

Dolly allows herself a good twenty-minute cry, then goes to the bathroom to splash cold water on her face. She reaches for a fluffy lavender hand towel and gently blots her face dry, looks in the mirror and lets out a cleansing exhale.

The past is hard and sad, rippled with complications and losses that anyone could have suffered. She might not talk about it often, or... *ever*, but it still lives with her today. There are places that it hurts to look, moments she wishes she could forget. Parts of her story that time was supposed to heal, or erase, but hasn't. Will it ever?

But there is also the present, and this is where she should be focusing her time and effort. On two amazing friends who have been her backbone these past few years. Friends who have helped her out of sticky situations and into dresses that she couldn't zip. Who have held back her hair, and lifted up her expectations of what it is to be a true friend.

There still remain the pieces of Sugar's Bend, and all she loved and lost there, which waft up and around her like the steam off Daddy's mugs of black coffee. But the now is a full picture, or at least one she's starting to paint and put together. And she's damn sure tonight won't be one to skip adding to it.

Dolly returns to her closet and pulls on her red Prada miniskirt and a black chiffon sleeveless top, laces up a somewhat comfortable pair of heeled black sandals. She doesn't know what the night will bring, but she does know this: there will be no texting Declan back. Not tonight, anyway.

* * * * *

It's hard to swallow the feelings Declan's message has brought to the surface as she heads out the door to meet John-John and Glinda for martinis. Extravagantly, Dolly opts for a taxi to take her way downtown and over to the West Side. While usually she takes the subway out and cabs it back after drinking, tonight she's feeling drained. The thought of standing under those harsh yellow lights and breathing in the stale air is unfathomable. She needs clarity and peace. It's worth any price, so thirty bucks actually seems cheap.

The cab pulls up to the Starlight and Dolly hands the driver cash, over-tipping. She steps out of the car, straightens her skirt, and checks her phone to find out if her friends are already inside. Five minutes later, she's pulling up a gold-painted chair in a dark, moody corner of their crew's favorite spot in the city. Not yet discovered by the hipsters, this little haunt shares a part-owner with many of New York's hot spots. She only heard about it in whispers from a model friend on a shoot; they did no press at the opening months ago and have no social media presence to speak of. As a publicist, that all seems insane to Dolly, but as a young person who loves to have the pulse on everything that's happening before it actually is happening, she *loves* it. As John-John put it once, "That lack of wanting to be known and yet being so worth knowing? It doesn't get more chic."

Glinda looks shiny in her usual way. Her always-platinum bob is brighter somehow in summer, and subtle pops of silver glitter glisten at the corners of her eyes. She is wearing a long, silky lavender dress with a dramatic slit that goes all the way up to mid-thigh, and the way she crosses her legs you can see nothing but skin ending in the lacing up of tan, chunky heels with about a million straps criss-crossing from toe to ankle.

"Hi baby," Glinda says, her voice like honey and sun rays. They cheek-kiss and Dolly breathes in the sweetness of her perfume, the faint hint of a cigarette she probably smoked an hour ago, and something like pears. Soft and fruity, maybe a lotion she's going to tell them all about tonight and pass out sample bottles of. Or maybe something cheap and silly that her dad sent in from Anchorage, for (*bless his heart*) that man would hang the moon in the perfect spot for her every night if he could. She is so close with her parents. Dolly is mildly jealous.

Glinda is about as radiant as her name and that's probably what drew Dolly to her from the start. When she was hired at the firm three years ago, everything clicked pretty quickly. It was the kind of friendship that a teenaged Dolly had always daydreamed about, but one she never thought she'd find. There are still moments, even now, that she wonders if she and Glinda will make it in the long run. Will there come a day when she is revealed to not deserve a friend like her? Someone so good, someone so true and so golden to the core.

Having a new close friend who isn't enmeshed in your past is a blessing, Dolly realized quickly into their relationship. With Glinda there's nothing to tiptoe around, nothing complicated to avoid or face. Their friendship grew easily, and without the haunts and taints of the others she had known before. And when Glinda introduced Dolly to her "gay husband" John-John, who had recently relocated from Miami, the trio cemented fast and blossomed into something solidly beautiful.

John-John looks light and happy tonight, in a striped boatneck t-shirt and white pants rolled up at the ankles. He has a fresh crew cut and is gushing openly about Roman, his new guy— (*"Y'all are finally going to meet him tonight!"*)—between sips of a gimlet that is ready for replacing. Like magic, another appears before he's had the chance to order it. None of them so much as look up to figure out why.

"I'm so excited we finally get to meet him!" Glinda exclaims above the up-volumed Amy Winehouse emanating through the speaker beside their table.

"I know right? How long have y'all been swappin' spit?" Dolly asks in John-John's direction.

"Damn near five months!" he returns, eyes glowing mischievously.

"You two!" Glinda throws her hands up in a gesture of surrender. "I swear, it only takes two cocktails and you're both talking like we're below the Mason-Dixon."

Dolly cracks up, nodding in agreement that no one pulls out her inner Southerner quite like John-John does, especially after a drink or two.

"What's going on in your bedroom, Glin?" She shifts the conversation back to her friend, instantly relieved when the response doesn't include Mr. Bar 6.

"Literally nothing," she says with a shrug. "Maybe if Sandra ever lets me hire a goddamn assistant I'll have time to go 'swap spit.' Until then, I'm married to my press contact list, apparently."

"Aww," John-John doesn't miss a beat. "I am so sad for you with your covetable career and naturally dewy complexion. And the fact that practically every guy in this bar is staring at your legs." He gives her a playful shove that she swats away, having noticed herself that the dress is earning her plenty of stares.

Just then, one bold bachelor wearing a blazer over a band t-shirt and a look of confidence reserved for the rich and mildly drunk, makes his way toward their table. He is intent on

Glinda, a fact obvious to all of them, and John-John and Dolly share a quick, conspiratorial glance in honor of the poor expectant guy who's about to be remanded back to his corner of the bar.

Glinda will never go for someone so predictable and hopeful, nor anyone who appears to have a drop of cash. She likes it dark and complicated. Poor guy doesn't stand a chance.

It's only as they're leaving that Dolly realizes for all their chatter about men, Michael hasn't come up once. She isn't sure if it's her fault or theirs, but she's also somewhat relieved. A break. Maybe that's what the sobs were about earlier. Maybe she just needs a break from everything rushing through her mind at lightning speed these days.

After the Starlight, they head to a club a few blocks up to meet Veronica. She is younger and a bit naive but her presence is always a breath of fresh air. Unlike the other models that Dolly knows around town, Veronica isn't hardened yet. She hasn't developed a surly attitude (or an eating disorder) and life still feels hopeful and fun to her.

Dolly hopes this young beauty with her flawless caramel skin and wide-set, deep brown eyes will hop off the modeling train before any of the above transpires. Start using her inquiring mind and passionate zest for knowledge to get ahead instead of staying on a career path based solely on her appearance. That she does this before a life in the fastest and hardest lane of all destroys her sweetness and replaces her vulnerability with pain and regret.

Some of Veronica's young friends are in tow, and the group eventually clears enough space on the floor to dance as one large unit. Dolly holds tight to the stem of her champagne flute, moving her hips slowly, careful not to bend far enough in any direction and hike up her already quite short skirt.

Eventually, Roman sweeps in to meet them and he's every bit as handsome and polite as she'd heard and hoped. Watching them steal kisses above the din and through the pulsing of the music stirs something hopeful and a little sad inside her. John-John catches her eye and mouths, "Cute, right?" to which Dolly grins and nods a vehement, *Yes*.

One of her dearest friends is falling, and the whole group is happy tonight. Maybe she should go outside, text her missing piece. Tell Michael she misses him and see what time he'll be back on Sunday. Throw herself back into the love she's been building and the one that has her future in its hands. At the very least, she could use a minute alone.

Outside of the club, the streets are alive in only the way that New York City sidewalks can be. People in their twenties huddle in groups, laughing loudly, making plans according to an incoming string of text messages. Kissing strangers or new love interests. Queuing up to get in. Piling up to get home. Just another Friday night.

All around her life is pulsing and energetic, free-spirited, lively, and fun. In her head, a weary stopgap. She came out here to text her fiancé, but now she hesitates. What would she say? He's off golfing on the Vineyard with his father, making deals or drinking bourbon or doing God knows what, and she suddenly feels miles away from him, miles away from this life they've pieced together, just on its cusp of really starting.

It feels good to be out in the busy streets, though. Anonymous and alive, alone for a few minutes of peace and thought. Dolly reaches into her bag for her phone and seeing a text alert makes her smile. Michael is thinking of her, too.

She taps on the words "new message" and her stomach lurches instantly.

Please just text me back.

The past, once more. And nothing from her future.

THEN

The thing about love is, once you're in it, it's a damn hard thing to find your way out of.

Dolly and Declan had been broken up for all of a month when the slow smiles and newly exciting flirtations started to creep back into their gradually repairing friendship. A little time and distance was maybe all they had needed, and before long they went from quietly, purposely passing each other in the hallways to making out in the cab of his truck.

Dolly knew they should probably be taking more time, more space, but she didn't care. It felt right to be back in Declan's arms. She had started to heal and was trying to move forward with her junior year. To fix things with Steph, and to focus on school work and cheerleading. But he was always just... there. Not only physically, but in every other way. When she lay down at the end of the day his eyes danced across the insides of her closed lids. When idle minutes ticked by in the afternoon, she would find herself staring at the phone, willing him to make it ring. Whenever something funny or sad or interesting happened, he was the first person she wanted to tell.

It was the fast and not-so-winding journey back to each other that later she would think on and wonder about. High school romance with its dramas and insecurities didn't quite seem a fitting description of theirs. Yes, they were a rush of Chap-Stick and eager hands, secret truths whispered in the dark and stolen kisses in every corner of this small town... but not just all of that. Things with Dolly and Declan were different.

There was more to this couple than they could know or understand at the time. It would all come together soon, though. Until then, they had, at least, each other.

NOW

Dolly takes a deep breath and makes a decision, months after deciding to sit still in the opposite of one.

Where are you? She types rapidly into her phone.

It's just about the most she can manage to say on three drinks and zero bites of food. The alcohol is just hitting her now, it seems, as she stands outside of the club. A wave of power over her fingertips, coming from deep within. Outside her control and making her act on emotion, on immediacy. She half-expects him not to respond, but her phone buzzes almost instantly.

My hotel, near Bryant Park. You?

These are the moments in life that we come back to again and again, wonder why we did what we did, and think on how or if we could have done it differently. But acting on impulse, Dolly does not think of the then, or what will be, she thinks solely of the now.

She responds with the name and address of the club that she is currently standing outside of in a very sexy outfit and manageable yet not low heels, having momentarily abandoned her friends. And he counters with a suggestion to meet for a drink at a quiet Italian restaurant not far from where she is. Dipping on the gang isn't a total faux pas, but she'll at least have to let them know she's leaving.

Dolly heads back inside the dark club to seek out her friends.

She's grateful for John-John's nearly excessive height that makes him easy to spot. "I have to go, honey! An old friend is in town and I totally forgot we were supposed to meet up," she offers.

The lie is just white enough to pass as a truth, even to herself. She kisses him on both cheeks, gives his new boy a quick squeeze, waves to Glinda who lifts her glass in response, and is gone. It's settled then. She is off to see Declan.

Taking the seven blocks in heels might have been a slight mistake, but the fresh air feels necessary. So many thoughts of Declan come rushing to her mind, and to her surprise, she thinks of Michael only fleetingly, and without guilt.

This is an old friend. This is just a drink. She tells herself these things on repeat as the city passes her in a blur. Declan playing guitar in the back of his truck, plaid shirt sleeves rolled up to the elbows. Stolen kisses behind the bleachers just before practice. It feels so long ago and yet so close to the heart.

And suddenly, there he is. Looking like the manly version of the boy she fell in love with so long ago. Standing outside a tiny Italian restaurant she's never been to, in white pants not unlike John-John's. He still wears a button-down shirt better than anyone, but this one looks more refined. Black linen with short sleeves. His hair is still sand-colored if a shade darker now, that one piece still falls out of place like it always did. The familiar smile broadens as he notices her, takes her in. It's upturned higher on one side like it always used to be. It's still him.

All she can manage is, "Hi." She breathes the word out and a smile follows close behind it.

"You look exactly the same," he responds.

Despite Facebook, despite photographs texted by mutual friends back in college, and all the other ways they have caught glimpses of each other over the years, she knows what he means. It's not so much a shock to see a familiar face staring back at you when you look at the person who used to be your entire world. It's more the stunning reality that that person is really here, really in front of you and that you don't know what else to say. He looks the same, too, in a way. But she finds she cannot speak.

Timidly, Declan holds out his arms for a hug. Dolly obliges wordlessly.

Inside the restaurant, she is suddenly famished. It dawns on her for the second time this evening that she never bothered to eat before leaving the house, so in addition to the glass of pinot grigio she knows she'll need to get through this meeting, she also orders a small Caesar salad and an appetizer sized bowl of penne primavera. He does the kind thing and orders a salad as well so she won't be eating alone, and she almost bursts out laughing at the realization that this will be the first time she ever witnesses Declan willingly eating something green. Instead, she eases into actually starting a friendly conversation with him.

"It is so good to see you, Declan," she says, finally. She can tell that like her he oddly, suddenly, feels at ease despite the randomness of all of this, the improbability of it. And also despite the fact that she made him wait so long for a response, the conversation begins to flow between them.

"So, how do you like living out here anyway?"

"I like it! It's definitely a little less glamorous and more difficult than I thought it would be, but it's good. I actually like the pace."

"I don't see how you keep up! I've been overwhelmed since I landed at JFK." They laugh; she can picture him desperately out of place, wide-eyed in the busy airport.

"You're here for work?"

"Yeah. Last-minute trip. Probably could've been an email, but you know how that goes." She shakes her heard. She doesn't.

"In my line of work, damn near everything has to happen face-to-face," she explains. "I probably spend as many hours schmoozing, dining, and stuffing gift bags as I do at my desk."

Declan smiles, catches her eyes. The candlelight flickers between them, casting a quick shadow across his face.

"That does sound exciting, though, Dolly. Like you always hoped it would be." There is a hint of sadness in his voice and she lingers just a beat, returning his glance before redirecting the conversation.

"You're staying near Bryant Park? Have you had a chance to wander through it yet? One of my favorite spots in New York."

"Not yet," he shakes his head. "I'll do that tomorrow, since you suggest it."

Neither one of them mentions the diamond on her finger, nor his sudden need to get in touch. Neither one gets into the hard stuff from the past, or broaches the last time they saw each other. She is prepared to bring up absolutely nothing difficult but continue to ride this easy wave of quiet, pleasant catchup with a handsome young man who is so different and yet also so familiar. To blot out the uneasiness that paints their entire story and just focus on the pasta, on the wine.

Dolly imagines what people in the restaurant are thinking as they glance over and notice them. Do they spot this young couple out on a Friday night at a low-key West Village Italian restaurant and peg them as nervous first-daters? Are they trying to eavesdrop on the conversation, reminiscing on their own early days as lovesick couples?

Looking around, the crowd is older and it's clear they're mostly locals at their familiar neighborhood spot. There are a few groups of old men with big, round bellies and unbuttoned jackets, caught somewhere between the nostalgia of Old New York when people dressed for dinner, and the reality of the moment which is that comfort is key.

With its red-and-white checkered table coverings and low-humming operatic background music, this is about the last place in the city that Dolly would have chosen to get together with anyone, let alone a gorgeous if stress-inducing ex-boyfriend. And certainly not in such a good outfit. (*The red skirt deserves to be seen...*) But Declan is comically unaware of anything out-of-order, as he lives in a city that is not quite so complicated.

But then he breaks it all. "Listen."

(*Never something you want to hear when you're trying to have an easy night out while avoiding the hardships of your past*).

"I owe you an apology, Dolly." (*Well, you owe me like 300 apologies, but which one are we going with tonight?*) "I should have been at your mama's funeral. I should have at least called you."

Dolly swallows hard, but the lump that's just formed in her throat won't budge.

"Yeah," she manages. "You should have."

"I—I didn't know what to say. And so I just hid out like an ass. I'm so sorry."

After a few moments, she nods. It's weird, but she gets it... sort of. What would she have felt, have done, had he lost his mother at this point in their lives, with all the distance between them? She probably would have at least reached out. Yes, *yes*. She knows she definitely would have. But a part of her understands how a person could have trouble doing it. The part of her that was always able to forgive him. Inside, she starts to unfurl just a little.

"I get it," she says, finally. "It's... it's fine."

It isn't actually fine yet, but she can feel that it will get there in time. A burden she has been unable to name for the past year and a half has started to lift, and she can feel it taking with it the corners of the heavier weight it was resting upon. The one deep inside her soul.

Dolly doesn't know what else she's feeling right now, but alone with him in a nondescript restaurant where she's sure she'll run into absolutely no one she knows, suddenly feels easy and natural. Exciting, even. The tears his text brought on earlier this evening feel miles away as the two order another round of drinks and laugh while sharing ridiculous stories about their colleagues or harking back on old friends from high school. They've moved back to the easy stuff for now, but a little promise of deeper conversations lingers. And she never would have expected this, but she's happy that they're here together.

Two hours later, they are standing on the street. Having poured themselves out of the restaurant and into the hot summer evening air, they both feel alive and new. Dolly feels sweat forming at her temples and dabs it lightly with the base of one palm, hoping he won't notice. Suddenly she questions why she had to wear her hair down and hot on her back tonight, wonders if he remembers running his fingers through it long ago. And then chastises herself for letting her mind go there when it shouldn't be, not even remotely.

Declan looks just like the city lights, she thinks, looking up at his face. His eyes are so bright and so aware of the world swirling around him, he almost looks like a kid again, if only for a second. She thinks on that voice of his that she's been listening to for the past few hours, a voice that feels like home. The hint of that old Southern twang she fell for all those years ago in her cutoff jeans remains on the edges of his now softened accent. He still talks slower than the guys up here and without that air of confidence (cockiness?) she's grown to expect. He still looks like that boy too, but his jaw is more chiseled now. His clothes fit the man he has become but they still fall sexy and easy on his body like the old ones used to do. She takes him in from here as long as she dares, afraid that if she speaks this whole beautiful enigma might just float away and she'll always wonder what it was for.

They are both wordless, maybe a little confused. She's engaged and he lives in San Francisco. Life is on its course for each and their paths don't match up, probably weren't supposed to cross.

Just when she's ready to call it a night with Declan and rejoin her posse at the club seven blocks south, looking out at the street to scan for cabs to save her aching feet, he says the second thing she never expected to hear.

"Your mama isn't why I needed to talk to you."

She looks up again, catches his eye.

"Okay..."

"The way we ended things—" The blaring horns of passing taxicabs and the shouts of laughter of passersby are distant, muddied, audial blurs. His voice with its remainders of a

Texas accent, though, is clear and direct. It fills her with a deep ache of longing she didn't know was there.

"I should have stuck around after, tried harder. You were…" he says, the past a wine-dulled dream she's not sure she wants to revisit.

How many nights has she wept over what might have been, especially in the wake of everything that happened between them, especially because of *her*? Deep down she must have known things were unfinished between them, otherwise she wouldn't have met him tonight. An apology pours out of him, the recognition that no matter what they should have at least remained friends.

Declan's voice breaks against the whir of passersby and wails of sirens. A couple of girls who can't possibly be legal to drink yet pass them by, one clearly about to vomit. Dolly looks at them, scantily clad in denim and lace, looks at the trash can on the corner of the block, at the light changing from red to green. Looks anywhere but into his eyes as her own fill with unexpected tears, hot and salty.

"I'm sorry, too." The words fall out of her before she even knows she means them, but of course she always has. As much as he is to blame for some parts of the whole mess, her decisions were big and painful to him, too. There is no clear villain in the teenage drama that unfolded between them. "I pushed you away," she finishes, knowing it's true.

Dec reaches in for a hug. It is their second one of the night and yet it feels so different from the first. Slowly, she wraps her arms around his still-narrow waist, pulls him to her for an embrace like she hasn't had in a long time. Here she stands with her high school boyfriend from small-town Texas on a downtown corner of Manhattan.

He smells of laundry detergent, the same brand his mother always used. And a new cologne, something more refined and musky than what she remembers. Dolly allows her head to find its place in the dip at the top of his sternum, just where it always used to go. A question flashes across her mind of how many other girls' heads have found the perfect resting place right here, but she bats it away quickly like a pesky fly. *Not now.*

They both hold on a bit too long; it's more than a friendly hug now. But all the things she can think to say to end it escape her. They jumble themselves up until she gets right down to it all: they've both apologized. And maybe now they both can start to heal.

The embrace reaches the point at which it's gone on long enough and they mutually realize that it's over. Desperate not to lose the connection she had no idea she needed so badly from him, Dolly takes a second trying to come up with a witty conversation recovery, but he does it himself. "So... You wanna help a confused country boy figure out this subway system of yours or what?" Declan asks, tasing her lightly like he used to. They both feel lighter now, and it's obvious that the space between them has shifted.

"Oh my God, Declan, it's not like you still live in a tiny town in the South! You can navigate a city, no? Anyway... your company won't let you expense some cabs while you're here? What the fuck! You need a new job!" She teases back, grabbing his hand anyway to lead him across the street in the direction of the subway he needs to catch uptown. The closeness already established, this feels like a natural progression.

"That or maybe I just want to spend a little more time with you?" He says it like a question, but they both know that it's not.

While earlier it was on both their minds if not on their lips, the ring on her finger is a distant thought for now. And before either one of them knows what they're doing, Dolly is hailing them a taxi and they're barreling up Eighth Avenue in a lip lock so natural, it's as if it hasn't been over a decade since the last one.

* * * * *

Dolly and Declan fall timidly and hungrily toward the couch, then move across the apartment into the bedroom together as one, slowly peeling off each other's sweaty summer clothes. The waiting bed stands silent aside from the gentle whir of a single oscillating fan that sits atop a ledge by the open window.

On every hot day they've had so far this year, Dolly has daydreamed about next summer and how incredible it will feel to enter an oasis of icy air at the new Brooklyn apartment after a long, hot day. To live in the luxury of a centrally air-conditioned, oversized, high-ceilinged loft where she'll never again have to deal with a window unit breaking down at the peak of a heat wave (*Why did Michael not bother fixing this before he left town?!*), or lament over the ineffectiveness of backup fans, oscillating or not.

But now it feels wildly natural and awakening to be grasping at sweaty skin in the dark, heavy heat of night. It's been extra warm this summer, but unlike the slightly neurotic, easily irritated New Yorker she's become, right now she doesn't mind it one bit. For the first time in what feels like, well, ever, she is physically catapulted right back to those Texas nights in the flatbed of Declan's truck. She can almost hear the Dixie Chicks cutting through the air between their breathless bodies, can almost feel the flip phone Mama and Daddy finally gave her that Christmas of junior year, vibrating across metal from the back pocket of the cut-up jeans that were not on her body where they belonged.

Having adult sex with your high school boyfriend is equal parts familiar and new. It's the same territory but the landscape is spotted with unknown curves and jolts, elongated slightly in certain places and now muscular in others. He is beneath her, his ankles wrapped around her own as if to hold her there, above him indefinitely. To clutch her close in any way he possibly can. She closes her eyes and opens them again, unsure if she wants to feel every wave of their connectedness without seeing, or if it would be better to watch the beautiful face she first loved reaching his climax, to search his eyes for as many glimpses of the past as she can find. To have that one visual memory of the deep love she has left behind.

Declan reaches up then, his hand outstretched toward her face. With his right wrist draped around the back of her neck, he slowly pulls her torso down, to seal the end with a kiss. She closes her eyes, deciding. *It will be better to remember this. Just like this, the feeling of him kissing me.* She is too lost in the roller coaster symmetry of her soaring thoughts and tingling body to let the guilt flood in. But it will come later. Even in patchy drunken glimpses, she can already feel that.

When they're done and the moans have subsided and turned into quiet sighs, he pulls her in close instead of turning away like Michael does (*Don't think about that right now!*), holds her whole person against his. They are one long, intermingled entity soaking sweat through a white sheet. They are not just now, of course, but then.

They are football games and heartbreak, folded paper notes scratched into looseleaf, and school-wide mortification. They are tears falling in milkshakes and late hours spent awake in bed thinking about each other long after the night was over. They are laughter by the creek and sex in the woods, the pit in your stomach when you find out what it feels like to fall in love and then lose it faster than you could have prepared for. They are every teenage American love story and yet absolutely no one's but their own.

He breathes warm and slow against the side of her neck, whispers something into her ear that she cannot hear. She doesn't want to ruin the moment by asking him to repeat it, so she just nods in silent agreement to something that she's sure is true.

The moon is so high and bright tonight it sheds a streak of white light into the room. Life is good and real and she is alive. These are the thoughts that skirt across her wild mind. Sure, the wine is talking some, but quietly. On a level she isn't quite ready to admit, even to herself, she must have known this could happen. Must have wanted it to, in some small and hidden way.

At six o'clock in the morning, Dolly wakes with a start, chilled and sticky, her body realizing it is still wrapped in places around Declan. Slowly she peels her skin from his, rolls away toward the opposite wall, and rises from the bed. If not for the digital alarm clock on her bedside table reading red numbers against the blackened din, she could have believed it was either five minutes later, or an entire year. The events of the night she's just lived through are very fresh and clear in her mind, but a sense of having been here before, having known this might happen, also sits within her.

She pads out to the kitchen and reaches into the cabinet for her yellow cup. One of her mother's quirky estate sale finds, Dolly has always cherished this cup with a past she won't ever know about. Etched out of bright glass in a fun and whimsical pattern, it features one tiny chip at its base and it cost exactly 10 cents. It is her favorite and it always will be, having randomly charmed her mother at that sale all those years ago.

Dolly relaxes best when drinking orange juice out of this cup. So, she pours some into it and takes a seat at the tiny table in her kitchenette. She must unpack the events of the night and figure out what she is going to do about the morning that is to come. But here in the waning moonlight, drinking orange juice out of her mama's little yellow cup, she is free to come to absolutely no conclusion. Outside of the fact that it is time to pick up some more orange juice, since she's just about run out.

THEN

As winter held firm, Dolly and Declan found their way back to a solid place together. Things with Steph weren't perfect, but they were healing. Dolly was so tired these days between cheerleading, school, editing the school paper, and keeping up with her social life that sometimes she wondered if she should cut back in some way. Declan obviously wasn't what she was willing to give up, but the day she quit the cheer team was also when her friendship with Stephanie would start to heal for real. It wasn't an easy decision to make, but she just couldn't keep up anymore. After doing so, she felt nothing but relief.

Slowly, Dolly and Stephanie got into a new rhythm of walking to school together, like they hadn't done since sophomore year. They would meet at the halfway point between the top of their two streets and enjoy some quiet, conspiratorial conversation and light exercise without the interruption of their parents, boyfriends, or other friends. It felt important to skip that morning drive, that time with Declan, and give it back to her best friend.

They were timid about opening up in their early talks, but one thing was quite clear between them: discussing the fight that had gotten them into this muddy stage of friendship was an absolute *no*. The girls were content to focus instead on mutual, lighthearted territory like all the cheer team gossip Dolly was missing now that she'd begged off for the semester. It was obvious that their own tiff a couple months back was nowhere near the radar of social upset or intrigue, as newer and even more ridiculous squabbles and rifts erupted amongst the rest of the girls in their social circle.

A few days before Valentine's Day, Dolly blew a kiss in the direction of Declan's house as she walked past it to meet Steph on the corner. She *missed* him; missed suddenly, weepily, how they had been over the summer. It felt so long ago and far beyond her grasp, those carefree days splashed with summer sun. Things were good between them now, building back up in a somewhat timid way, not dissimilarly to how things were rearranging with Steph. Every time she was in the vicinity of Declan, Dolly's body still felt electric. When they kissed, she still saw tiny stars shooting across the backs of her eyelids. Their breakup had left a mark, sure, but not one that could replace or ruin all the good. What she wouldn't give to just get more time with him though. Hopefully, spring break would be here before they knew it. Maybe that would allow them some extra freedom to be together.

Dolly paused at the end of their street and waited for Stephanie to arrive. As always, she was all legs in a short corduroy skirt and knee-high boots with those shiny auburn curls cascading down her slender shoulders. Steph had really grown up in the past two years from a knobby-kneed kid with a space between her two front teeth who loved sports and didn't mind getting in trouble for staying out too late competing with the boys. A year and a half with a retainer, some decent frizz serum, and the physical and social benefits of cheerleading since the fall of sophomore year, and Steph was practically a new person.

Despite the issues their friendship had faced, Dolly looked up at her best friend and felt suddenly, awkwardly moved to tears. "Dolly! What is it?" Steph asked, her mouth unsure whether to smile or not, her lips parted in the faintest quiver.

"I just love you," Dolly said quietly, and Steph came closer and pulled her into a hug. Months later, when she needed her best friend the most, she'd come back to this moment and remember. That sometimes, even when you think they've walked out, a true best friend can never really leave you. Not as long as the memory of what you had doesn't.

NOW

After about an hour lost in thought and flipping through the pages of an old issue of *The New Yorker*, Dolly rinses her juice cup. With now-sober eyes she looks about the apartment and suppresses a chuckle at how obvious the details of her night are. They read like the pages of a choose-your-own-adventure book where the choice being made was to betray one's fiancé. The chain lock is latched and the umbrella stand beside the door is off-tilt, having been knocked aside during their passionate, handsy entrance.

The tiny red skirt lies feet from the door and inches beyond that are her shoes. A trail of clothes and accessories—here, his belt; there, her cell phone—litters the shortest route to the couch and then the bedroom, and all around the air is thick with heat and the scent of sex. Despite having cracked open the bedroom window, the lack of air conditioning is obvious now in the fresh heat of morning. Last night is over, but in the light of day the betrayal continues.

Dolly knows she doesn't have long to figure out how to tactfully get Declan out of the apartment and start cleaning up. She also knows that she has some major thinking to do, but it'll have to wait. Michael didn't specify when he'd be returning. These weekend jaunts typically return him directly to the office on Monday morning, but she doesn't want to risk it. Michael could always get home early and come bounding eagerly over to her apartment, excited to share news of a closed deal or just to hug her, to put on a pot of coffee and ask her about her night.

She chastises herself for thinking so carelessly of Michael, a man she loves. The man she is supposed to marry. He might put his job and his mild obsession with working out before her sometimes, but this is New York—who doesn't do at least one of those things? What is wrong with her that she can't make herself feel the guilt she is supposed to, that she doesn't long for Michael the way she should? That she isn't hunched over in a corner sick with anger at herself. Instead all she can think of is Declan's deft hands on her body.

Lost in thought, Dolly has started to pick up around the apartment, folding and smoothing the edges of Declan's discarded clothing and creating a pile of them on the velvet couch. She throws open both living room windows and starts up the oscillating fan to move it around the space. Once the living area is tidy, with couch cushions fluffed and obvious evidence of last night's infidelity cleared, she moves on to the kitchen. Here, she sweeps the floor, wipes down the countertops, and replaces the dreary dish towel hanging from her oven handle with a crisp one featuring her monogram in yellow thread against white waffle knit.

It starts to feel like eons have taken place between her early-morning departure from the bed and this moment of looking around at a clean apartment. Dolly has to smile then at the thought of one thing both of the men in her heart seem to have in common: a propensity toward sleeping off a hangover for far longer than she ever could.

Filling a fresh glass at the tap, she moves light-footed toward the bedroom and turns the knob, feels the familiar shift of floor boards beneath her feet as she crosses the threshold into the room. There he lies, her high school boyfriend, snoring softly with his back to where she stands. Her white cotton sheet is the only thing covering him, and just to the waist. His back is wider now than it used to be, the muscles more developed, but only slightly. From behind, in sleep, he looks almost exactly like he did then. She watches the ribs expand and contract with each breath, takes in the sandy blond hair that, while straight, never seemed to go exactly where Declan wanted it to, and still doesn't. She wants to twist it in her finger a while, wants to bury her nose in the nape of his neck.

This particular view, watching Declan sleeping from behind, is especially familiar. In this moment Dolly realizes that the last time she got to truly take him in, observe him in a moment of peace and quiet, he was resting exactly as he is now. It was right after everything... when they finally had some time to rest. That day comes back to her in a flash of colors and sounds, of tears and light blues, the smells of blood and antiseptic.

She remembers it from time to time in both agony and tiny slices of joy. A day that could have been, maybe should have been, the most important in their lives. Well, it was, actually, but not for the right reasons. So much has transpired between then and now, but in this moment all Dolly can see is that back, at once muscle-ridden and bony. All she can think of is what might have been.

(And maybe, what could still be?)

THEN

Reluctantly, Dolly had invited Mama in and accepted the piping-hot cup of tea on offer. She sat with her legs bent up toward her chest and her sweat-soaked hair pulled back into the sloppiest ponytail in three counties.

"What am I going to do about all this?" The words came out before she could edit or think them over.

For the first time ever, Sally Weston, whose support and love had stretched out over every child and now teenager in the neighborhood for years, was silent.

The woman with all the answers had none.

NOW

Dolly watches Declan quietly in slumber until the reality of the approaching day sets in and she begins to contemplate how she will wake him up and get him out. First, though, she creeps across the room toward the bed, places the glass of water that is in her hand onto the bedside table, and sneaks in between the sheets.

She puts her nose to the nape of his neck after all, not quite against it but grazing its surface. The scents of sweat and alcohol mingle together with the cologne he applied at least twelve hours ago. She closes her eyes and remembers the rest —leather and dirt, cut grass and cheap beer, the aromas of romance and high school that emanated off him back in the day.

When enough time has passed that the weight of guilt begins to push heavily upon her psyche, Dolly reaches her left hand toward his cheek, stroking it gently as she whispers that it's time to wake up. He startles in waking, turns to face her, his eyes studying hers and not ready for words.

She isn't either, and there they remain a minute longer, stares catching each other's, dancing somewhere between the past and the now. Before she can come up with the right way to end all this and get him out the door so she can *think*, Declan comes out with the one thing he should have said last night and didn't.

"Are you engaged?"

It doesn't take a genius to intuit that the four-karat diamond resting on her left ring finger means that she is permanently attached to another man. In another world, under other circumstances, she can imagine feeling bitter with Declan for asking, and even vindictive here in a positive reply. But instead the simple word that comes out feels weird. It bears with it love for another man but a lot of other conflicting thoughts she didn't know she had until last night.

"Yes." Her voice sounds dry and a little pained.

There is relief and sadness with the affirmation. There is the knowledge that the man who gave her the ring is a good one, that she will have a good life with him by her side. There is also the hollowness that last night has created; because now there is a hole inside her engagement. A gaping one at that.

And although Dolly loves Michael and knows she wants to marry him, what happened last night did happen, and it was for a reason. Right? Her past with Declan is murky and complicated, but for all his mistakes, he could have also been "the one." How does she reconcile the decisions she made with the soft blue eyes darting back and forth between her own? How does she explain that she remembers loving him, but that her future belongs to someone else?

She doesn't know how to say any of this, isn't even sure what she feels. So she busies herself with getting up and out of bed, handing him his things in the living room, leaning in for a hug goodbye. Now she looks at him, the bright eyes she never stopped loving burning holes into her face. She can only imagine how she looks to him now, pathetic and torturous. Cruel.

Dolly has no idea when or if she'll ever see him again, and the sudden thought is melancholy.

"I guess I'll see you around then," he says, and she can feel the sadness in his voice, too. Last night *did* mean something, and she can't place her finger on what. Was it just sex with an ex, the most basic of self-inflicted cruelties? Was it just getting lost in memory, missing their young selves, or was it more? In the light of day, with a clear head about her, Dolly is starting to realize that the past might do better to rest right where it lies.

"I guess so, Dec," she says as he leans in to place a brief kiss on her lips, before stepping into his shoes and heading out the door. Dolly walks over to it, her bare feet soft against the glossy hardwoods. She presses the door fully closed until it clicks, and leans against its metal fortitude. She sighs hard, unsure whether to laugh or cry. It's the second time in less than twenty-four hours that the biggest thought she can decipher from the rest is how much she wishes she could call her mother and talk about everything that is happening.

Silently, she glances upward and nods. Mama might not be here, but Dolly feels in her bones that she can see what's going on. She has no idea what her mother would make of all this —her proper and sweet Southern daughter sleeping with her high school ex when she's engaged to be married to another man. But she knows one thing for sure: Mama would stick with her while she figured it out.

A few hours later, Michael makes a surprise Saturday afternoon return and Dolly's first thought is relief that the apartment is clean and shows no obvious signs of cheating. In his usual way, her fiancé turns his key in the lock and enters as if he owns the place, startling momentarily at the sight of her, so obviously hungover on the couch.

"I thought you'd be at yoga—hi!" explains the confused look on his face as he makes it across the floor in three strides and lifts her up into a hug.

"Hi," she whispers back, reaching up one hand to frame the

side of his face in it. Michael is clean-shaven and smells like spring rain. There are tiny beads of perspiration forming on the back of his neck and she feels suddenly re-aware of how hot it is in this damn apartment.

"Do you wanna go to your place?" she asks. "It's hotter than Hell in here!"

"We can, but I'd much rather warm up than cool off."

The silly line, she thinks, is just a precursor to what marriage will be like. How do married people come on to each other, anyway? It's kind of a scary thought. She has sat through business lunches actively keeping her jaw clenched shut to avoid letting her mouth hang open in shock at hearing women in their thirties and forties admit that they have to schedule sex with their husbands. Like, in their actual Blackberry calendars. These days, both she and Michael are pretty much always up for it, but sometimes his lines make her want to roll her eyes more than take off her clothes.

Are these quirks the parts of a person you grow to love more and more as you grow old together, or the things that eventually create cracks that lead to wedges? It's a ridiculous train of thought she knows, looking up at her handsome fiancé whom she can feel growing hard against her leg. Any girl in Manhattan would be lucky to land a guy like Michael, not only in the bedroom but with the power vested by New York State.

So, why does she suddenly feel awkward? She goes through the motions of sex with Michael at first now, eventually getting into it and climaxing quietly with her hands running up and down his spine. She lies in bed beside him afterward on sheets that have been changed since this morning. It's only after she has sex with her future husband that Dolly registers she has slept with two men in less than 24 hours. And like one blow hitting right after another, she realizes that this one is supposed to be the only man she looks at, ever again.

Feeling desperately sorry all of a sudden, and terribly confused, Dolly buries her head into his chest and whispers, "I love
you." Maybe if she can hear it back, she'll be able to erase what
happened last night, be able to move toward forgetting it all?

But when he returns the sentiment, smiling in postcoital bliss
like a teenager himself, Dolly feels even sadder than she did
before. In front of her eyes, stretched out naked and vulnerable in her bed, is a good man with a good heart, who will
treat her well. Who was there for her when her mother died,
even though he was only a brand-new part of her life. A man
who has never walked out on her when times got tough. He
is beautiful and kind, and all he wants in the world for her is
joy and success. She is lucky to have him, oh, *lucky*. The word
imprints in her mind; she wants to whisper it, to hear it in her
own voice. She closes her eyes and sees it in swirls of purple
and blue.

You are lucky to have him, Dolly, the voice comes from within.
Don't fuck it up.

GOODBYE

Everything turns black. The deepest black she has never known.

Paramedics and police arrive in minutes and a team of highly skilled professionals pull Sally from the wrecked SUV. Her not-quite-lifeless body is placed on a stretcher and an ambulance screams its way down the main road to Sugar's Bend Emergency ICU sooner than Avery Longman, Stephanie's kid brother, can even get his statement out to the police.

At SBH, the doctors try to revive her unsuccessfully. Dale will have a chance to say goodbye to her sleeping eyes, to confirm the identity of the body because that is all she will be by the time he is allowed in the room. He can't know it, but she sees him there one last time.

"I'm here, sweetheart, I'm here," he blubber-screams from the doorway over the beeps and whirring, the shouting doctors. A nurse blocks his entrance at the threshold of the door. "Please," her panicked eyes dart back and forth as she hisses, "Please, sir, wait outside."

Dale can only hope this is because there is a chance; he doesn't want to understand it's because there actually isn't. Minutes later, he hears those words hollow and scary like he has so many times in the movies or on TV. "Time of death 8:42." *Just like how they say it on 'Greys' Anatomy', baby!,* he wants to tell his wife, forgetting for a split-second that the death is hers.

Defeated and apologetic, the medical team slowly exits the

room, the protective, harried nurse with the darty eyes reaching out a hand toward his shoulder as the head doctor mutters his apologies. *We tried everything, but it was too late.*

Fuck their trying, he thinks bitterly as he enters the room, finally; as he crouches over her tenderly as if not to hurt her, not to cover her nose or mouth. He can taste the salty tears before he knows they're flowing, sees them fall onto her face in a stream. "Oh, God," the words form from somewhere deep inside. "Oh... oh, God. I am going to miss you, sweetheart." He cups her cheeks in his palms, holds her in this way, one last time.

She is gone but remains in the room just a moment. Her pull to the light of what's next is strong, but in her mind, in her spirit, she wraps her arms around the man at the center of her world and says a silent promise to never be too far away. He cannot feel or know this final embrace, but as the years go by he will comfort himself by hoping something like it was happening. *What a life. What a life they had.*

He has to leave the room eventually. Their time is officially up. With a silent prayer, Dale Weston takes one more fleeting look at his beloved, and turns away toward the hallway. The white fluorescent lights are jarring and the smell of Hospital— that notable blend of chicken soup, antiseptic, and sickness— hits strong.

Life as he knows it is over. But even worse, so is the life of the one he loves most in the world.

NOW

Late summer in New York is beautiful in a way Dolly never expected before she lived here, back when she was a teenager with a far-away dream. She imagined angles and corners, a twisted and elegant reality emerging in grayscale as far as the eye could see. Never did it occur to a seventeen-year-old Dolly that there would be so many trees and flowers here.

Today, the seasonal dwindle of flowering trees that dots the sidewalks seems to be almost showing off. The daylight lasts luxuriously late into the early evenings now, dripping a honey-hued glow across the rooftops. This morning, she can see from her window how the early light makes puddles left over from a pre-dawn rain twinkle. Anyone who dubs this city a "concrete jungle" doesn't know what they're talking about, because Dolly Mae Weston, a newer but enamored Manhattanite, can attest to the fact that in spring and summer, there is so much nature mixed in with the buildings, it will take your breath away. She hasn't even left the apartment yet, and that buzzing summer beauty is tossing itself all around the windows like a song.

Dolly is filled with mixed emotions (mostly good) about heading off to her rescheduled wedding dress appointment. It's been a long few weeks trying to push Declan out of her mind, trying to shove him back down deep inside where he belongs, with the rest of the memories she no longer has a use for. She is still not sure what made her do what she did, and she knows that she should come clean to Michael, but she hasn't figured out what to say yet. Moving forward with wedding planning seems like a way to show her commitment rather than tell it, and that's about all she has the wherewithal for right now.

Mostly, she feels happy and light. Hopeful, too. She is wearing the vintage Cartier watch her parents gave her for college graduation and a pair of black cigarette pants with a white silk Joie top French-tucked on the right side. She slips into her favorite Louboutin driving mocs (a gift from Sandra last Christmas), and kisses Michael's forehead on her way out the door. She will never understand why that man prefers this overheated, somewhat cramped (he says cozy), apartment over his luxurious one downtown. But while she's still here, they may as well enjoy it. She loves this place and knows she'll miss it at summer's end when the boxes are all packed up and the floors swept clean one last time. When she moves out, and in turn grows up more than she's ever done. Says goodbye to her single self and becomes the woman of somebody else's house.

Down to the lobby and out the front door she goes, deciding to brave the subway this morning with the full knowledge that she'll be cabbing back after too many glasses of champagne with John-John and the girls at the appointment. Dolly allows herself to get lost in the excitement, the utter day dream of heading to one of the most esteemed bridal ateliers in Manhattan to pick out her wedding dress. Even though she might not have had those childhood daydreams about her wedding day that so many other littles girls do, she feels the weight and the joy of the occasion looming.

Dolly might not have pictured a wedding dress, per se, but she did have couture dreams as a child. There was a small dress shop in Sugar's Bend, and she remembers passing it hand-in-hand with her mother. If she closes her eyes for a moment she can picture the thick chiffons and heavy silks, the puffed sleeves and extra-long trains a couple seasons past chic on display in the front window. And most treasured is her memory from that day at Neiman's with her mom and the dress they fell in love with together.

Now, thanks to the internet and social media everyone thinks they're fancy, and even the cheap bridal shops do their best to stay on-trend. But the beauty and promise of today brings with it the nostalgia of a time gone by, a time when she pictured herself in those dresses staring back at her from inside the dusty windows. She always knew she was meant for more than such a small town had to offer, but as an innocent little girl, that shop window was enough to make her smile with a large and burning hope.

She was never really chasing a wedding, but a life of glamour. Those magical moments staring into the bridal shop window were more about a hunger for anything and everything couture. By far, a no-name bridal gown was the highest fashion anyone could really hope to see in Sugar's Bend itself. Dolly grew up with a silent understanding that her place was to be among tastemakers. Her dreams had very little to do with a man but everything to do with fabric and luxury. Now, as it's turned out, she'll have both.

The thrill is tingling inside her. If there is one group of people who could make the tragic void of her mother's absence bearable, it's this one. Dolly smiles wide as she turns the corner toward the bridal shop, sees them standing out front in sundresses and shorts with balloons and booze. The perfect mix of cheesy and chic, her work-wife and industry husband, and their closest other friends, stand outside the door looking like heaven. To a girl who's lost her mother, a support system like this means more than anything else could. Dolly squeals as she approaches them, anticipating the moment she's about to experience.

"Let's do this, y'all!" she says, giving them each a grateful squeeze, one after the other. John-John pulls open a heavy glass door and the six-deep crew enters the salon, ready for whatever might happen next.

In the cozy atelier, Dolly pans the length of the two silvery leather couches before her to take in her New York family. John-John has never looked at her with such pride, with such promise. She tries dress after dress to their constant enthusiasm, but there's one in particular that she's been eyeing most heavily from the start. And when she comes out in that ivory silk sheath with its generous train, even Glinda, who is a bit of a marriage-phobe, sheds a tear.

"You look like Greta Garbo!" John-John tops off the girls' champagne flutes before walking toward Dolly for a closer look at the detail. "Turn, honey," he instructs. The open back of the gown shows off her tanned skin; the bottom swishes with her movement.

"How do you feel?"

Dolly turns back to take herself in, to admire the dress as her friends are. She can admit to herself that she does look beautiful, that the shiny silk hugs her minimal curves in a way that no dress ever has before. That, she feels a tear forming as she realizes silently, her mother would *love it.*

"I feel like I need more time," she admits, catching John-John's eyes again.

Something akin to panic flashes across her friend's face, but he doesn't acknowledge it out loud. "Then, that's it. Let's get you changed and think about it over lunch."

"Okay," she nods, afraid if she looks up into his eyes again, she'll cry. "Thanks, guys," she mutters in the direction of her friends. "I guess we'll have to book another appointment."

"I could get used to this!" Veronica nods, lifting her glass. "I'm definitely in for round two!"

Twenty minutes later, they tuck into a corner booth at a café around the corner and order a round of prosecco and a bunch of appetizers to share. Dress shopping might not have gone how she'd envisioned it, but looking around at the smiling and supportive faces of her close friends, she still feels the day was a success.

* * * * *

If she's honest, shopping for a wedding dress without her mother there was harder than she expected. Now that hours have passed, and she's moved on to her second glass of French rosé, feet up on the coffee table, she can admit this to herself. Being surrounded by her dearest New York friends on the occasion when she is expected to select a gown for the absolute most important day of her life rendered her feeling guilty and —oddly—a bit lonely.

John-John and the girls were delicious, even when she tried on a ball gown for Michael's sake that they all knew was wrong. And lunch afterward was relaxing and fun, but now she is so tired and confused, her head spins.

Tonight Michael has Yankees tickets and Dolly declined his invite to join because she needed time to herself. And, if she's honest, really, a break from life. It's getting harder and harder for her to differentiate between her feelings about what happened with Declan and classic cold feet. When Michael is in the room, and she looks over at him, she is consumed by all the feelings. Michael is comfort. He is warmth and sturdiness; her future wrapped up in a Tiffany bow.

But when she's left alone with her thoughts, confusion

mounts. Memories of Declan then and now come crashing into her mind... flashes of sweat and laughter, the ripping off of clothes. The tenderness with which he held her face between his hands, the little details she didn't linger on and wished she could have. The pretending that this place was theirs, if only for a night.

What has she become? A cheater. That much is clear even though it hurts to admit. In the moment, she told herself that it didn't count as cheating if it happens with someone from your past. If your number doesn't go up. The wine blurred the edges of her reasoning and the past lured her in with a magnetism she couldn't have denied. In the weeks that have unfolded since, he's called a few times, and she's been pleased with herself for not picking up or returning his calls. But now that she is purposely avoiding outings with Michael and refusing to pick a wedding dress, she sits with herself in the dark and has to wonder why.

* * * * *

At nine-thirty, there is a soft knock on the door and a weighted pause. Dolly has fallen asleep on the couch, shrouded in an old chunky scarf of her mother's. A rapid succession of worst-case scenarios flash through her mind as the knock wakes her—it's a murderer, it's Declan, it's a drunk neighbor she'll have to deal with through gritted teeth. Michael never knocks, so it can't be him.

Dolly tiptoes across the floor gingerly and presses her face up to it, blinking into the peephole out to the hallway. She sighs in relief and reaches down with one hand to unlock the door. There, in fitted sweatpants and a tank top he's likely fashioned himself out of an oversized vintage tee, is John-John with a bottle of wine.

"What are you doing here?" Her voice sounds croaky and tired.

"My bitch is getting married at the Plaza in less than a year and can't pick a dress? We obviously need to talk."

Dolly sighs, lets him into the apartment. *He's right, he knows...* She hasn't even said anything yet and already feels better because she has been seen and understood. All of the hiding and secrets, all of the colorful lies and the ones made only by omission. Someone cares enough to see through her facade and reach out. Finally, the moment has come to unburden herself; the moment to revisit it all herself... the moment to make some decisions.

THEN

The summer between junior and senior years was oppressively hot in the way that only Texas knows how to do summer heat. Day after day, that unrelenting, overwhelmingly intense air hit you in the face the second you stepped outside. It filled your nose and your mouth, turned silk and linen to an instant mess of wrinkles. It was staying-inside weather, unless you had a real reason you needed to do otherwise. And Dolly, decidedly, did not.

On a seemingly unremarkable Wednesday around noon, Dolly reclined on the living room couch wearing her lightest-weight sundress, even its thin material a cruel barrier between herself and the air conditioning. A window unit whirred at a constant pitch throughout the open kitchen and living room area, but the heat somehow managed to seep through every crack and corner of that dang house. Their central air was two decades old and not cutting it, so Daddy had picked up extras for the main area of the house and the bedrooms. Still, Dolly was miserable even though everyone else felt it was working.

Dolly's now-waist-length, dirty blond hair that usually fell straight down her back had taken on a surprising wave in the recent months. Today it sat piled at the top of her head where she'd collected it into an absolutely massive chignon earlier in the morning. A few tendrils had fallen around her temples, but the rest of it knew better than to budge.

She flipped idly through the television channels, willing Declan to call. But if there was anything she'd learned by this point in their relationship, it was that you can't make a man do something he wasn't planning to do already.

Correction: a boy.

You can't make a selfish teenage *boy* do anything that wasn't his idea. And if it comes to light that things won't necessarily happen on his exact terms, then you'll be lucky to have him show up at all when you need him around.

Maybe it was fear and maybe it was the deep-seated insecurities that life (and his parents) had set up in him from a young age. A few years on down the road when Dolly would fall into bed with heartbreaker after heartbreaker, each with his own complicated emotional problems or complete lack of empathy, she would think back to this week—actually to this very day—of her life, and wonder if her destiny was to be matched with men who didn't get it.

That song he had written for her last year and strummed on his guitar in the back of the truck that midsummer night came back to her now in waves, but mostly just its lyrics. It had been months since she'd heard him sing it, but the words were still a jumble in her weary mind. Sometimes she caught herself mouthing them silently, a personal plea for life to go back to what it had been, or at least morph into what it could be:

...And I will wait for you // And I will see this through // And you will not see me break free.

It used to feel like they were written in the stars, but now the writing was on the wall. While she was spending more and more time relaxing and trying to make the most of this last high school summer, Declan was out with his friends as often as possible. Later he would come crawling into her bed, telling her how much he loved her but it was always hours after she wanted him around. She could feel what was coming next from a mile (or now, a day) away. And it broke her heart into enough pieces that all she wanted to do was turn off the words playing over and over in mind.

But she couldn't. Because when you're young and in love, sometimes you can't turn away even when it hurts worse than you ever could have imagined.

And we will stick this out // And we can withstand doubt // And we can reach forever, Dolly...

NOW

John-John collects his friend into the kind of hug that only someone who truly knows you and loves you with all of your flaws can do. It's pretty miraculous that she hasn't even hinted at anything being wrong, but he can tell. He can see her mess and he's come here to help her tidy it up, to give her the chance to unburden herself. She deserves that, doesn't she?

Dolly has been distant lately but she could easily explain that away by saying she wants to give him and Roman space to develop their relationship. Not picking a wedding dress on the first big day of shopping also wouldn't have been the biggest deal if it was an isolated event. But John-John knows his best friend better than anyone does, even her fiancé, he dares to admit. And there's more going on with her lately than all the well-meaning check-in text messages or nights on the town could fix.

So here he is with chilled rosé and an open mind, delivering one pointed final squeeze before he pulls back, holds up the bottle, and declares, "Let's open this sucker and have a chat."

The words spill out of Dolly in a rush of passion and pain. She explains about her complicated past with Declan, how they started and how they ended. All of the tiny pieces of her heart that stayed behind in Sugar's Bend when she moved up here to put it all behind her.

She tells John-John about her mother for the first time, *really* tells him. "After my best friend from high school and I fell out, my mom was truly my only friend for a long time. Honestly… until I met Glinda, and then you." He smiles warmly.

"Even in college, I trusted no one," she goes on, just above a whisper. "I went out and got wasted and went back to boys' dorm rooms. Slept around, smoked weed, went shopping. I hung around, but I never got close to the other girls. I just couldn't."

John-John inhales deep, blows it out slowly from puffed cheeks. He understands.

"You and I might have more in common than you think," he winks as he embarks on the details of his own college experience. They've touched on their differing experiences being from the South. She knows he grew up in Arkansas. She could tell he was from the South the second she met him, as he still carries the tiniest hint of a Southern twang in his voice. It comes out like hers does, in random expressions that he can't give up, once he hits his second or third cocktail, or when his emotions are strong.

But as she knows, he is not the product of incredibly sensitive or understanding parents. Dolly had no idea before today if his father even speaks to him now that he is openly gay and makes his living as a makeup artist. Now he details their broken relationship and recounts what it was like at the very conservative university he attended in South Carolina. Her throat feels itchy with empathy.

"I couldn't let anyone in because I had this big secret," he says now, clearing his own throat and then lubricating it with a big swig of the wine.

"Same," she nods, reaches out to squeeze his hand. "Exact same."

A comfortable moment of quiet reflection passes between them before they return to the issues at hand. "So what's going on now, then?" His eyes search hers for a reason that she won't pick a dress, hasn't been herself in months.

"Well," she breathes out, "For starters, I slept with Declan three weeks ago."

"Oh, boy." She expects a chastising shake of the head or at least another moment of silence, but instead John-John bursts into laughter and then covers his mouth in a mock-gasp. "Why, Dolly Mae! I declare," the deeply accented teasing drips with empathy and love, and the chance to laugh about this mess she's created is too good to pass up. Dolly begins to crack up herself at the absurdity and the inevitability of the whole thing.

"When *exactly* did this happen?" John-John asks when their boisterous laughter has slowed and quieted to conspiratorial chuckles and grins.

"The night you introduced us to Roman," she confesses, eyes downcast for a moment.

He nods, putting the pieces together and taking another sip of wine. "So, *that's* why you ran out on us," his smile remains infectious and she can't help but focus on the positive here. Which is why his next question comes as almost no surprise whatsoever:

"So, how was it?"

"Honestly? Even better than I remembered."

THE OTHER GIRL

Dolly and Declan had been seeing each other with decent frequency over the weekends and after practice until the summer hit and everything went quieter and colder between them despite the heat outside. The world was a new place for Dolly these days and sometimes Declan seemed to be on board while others, he was making his own plans.

That early August afternoon Dolly lay on the couch flipping through the channels with a boring magazine splayed out on her stomach, her legs bent into triangles with her feet propped up on the coffee table next to a large glass of ice water. Her mother wasn't due home from her errands about town for another hour or so, but suddenly the urgent pressing need to have her here, *now*, overcame Dolly. She knew she should call Declan, too, and he'd want to be here despite their recent semi-distance, but first and foremost, she needed her mama.

No one was quite prepared for what was about to happen, but happen it would. And there was nothing they could do to prevent it, but maybe by facing it, they could start the healing process, even as things all fell apart.

* * * * *

The wallpaper was mauve with little white flowers, a pattern not unattractive but also not something that would have been her first choice. There was an off-white curtain hanging from the ceiling with one small mark on its upper left corner. She fixated on that one spot every time the waves of pain came in too strong to bear. There were so many people in the room saying different things and moving around in a blur, at times it felt like a dream.

Maybe it was a dream. Maybe this whole season of her life had been ripped out of the unconscious nighttime musings of a lovesick, overwhelmed teenager. Maybe her physical ailments and the complicated layers of disagreement with Declan would disappear if she could just open her eyes and shake it all off.

But in the actual here and now, Dolly could hear her mother saying encouraging words and could feel Declan's quiet presence beside her, locking eyes with her every time she looked his way. Mouthing "I love you" when she needed the reminder the most. And then with screams all around, they witnessed bursting into the room the girl who would change the course of their love, of their lives, forever.

Seven pounds, eleven ounces and sporting the sweetest little patch of blond curls at the top of her head. Ten fingers, ten toes, and eyes so icy blue it almost hurt to look into them.

Dolly looked down at the tiny creature for the first time and burst into uncontrollable tears. She was so perfect and beautiful, every bit the dream come true. But it was a dream meant for another time, another place... maybe even another man? What dream was this, after all, that had splintered their relationship while giving them the best gift they could ever want?

All throughout the back end of junior year as her middle had grown steadily beneath oversized hoodies and later, floaty sundresses, Declan had taken every chance he could to cuddle up and whisper to her belly. When she'd first told him the news, it had come as a shock. But he was a good boy, and he loved her, and he would do "what was right," he said.

But that was just it. There was nothing "right" about this.

They were a couple of high school kids with no money and no-where to live as a family. His parents had gone from enraged to ashamed to excited, and wanted Dolly to come live with them and raise the baby at their house. Her parents thought that was outrageous. They pushed for adoption, knowing their only daughter had so much more to accomplish. But they also knew it wasn't their choice to make.

These past few months the disagreement over what they should do had caused a rift between Dolly and Declan. Angry over her unwillingness to march, rotund, down to City Hall, Declan had turned away emotionally and physically.

Well, that wasn't fair. He had come to her doctor's appoint-ments and left mint chocolate chip sundaes on the front porch of her home, knocking three times and turning to leave so as not to see her barefoot and pregnant, so as not to feel his heart breaking more and more with each day that she refused to marry him.

But in the hours after the birth of their daughter, everything was peaceful and dim. They kept the lights low and De-clan rubbed her shoulders tenderly, sniffling with joy in lit-tle bursts. Both sets of middle-aged grandparents took brief turns nuzzling the little girl they were afraid to get too close to while they awaited their teenage children's decision. And then the young couple was left alone with the simple white noise of the persistent air conditioning and the occasional tap on the door and click of the heels from the on-call nurses to check that Dolly and the baby were doing well.

Every now and then they would trade off napping for an hour, each taking a long turn holding their daughter so the other could sleep off some of the emotion, some of the hardship.

During Dolly's turns allowing him to sleep, her gaze would shift between the newborn in her arms whose little face was scrunched up in dreams, and the shirtless back of her gorgeous boyfriend, taking his nap on the small cot that had been dragged into the room, turned away from her in fetal position, etching those muscles and bones into her memory forever.

She watched him now, ribs expanding as he breathed in sleep. Wondered what he dreamt of, what his thoughts would be on waking. Wondered if they could take this little girl home and raise her. If they'd be okay at that; if they should even try.

* * * * *

On the same day that Dolly had their baby, a woman down the hall had given birth to a baby girl whose heart had only beat for mere minutes after her arrival. It had been a healthy pregnancy, they heard in whispered murmurings, and there were numerous details of the tragedy making their way up and down the maternity ward. The night after giving birth to her daughter, Dolly took a triumphant walk down the hall to ease the swelling in the bottom half of her body and demonstrate to her doctor, and to Declan, that she was ready to go home despite having lost some blood and feeling woozy after the birth.

The hallway was tiled lemon-yellow and the wall decor was sparse despite how populated the ward was. Dolly made her way down toward its end, having left her unnamed baby in her boyfriend's arms for what she didn't quite know would be one of the last times. As she approached the nursery she noticed a woman with tousled blond hair, standing up but leaning against the wall at the edge of the window into a large room filled with tiny, wheeled cots. She had a rounded middle and was in a hospital-issued gown like the one Dolly wore, clearly having recently given birth as well. The woman was looking in on the babies with tenderness and ease, the hint of a smile at the corner of her lips, her eyes misty.

Dolly thought small talk might help her own confusing feelings, so as she approached the stranger she asked, "Which one is yours?"

The woman, caught in her own thoughts for long enough to almost not respond, looked up confused and said nothing. Dolly motioned with her left hand in the direction of the glass that stood between them and the babies.

"None," the woman said, taken out of her reverie and into an unexpected conversation that Dolly could tell, suddenly, she didn't want to have. "None... none of them."

"Ah, okay. Sorry."

She didn't know what she was sorry for, exactly, but something in the woman's eyes started to tell the story faster than Dolly could even face her terrible mistake. "Oh!" Dolly exclaimed, connecting the hideous dots of rumor with the obvious aftermath of tragedy. The woman with the matted hair and swollen eyes looking out on the babies, none of whom were hers... must be one and the same with the woman whose daughter had only taken a few breaths, whose heart had stopped just after her birth.

"I am so, so sorry," Dolly breathed, feeling her own tears forming, too. This woman must be Claire, whom she had prayed over just earlier, holding hands with the on-call nurse who shared just enough of the grim details to explain why there was so much going on in the hall, why she'd been late with Dolly's meal.

This painful errand was looking in on the other healthy babies and starting to heal her own heart with the purity of their sweetness, starting to rebuild her faith in life with the reminder that there was still beauty in this world despite the incredible swell of loss in her own.

Dolly understood all of this without a word being said. And understood, too, that unlike herself, Claire was ready to be a mother. Because right there in the ultimate moment of desperation and hardship she found the space in her heart to comfort the teenager while crying over her own loss.

Claire said slowly, "That's okay, sweetheart. It's okay..." and held out her arms to hug the bawling teen.

And there they stood—two swollen, exhausted new mothers in hospital gowns, embracing and weeping as their noses ran into each other's unwashed hair. Feeling all the hard and tenderest things in the world while thick, woolen socks protected their feet from the icy-cool of the tile floor. The only part of them, really, that *could* be protected in this moment.

But they had found each other, which was starting to feel like something.

"I'm so sorry," Dolly whispered again into Claire's ear. "I wish there was something I could do."

But there was something she could do, of course. And after giving Claire a final squeeze with the promise of a visit tomorrow morning, and ambling back to Room 3 where her boyfriend and their child awaited her return, Dolly mulled over what would at once be the simplest and most difficult choice of her young life.

You made the right choice, Doll, Stephanie would say as they passed an ice cream cone back and forth just two weeks later. In the quiet stillness of the hospital room, she couldn't imagine how much that simple affirmation would mean, or that she'd get it. For now, all she had was the agonizing part. The decision-making part and its immediate aftermath to follow.

That night, Declan and Dolly stayed up every hour they could, holding their sweet baby girl and breathing secrets about life into her tiny ears. They refused to send her to the nursery for a break, preferring to enjoy whatever time they had left together with her. They pulled back the little cap atop her head to kiss that one swath of curls every chance they could get, wanting to memorize every little detail.

He agreed, of course he did, that they couldn't get married. He finally understood that this wasn't going to go like it did in even the best movie. If they wanted a chance, and if they wanted to give their daughter one, they would have to say goodbye.

In the morning, they sat with Claire and her kind, tired husband, Cliff, and went over the details of the arrangement. The conversation was dizzying and exhausting, and as much as Dolly just wanted to hold onto her baby as long as she could, she also couldn't wait for it to all be over. It would be a closed adoption for everyone's sake; the child would be given the chance to contact them as a teenager if she chose to. It sounded so final, so scary, even though she knew it was what she had to do.

Dolly held her tiny daughter, warm and sweet, and waited for the hard parts to be over. She'd be waiting forever, though, she almost knew.

Everyone got up and left the room to give Dolly and Declan some final moments alone with their daughter, and again the young mother fixated on that mark in the upper left corner of the curtain that hung from the ceiling. She was trying to be strong for Declan's sake, and for the baby's, but words blubbered out of her mouth like the tears streaming from her eyes.

"I can't believe this is goodbye," she managed to get out. He, sitting edged beside her on the bed, put his right arm around her, pulled her in close. She could only imagine that inside he wanted to blame her, wanted to remind her it could have been different if she'd married him. But instead, ever the gentleman and maybe even a more mature version of himself than he'd been just three days prior, he responded between her heaving sobs.

"It's only goodbye for a little while, baby. We'll see her again... along down the road." The teenagers and their too-soon born child sat, a unit of three, quietly for a few more minutes. The only sounds in the room above the whirring air conditioner were their sniffles. The baby slept peacefully in her mother's arms.

There was a quiet knock then on the door, and Dolly steeled herself from the pain of the final send-off that was to come. It *was* Claire, but she would only stay a minute. "I have a favor to ask of y'all," she said quietly, her warm voice just above a whisper. "And then I'll leave you to say goodbye while we pack up our things..."

Dolly looked up at her, took her in. Already Claire was putting on the brave face, righting herself to be a mother. She'd just lost a child herself and was aching, but she had showered, blown out her hair, put on a bit of makeup. She wore terry cloth sweatpants and a matching zip-up, youthful but tasteful in all black. Her eyes displayed subtle crow's feet at the edges, wide and warm as she smiled at them, grateful and kind. "I was wondering if you'd name her for us, so she'll always have a part of you with her."

It was touching and painful... a final act of gratitude from one aching mother to another. What was unsaid was that this woman had come to the hospital preparing to bring home a daughter by one name and was now leaving with another child, one she didn't grow for nine months, one she hadn't dream-bonded with over pints of ice cream and bad TV. What was unsaid was that the ache of loss had shifted from just Claire's to both women's.

Claire and Cliff were gaining a daughter but burying one as well, so this wouldn't be an easy time for them, either. And yet, showing who they were from the inside out, and what kind of parents they would make for the baby, they cared only in this moment about Dolly and Declan's pain, about their loss.

In one final gift of thanks, they tasked the young parents with naming the daughter that wouldn't replace their other one, but would turn them into parents nonetheless. The adoption would help fill the massive hole at the center of Claire and Cliff's lives, their hearts, while leaving the teenagers' gaping wide open.

They didn't have to think twice about it, or even discuss it aloud. Dolly and Declan looked at each other and smiled through their pain, then turned back to the woman who would be their baby's mother. "This is Hannah Jane," Dolly said softly, "your daughter."

NOW

Talking to John-John eased the loneliness Dolly's been feeling from her heavy secrets both distant and fresh, but it didn't do much to help her find a solution to her situation. *Situations, plural,* she thinks. *Michael and Declan. Declan or Michael? Neither? Can't be both.*

Michael texted her last night from a bar after the game, but she was already sleeping and doesn't see it until this morning.

Missing you babe. AM coffee?

Her heart lurches and Dolly can feel the tightness in the back of her throat. Michael. Her Michael... she hates to have a secret from him, but if he knew even a stitch of what's happening, it could ruin everything. Is this why she couldn't pick a dress? Or is it something more? *Maybe,* she thinks, sitting up and pulling her knees to her chest, *it's something less. Maybe that dress just wasn't it.*

The thin white topsheet has come undone from the bottom of the bed and is crumpled by her side. Dolly pulls its edges taut, smooths the top. There's this thing in her that always feels compelled to fix things, make them straight. That's why she was better than hiring a professional organizer to help Daddy with the house and also why she's never been able to deal with having a roommate, opting instead to live in a smaller place on her own, and pay more for it, too.

Dolly has tidied up practically every night of her adult life before crawling into bed, and in the morning if there's ever a dish or a throw pillow out of place it's the first thing she handles before putting on a pot of coffee. This is just innate in her not only as a Southern woman but as her mother's daughter. You can't right every wrong in life, but you do your damnedest to use what you have to fix what you can. Today, the apartment is swept, mopped, straightened up, and showroom quality within forty minutes, but Dolly is still no closer to figuring out how to fix things with Michael.

Talking to John-John about Hannah, whose name she had not spoken aloud in years, felt natural and cathartic. The weight of that burdensome tragedy has been hers and her family's alone all these years. Mama used to bring it up in the early days, but learned quickly that Dolly couldn't talk about it. Daddy has known better than to go there—ever.

Stephanie was always the person she could talk about Hannah to, guiltlessly and alone. Steph would listen and nod with empathy, would tolerate the tears. And best of all, she always, *always* reminded Dolly that they'd done "the right thing." That clean, sure confirmation was exactly what she needed to come back to as they made their way through senior year. *You did the right thing*, or you wouldn't have cheerleading now and college to look forward to. *You did the right thing*, or that baby would be living in a cramped house and you'd be under the same roof as Declan's awful mother. *You did the right thing for everyone*, Steph would remind her again and again, like warm shower water washing over her every sorrow. If they are never friends again, she will always have that to look back on, to be grateful for. Confirmation, and love.

And Declan? Well, in all their carefree fun last month, she wonders why they couldn't talk about the baby either. Then again, what is there to say? The adoption is closed, the child is no longer a baby at all. Hannah Jane will be twelve years old soon, and is living somewhere in Texas (*Right?*) with Claire and

Cliff Anderson as her parents. Dolly has no idea if her daughter knows about the overwhelmed teenagers who brought her into the world and gave her those ice-blue eyes. If she does, is there a part of her missing like there is for her birth mother? Or do the wounds seal up, disappear easier when you're young?

Dolly picks up her phone and punches out a brief text to Michael. She's no closer to selecting a wedding dress, but she has more important things to take care of first.

Yes, come over. Would love a venti! Let's talk... xx

* * * * *

Two hours later Dolly has already downed an entire pot of home brewed coffee and changed her clothes three times, when a rapping at the door startles her out of her Sunday morning work catchup. She's got client files splayed out on the glass coffee table with pastel sticky notes adding a sort of collage-like beauty to the chaos that will unfold tomorrow morning back at her desk.

Before she can rise to check who's at the door, it opens and Michael walks in.

"Why did you knock, silly?" she rises, walks toward him for a hug. Michael shrugs but is quiet. He has her venti in one hand and his tall in the other.

"I don't know," his words are self-conscious in contrast with his broad-shouldered presence.

"You seem a little off." Dolly looks up and catches Michael's eyes, which are tired. New creases she hasn't seen before seem to have developed recently and he is wearing his glasses, which he rarely does. She knows he went out after the Yankee game last night and is probably slightly hungover, but it's clear there's more going on as well. It is her turn to steer the conversation.

"Come sit," she says and takes him by the hand, leads him to that familiar velvet couch where so many of their moments have taken place. And, too, she thinks with a quick shudder, where her recent betrayal of his trust went down, or at least part of it.

"What's going on?" she asks him, feeling suddenly, desperately panicked about their future. All along her confident, if quiet, husband-to-be has been the bedrock of their relationship. He might be a man of little emotional color or dramatics, but he has always made it clear that he loves her and isn't going anywhere. Now the complications that she has brought into their connection are bleeding out onto him, she can see that. A wound she thought she'd covered and started to work toward healing lies open in their midst.

"You tell me," Michael counters, the soft sadness of his features hardening. He sits up stiffer and removes her hand from his thigh, taking a long swig of his coffee, which he drinks black. The lid is off and its piping steam reminds her briefly of her dad. Michael sets the takeout coffee cup down on the table in front of them and pointedly crosses one ankle across the opposite knee. Resting his elbows on that leg, he places his chin on his hands. His eyes are wide open and probing, fixed on her. His body language says, *You have a secret—let's hear it*, even though Michael is far too WASPy to match the sentiment with actual words.

Dolly sits up straighter too, puts her hands in her lap. "I don't really know where to start," she says, feeling the quick urge to run away, but swallowing it. Knowing she can't make this about his reactions anymore, but has to dive into her truth.

All this time they've been together, and in fact for all the years before that, Dolly has pushed her thoughts of Hannah down deep below the surface. The baby is never mentioned because it's the part of her history where it just hurts too damn much to look.

Even on the drive to Mama's funeral, Dolly could feel the baby's name on the tip of her tongue. She felt this irrational pull to sit down at a computer, anyone's laptop, maybe at a random Starbucks a few miles off the highway, and frantically look up Claire Anderson on Facebook. To find her daughter's replacement parents and inform them that the world was just a little grayer now, that the baby's biological grandmother was gone. Maybe to see a picture of the child she'd grown inside of her for nine confusing months, to feel a connection to the next generation of Day women in losing the one that came before her.

She did none of that, obviously. Instead she drove through the pain, her tears streaming down her cheeks in hot rivers all the way to Dallas. She stood stiff-lipped at the funeral in a plain black dress she now cannot picture. She hooked the bend of her arm onto the bony elbow of her grandmother who was radiant and bereft in black crepe. They wept together, each feeling the hollowness of a loss so profound from two sides.

The elderly woman was used to funerals, naturally, because her friends had been dying off in fits and starts for the last two decades and even before that. Her parents were gone, and so were her siblings now. But no mother should ever have to bear the weight of losing their own child to the great beyond. It's a pain not imaginable until you've gone through it, and Cara Day could hardly stand its blow.

For Dolly, who leaned equally on her now frail, eighty-year-old grandmother with crystal blue eyes hiding behind the largest Chanel sunglasses in the entire state of Texas, the loss was just as great. To lose your mother is to be robbed of what is most essential to you. Mother is home and reason, reliability and truth. She still had her father and her grandparents, but the new hole in her heart where her mother used to be felt un-fillable, permanent. And she knew then, as she knows now, that seeing the baby (who would no longer be a baby, but a no doubt beautiful preteen) wouldn't fix it.

"I had a baby when I was seventeen years old," begins the confession that will keep the two of them inside all afternoon, talking and holding each other, finding their way through questions and silences, moving back toward their own nest they have created in New York City. She bares her soul to Michael about the fear and the beauty, of spending the winter and early spring of junior year terrified that she had some sort of stomach disease as she was nauseous almost daily, with absolutely no appetite whatsoever and constant bloating. Only to find out right before spring break that she was actually carrying a child, not a tumor, in her midsection.

"I was terrified. Telling my parents was the worst thing I ever had to do..."

"What about telling the guy?" he asks, a fair question but one that's hard to answer.

"He was... conflicted," she settles. "I didn't want an abortion, but I knew that I couldn't raise her. I wanted to graduate and move to New York and build a life... *this* life," she emphasizes, looking up at her husband-to-be, reaching over gently to place her hand on top of his. "A life just like ours."

Michael's large eyes are doe-like and soft in the waning afternoon light that drips across her apartment. He has been crying. "You must have been so scared."

"Being pregnant at sixteen was terrifying. Not only that, but it was a small town. In the South. I could practically feel the gossip dripping off their tongues when I walked down the hallways with a baby bump. You can only hide one of those for so long!"

The moment of levity and the shared smile is brief. Dolly goes on to tell him about Hannah's adoption. She leaves out the fact that the father wanted to marry her; mentioning that part of the story seems unnecessary and cruel.

"Where is she now?" Michael wonders aloud.

"I don't know... probably in East Texas somewhere still? I have no way to know for sure." She chokes back tears. It's been so long since she allowed herself to really think about all this; now it's rushing back so fast she can hardly keep up with the emotion. "It was a closed adoption. I've never gotten any information. Or pictures."

"Will you ever see her again?" It's the one question she wishes more than anything she could answer.

"I have no idea," her words are hollow in the otherwise silent apartment. "That will be up to her... later."

She catches his eye now. He looks up at her wordlessly. She gives his hand a tight squeeze that he does not return.

Michael has expressed empathy at her loss, but his eyes now reveal something else, too. Maybe this is all just too much. Unexpected and aching, a newly discovered chapter in her story. Or is it... betrayal? Jealousy? Over the part of her life—baby-making—that he planned to be the only one to share with her. That has been taken from him, and he never saw it coming.

Dolly's small apartment feels suddenly huge, bottomed out and open now, its borders and edges expanded to contain the emotional abandon she's unleashed into it. It was never in her plans to tell Michael about Hannah, or about Declan for that matter. She digs her pointer finger into the velvet fabric of the couch, tracing circles by her side. One, two, three... ten. Twenty. How long can she stall, fixating on nothingness?

Now that half the truth is out, she knows what she has to do. Because there's no way she can marry this man without letting him know the whole story, without affording them both the chance to see if they can get past her cheating and move on toward their future. The shame of what she did feels like an insurmountable mountain splayed out before her, the path to her future stretched up and over it—with a misty ending she cannot see. Dolly can't figure out how to say the unsayable, how to confess to her future that she has recently, potentially, ruined everything with the presence of her past.

"Declan was in New York about a month ago," she confesses, barely above a whisper.

"Who's that?" Michael asks.

"The baby's father," she says. "My high school boyfriend."

Michael inhales so deeply and audibly she isn't sure if he's going to let out a shout or stand up and storm out of the apartment, but something big is coming next. She sits nervously on the edge of the couch, her head resting sideways on one hand as she waits for him to make the next move.

Instead of saying anything, or letting her go on, Michael rises slowly and deliberately, makes his way over to the kitchen. She makes to follow him but he holds up a hand to say *Don't*, before she can actually move. The minutes tick by at a snail's pace as she hears the unscrewing of a couple of caps, the pouring of liquid, the clink of a spoon against the side of a glass. Finally, Michael returns with a cocktail in each of his hands, placing one on the coffee table in front of Dolly and taking a quick, palate-whetting sip of his own.

"I don't want to know, babe." He shakes his head so slowly and subtly the move is almost imperceptible. "If nothing happened, it won't change the past you two have... and if something happened, I don't want it to change *us*. But I can't un-know it... so just, just don't tell me."

Dolly is stunned for a moment, but isn't this like Michael? Dolly thinks for a moment how utterly ridiculous all of this must seem to her fancy New York fiancé. She wonders at what might have happened if he'd ever gotten a girl pregnant in high school. Surely, his father's money and power would have "taken care of it" straight away and it wouldn't have been spoken about ever again. But she knows better than to imagine any of that anyway.

Michael doesn't have skeletons like this dancing in his closet, and she feels ashamed of her own. Dolly wants with every fiber of her being to tell him that he needn't worry because nothing happened, but that would be a lie. So instead she reaches for her glass and holds it out toward him in a feeble gesture of "Cheers," which he returns with a wry smile.

That night they order in Thai noodles and watch movies until they are both asleep in their clothes on top of the sheets of her bed. It was the hardest conversation they've ever had and yet, somehow they both feel lighter. She has been given the gift of a man who loves her too much to want to know what she's done. And he, for tonight anyway, can start to look beyond the past with a feeling of hopeful resolution.

THEN

In the weeks after the baby was born, everything changed dramatically for Dolly. It was a blessing and a curse that school picked up not long after she gave birth. She was able to throw herself back into schoolwork and even cheerleading without missing a beat. Staying busy helped fill the void that Hannah had left behind. Well, it sort of helped.

Sometimes Dolly felt like she was floating around somewhere outside of her body while the other girls gossiped in clusters on the bleachers and scattered across the town green. She did her best to keep up socially and act normal, to fit in. She lost the belly quickly with youth and stress on her side, but no one had prepared her for the weeks of postpartum bleeding that would make her a slave to the maxi pad, nor the constantly aching breasts that leaked and hardened for a baby who wouldn't have a chance to drink the milk. These were stops on the lonely path she walked daily, dragging herself through a "normal" small-town senior year while recovering physically and emotionally from the birth of a child she would never know. All of the regular high school girl things that used to matter so much now seemed trivial.

After everything she and Declan had endured together, Dolly expected him to turn away from her. Instead he was, shockingly, an enduringly lovesick romantic. The guitar was broken back out; he was writing songs about her again. Dolly still loved his eyes and his hands, the way he made her feel. But the fact that she had come close to creating a little family with this sweet almost-man was too hard. Sometimes she railed against herself, wishing she had made the other choice. Cursing herself for being so selfish as to choose chasing dreams out of this town, over living a good and honest life right in it.

Dolly tried in those early weeks to figure out a way they could be together again; they were back to their old ways of sneaking around quite quickly. One night toward the end of September, the Westons headed to Dallas for the opera and an overnight stay with Sally's parents in Highland Park, leaving Dolly alone in the house. Declan told his parents he would be staying at Flynn's house and instead arrived at hers at seven on the dot. There was a bouquet of pink flowers in one hand and his lightly packed knapsack in the other. He looked disheveled and sexy, with eyes hopeful and his mouth half-open in an expression she couldn't quite read.

It was early enough in the fall that the air outside still felt summery. The screen door was all that separated them, and she watched him through it at a distance for just a moment before getting up from the living room couch to turn its lock and let him in.

Looking at him now, she could kind of see what he had meant in thinking they could keep and raise their daughter. He looked older now, wiser. Less like a boy. Maybe he *was* ready to be a parent, maybe he was ready to grow up. Maybe her dreams about New York, about magazines, Balenciaga and Dior, Barney's and Zabar's, the Plaza and the Mandarin Oriental... were ridiculous. Maybe she'd never have a charming third floor walk-up or elegant men with III's on the ends of their names to buzz in. Maybe she was made for this small town with its quiet flow in and out of the new and the trendy.

Dolly drank him in like lost time, like distance and fallen tears. He smelled like cedar, having no doubt borrowed this old t-shirt from his fathers' attic stash. Together they moved back toward the couch, him placing the flowers on the coffee table while she wordlessly unbuttoned his jeans. The weight of his body on top of hers felt like home as she reached up behind her head to switch off the end table's jarring lamp. Together in semi-darkness their bodies moved slowly, a dance of longing, a dance of loss.

They were two teenagers in a nameless fight against their feelings. Drawn together by the tragic consequences of a choice they'd made right here on this couch. Her body had started to heal and she felt ready to make love again, but it was a long time before they actually got to that. He kissed her slowly, leaned back a moment and smiled in his way. Lifted her t-shirt from the bottom, pulled it over her head and off with one hand. This was the first time he had laid eyes on her body since she'd given birth, and its shape was different now and softer. Somewhere in this county, or maybe the next one over, was a nearly two-month-old baby girl who had lived just below this rib cage. Somewhere in their past, they had made her with their bodies. The thoughts collided and dispersed as he kissed her harder and longer. He was trying to fight back the words that wanted to spring forth. He couldn't find their perfect form. He was trying to be the man his father would have expected him to be, the rock she needed. Strong and silent.

They were not even supposed to be together anymore, had both told their parents they were no longer going to see each other outside a group setting. But tonight he would prove to her that he had what it took to be there for the long haul. With everything they had faced, he found that now he loved her even more.

But then again, could love ever be enough?

They made love that night slowly in a darkened room, the blue light of the television screen illuminating each other's faces whenever one of them opened their eyes to take it all in. When they were finished, he collapsed beside her, pulled her in to be the little spoon. "I never stopped loving you," he whispered, his right hand traveling down the curve of her bare spine. "I never will."

But inside, Dolly knew. This would be the last time. It took every bit of strength she had left inside to turn around tenderly, to look him in the eye as she told him. Softly, she ran her fingers through his messy hair. "I love you, too, Dec." The words were not enough; they didn't convey the whole story. "I love you so much... but I just can't."

"You can't what?"

She willed him not to let go even as she pushed him away for what would be one final time. "I'm not strong enough to do this. I don't know how to face you every day when I made you agree to give her up!" It was only in letting the words out that she realized how she felt. They were forming just as fast as the truth was.

He coughed, trying to steady his voice and failing. "I need you," was the most coherent thing he could muster.

"But I need you to understand that trying to stay together would hurt too much." She didn't want to hurt anymore. She just wanted to forget.

They said goodbye on the doorstep, both red-eyed and incomplete. The sleepover cancelled, their hope cancelled. "Just think it over," he breathed, collapsing into one more hug, pulling her waist side to side with a sway that they both could have fallen into all night.

"I will, Dec," she said finally. "I just need some time." If their first breakup had been shattering, this one made it feel like every piece of the world had lost its matching bit. There would be no more innocence, and no neat resolution because she had handed their baby away when he wasn't sure it was the right plan, and now he still wanted to love her anyway.

* * * * *

Dolly wore black and kept her head down. Did her homework and read in silence in her bedroom. Spoke to no one of Hannah and faked her way through parties and class, dinners with her parents, and movies with her friends.

Senior year dragged and flew. She filled out and sent off college applications to the attempted cheer of her parents' reassurance. She did all of this with the knowledge that her world would never be the same again. For now, she was a mother, and handing the baby over to someone better equipped to raise her wouldn't change that.

She and Steph were hanging out a lot again, and slowly she reassembled a steady if quiet social life with the neighborhood kids. But despite being right there next to them, she was always a small distance apart. Dec was often around and she could see his feelings written all over his face, could feel the words left unspoken between them. But she knew there was no going back and fixing any of it, so turning away seemed the best plan.

And that's exactly what she did. Declan tried in turn to give her space. She knew it was as hard for him as it was for her, so they both kept conversations light and brief whenever they were in the same room together.

When the acceptance letter arrived from Fordham University in New York City, Dolly smiled so broadly and authentically she almost felt guilty. Her dream was starting to come true and there was nothing anyone could do to hold her back. This felt like another chance. This felt like forgiveness.

She was hopeful about her future as the months flew by and the dorm room essentials were purchased and packed up. Sally flitted about the house in a whir of pride and the bitter-sweet retelling of her favorite childhood memories of Dolly. Her little girl was leaving and she was equal parts excited and melancholy.

They decided to road trip it to New York so they could haul all of Dolly's things in one go and pass through parts of the country none of them had seen before. Sally wanted to see the historic buildings of Savannah, Georgia and eat falafel in Washington, DC. Dolly wanted to take the fastest and surest route they could, but watched lovingly, anyway, as her parents decided on places to stop and "make a day of."

The early August morning arrived and presented itself like a low, aching yawn to the almost-college student. The final suitcase was shoved into the trunk and she reached down to scratch a new mosquito bite that was creating a nagging itch at her ankle. As she stood up to turn back into the house and get her parents, Dolly took a good long look at this home where all of her life had unfolded up to this point.

On the front porch was a swing she hadn't sat in for far too long. At the top of the two columns there by the front door were a few cobwebs that she should have swept away. The window boxes and shutters, the perfectly manicured lawn, and the smart little mailbox engraved with a *W* seemed to all smile back at her, telling her it was time; this was good. Through the screen door she could hear her parents arguing about how long their packed sandwiches would stay fresh in the cooler and whether or not they'd remembered to confirm with Mrs. Birch next door about bringing in the mail while they were out of town.

It all felt so... normal somehow, despite everything that had happened that past year. Like she was winding up exactly where she was meant to be, even though the sinuous path she'd taken to this point had been a total, gut-wrenching detour from the course she had planned.

A *year*. The thought came whirring at her, a surprise to her cognitive mind though it must have been hanging out there beneath the surface for weeks. Tomorrow, her little girl would turn one. For almost a year, she had been walking around, going through the motions, living her last teenage chapter in this cozy, loving home. All the while, actively pushing away the thoughts of the tiny human who had lived inside her for months. Dolly felt for a second like she might puke.

The world is an ugly place where things happen that you cannot fix. Her parents were coming closer to the doorway and she didn't want them to see her cry, so she turned away and started walking away to go fetch the newspaper from the end of the drive. When she stood up with the newspaper in hand, her face all salty tears and red cheeks, she was startled to see Declan standing beside the car.

"You weren't thinking of leaving town without saying goodbye to your old boyfriend, now were ya?" There was that classic Declan eye-glimmer, that crooked smile she missed. He was teasing, but neither one of them could say for sure if she'd planned to do just that.

She tried for a second to come up with a witty response but couldn't, so instead she walked toward him quietly, fell into him for a hug. Her bronzed arms wrapped around his waist and held on so tight she didn't know how she'd ever get them undone. She buried her face in the Tide smell of his t-shirt, listened to his breath by her ear, willed her mind to never forget exactly how this moment felt.

"God, I'm going to miss you so much," she said finally, not realizing she was going to say it until the words fell out. She could feel his chin move against the top of her head as he nodded in agreement. "And I miss her, too," she said more softly.

"We are going to miss her forever, baby," he whispered. "But Dolly, we did the right thing... *you* did the right thing."

They stood at the end of her driveway and swayed back and forth slowly in an embrace neither one wanted to get out of, wordlessly feeling the pain together of an anniversary they would never be able to forget. Knowing that they'd done what they had to do for their daughter and for themselves. And too, feeling so completely powerless at the hands of the loss they had instilled on themselves.

"I wish you didn't have to go," he said, but before she could respond he finished, "but you do. It's the right thing." There it was again. *The right thing.* Even if it was true, she allowed herself to wonder for a moment what life would look right now like if she'd decided to do the "wrong" things? Would it be all that terrible? She couldn't imagine it would, to be honest.

She allowed herself then to picture pudgy baby legs and a blow-up pool out back. Saw herself baking a first birthday cake and tying strings onto paper hats. Could imagine taking classes at the community college two towns over, saving for their future by rotating childcare between their mothers. None of it seemed all that bad. Then the fantasy vanished as quickly as it had come on.

"If we're supposed to be together, we will be," she said, her eyes begging his to say they would.

"It's as simple as that, Dolly Mae," he replied, leaning down to kiss her forehead. "Now git on up to New York. The sooner you go, the sooner you can come on back."

NOW

Since Dolly confessed her past to Michael, they have been quietly at ease. While he's been busy at work and the gym, that's nothing new, and Dolly's unconcerned. She's managed to put Declan back in the mostly forgotten corner of her heart. This time it doesn't hurt as much. Maybe that's because she's (sort of?) come clean to Michael about what happened, but probably it's because she has set herself free from the grip of her deepest and heaviest secret. Harboring that truth was weighing her down for years; now she feels lighter than she could've anticipated.

The word is out and she feels new. Like fresh skin growing beneath a healing wound, she is delicate and vulnerable, but no longer in such harsh pain. Michael has proven that she is still lovable despite her complicated past. That having a baby at seventeen doesn't make her dirty or bad or marred. He has accepted it without needing to pry. He has asked no more questions. He has made love to her several times a week, whether she is morning-breathed and running late or doll-eyed in a cocktail dress. He has been strong as only he can be.

And she has been doing what she does best. Floating around her apartment in the evenings and weekend mornings when she isn't at work. Piling and packing and deciding what will come with her into their new life and what will stay in the past. They have agreed to pause wedding planning for the moment because they're ahead of schedule, and to focus on the move instead. Dolly would be lying if she told herself she isn't a little relieved for that break.

One thing at a time... One thing at a time.

In the months since Dolly and her father had their weekend in Sugar's Bend to purge, box up, and move forward from their old life, things have changed within their new ones. Daddy is officially living in his shiny new condo in the center of town and even, Dolly suspects, has taken up with a girlfriend. She can't be 100% sure, but he's seemed busier than usual recently, less frequently answering her calls and more likely to return them at a later time. And she's pretty certain she heard a woman's voice in the background the last time they spoke on the phone.

She is happy for him, if it's true, even if the initial realization was a shock. She wants her father getting out there and enjoying life, and he's always been happiest in the company of others. These past couple years of solitude have been tough on him, and the timing feels right. Appropriate.

The remains of her childhood rediscovered those few days in Sugar's Bend have long since been sorted, donated, or held onto and packed away. Her Manhattan apartment is undergoing a similar transformation from overstuffed to streamlined, another big move pending. Dolly has managed to move past most of the visceral reactions she had to the important items she and Mama had left behind and incorporated what she wants into her life here in New York. At this point, she's pretty sure that everything she needs to bring to Brooklyn is sitting somewhere in this small collection of rooms; has been seen and touched, sorted or displayed, and is accounted for.

So, when Daddy calls her up one Saturday morning and tells her he found something of interest, and he mailed it to her a few days ago, Dolly's heart leaps. Immediately her mind goes to the box of sentimentals that she wasn't ready to handle that emotional spring day, and sure enough that's just where it was. Nestled in the back of her date book from the year Dolly left for Manhattan, paper-clipped to a photo of her and Mama, Daddy has found a letter that he suspects Sally never really meant to send.

"I remember your mama told me she'd written a letter to give you that morning when we dropped you off at school, but in the end she decided to just let you fly. That if you wanted advice, you'd ask for it." He takes a weighted breath. She hears the air over the phone as it sucks in, pushes out. "I'm sure she's somewhere kickin' me right now for letting you see it, but I went ahead and read it, nosy as I am, and I think you need to, too." After a pause he continues, "Think it might help."

They say goodbye, hang up, and Dolly decides to go downstairs and outside to run a couple of errands but also, really, to check on the status of the mail. She throws on a floor-length sundress and slips into her favorite slides. Pulls a hat over the mess that is her day-after-Friday-night hair and takes the stairs two at a time to the lobby. The box is still empty, so she proceeds out through the double glass doors.

Outside, it's instantly clear that summer is holding on tight to these early-September days. The air is balmy and resting in the mid-80's but feels warmer for all the tightness of living space, for the confinement of buildings lining up on either side of you, stretched up to the sky. If the streets weren't so damn loud and busy here, she could almost close her eyes and pretend she's back in Texas.

Dolly stops at the fish market down on the corner and pays for a pound of salmon just in from Long Island early this morning. On a whim she picks up peonies from outside the small grocer next door before heading home. The mail never arrives until around noon, but she paces back and forth in front of the building anyway. The anticipation of unlocking a secret part of her relationship with her mother gives her a levity she hasn't felt in months.

Relenting, Dolly heads back upstairs to put the fish in the fridge and the flowers in a vase. She catches up on a few client emails and texts John-John to see what he's up to tonight. She stands in the kitchen dipping rice crackers into garlicky hummus for what feels like forever until a woman in blue with a cart full of possibility shows up outside of the building and Dolly watches from her kitchen window above as she enters the lobby to drop off the mail.

The envelope is marked Priority Mail and on its front Daddy has scrawled, "Please listen to her" in permanent marker. Dolly holds it to her chest a moment and then tenderly pulls back its edges to reveal the note within.

Inside, she finds the letter Daddy spoke of on the phone. Not dated, and written in Mama's famously flawless cursive on the lined paper that was clearly torn from the back of a day planner. Even though she never gave the letter to her daughter, it's now as if she speaks to her from the grave, and so Dolly dives into the last words she'll ever receive from her mother.

* * * * *

She had planned to bake the salmon in lemon and dill, letting its edges brown with butter and serving it atop fluffy basmati rice, out on the fire escape. To pour generous helpings of sancerre into glass juice cups so as not to break her finer stems and sit outside watching the sunset over Manhattan with Michael tonight. But a new sense of purpose takes hold, and empowered by her mother's eleven-year-old letter, Dolly decides the salmon has been outvoted.

Tonight, they're going out.

The scene at The Penrose, her favorite local whiskey joint, is predictably lively and delicious. The long and winding bar is crowded; they have to wait twenty minutes before two leather topped stools are relinquished and they can sit down and peruse the menu. 70 whiskeys would be overwhelming to some girls, but Dolly grew up in the South. This is just like being a kid looking behind the curved window at an ample selection of ice cream flavors: exciting, tempting, and totally doable.

Michael, raised by an aficionado of all the fine things, and better traveled than anyone she's ever met, greets every exploit of indulgence with confidence and maybe a touch of amusement. They each pick a whiskey and a cocktail to follow, settle quickly on sharing the cheese platter and a kale salad to start, and then pause reflectively once it's ordered.

"Why the change in plans?" He finally asks, after they've both taken in the scene a beat too long.

"Oh, I just didn't feel like cooking," she lies. Inside her, the truth of her mother's letter swirls like a snowstorm picking up speed, crystalizing every piece of her reality. At the same time, she wants to either read it aloud to him on her trusty velvet sofa, wine glass raised and hot tears escaping down her cheeks; or bottle up its essence to store in a tiny, secret corner of their world, never to let him in on what is so fundamentally precious to her. The last she'll ever get.

"Maybe I just needed to get out," she concedes, to which Michael nods in approval. Always flexible, always agreeable. Always ready to check off whatever box she presents.

The whiskey glasses are placed before them by a check-shirted, handsome young bartender with a crooked smile. "Cheers," he says almost as an afterthought, reaching to his left to gather garnish or mixers, some out-of-sight detail for the next round of drinks he'll be fixing.

"Cheers," Michael repeats, looking at his wife-to-be, and they both clink and smile, each taking a long, low sip. The whiskey brings a heat and thickness to her tongue, to the roof of her mouth, burns slightly going down her throat. Tastes like college summers back on Mama and Daddy's porch.

Dolly glances down at her engagement ring, heavy and promising, sparkling in the waning sunlight of early evening that reaches their end of the bar through large windows. With everything they've been through this summer, all the hard parts and the quieter moments, it's become crystal clear to her today how they need to move forward.

"Michael," she starts, finding her moment between the first sips of their cocktails and the arrival of the food. She catches his eyes, dark brown and eager, takes in his questioning expression before catching her breath and diving in. This is the moment to let him know. She's finally ready.

LATER

The moon is a bright beacon of joy tonight, resting in a quiet and nearly black September sky dotted with glinting stars that go on and on. Dolly shivers a little inside her woolly cardigan, pulling the sleeves down to cover her hands. It's dipped down to around 50 degrees, a temperature that her homegrown Texan self would have thought downright freezing not too many years ago, especially for this time of year. The relentless chirping of crickets rises up from every corner of the landscape. They are unseen and yet so very present, their sound a kind of music in the late summer atmosphere.

Dolly wears a forgiving white dress under her sweater, one that feels light and soft against her sun-kissed skin. She holds a mason jar of room-temperature tap water in one hand, wearing thin canvas sneakers on her still-tanned feet. She stands self assured and peaceful in the foothills of one the most beautiful places she has ever seen, thinking for a moment back on that naive teenage girl who once stared back, hopeful and green, at her reflection in the mirror.

Did she think she'd ever see Vermont, did she know enough to care that it would be this wondrous? Was the big world she so dreamed to conquer only something that stretched out as far as the limits of that twenty-two square mile island she's called home since the age of eighteen? Was the career she pushed so hard to create and grow an illusion of joy, or was it the groundwork to a fulfilling future?

Come explore the world with me, was at once just about the most romantic and ridiculous thing she'd ever heard. But she took the bait nonetheless and tonight, here she is. Dolly has four clients now in her own little firm and they are being handled meticulously by Glinda and Veronica while she and the man she loves take a much-deserved vacation. Their office is small, tidy, and stylish. The team is dedicated and well compensated. The bills are paid and the workload is manageable. She has built the New York Dream. Laid the groundwork for it to unfold upon, anyway.

Dolly has finally found that happy place where work and life can coexist amicably and has learned that if you allow some of each column to seep into the other, you will be fulfilled in the office and at home. It takes a strong life partner to help you reach this revelation. She's grateful to have one.

And he has come into himself as well, leaving the corporate tortures and the space where excellent money meets soulless labor. Opening up his own business too, that puts the down-and-out to work and lines their pockets appropriately while making a positive impact on the community. A good man. He was always a good man.

Together, they have merged their separate ways and put together an extraordinary life.

But it isn't just the two of them anymore, because inside her has sprouted their future, too. At first she felt guilty and wistful, glowing in the knowledge that there was a human life in her once more, when the first time was wrought with so much hardship and confusion. And she longs for that first baby sometimes, especially late at night. But she has, in time, made a kind of peace with the past and the understanding that her fifteen-year-old daughter is living a beautiful life in Texas that she could not have given her back then. A tiny flicker of hope lives in her, too, that one day in a far-off future, maybe her children can know each other and be friends.

Maybe that's too much to hope for, but she's been given every reason to think that hope is the one thing that gets us to where we need to go. Dolly hoped for forgiveness and he hoped for a fresh start and together they hoped for a chapter that would bring more joy than pain. And now only two years later they are married and the world is starting to show them just how beautiful it can be when you give real love a chance.

Their wedding was perfect. She wore a sheath dress with shimmering detail that her mama would have just loved. The ceremony was small and quiet, a change from what she had envisioned in recent years. Her hair lay long and natural in waves past her shoulders and her makeup was light and dewy. Steph was there, clinking glasses and sharing laughs with her New York friends, beaming ear-to-ear to watch her oldest friend —their relationship freshly rebeginning in a soft and gentle manner—marry her beloved.

The memory of that magical day is one Dolly will carry with her forever, and she can't help but smile when she pictures him, broad and beautiful in a white shirt and rolled-cuff slacks waiting at the top of the aisle for her. So simple and sweet, the way they were always, *truly,* meant to be.

Now he is tinkering with something back there while she takes out her phone, sends a quick photo text to Daddy and Faye, his new wife. *Missing you! Absolutely gorgeous here,* she captions the selfie they took over dinner, before hitting send.

"Babe!" she hears, a laugh in his voice coming from the other end of the vehicle. And as she walks his way, he jumps down to help her up, placing a protective and proud hand on her growing belly. She can hardly contain the gasp that comes out as she looks up and sees tea lights and heavy blankets, a local Vermont pie in a brown box tied up with twine.

She places her own hand on top of his as they're both treated to the thrill of a kick from deep within. Stopped in thought for just a moment, Dolly lets herself take in the scene. Then looks back up into the eyes of the man she married, the aching love for him and what they are going to build together in this life shining out in the grin she can't contain.

"Well," he asks, eyes smiling as he nods toward her belly, "Y'all gettin' in or what?"

EPILOGUE

Dolly,

We leave tomorrow to drive you to New York City and the feelings that swirl inside me are complicated and so intense. I am immensely proud of all of your accomplishments, and I know on every single level, from the depths of my soul, that this is the right move for you.

But I worry... about subway systems and bad men who take advantage of kind-hearted young women. About you forgetting your roots, or your manners, or both (I know you won't—I know you won't!). I worry most about me, sure I do. Because the souls we bring into this world just about always hang out right beside us, even when they aren't there. (Don't you understand this already, even more deeply than I do...?)

I hope you find success and beauty and wonder, enough to bottle up and then bring on home to us. And then more importantly I hope you don't do that... that instead, you find an anchor that will keep you right there, or wherever it is that you truly belong. I hope you will trust in my love and your father's enough to know that we are always just a phone call away, just a heartbeat away. And that no matter how much time life gives us together, I will be right by your side now and forever, whether we are in the same town, or farther apart than we'd ever dreamed to be.

Life will catapult you further and further ahead, and as your mama I will always wish you back closer. But I beg of you this one thing, always, my darling: that you do not let me (or anyone) hold you back. Not my love and not my hopes for you; not anyone's priorities.

I will love you from afar, just as I loved you under my roof.

Please, go give yourself the beautiful gift of living fully and completely outside of my arms. And if any part of the next chapters of our lives makes you choose between the now and the then, I pray that you will choose what you truly want and not what anyone else thinks you should. That you will keep moving, keep growing, keep becoming the person that you are meant to be.

I trust I've given you the basis of a mother's love you need to make your way in this big world that is ready for you. (You're ready for it, too. You are, you are). So, please, my sweet daughter, don't choose looking back and don't choose Mama's arms, even though they're always open.

Selfishly, I would choose for us to always be as we have been to now, figuring it out together under this roof in this little old town. But the mother in me knows it's time to tell you what you ought to do next. And I pray you will let me love you from afar, that you won't spend too much time looking in that rearview. Make your changes, fall in love, and run as far forward into this new life as you need to, baby girl. Don't worry about looking back. You've held this dream in your heart for far too long to not make the most of it.

Lord, I pray for the strength to believe the things I'm writing. To stay firm in the knowledge that you are ready for your new life and everything it will bring with it. Let me love you from afar, sweet girl, and let my arms be a memory when you need them. Let me visit you in your dreams but give you peace and distance when you wake. Let me bid you luck on your journey into a life so far removed from what we've built together. Let me love you.

But also,

Let me let you go.

ACKNOWLEDGEMENTS

While the actual writing of this book was in large part a solitary effort, it would have been an impossible feat without the help of so many important people in my life.

Firstly, I would like to thank my whip-smart and endlessly kind editor Sara Bowne for her early enthusiasm over this project and all of her hard work on it along the way. *Let Me Let You Go* simply would not and could not have been what it has become without her tireless efforts. I cannot wait to have a drink with you in New York one of these days, Sara! We deserve it.

Thank you to James and Mychelle Humphris for the use of your truck for my cover art, and to hugely talented photographer Elisabeth Millay for letting me use her New York skylines. Thanks also to cover model Sienna Cartier for lending your look and your heart for the cover: you captured Dolly perfectly. I am so grateful for your efforts on this project and also for your presence in my family's life as a dear friend.

I will always look back lovingly and with gratitude on my young and single days in New York City. There is truly nothing like those memories. Thank you to my New York friends Kate Auletta, Andrew Lutjens, Monique Meneses, Stephanie Nodzo, and Nadine Taylor for always being down for a laugh, a cry, a happy hour, a chopped salad, or a shopping excursion even when we were broke. The same can be said for high school friends who bridged the gap from Long Island to Manhattan beautifully—Jackie Tobin Connor, Cristina DiVuolo Marino, and Alani Puca—I loved being young and hopeful with all of you and will never forget that special time in my life.

Speaking of high school, thank you Suzie Benko and Rachel Arnold for making it bearable. And to Pookie, I'm so glad I got my way and turned you from friend to sister. The master plan was executed perfectly. Madelaine Snodgrass has been a constant voice of reason and source of support and love since we met in Texas what feels like yesterday. Ashlynne Dezelske pushed me almost as hard as my husband did to stop wasting my time and write this book. Thank you, my dear friends.

Thanks also to early readers Renee DeBussey and Brittini Peavey for your invaluable insight as fiction lovers and women living in the South. And to the Roswell Mom's Book Club and my lovely "Babes" within it. It was you all that gave me the spark of reminder I needed that people still want to read fiction—love stories, too! I had the idea for this novel months before I met you girls, but it was our wine-filled book chats that ignited my early writing process with confidence. I will always be grateful for y'all.

I would like to thank the string of badass female bosses I have been lucky (and stressed) enough to work for. Thank you Kerriann Flanagan Brosky, Lisa Pulitzer, E. Jean Carroll, Tina Gaudoin, Michelle Steinberg, and Jen McCrady for pushing me— sometimes to the point of tears—to be a stronger writer and a better person. You were all so influential to my professional development and I am lucky to have had you each in my life at the times when I did.

Working on this book with two small children at home was a challenge to say the least. I owe an unpayable debt of gratitude to babysitters Megan Leisses and Megan Farthing. Thank y'all for loving our girls as we do, and for putting up with my haphazard scheduling requests.

If you can believe it, my parents are just as awesome as Dolly's and I am convinced that none of the best parts of my life would have happened without them. Thank you, Mommy and Daddy, for not just believing, but *knowing,* that I would become a professional writer and fulfill that lifelong dream. Thank you for loving me as I am, and for cheering the loudest for me all along the way—even during my failures. I love you and our original five (including my two shugs I was lucky enough to grow up alongside) enormously. And thank you Kurty for your generous storytelling and listening ears.

An immeasurable thank you to my loving and supportive husband Josh for making me quit all of the nonsense to focus on this project, because he believed I could do it and he wasn't going to let me let myself down. I have found a man to share my life with who is equal parts fun, steadfast, and hopeful. This is rare and special, and I do not take it for granted ever. I love you endlessly, Hunzy, and I am grateful for our life every single day.

And finally, thank you to my beautiful children Willow and Marigold, who have put up with Mommy's passion project and the time it took away from us because you love me and want me to be successful. I hope that I am proof to you that women don't have to choose between their greatest desires; mine were always to become a mother and a novelist and now I am proud to say that I am both. I love you girls with all my heart and I am so grateful to be your mommy. I hope you know that wherever your wildest dreams take you, I will be lifting you up to help you reach them, all along the way.

Made in the USA
Monee, IL
26 October 2020